FULLY INVOLVED

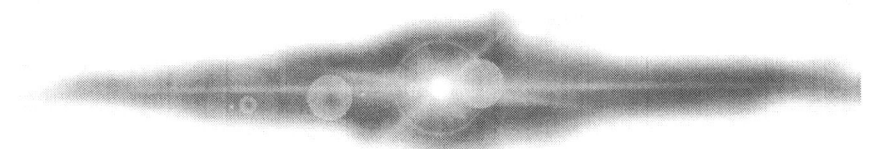

LINDY BELL

Day Agency Publishing
Salt Lake City, UT
84065

Editor: Sean Linton
Cover Designer: Fran Plat • Eden Graphics • www.edengraphics.net
Interior Print Design & eBook Design: Dayna Linton • Day Agency • www.dayagency.com

Library of Congress Control Number: Pending

ISBN: 978-1-7365604-0-2 (Paperback)
ISBN: 978-1-7365604-1-9 (Digital Book)

First Edition: 2021

10 9 8 7 6 5 4 3 2 1

Printed in the USA

For my brother, Fire Chief Larry Bell (Retired)
Thank you for your dedication to and love of the fire service and for
telling me about Larry Kraus, the inspiration for this book.
While Fire Chief, you were the epitome of what a great fire service
officer should be and made the care of the men and women under your
command your first priority.

I appreciate your untiring patience answering my many, many questions,
sharing your in-depth knowledge about firefighting and the men with
which you served.

You are an inspiration, not just to me and others, but to all those
firefighters who served with and for you during your thirty-five years of
service with the Abilene, TX Fire Department.

This book is what it is because of you.

My appreciation and recognition also go to my nephew, Zac Bell, paramedic and driver with the Mesquite, TX Fire Department. I am so proud of you and the exemplary service you provide and the example you are.

IN MEMORIAM

LARRY KRAUS
Senior Firefighter, Abilene Fire Department
Line of Duty Death: 9/28/1988

Abilene, TX — On September 5, 1982 a telephone transformer exploded, covering the area around the pole with oil and igniting a fire. After firefighter Larry Kraus pulled a booster line and attacked the fire, his bunker gear and booster line became coated with a large amount of oil from the transformer. The fire was quickly tapped out, and Larry began cleaning his gear and the booster line. A utility representative arrived on the scene and during his assessment informed fire personnel the oil contained polychlorinated biphenyl (PCB), a toxic, cancer-causing chemical. The site was soon secured for clean-up and decontamination.

Over the next several years Larry began experiencing an increasing amount of unexplained health problems. In September 1986, he was diagnosed with an aggressive form of malignant lymphoma. During the next two years, Larry endured a variety of treatments including surgery and chemotherapy, all to no avail. On Wednesday, September 28, 1988, Senior Firefighter Larry Kraus died at Abilene's Hendrick Medical Center. He was 32. Autopsy and toxicology tests confirmed the presence of elevated levels of PCB isomers.

In 2016, the National Institute for Occupational Health released a study of over 30,000 firefighters stating that not only are firefighters at a greater risk for cancer diagnoses (9% increase) but are also succumbing to cancer-related deaths at a 14% higher rate than the general public in the United States. According to the International Association of Firefighters, cancer has surpassed heart disease as the leading cause of death among firefighters. Between January 1, 2002 and March 31, 2017, 61% of career firefighter deaths in the line of duty occurred as a result of cancer, compared to 18% from heart disease in the same time period. In 2016, that number rose to 70%.* *Fully Involved* is inspired by Firefighter Larry Kraus who is one among hundreds of firefighters who have been exposed to toxic chemicals while on duty, resulting in untimely deaths.

By writing this book, my hope is to increase awareness of the unseen dangers firefighters face every day and to a glimpse "behind the station walls" of the fire service family and the unparalleled level of support these brave heroes provide — not just to the public — but to each other.

The level of devotion provided by fellow firefighters and the final honors depicted in this book are typical and are testament to the care and dedication exemplified by fellow firefighters to members of the fire service brotherhood.

* "Cancer, Leading Cause of Death in Firefighters" by Ryan Shaffer, January 11, 2019

AUTHOR'S NOTE

FULLY INVOLVED IS A work of fiction. Any resemblance to actual events or persons, living or dead, is entirely coincidental. Firefighter deaths from cancer, however, are very real. The idea for this book was inspired by the untimely death of Firefighter Larry Kraus whose death from cancer was considered in the line of duty.

FULLY INVOLVED

T HE START OF A new school year was never easy. Katie thought her anxiety level would have mellowed by her third year of teaching second grade, but the seemingly chaotic condition of her classroom was proving her wrong. Her eyes narrowed as they fell on the new reading corner in the back. The bookcases definitely needed some tweaking. She didn't like chaos. She heaved a sigh and blew a wayward wisp of auburn hair out of her face. She stood in the middle of her classroom, hands on her waist, and turned slowly, making mental note of things still to be done before the open house that night and the start of school tomorrow.

She picked her way through the rows of tiny desks to the reading corner, made some adjustments and stepped back to survey her work. Cocking her head to one side, she chewed on the thumbnail she'd just broken, tucked a stray bit of auburn hair behind her ear and groaned. "It's still not right." This was turning into a bigger chore than she had imagined, and she still had lesson plans to finish.

Sally Morton paused outside Katie's classroom door, hearing muffled voices from rooms of other teachers working, and rolled her eyes as she watched Katie work. Sally stepped inside the door just as Katie stopped to deliberate her furniture arrangement. In spite of herself,

Sally's attention was drawn to the bright colors and decorations splashed across Katie's room which felt warm, exciting and completely inviting. Katie Garrett. Little Miss Perfect. Everyone at Birmingham Elementary talked about how nice Katie was, how sweet Katie was, how great Katie was but not Sally. She congratulated herself on being smart enough to see right through this soft-spoken impostor.

Sally's eyes glittered catlike as the sound of heavy furniture scraping across the floor drifted into the hallway. What was she up to though? Sally strolled further inside to get a better look.

Katie stepped inside the small space that she'd intended to be an enticing reading corner but in spite of the cheery braided rug and a couple of brightly-colored bean bag chairs, turned out to be more of a black hole surrounded by bookcases. She grunted as she tugged on one of the bookcases and jumped when she heard someone say, "Having a little trouble?"

Katie peered around the edge of the bookcase.

She grimaced slightly as she tried to maintain a pleasant look. "No. I've. Got. This," punctuating each word with a shove of the bookcase.

Sally smiled like a cat who'd spotted the canary's cage open. "Ah, so I see," she said before sliding gracefully into one of the small chairs at the nearest table.

Katie huffed and tugged on the bookcase one last time before stepping outside the reading area and nodding. She moved another bookcase slightly which added more light into the nook. "There. That should do it," she said under her breath, smiling with satisfaction.

"To what do I owe this honor?" Katie asked, reluctantly turning her attention to Sally.

"Just thought I'd see if you are ready for tonight," Sally replied, looking languidly at her set of highly polished fingernails.

Katie eyed her own broken nail and ran her fingers through her hair at an attempt to look more presentable. She had been stung numerous times by Sally's directness and knew Sally wouldn't let anything go until she had an answer, and she was waiting for an answer now. Katie eyed her closely and hesitated before replying cautiously, "I'm as ready as I'll ever be."

"Well, me too. There's just so much to do," Sally said, shrugging her shoulders with a dramatic sigh.

Katie had seen that shrug before. Sally had been a high school cheerleader, and she used the same dramatic sigh, helpless shrug of the shoulders and delicate little pout when she had flirted, and the guys had fallen victim to her spell. Katie had watched Sally use those tactics with Andy, Katie's especially handsome firefighter husband. This was before Sally knew Katie and Andy were married. Katie had been so proud of Andy while watching the exchange with Sally, because she'd never seen him act so coldly. He'd parried and dodged Sally's advances effortlessly as if it were a boring game he'd won a hundred times, but Sally never caught on.

In her first year of teaching and newly married, Katie felt self-conscious and unsure of herself. Half teasing, half not, she'd tried to laugh it off when she said to Andy, "It's a good thing we're married. I was getting a little jealous watching you and Sally."

Andy's strong reaction surprised her. He'd pulled her close and said firmly, "Katie Garrett, I don't want to ever hear such nonsense again. You're the one I love. Not Sally, or anyone else. Got it? I love you because you're *you*."

He'd looked at her, his eyes blazing, and then smiled his most dazzling smile right before he'd kissed her. She could still feel the power of that kiss and see the love burning in his eyes.

"So, is that handsome husband of yours coming tonight?" Sally asked, her eyes flickering down to her neatly-pressed capri pants that she stroked with her thumb.

Torn from her romantic reverie, Katie gave a surprised start and then reached for some books to cover her reaction. As she slid them onto the bookcase shelves, she replied just as casually, "Why, yes. Why do you ask?"

Sally waited until Katie finally turned. Holding Katie's gaze for several seconds, Sally replied coolly, "No particular reason. Just thought he might well . . . you know . . . be busy."

Katie didn't understand the meaning. She studied Sally, meeting the haughty look in her eyes, before answering. "Well, he is busy, but no more than usual. He'll be here."

Sally snickered under her breath and stood. "Well, good for you."

Katie clenched her hands tightly to her side as she strode to within a few feet of Sally. "Okay. What is it? You're about to burst. Just say whatever it is you're so anxious to say."

Sally's eyes gleamed when she leaned toward Katie and said, "It looks like Andy must have a new partner. She's attractive. I'd even say very attractive. Blonde, athletic. They sure were having a good time when I saw them at the grocery store. So much fun in fact, Andy didn't even notice me, and we were on the same aisle!"

Katie frowned as her heart pounded painfully. Andy hadn't mentioned anything about a new recruit at the station.

"Oh, and one more interesting thing," Sally said, having gotten the reaction she wanted, "She had a police uniform on." Sally turned and waved smugly before she walked out the door.

Katie breathed a sigh of relief after Sally left, flexing the fingers she'd unknowingly clenched. Of course, there was a reasonable explanation. Andy did grocery shop while he was on duty, but normally with his partner, Sean Hedrick, the rookie who cooked for C shift. The question was, why hadn't Andy told her about this policewoman? He usually told her about everything that went on at the fire station in detail, and in his enthusiasm, she typically heard a lot more than she wanted to. Strange that he would leave this detail out.

Katie shook her head. She was letting Sally's insinuations get to her. She couldn't help but think back to the beautiful blonde in the extremely tight and very short dress at their wedding reception three years ago. Katie could still feel the heat of her glare when Andy ended their conversation to return to Katie's side.

Katie's phone rang, and she jumped.

"Hey, beautiful."

Her heart skipped a beat, and then she smiled, hearing Andy's voice. "Hey yourself."

"Thought I'd check in. Ready for tonight?"

"Definitely," Katie paused and then said in a rush, "Well, if I can get everything finished."

Andy laughed. "You will. I'm not worried."

Katie detected something different in Andy's voice. "Andy, you okay? You sound different."

Several seconds passed before Andy replied. "No worries. All's good — just checking in."

"Well, we're on — unless of course, you have something else planned," Katie couldn't help adding, the police blonde still on her mind.

"Now, what else would I have planned?" Andy asked, irritation creeping into his voice. "This has been on the books for weeks. Besides, I wouldn't miss it. I love seeing my wife shine. Okay — gotta run. Almost to the office."

"All right then, but Andy, I'm just wondering. Is there anything new going on at the station?"

"New at the station? What do you mean?"

Katie felt foolish even asking. "Sorry — never mind. I'll see you this evening."

"Everything okay?" Andy asked. "What's up with all the questions?"

"Everything is fine. I just have a lot on my mind."

"Alright then. Love you forever," Andy said, waiting before he hung up.

"Love you forever too," Katie said and heard Andy click off.

The first day of school was tomorrow, and her classroom and first week of lesson plans still needed some last-minute touches, but now, there was a lot on her mind. It was going to be hard to concentrate.

Katie paused, as she stood in the middle of her room, thinking of Andy. He was more than she'd ever dreamed of having in a husband. Like in high school, when she hadn't been good enough to be elected cheerleader, she still wondered if she was good enough for Andy. Her college roommate, Gwen, had said that Andy was "the catch of a life-time" when he proposed. Katie agreed. He was handsome, outgoing, thoughtful, fun, and charismatic. He made her feel like she was the best and most amazing thing in his world. She'd never dreamed, watching him on the softball field the night they met, that she could ever gain his attention — and even more amazingly — his affections. But she had, and she loved him more than she'd thought it possible to love someone.

ANDY ENDED THE CALL with Katie as he pulled into RITE2U's parking lot. RITE2U occupied a small office in old downtown Abernathy, not far from the fire station. His second job as a delivery driver job was ideal. Andy loved being able to drive around the city, deliver packages, and visit with the wide variety of RITE2U clients. The old-fashioned bell hanging over the office door clanged abruptly as he bounded through the door. The office was deceptively small with workstations and various machines strategically placed to get the most use from the space. RITE2U was the largest courier and delivery service in the region. Charlene, the office manager, looked up as Andy entered. Mr. Henderson, RITE2U's owner and manager, sat in his office beyond Charlene, staring at a computer screen.

"You're late," Charlene stated matter-of-factly.

Charlene treated everyone in the office, including Mr. Henderson, the same, and no one doubted she was actually the one in charge. Andy had tried his special charm on her several times, but the best he could muster from her was a bored shrug or eye roll.

Mr. Henderson looked up, hearing Charlene's light reprimand. Andy spoke to Charlene as he passed her desk, and Mr. Henderson couldn't help but grin when he saw Charlene's round face crinkle with pleasure.

"Busy day," Andy said as he wiped beads of sweat from his forehead. Charlene glanced up briefly and nodded, scanning envelopes and packages into her system as Andy pulled them from his box.

"This it?" she asked, dropping the last envelope into the bin.

"Yes, ma'am," Andy replied, moving quickly aside for her to step back to her desk.

"You're good to go then," Charlene said without looking up. "Clock out."

"OK, thanks." Andy turned toward the break room and checked his watch against the clock's stamp and flinched. He hadn't realized how late it was. He punched out, then walked briskly back through the office and gave Charlene a quick wave before he was out the door and headed to his truck.

Andy breathed deeply of the early evening air, crossing the parking lot to his truck in quick strides. He was about to start the engine when a sudden stomach cramp bent him double. He managed to start the engine, fumbling for the controls. He punched the air conditioning up and adjusted the vents so cold air blew over him. He squirmed in pain as he clutched the steering wheel tightly with one hand and grabbed his stomach, wadding his shirt in a white-knuckled fist with the other. As suddenly as it came, the cramp was gone, leaving him gasping for air. He took several ragged breaths before raising his head slowly to glance around and make sure no one had seen. Thankfully, the parking lot was empty save for Charlene and Mr. Henderson's cars.

Andy worked to catch his breath. These attacks were coming more often, and with each, the pain increased. This had been the worst so far. He thought back over the past several months to when he'd first started experiencing an occasional stomach pain or spasm. He had pushed each one from his mind, but now, they were happening several times a week and getting to where they couldn't be ignored.

After several minutes, Andy was able to breathe easier. He cautiously sat up and pulled the rearview mirror around to look at himself. His normally-tan face was colorless and drawn, his blue eyes were red and watery, and his hands were trembling. He couldn't let Katie see him this way. He ran his fingers through his hair, then wiped the sweat from his face. He took a deep breath, placed the truck in gear and backed out.

ANDY'S TRUCK WAS ALREADY in the driveway when Katie arrived home. She walked to the front door with her key out, but the door swung open at her touch. The late evening sun still shone, but the house seemed gloomy. Katie reached for the lamp near the door and flipped it on.

"Andy?" she called, dropping her purse and satchel on the table. No answer. She picked up the mail and sifted through the stack before dropping it back onto the counter.

"Andy?" she called again. Still no answer.

She slipped her shoes off and swung them from the tips of two fingers as she walked down the hall. She stepped into their bedroom just as Andy came out of the bathroom, fresh from a shower. A towel around his waist but still beaded with water, his broad chest and muscular arms, flexed as he grabbed her in a wet hug. He smelled of soap, his damp skin still warm from the shower.

"Hey, beautiful!"

"You're soaking wet!" Katie squealed as Andy lifted her up and swung her around. She laughed as she looked into Andy's electric blue eyes, crinkling with pleasure. He set her gently down but before she could say anything, his warm lips covered hers, tenderly at first and then more intensely as he pulled her close, her body fitting willingly to his. Katie felt her heart race and her breath quicken as Andy's strong arms held her so tight she could feel his heart beating.

Andy grazed her lips with another lingering kiss before leaning back and grinning into her flushed face.

"That was some welcome home, mister," she sighed happily before opening her eyes.

Looking into Andy's face, she could tell something was wrong. The smile on her face turned into a frown and then a look of concern.

"You look pale."

Andy dropped his arms and walked quickly back to the bathroom. "I'm fine," he said, an edge in his voice.

"You sure?" Katie ventured, peering into the steamy bathroom.

"I said I'm fine," Andy said as he snapped a tee shirt over his head. "Why can't you just take me at my word. I'm tired of being second guessed on everything." A sudden flush of anger covered his face as he turned on Katie.

Startled, Katie took a quick step back. "No one is second guessing you," she tried to assure him in a soft voice. "You just don't look like you feel well."

"Again, I am fine," Andy snarled, brushing past her. "Don't we have an open house to get to?"

Katie stood motionless, her damp clothes clinging to her, watching as Andy finished dressing with intense, deliberate movements before he turned to pin her with a glare. Besides that one look, Katie noticed, Andy had pointedly avoided eye contact.

She was genuinely puzzled. They hadn't had many fights since getting married, but lately the least thing set Andy off. The first time he'd gotten angry like this was a couple of months ago. Katie remembered it vividly since it had been so out of character for him. The Fire Department softball team had won a resounding victory over a major rival. Andy had played a great game as short stop, and they were driving to meet the team and their spouses at dinner to celebrate. Katie enjoyed these after-game dinners as much as Andy, but that particular evening, she mentioned needing to leave a little early since she had a teacher work-day the next day. Anger had suddenly flooded Andy's face red before he turned on her. "Are you deliberately trying to cut my time with the team short?" he'd exploded. "You know this is something I look forward to every week. Are you going to ask me to stop playing next?"

She had fallen against the seat, stunned. Andy knew she enjoyed the dinners. Leaving early that night was an exception. Andy had ranted until they'd gotten close to the restaurant and then just as suddenly as it began, his fury ended with him sheepishly contrite for losing his temper. There had been other smaller fits of anger, but the episode tonight was the worst since that night.

Katie opened her mouth but closed it again when Andy huffed out of the room. She felt the air escape her lungs as she fell against the closet door. Several minutes passed before she glanced at the clock, and seeing the time, she tried to shift her focus to the evening ahead. She looked down the hall after Andy. What had just happened? Had she done something wrong?

———

GUILT SAT ON ANDY's shoulders like a rock. He'd hoped taking a shower would help him look better than he felt, but it obviously hadn't worked. He closed the car door behind Katie and slid into the driver's seat. She sat silent, pensive, staring out the passenger window as he pulled out of the drive and turned toward the school. Oh, how he wished he could take back what he'd said. He'd lashed out before he'd realized what he was doing. While trying to ignore the increasing pain, even the smallest things were frustrating him, and in that frustration, he was lashing out at the closest thing to him. Tonight, that happened to be Katie, who already had so much on her mind.

Katie hadn't said a word since he'd stormed out of the room, and he couldn't blame her. His fingers tapped nervously on the steering wheel. He fought the urge to pull over and tell her about everything — the shaking hands, the dizziness, the painful stomach cramps and everything else, but he couldn't. Not tonight. Besides, he didn't want to add to her worries. He was supposed to take care of her.

Cautiously Andy asked, "Ready for tonight?"

Several seconds passed before Katie finally mumbled, "I think so," and continued to stare out the window.

Andy was keenly aware of Katie's nervous silences when she was stressed. The start of the school year was always a trying time for her whether preparing for her new class or dealing with Sally. Andy cringed. He'd hoped, without success, that Sally might change schools over the summer.

Andy's attention snapped back to Katie when he heard her ask softly, "How are things at the station?"

A small frown creased Andy's forehead. He was puzzled at Katie bringing the station up for the second time that day. He was usually the one to talk about it. Unsure of where this was leading, he said cautiously, "Well, they're fine. Nothing exciting except Hedrick has been preparing some amazing meals lately. We sure lucked out when we got him. That guy can cook."

Andy glanced at her but the look on her face was totally unreadable. She turned to look out the window once more.

Andy tried again and with a soothing voice said, "I wish I'd had a teacher as pretty as you when I was in school. If I know anything, I know those kids are lucky to have you for their teacher."

Silence was her only reply. He continued nervously tapping the steering wheel and waited, hoping she'd say more, but nothing broke the strained silence.

After parking, Andy made a quick dash around the car and opened Katie's door. The surprised but pleased look on her face made him smile. As she got out, he whispered in her ear, "Katie, honey, I'm so sorry about earlier."

His blue eyes sparkled and his lips turned into a tentative and apologetic smile. Katie offered a small, hesitant smile in return. Andy pushed the car door closed and took her hand firmly, but gently, in his own. He wove his fingers with hers and pulled her close to his side. He felt the tension in her begin to relax as they walked toward the door.

Andy leaned in close to tell Katie how beautiful she looked but was interrupted by a cooing voice behind them. "Well, hello, Garretts! Don't you two look cozy."

They turned as Sally sidled up to them. Andy scowled and looked away, as she fell into step beside them. He opened the door for Katie as they reached the building, then stepped back to give Sally a wide berth. Instead, she stepped close, trying to brush up against him as she skimmed past him through the door. Andy held the door and nodded to a few other arrivals before catching up with Katie. Taking her hand, he ignored Sally and firmly steered Katie toward her classroom.

"What's going on?" Katie asked as they reached the door.

"Nothing, nothing," Andy answered. "I'm just anxious to see your room."

He turned away as Sally tried to get his attention before disappearing inside her room.

Katie sensed Andy's tension and squeezed his hand as they stepped inside her room. She realized Sally must have done or said something that bothered him, and she wished, not for the first time, that Sally was at another school.

Once inside her classroom, Andy smiled as he turned in a slow circle admiring her room, his eyes shining with pride. Katie watched Andy, remembering the night they'd met vividly. It all happened so fast, and she still couldn't recall the exact sequence of events. All she remembered was after a game between Andy's and her brother's softball teams, their paths crossed. Andy was headed straight for her and without her stopping completely, there was no way to avoid him. Her eyes had locked onto his face, so strong and handsome, highlighted by sparkling blue eyes and boyish good looks. He had a short, upturned nose and lips that seemed to be twitching with mischief at something a teammate was saying. A red Fire Department cap sat on top of wavy brown hair and his firm chin boasted the most appealing bit of soft brown scruff Katie had ever seen. She was mesmerized, and even though she managed to keep walking somehow, she couldn't take her eyes off of him.

Before she could talk herself out of it, Katie stepped right in front of him. He ran full force into her and to catch himself from falling, he'd grabbed her arm. She could still feel the thrill of that first touch. Their faces were only inches apart, until Andy steadied himself and stepped back. The two groups kept walking but some of Andy's teammates, Katie noticed, grinned or smirked as they passed by.

Katie's heart hammered, wondering what was going on behind those electric blue eyes focused so unwaveringly on her. Under the intensity of his look, she hadn't been able to think of a single thing to say and immediately regretted her boldness. She looked frantically around trying to find a way out of this awkward situation she'd ridiculously created for herself. What seemed like hours had only been a few seconds. The frustrated look on Andy's amazingly handsome face had been replaced with a look of pleased surprise.

She'd turned quickly to leave but felt his hand on her arm.

"Wait," he'd said softly. "I don't believe we've met. My name is Andy, Andy Garrett."

Katie looked up and couldn't force even a squeak past her lips. He'd put out his hand and with an impish grin said, "And you are?"

"Katie," she remembered whispering. Andy had taken her cold hand in his warm one and smiled.

"It's nice to meet you, Katie. Did you enjoy the game?"

She could only nod.

"I love softball," he said, standing there as if he had nowhere else to go. "What brings you out tonight? Do you have someone on the other team?"

Again, Katie remembered only nodding but forced herself to clear her throat and said, "My brother. My brother is on the other team."

"Ah. He's probably not too happy, being on the losing side this time."

Before she thought, Katie blurted out, "No, that's okay. His team loses a lot."

Andy had tossed his head back and laughed, which gave Katie the courage to look at him and smile.

"That's awesome, but don't let him hear you say that," Andy said, chuckling again.

Andy had hesitated then and seemed a bit nervous when he said, "The team usually goes out for a bite after the game. Would you like to join us? I think I heard it's burgers tonight."

She was stunned. This amazing guy was asking her out? She must not have heard right. Besides, she was stupidly nervous around him.

She hadn't even been able to make basic conversation, but she'd wanted to go — she'd wanted to go so badly.

"Thank you, but I'm studying for finals next week and need to get back," she'd replied. "Congratulations on the win. It was nice to meet you." Proud that she'd made sense, she walked away and left him standing there.

Katie smiled at the memory as she shuffled some papers on her desk. She glanced over to where Andy stood, studying her closely. Blushing, as if he'd been reading her mind, she asked, "What are you doing?"

"Studying."

Puzzled, Katie said, "Studying?"

"Yep. I'm in a classroom, and that's what you do in a classroom. Right?"

"Well, yes," Katie replied, cocking one eyebrow. "And just what topic would you be studying then?"

Andy grinned and started walking toward her. "I am studying my best friend who — lucky for me — happens to be my wife, who also happens to be gorgeous."

He stopped in front of her desk and, looking her in the eye, said, "Katie, I really am sorry about earlier. That came out of nowhere, and I regret it. I know how important tonight is to you, and I am truly sorry to add to your stress. Will you forgive me?"

He hung his head but peeked up at her with a twinkle in his eye.

"Oh, Andy, you know you're forgiven, but — "

He looked at her with sudden concern. "But what?"

"But you would tell me if something was wrong, wouldn't you? Or if there was something going on at the station or anything else, wouldn't you?"

Andy blinked. He didn't want to lie, but he didn't want to worry her either. He stepped around the desk and, taking the papers from her hands, laid them on the desk and clasped her hands tightly. Looking her in the eye he said, "You have my solemn word."

He raised both of her hands to his lips and kissed them tenderly.

Katie blushed with pleasure. "Then, one more thing."

Andy leaned closer. "Yes?"

"Thank you for the beautiful flowers." She nodded to the bouquet of flowers, gracing her desk. The card read, "Flowers for my beautiful lady. Good luck, Mrs. Garrett."

Andy smiled. "You, my dear, are most welcome. Now, you'd better get busy."

Andy resumed his observation of her room, while Katie straightened her desk. Focused on the task at hand, Katie didn't look up for several seconds, and when she did, she noticed Andy was moving stiffly, his hand pressed tightly to his side. When their eyes met, he straightened and quickly smiled the brilliant smile he saved just for her.

Katie was glad he was here. Andy's support meant the world to her, and he'd promised this year, as he did every year, to stay in the background and just watch. "This is your show, Katie dear. I'm merely a supporting player, happy to follow your lead."

But Katie knew before the night was over, he'd be right in the middle of everything, and that was exactly where she always wanted him to be.

KATIE LAY IN THE dark, anticipating the alarm. The sheets were soft against her skin, while the warmth of Andy sleeping next to her was soothing. She had slept fretfully, anxious for the morning to come. Growing up, it had never occurred to her that teachers were nervous on the first day of school but now, she knew better.

Andy had also tossed and turned all night, which hadn't helped her sleep. He usually slept silent and still, but last night he had been all over the bed and even moaned in his sleep once or twice. Concern crossed Katie's mind. Something was going on with Andy she couldn't figure out but after his assurances last night, she was confident he'd tell her if anything was ever wrong.

Last night had been a tremendous success — all but one student and set of parents had come. Her room had turned out just as she'd envisioned it. Her 'second grade stars of the universe' theme had been a big hit with parents and students alike. They'd especially liked the stars of the universe bulletin board, which featured stars with the name of a student on each and placed among 3-D cutouts of the solar system planets. The parents had already shown their appreciation for her knowing so much about their child. She had turned on the rotating universe for Andy after everyone had gone and received a big thumbs up and huge grin from him. It would be fun to see the students' reaction when they saw it rotating across the ceiling for the first time. Katie smiled into the dark.

As Katie predicted, Andy had become the central figure of the evening, meeting each student and their parents, introducing himself with a charming smile as Mrs. Garrett's husband. He had ingratiated himself with everyone, something he always did easily. Katie had learned of Andy's reputation as a ladies' man soon after their first date but had already discovered why he was so popular and the ladies found him so attractive. He was handsome, no question there, but he was also outgoing and fun. He never seemed at a loss for something to do, and Katie felt herself carried along in the wake of his magnetism, which was outweighed only by his kindness.

It seemed as if Andy had saved every romantic idea or thoughtful deed until he'd met her. Anything remotely capable of sweeping a girl off her feet — cards, gifts, phone calls, romantic dates — Andy had sent her way. She couldn't imagine anyone more personable, charming or sincere than Andy. After he proposed, Andy confessed to her that he had purposefully cultivated a play-boy reputation during and right after high school to fend off girls and any kind of commitment. He said he'd never wanted to commit to a relationship before — something to do with his mom. He told Katie he had worked hard to maintain his freedom, but all that changed when he met her, and now, commitment, he'd assured her, *was* what he wanted.

It didn't seem possible they had already been married three, very happy years, but today was the first day of another school year. She rolled over and looked at the clock. 5:45 a.m. What's fifteen minutes? she thought, as she tossed off the covers and sat on the edge of the bed. She looked over her shoulder at Andy. His soft breathing and the childishly-innocent look on his face made her smile. She leaned over to brush some hair from his forehead and kiss him softly on his stubbly cheek. He stirred but didn't wake. His gentle slumber and soft scent tempted her back to bed, but not this morning. She couldn't be late the first day of school.

———

ANDY'S ARM FLAILED BLINDLY, reaching for the alarm when it went off fifteen minutes later. He rolled toward Katie's side of the bed but found it empty. When he looked at the clock again, it was 6:45 a.m. Groggy, he laid there a few more minutes until he remembered today was the first day of school, and Katie usually didn't sleep well the night before. The smell of coffee drifting in from the kitchen confirmed she was up. He rolled out of bed and pulled on a pair of warm up pants before making his way to the kitchen.

Hearing him, Katie turned and then burst into laughter.

"What?" Andy said as he stepped onto the kitchen's cold tile and opened the cabinet to grab a coffee mug.

Katie leaned against the counter and giggled as she took a sip of coffee.

"If you could only see yourself. You look like you wrestled a bear last night and the bear won. Every hair on your head is standing on end."

She was right. He hadn't slept well, but he rubbed his hands over his hair, pretending to be hurt. He knew he must look a fright.

Katie took a last sip of coffee and poured the rest down the sink. Grabbing her lunch satchel off the counter, she said, "Sorry, got to run."

She patted Andy's cheek and gave him a quick peck on the lips as she went by but then stopped abruptly and came back. With a coy smile, she stood on her toes and gave him a gentle kiss on the lips as his free arm circled her waist and pulled her close.

"What was that for?" he asked with a grin.

"For luck and because I love you," Katie said, heading toward the door. "Bye."

"You're going to be amazing today, Mrs. Garrett!" Andy called after her.

Andy smiled into his steaming coffee cup, the rich aroma tickling his nose. Katie had brewed it extra strong, just the way he liked it. His outburst seemed to have been forgiven. He was one very lucky guy.

K ATIE WAITED BY HER classroom door, excited to greet her students.
"Good morning, Samantha. Good morning, Thomas. Good
morning, Sebastian." She smiled brightly and greeted each by
name as they filed in. Their eyes went wide with wonder seeing the
universe swirl across the ceiling in a revolving light show while soft
music played from a hidden speaker. Students found their desks with
the help of rocket-shaped name tags, their names written in big block
letters. She and Andy had placed them on each desk last night after the
students left.

"Good morning, Laura. Come in, Janice," Katie continued, calling each by name as they filed through the door. "Please find your desk
and take a seat."

She looked down to see one last student hovering at the door.
He hadn't been there last night, and the only name not matched to a
face had been Lucas Matthews. Lucas looked tired. His clothes were
unkempt and too small, and his long, blond hair was tangled and
unruly. The golden flecks in his brown eyes, though, glowed with gen-
tleness and kindness. He looked up at her expectantly.

"You must be Lucas Matthews," Katie said with a warm smile.

Lucas nodded. "Yes, ma'am," he said softly.

"We're glad you're here. Come in and find the rocket ship with your name. That will be your seat."

Lucas gave Katie a small smile before stepping into the room. She watched as he looked around nervously until he found the desk with his name and slid into his seat. Lucas didn't bring any of the required school supplies or, Katie noticed, lunch. She made a mental note to pick up extra school supplies that evening and to make sure he had something to eat at lunch.

Closing the door, Katie moved to the front of the room and sat at a low table. She surveyed the faces watching her.

"As a reminder, my name is Mrs. Garrett," she began as she switched off the music and the universe circling the ceiling. "I am your teacher this year, and I'm excited you're here because we have a lot to learn and a lot to discover. I look forward to getting to know each of you. To get things started, let me tell you a little bit about myself."

She wrote her name on the monitor that projected the image onto a screen on the wall. "My name is Katelyn Garrett, but my students, and that's you," she said, pointing at each of them and smiling, "call me Mrs. Garrett." She picked up a pink carnation and twirled it around. "My favorite color is —"

"Pink! Pink!" several of the students said excitedly.

Katie nodded and smiled. She stopped again and held up a book. "That's right! And my favorite subject is . . ."

"Reading! To Read!" several chimed in at one time.

Katie laughed. "That's right. You are all so smart. Now can you guess my favorite food?" Katie grinned as the students looked at each other, puzzled.

"Okay — that's a hard one. My favorite food is — Italian food!"

The children clapped as they cheered their agreement with her choice.

"Are you married?" the little boy named Sebastian blurted out.

Katie laughed. "Yes, I'm married. My husband's name is Andy. He's a firefighter and paramedic for the City of Abernathy."

When Katie said firefighter, their faces lit up with excitement. One little boy's hand went up and started waving frantically.

"Yes, Caleb?"

"Does he drive a fire truck?" Caleb asked, eyes round with interest.

"No, he's not the one who drives the fire truck, but he does ride in the seat right behind the driver when they go to fires."

"Whoa," Caleb said, obviously impressed.

Another hand flew up.

"Can we see his fire truck?" Lucas asked excitedly.

Pleased Lucas was taking part, Katie mused aloud as if thinking hard. A field trip to the station was already being planned, but instead, she acted like it was going to be a challenge. "I think that might be arranged, but," she hurried to add as the class erupted into excited talking, "but — first, we have to learn and study hard. Only after we do those two things, can we visit the fire station and see the fire truck. Is it a deal?"

"Deal!" they all shouted in unison. Katie smiled at their eager faces.

After his excitement about visiting the fire station, Lucas retreated into himself, not engaging with the other students for the rest of the morning.

After an overview of what to expect each day — recess and a round of reading and math exercises — it was time for lunch. Katie noticed Lucas made sure he was last in line when the class filed out.

Katie slipped the cafeteria cashier the necessary money for Lucas' lunch. Since it was the first day, Katie carefully guided her students through the line, making sure they knew what to do. She made sure

Lucas picked up a tray of hot food before he sat at the table assigned to their class. Katie stood in the door to the cafeteria and watched, smiling and speaking to other teachers as they brought their classes through. Katie watched Lucas as he sat at the same table with the other students, but he sat on the end and well apart from everyone. Ignoring their chatter, he devoured the food on his tray quickly until everything was gone.

Katie's heart went out to Lucas. He reminded her of what Andy had told her his childhood was like. Whatever she could do to prevent another little boy from going through what Andy had, she was going to do.

It had been hard for Andy, but he'd gradually confided in her how he'd grown up. He and his mom had been close until Andy turned ten, then his mom married a man who verbally abused and bullied Andy until he graduated high school and left home. The abuse was brutal and intimidating, and his mother never once intervened on his behalf. Andy had been a star athlete in high school, especially in baseball, but his mom never came to a single game or acknowledged his accomplishments in any way. At age ten, Andy had been emotionally abandoned to make do on his own. Katie's heart ached for Andy as he told her so many painful stories from his past, and her love for him only grew as she realized what an exceptional person he had turned out to be.

The afternoon passed quickly, and when the dismissal bell rang at 2:45 p.m., Katie was tired, but happy. It had been a great first day. She walked her students out to the designated pick-up area while keeping an eye on Lucas, hoping to meet one of his parents. As she watched, he walked out of the gate with the others, but instead of going to the pick-up area, he turned to the left, walking through the lines of students from other grades. Katie hurried to catch up to him.

"Lucas!"

He stopped and turned.

"Where are you going?" she asked as she knelt beside him. "The buses and parent pick-ups are over there."

"But I live over there," he said, gesturing in the general direction of some old apartments. "My mom said to meet her at home when school was over."

"I see," Katie said. "Would you please tell your mother I would like to meet her? She can come by one day after school, and you can show her our room."

Lucas' head jerked up. "Am I in trouble?"

"Oh my, no," Katie rushed to assure him. "I would just like to meet her and tell her how glad I am you're in my class."

Lucas studied her. Katie could tell he was unsure.

Katie changed her direction. "I'll tell you what. You decide when you want to ask her to visit. You may want to wait until you have some work to show her, but I'll let you decide. How does that sound?"

Lucas looked at her, still unsure, but finally, he nodded slowly.

"Great!" Katie said. "When you're ready, tell her your teacher, Mrs. Garrett, is looking forward to meeting her."

Katie stood and patted him on the back. "Okay then. See you in the morning."

Lucas nodded and shuffled off. Katie watched him for a few seconds before returning to her other students.

Her phone buzzed as she walked back to her room a few minutes later. She smiled when she pulled it out of her pocket and saw Andy's name.

"Hey there!" she said, smiling.

"Hey there, yourself. How was the first day?"

"Actually, it was a great first day. I'll tell you all about it. And — you'll never believe it," she said with a tease, "they want to see your fire truck! They were so excited when I told them I was married to a real firefighter."

Andy laughed. "I will be honored to give them the grand tour."

"That means we'll have the best tour guide in the department then," Katie said with a chuckle. "One thing though, I have a little boy who I can tell needs some extra attention. The only part of the day he really interacted with the group was when we talked about the fire station. Would you be up for a little more one-on-one time with him than just the tour? I'll need to get his mom's permission, but —"

"Come on," Andy scoffed, "you forget who you're talking to. Aren't you the one always telling me I act like a kid? I bet he and I will get along great."

"Of course! What was I thinking?" Katie said, laughing as she reached her room. "I'll miss you tonight." She thought ahead to the evening alone, and Andy at the station.

"I'll miss you, too. I always do. You're much better company than these knuckleheads."

Katie laughed. She knew Andy loved being at the station and enjoyed the company of the guys. She didn't think there was anything he didn't love about being a firefighter, except possibly Lt. Bentley.

"I tell you what," Andy said conspiratorially.

"What?" Katie responded, smiling.

"Even though we can't go tonight, how about our usual tomorrow night?"

"And by our 'usual,' would you happen to mean our traditional first night of school dinner at Gessupi's?"

"Oh? Do we have another usual?"

"Let's see . . . what about our first baseball game of the year hot dog and ice cream sundae at The Sky View Drive-In or the first football game of the season barbecue at —"

"Okay, okay, you're right," Andy laughed. "So, allow me to provide a little more definition to 'our usual' in this particular case."

Andy cleared his throat dramatically. "Mrs. Garrett, would you do me the honor of dining with me tomorrow evening at Gessupi's Italian restaurant in celebration of the first day of school? The favor of a reply would be greatly appreciated."

Katie laughed, "You're such a clown. But of course, Mr. Garrett, I most happily accept your invitation. Do you want me to make reservations?"

"Oh ye of little faith, Mrs. Garrett. I made reservations last week."

Katie smiled. "How do you always manage to remember?"

"Don't you know by now? It's *any*thing for my girl."

Even though Andy had said those words before, Katie's heart fluttered to hear them again. "I love you, Andy Garrett. So much."

"I love you too, Katie Garrett. Forever." Andy said.

"I can't wait until tomorrow night," Katie said softly. "And not just for Gessuppi's either. I'll miss you tonight. Be safe."

Andy replied, "I'll miss you too, my dear Katie. Bye."

ANDY GASPED AND LURCHED awake. His chest was heaving and his heart racing. An explosion of light propelled him out of bed, and he was almost relieved to hear the station's alarm.

"Garrett, get a move on!" Lt. Bentley yelled as he rushed past the door.

Andy shook his head, trying to clear the haze snarling his mind. He threw on his uniform t-shirt, then half ran, half hopped into his coveralls, bringing up the rear as he followed the others down the narrow hall to the engine bay. A quick glance at his watch showed 1:36 A.M.

The rumble of the powerful diesel had begun to echo around the cinder block walls when Andy skidded to a halt at the back door of the engine's cab. He jumped into the boots and bunker pants he'd left rolled down and ready the evening before, slipping the straps up and onto his shoulders with a sharp snap. The dispatcher's message came across the intercom again: "Engine One, Truck One, Engine Two, Engine Three, Ladder Three, Battalion Chief 303. Structure fire. 740 South Iverson. Caller reports heavy flames." The bay doors arched overhead, screeching with the harsh squeal of metal against metal as they banged to a stop.

Andy grabbed his bunker coat from where it hung on the open cab door, pushing one arm through the thick sleeves and then the other. He jumped into the cab, landing in the seat with a heavy thump and started closing the fasteners on the front of his coat. He pulled his door closed as the other doors slammed shut.

The siren wail started low and built to a crescendo as the red lights started circling the walls. No one talked as they adjusted their coats and pulled on their headsets. The team in the ambulance were making their preparations and readying to pull out ahead of the engine. Andy's heart beat fast, and he fumbled with his headphones as he tried to slip them on. He stopped short when he realized his hands were shaking. He glanced around quickly to see if anyone had noticed, but everyone was too preoccupied. He took a deep breath and put his headset on, adjusting the microphone in front of his lips. He reached into his bunker coat and pulled his heavy gloves from the pocket. He took a quick swipe at the cold sweat beading on his forehead before he shoved the gloves into his lap and pressed his hands together. He was rarely nervous anymore, but he shook his head, telling himself it was just an adrenaline rush.

Lt. Bentley acknowledged their departure back to dispatch via the radio, and the engine shifted into gear. Andy frowned as he looked down through the half-lit darkness at his tightly clasped hands continuing to shake.

As STATION OFFICER, LT. Mike Bentley sat in the seat next to the driver. Even in the dark, Andy could see Bentley's jaw muscle clench and unclench as he jotted down information from dispatch. Bentley's clenched jaw and the fury it typically foretold were all too familiar.

Since Andy's assignment to Station Two six months ago, he and Bentley had been clashing frequently, from verbal sparring to Bentley's relentless harsh scrutiny of Andy and everything he did. The escalating tension was creating an uncomfortable atmosphere at the station. It was evident that Bentley's mission was to vent every frustration at Andy, making sure Andy felt every possible shred of anger. Andy sighed. He'd had high hopes for his career, but having to deal with Bentley's continual complaints to command about him made it look like he would remain a first level firefighter for the foreseeable future.

Andy glanced to his right where Sean Hedrick, the station rookie, sat in the seat behind Bentley. Head out the window, Hedrick was straining to see the first sign of fire. Andy grinned and shook his head. Hedrick had been with C shift for four months now, and even though other stations had fought to get him when he graduated from the academy, Station Two won out. Being a rookie hadn't mattered when it came to Hedrick, so long as he delivered on his reputation of being an outstanding cook. He hadn't disappointed in that department but still — he was a rookie.

"Rookie," Andy said into his mouthpiece. Hedrick jumped and pulled his head in the window, a question on his face.

"Coat," Andy said nodding at Hedrick's unsnapped and unzipped bunker coat. "Button it up."

Hedrick's eyes widened as he looked down at his coat and offered an apologetic grin. He set his helmet and gloves on the floor between his boots, snapping and zipping his coat closed. Andy gave him a thumbs up and then peered ahead, trying to see past the glow of the dashboard lights.

———

THE ENGINE TOOK A sharp right turn onto a residential street, and the siren squelched abruptly while the red lights continued spinning. Battalion Chief Curtis Rogers pulled onto the scene at the same time, assuming a command position a short distance from the fire ground. He began directing the laying of hose lines and personnel deployment. The structure involved was a two-story house with flames showing from its first-floor windows. The glow was already bright enough to light up the surrounding houses.

Andy hefted his air tank onto his back and pulled the straps tight over his shoulders. Bentley was doing the same when Chief Rogers came over the radio: "Offensive. This is an Offensive fire. Engine One, Engine Two, attack. Family members and pets accounted for. Fire is Charlie/Delta side."

As Rogers continued his directions, Andy and Bentley slipped their masks on and secured their hoods before attaching their breathing apparatus. With helmet strapped into place and gloves on, Andy lifted the hose nozzle. He could feel the pulse of the pressurized water in the taut hose. He grasped it firmly with his thick gloves as Bentley stepped in close behind him. The hose was heavy, and it sagged with the weight of the water as they began dragging it toward the house.

The mask and hood enveloped Andy in the vacuum of a sudden hush. Each breath through his mouthpiece sounded raspy and loud. He blinked hard and blinked again, fighting the already steady stream of sweat treading its way down his forehead. Bentley pushed Andy roughly forward and with a tug on the charged hose, they stepped through the home's front door. Andy maneuvered carefully through the unfamiliar rooms, drawing closer to the glimmer of orange he could barely make out through the thick smoke. As they drew closer to the flames, blistering heat radiated around them. Andy stopped and braced his boots on the hardwood floor. Moving the lever on the nozzle to open the flow of water, Bentley stooped low, close behind him, working to hold the charged hose steady. Andy immediately heard the hiss of the pressured water hitting the flames as it escaped the confines of the hose and instantly, a billowing cloud of scorching steam enveloped them. They moved forward slowly and methodically, directing the water toward the flames, aiming the hose toward any sign of a flame or spark until the fire was completely tapped out.

With the flames extinguished and smoke hanging thick, darkness surrounded them. Andy took a deep breath and shut off the stream of water from the hose. He took a step back and fell against Bentley, who had been following too close behind. Startled, Bentley jerked back, and Andy could feel the strength of his glare even through the smoke. Bentley pulled on the hose and Andy could tell he had turned to retrace their steps to the front door, but Andy hesitated, reluctant to leave until he was sure no hot spots lingered. Using the brightness of a spotlight now shining through a ventilation hole created by Truck One, Andy carefully started moving the charred remains around with the toe of his boot.

The hose jerked in Andy's hand again, harder this time, as Bentley gave it another yank. Frustrated with Bentley's lack of attention to detail, Andy continued checking for live sparks until he was satisfied all were eliminated. Only then did he follow Bentley out the door.

Once outside, Andy pulled off his helmet, his mask and finally his hood as he strode to the engine. Bathed in sweat, he braced himself against the engine's side and gulped down lungs full of sweet, fresh air.

Sweat ran down the bridge of his nose, dropping off to join the water already running in the street. When Andy straightened, he saw Hedrick down the block, attempting, unsuccessfully, to disconnect one of the hoses from a hydrant. It looked like the rookie needed some help, so Andy made his way down to him. They were able to disconnect the coupling, and Hedrick gave Andy a quick nod of thanks as they pulled the heavy hoses onto the hose bed. The noise created by the firefighters seemed extra loud in the pre-dawn quiet as knots of curious neighbors finally made their way home.

Once tools and equipment were stowed, Bentley confirmed with Rogers that Engine Two's work on scene was complete. Andy, along with the others, eagerly shed their hot bunker coats and discarded them onto the floorboard as the familiar smell of acrid smoke filled the cab. Andy clicked his seat belt on over his bunker pants and adjusted his headphones. He looked around as the others did the same, and he couldn't help but grin. Oh, how he loved this job.

"Engine Two, back at station." Bentley radioed into dispatch just as the brilliant rays of the rising sun peeked over the horizon.

The engine backed in as one of the large, silver bay doors rolled opened. The engine bounced and then bounced again while it rolled over the drainage dip between the street and the drive. Station Two was one of the first fire stations built in Abernathy, now in an older part of town. Made of dark red brick, it nestled onto its tree-lined street just around the corner from a light commercial area. It might have been old, but it was homey. And in spite of the many coats of paint, the worn spots in the floor tile, the sticking cabinet doors and slow-running showers, it was affectionately known by its firefighters as 'The Deuce.' The new Station Two, currently under construction, would be welcome, but hundreds of firefighters had called this station home, and those they served with and beside have become family.

The driver slowed the engine for a short stop as Andy, stifling a yawn, released his seat belt. His hand was already on the door handle when Bentley barked out, "Garrett, get the exhaust hose."

Andy stifled a reply but rolled his eyes as he opened his door and jumped into the early morning heat. Attaching the exhaust hose was his regular assignment. He didn't need to be told.

Fall wasn't supposed to be far away, but the summer's heat was refusing to make its exit. The heat had intensified overnight and Andy's dark blue Abernathy Fire Department t-shirt was sweat-soaked and his bunker pants felt like ovens on his legs. He stepped into the shadows of the open bay door and retrieved the exhaust hose hanging from the ceiling. Sliding it across the overhead railing, Andy quickly connected its nozzle onto the engine's exhaust to prevent diesel fumes from escaping into the bay.

He positioned himself so the driver could see him in the large side mirrors and keeping step with the engine, signaled as the driver expertly backed the engine. The high-pitched beep of the back-up alarm was soon accompanied by the reverberating rumble of the diesel engine as it entered the bay. Andy sliced his hand across his throat to signal stop, and the cab doors swung open as the driver killed the engine. The three firefighters jumped to the ground, their thick rubber boots hitting the concrete floor, one solid thud after another.

The crew looked at each other and shook their heads as Bentley headed to his office, leaving them to prep the equipment for the next call.

Jernigan, the driver, looked at Andy and shook his head. "I wouldn't want to put him out any and ask him to help," he said with a snide grin.

"It'd be a waste of breath," Andy chuckled. He turned to Hedrick.

"Rookie, looks like we need to introduce you to a few more fire hydrants. I'd hate to leave a hose behind because you couldn't get it unfastened."

Hedrick did his best to ignore Andy's banter, but Andy couldn't help but razz him a time or two while they worked, resulting in a red-faced Hedrick and hearty laughs from Jernigan. While gathering the discarded bunker gear, Andy happened to glance at the office window that overlooked the bay and caught Bentley scowling at him from behind his desk. Andy couldn't help himself. He broke into a huge smile and waved furiously at Bentley as if he were a long-lost friend. Bentley's face turned a deep shade of crimson, and Andy thought, with a chuckle, he was literally going to explode.

ANDY CAME TO AN abrupt halt as he rounded the corner of the engine, stopping just short of the array of tools Hedrick had laid around him on the concrete floor.

"Rookie, you might want to think again about where you're laying things," Andy said with a grin. "Oh and, you missed a spot."

Sean Hedrick sat on the running board of the engine cleaning tools used the night before, carefully laying them in an arch around him. He jerked his chin at Andy in mock defiance but kept working.

While Hedrick cleaned the tools, Andy gathered the bunker coats, pants, gloves, and helmet hoods from where they'd been thrown in a pile behind the engine. Helmets were left on their owners' seats in the cab. Andy carried the gear to the back of the bay and threw the first set into the extractor unit they'd received a couple of months ago. It had been a big deal to Chief Hamilton that every Abernathy station get an extractor which was the latest technology in deep cleaning bunker gear. Previously, Abernathy bunker gear had been cleaned only once a year but now, gear went through an extractor after every incendiary incident and every firefighter had been issued a backup set.

After stuffing the gear into the extractor and starting it, Andy pulled extra bunker coats and pants off their pegs on the back wall of the bay. The coats, matching those in the extractor, were stenciled with each firefighter's name across the bottom in reflective tape. Andy hung the appropriate bunker coat on the door of the cab where each firefighter sat and set the pants just outside the door, rolling them down so they were ready to step into. Lt. Bentley's gear went to the officer's seat on the front passenger side, gear for the engine's driver, Keevin Jernigan, went to the driver's door. Andy's own gear went to the door behind the driver while the rookie, Sean Hedrick's gear, went behind Bentley's. There was less than an hour left on shift, but they were to be ready at all times. The first task complete, Andy went to the back of the engine and stepped up and onto the hose bed to check the hose.

Jernigan, Hedrick, and Andy worked silently in tandem until Jernigan wrote the final entry onto his checklist, and Hedrick pulled the last compartment door shut.

"You working at RITE2U today, Garrett?" Jernigan asked, breaking the silence.

"Yep," Andy answered over his shoulder as he finished adjusting the last hose. He stifled another yawn as he stepped down from the back of the engine. Eying the hose stack, he stepped back up and straightened a couple of rolls one last time. Andy fretted. He felt tired — unusually so. He wrestled the last stubborn hose into place and jumped down.

"Got a date tonight, Romeo?" Andy asked Hedrick as they headed toward the living quarters.

Hedrick's face went a light shade of red as he frowned while Andy's mischievous grin widened. Hedrick's gaze had recently fallen on Mandy Fitzhugh, a sweet little ER nurse, but he couldn't put two coherent words together when he was around her. Andy noticed Hedrick's frown and thought he might be giving Hedrick too hard a time but then again, probably not.

Hedrick shrugged and tried to sound disinterested. "Nope."

"Sure, Rookie, sure," Andy and Jernigan chided as Hedrick turned a deeper shade of red.

They filed through the hallway toward the living area but were stopped by a freshly-showered Bentley.

"What's up, Lieutenant?" Jernigan asked. "We're almost out of time to shower within regs."

"You guys go ahead," Bentley said, eying Andy with a dark gleam. "Garrett has some more work to do."

Jernigan furrowed his brows. "But, Lieutenant —"

"Showers, gentlemen. Now," Bentley said, cutting Jernigan a hard look as he headed toward Andy.

Jernigan and Hedrick moved on but glanced back with concern.

Bentley stepped to within inches of Andy and with a smirk said, "Garrett, let's take another look at that hose bed. I don't think the hose is stowed right."

"Is that so, LEW-tenant?" Andy said with a cocked eyebrow, stepping aside and with an elaborate motion of his hand said, "After you."

At the back of the engine, Bentley stepped onto the running board and surveyed the hose laid in perfect alignment per departmental specifications.

"Looks like this one's wrong," Bentley said as he yanked the end of one hose, sending a large section onto the concrete floor. "Get it right this time, Garrett."

Andy gave a start when the hose hit the floor, and he fought to control the fury engulfing him as he watched Bentley swagger to the door. Andy stood motionless, remembering his stepfather Donald ripping the blanket and sheets off his bed one cold morning before school. An ex-Marine, Donald's face was red with fury as he towered over Andy. "Do it right, kid," he'd snarled. "No breakfast until it's perfect. I don't care how many times it takes." Andy remembered shaking, not only from the cold seeping through his thin pajamas, but from fear as he cowered under the barrage of abuse Donald continued to spew as, quivering, Andy tried to make his bed. Most vivid of all, was seeing his mother watching from the door; just watching, before she turned and walked away.

Andy balled his hands into fists, his eyes fixed on the tangled hose at his feet. He forced himself to take a deep breath before reaching for the hose and lifting it onto the hose bed. He arranged it correctly, again, exactly as it had been before. He checked his watch. He only had five minutes to shower and comply with regulations of showering within an hour of returning to the station.

He pulled his shirt off as he stepped into his room, and his glance fell on the tangle of sheets he'd left piled on his bed. Remembering his hands shaking that morning, Andy dropped his shirt on the bed and held them in front of him, palms down. They were smudged with grime and soot, but steady. He turned one over and then the other. Normal. He didn't remember when they'd stopped shaking, but they were fine now. He also remembered feeling foggy too. He shook his head, pushing the memory away, but it only caused the smell of smoke and soot to float in the air around him.

Reaching for the worn wooden door of his locker, Andy pulled out the Class B uniform most of the guys wore around the station: navy blue polo, navy twill pants, navy blue socks. Classic and clean, he loved every stitch. His badge gleamed above the left chest pocket and *A. Garrett* was embroidered above the right. His paramedic patch was stitched at the top of the right sleeve and the Abernathy Fire Department shield at the top of the left. Gathering the clean uniform,

Andy headed to the showers, the room heavy with steam, but both were in use.

"Hedrick!" Andy called, "You'd better be finished by the time I walk in there. You do remember, rookies shower last — right?"

He waited. Nothing but the spraying of showers answered. "Are you hearing me, Rookie?" he said a little louder.

Hedrick's face, dripping with water, poked around the partition of the furthest shower. "Sorry, thought I heard something. Guess not," he said with a mocking grin. His head disappeared behind the partition and a few seconds later the water shut off. He reappeared with a towel wrapped around his waist, his chest still wet. "All yours."

Andy stepped onto the wet shower floor. He didn't have time wait. Even though this was the worst of the two showers with its weak water flow, the warm water felt soothing as it rolled over him.

Ten minutes later, Andy stepped into the kitchen as the bay door banged open. Canfield and Hart, the ambulance crew, burst into the room, returning from a medical run.

"I'm telling you, it's going to be Everett," Canfield was arguing. "That kid has a rocket for an arm, and he's fast — really fast."

Canfield scurried behind Hart, attempting to keep up with his long strides.

A man of few words, Hart just grunted his typical reply, "Humph."

Andy rolled his eyes, watching Canfield trail Hart, talking non stop.

"Guys. Really? Again? This is old news," Andy called after them as they passed.

"Old news?" retorted Canfield as he turned and walked a few steps back toward Andy. "Just because it's not baseball, Garrett, doesn't mean it's not a hot topic. Football season is just getting started, so get used to it."

"I might remind you, this debate has been raging ever since the season ended last year," Andy said as Canfield walked away and disappeared.

Andy pulled a bag of coffee out of the C shift cabinet as Jernigan and Hedrick strode into the kitchen. Hedrick was busily stuffing his uniform shirt tail into his pants.

"What took you two so long?" Andy said as he punched the brew button.

Ignoring Andy's comment, Jernigan and Hedrick pulled out several mismatched coffee mugs and set them beside the brewer.

"Everything okay?" Jernigan asked, eying Andy. "What'd Bentley want this time?"

"Nothing," Andy said flatly.

Exchanging knowing glances, they each pulled out a chair and took a seat around the table. Bentley stalked into the kitchen and surveyed each man in his version of a military inspection, then grabbed one of the larger mugs waiting by the coffee pot. He put it under the brewer and filled it to the brim.

"Gonna leave any for us, LEW-tenant?" Garrett said with a roll of his eyes toward the others. Hedrick and Jernigan waited silently, their eyes first on Garrett and then on Bentley.

Bentley's back stiffened when he turned to see a devilish smile spreading across Andy's face. Bentley's glare deepened, and he opened his mouth to respond, but before he could say anything, Hart burst into the room, struggling to button his uniform shirt.

"Coffee ready?" he asked nonchalantly as he strode between the table of men and Bentley's rigid frame. Tension crackled in the air as Hart took his time filling a large mug.

"Smells good," Hart said, turning to lean against the cabinet. He took a sip of his drink, seemingly oblivious to what he had interrupted.

Bentley shook his head and walked back to his office.

Hedrick stood to start another pot, but Hart hadn't moved.

"Why do you do that, Garrett?" he asked, his focus on his coffee mug.

Andy eyed Hart. His entrance hadn't been quite so random after all.

Andy shrugged. "I don't know. You might say it's because I can, but mostly it's self-defense."

Canfield sauntered in and joined the group. "What'd I miss? Garrett razzing Bentley again?"

"Who me?" Andy asked with wide-eyed innocence.

Jernigan shook his head. He grabbed a mug, poured a cup, handing it to Hedrick, and then poured another for Andy.

"Get outta here, Garrett," Jernigan said. "You know you love giving Bentley hell, but you also know it makes it tough for the rest of us."

"Guys, I know. I'm sorry, but he can't relax and let things — especially me — just be. But I promise," Andy said, looking around the table, "I'll be good."

The others exchanged sideways glances. They knew better. Andy thrived on the conflict, especially when he knew he could get the better of Bentley, which he usually did. Things weren't likely to change any time soon.

The back door of the station banged open as several guys from the A shift strolled in, exchanging good mornings, some carrying their bedrolls and duffel bags.

Back in his room, Andy grabbed his own duffel bag and headed to the door. He had to get going. He had a full day of deliveries at RITE2U before dinner with Katie. As he turned toward the door, he suddenly felt an intense wave of dizziness. He steadied himself against the door frame and blinked rapidly, trying to stop the room from spinning. The sensation passed quickly, but it left him feeling weak.

Jernigan strode past but saw Andy chalk white and stopped. "You okay, man?"

Andy nodded stiffly. "Yeah. I'm good."

He stepped past Jernigan and moved through the kitchen toward the back door.

The warm air was stifling when he pushed the back door open, and it didn't help clear his head. He tossed his duffel bag onto the floor of his truck, cranked the engine and dialed the air conditioner to full blast. He sat, letting the cool air blow over him. His hands were trembling again and as he shifted the truck into drive, he reached for his cell phone. He knew what he needed. He needed to talk to Katie. She always made things better.

IT HAD BEEN A busy day at RITE2U day, but it had gone fast. Andy was looking forward to dinner with Katie — just the two of them. Even after the dizzy spell that morning, he felt truly happy and was in a good mood; a welcome change after the past few weeks. He hadn't been feeling like himself. It had been hard to maintain the facade at the station but even harder at home. He'd let his irritation get the better of him several times, but not today. Today, he felt great. He had finally decided to call Dr. Payne's office for an appointment but now, he felt so good, he didn't see the need. If he started to feel bad again, he'd make the call. Tonight, they were celebrating Katie's first day of school, and he'd celebrate feeling better. Andy pulled into the drive and was surprised to see Katie pull in behind him.

"I thought you'd already be home," Andy said as he swung out of his truck.

"I had a few errands to run, but I did hurry home. I've got a hot date tonight," Katie said, laughing as she closed the distance between them.

"I like the way you think," Andy said, putting an arm around her as they walked up the front steps.

"I'm tired but I think I'm even hungrier," Katie said, plopping unceremoniously onto the sofa.

Andy eased down beside her. He really wasn't hungry but said with a grin, "Gesuppi's is always a great cure for hunger."

"What time are the reservations?" Katie asked, looking at her watch.

"6:30," Andy said, glancing at his watch too. "It's 5:45 so we'd better get a move on. It will take us awhile to get there with traffic."

"I wish Gesuppi's was closer."

"Oh come on," Andy teased. "You'll have the best company in the world to entertain you on the way."

"Entertain?" Katie said with a coy smile. "That *is* the operative term."

"Come on, you," Andy said with a grin as he stood and pulled Katie to feet. "Let's eat."

Thirty minutes later, they pulled into Gesuppi's full parking lot. Gesuppi's was a local favorite, and it was special to Andy and Katie — it was where they'd had their first date and several months later where Andy had gotten to one knee and proposed. The full complement of waiters had cheered when Katie said yes. Mr Gesuppi had even stepped in and catered their rehearsal dinner as a wedding gift since Andy's mom wasn't around.

Mr. Gesuppi himself, a short, round-faced, jolly man, greeted them at the door with a hearty, "Ciao, my friends!" He pulled Katie close giving her an Italian air kiss to each cheek. Andy laughed as Mr. Gesuppi shook his hand and clapped him on the back in greeting. He escorted them to their table, winding through the main dining room full of patrons.

Katie breathed hungrily of the air that swam with rich Italian aromas and fresh bread. The dining room was dim except for sconce lighting on the walls and small votive candles on the tables. Their table, a special request of Andy, was tucked away in one of the back nooks and provided a greater degree of privacy. Mr. Gesuppi pulled Katie's chair out with a flourish while Andy pulled out the chair across from her. Handing them each a menu, he exclaimed jovially, "Enjoy, my friends."

With a wave of his hand, he was off to see to other guests. The low hum of voices was softened in this reclusive spot. The soft glow of the candles made the setting intimate.

Andy grinned at Katie as they opened their menus. Lifting the menu to hide her face, Katie pretended to read the offerings.

"Hmmmm," Andy mused. "Whatever am I going to have?"

Katie sighed dramatically. "Oh my, I just don't know what to order."

Giovanni, their waiter, walked up at that moment with two glasses of sweet iced tea. Setting the glasses on the dark wood table in front of them, he looked between them with an eyebrow cocked and asked dryly, "The usual?"

With a humph, Katie's menu fell forward revealing a teasing smile. "You might at least let us pretend to think about it first."

"Sure, sure. I don't have time to indulge you two," Giovanni countered with a grin.

"The usual for both of us, Gio," Andy laughed.

"Very good, sir," Giovanni said with a slight bow. He picked up the menus and hurried away.

"I love coming here. Thanks for remembering and for making the reservations," Katie said as she placed the white linen napkin in her lap and smiled at Andy.

"My pleasure," Andy replied with a wink. "So, the year is off to a good start?" he asked with a grin as he placed his own napkin in his lap.

"Yes — I am really pleased. It's a great group of students."

"I've said it before, but I'll say it again. They are mighty lucky to have you as their teacher." He shrugged his shoulders matter-of-factly. "Just saying."

Katie glowed at Andy's praise. "You are a bit biased though, don't you think?"

"Nope. Just stating the facts."

Andy took a sip of his sweet tea and set the glass back on the table. "Tell me about the one student you mentioned who might need some extra attention."

Katie's face lit up. "His name is Lucas Matthews. From what I've been able to figure out, he lives in a run-down apartment complex near the school with his mom. It sounds like it's just the two of them —"

Before Katie could go any further, Gio appeared with their food. For Katie, it was eggplant Parmesan with angel hair pasta and marinara sauce; for Andy, a towering serving of meat lasagna, both entrees complimented by a crisp salad and hot bread. Conversation slowed while Katie hungrily began, but Andy managed only a few halting bites. After several minutes, Katie noticed Andy absently pushing his food around on his plate. He hadn't made a dent in either his salad or lasagna.

"Not hungry?" she asked, her fork in midair.

"Not particularly. I guess I ate a snack a little too late this afternoon," he chuckled.

Katie studied him. She'd never known him not to eat when food was in front of him, especially lasagna at Gessupi's.

"No worries," Andy hurried to add, seeing her hesitate. He pushed his plate to the side. "I'll just get a to-go box. I may need a midnight snack."

Katie put her fork down and looked at him closely.

Andy's smile faltered slightly as he patted Katie's hand laying on the table. "Come on. Eat up. I'll have mine later."

Katie furrowed her brows. "Andy —"

"I'm just not hungry right now. Okay?" He tossed his napkin on the table and turned his head, leaning back in his chair.

Confused at another sudden change in Andy's demeanor, Katie stifled her reply and trained her eyes on her plate. She picked up her fork and took a few halting bites before putting her fork down. She wasn't hungry any longer.

Smiling, Gio bounced up to retrieve their plates. Seeing them still mostly full, he looked questioningly between them.

"Can we have a couple of to-go boxes, please?" Katie asked. Andy sat with his eyes averted, playing with the corner of his napkin.

"Of course," Gio murmured, sensing tension in the air. He picked up their plates and turned toward the kitchen.

Strained silence hung between them as Andy paid the bill. They picked up the to-go boxes and wound their way back through the main dining room to the front door. Seeing their dark looks, Mr. Gesuppi bid them good night with a troubled smile before turning to greet new customers coming in the door.

Andy got in the truck as Katie opened her door and slid into the passenger seat. The engine roared to life as Andy backed from the space and knocked the shift into drive. Katie sat quietly, not knowing what to say, or, if she should say anything. She took a couple of quick, sideways glances at Andy, whose expression remained grim. He didn't speak or even look at her as he rapidly covered the miles home.

It had been such a wonderful evening. What had happened this time? Katie mulled the question with growing agitation. Whatever was going on with Andy, it had been going on for too long. But what exactly *was* going on? What was Andy hiding? His anger was flaring more often, and his outbursts were as irrational as they were unexpected. He was putting her on edge, as much as he apparently was on edge himself. Andy could be his sweet, loving self one minute, and the next minute completely unreasonable with anger. Frustrated and concerned, Katie glanced at him again. His expression hadn't changed. She watched the road as it fled beneath them and wondered, where exactly was their journey leading them?

———

ANDY PULLED INTO THE drive and shut the engine off. This might not be the right time, but she had to say something. "Andy."

He didn't acknowledge her.

"Andy," she persisted but still no response. "Andy, what's going on? This isn't you — this isn't the kind, sweet man I love. Please tell me what's bothering you."

Andy folded his arms on top of the steering wheel and laid his forehead on top.

She placed a hand softly on his shoulder. "Please, talk to me, Andy."

He was silent for what seemed like ages. In a muffled voice, he said, "Katie, please. Just leave it alone for tonight. Please."

Katie tensed. His voice sounded hollow and ragged, so unlike the typical, vibrant Andy. Her heart pounded as fear and uncertainty burned inside. She wanted — no she needed — to know what was wrong but she didn't want to push him. He sounded broken.

She thought for several minutes, weighing what to do, but knew the right thing, for now, was to give Andy some space. She patted his shoulder gently and said softly, "Andy, I love you."

She waited to see if he would respond, but when he didn't, she slowly opened the door and walked to the front door. She turned the lights on in the living room and the kitchen, placing their food in the refrigerator. She changed for bed and slipped between the covers, curling into as tiny a ball as possible and squeezed her eyes closed. What was happening? She was confused and didn't know what to do. Tears spilled onto her pillow. Even though she was exhausted, she knew sleep wouldn't come, not until she could feel Andy next to her.

———

ANDY'S SHOULDER BURNED LIKE fire where Katie's hand had rested, and her words still echoed through his mind. He could talk to her about anything. Why couldn't he talk to her now? What *was* wrong with him? He tried to ignore the pain and nausea that had come on him at dinner as he attempted to sort through the chaotic feelings roiling inside him. He grimaced and groaned out loud with both pain and exasperation. Things were spiraling out of his control. He'd just have to try harder to keep himself in check. He'd make things right — he had to — but that might mean asking for help, something he had never wanted to do or been good at doing.

He had no idea how long he sat in the car, but the pain and nausea finally passed, and he seemed to have his emotions under control. He looked toward the house. Katie was probably asleep. He hadn't responded when she'd told him she loved him. It was one of their agreements when they got married — they would never go to bed angry or without telling the other they loved them. He wouldn't let her down again. He could remedy this failure at least. He slowly opened the car door and eased out, his body feeling stiff after sitting so long.

He locked the front door behind him before making his way down the hall. Katie lay in bed, the covers lightly outlining her still form. Andy bent over her and softly brushed back a bit of hair that had fallen over one cheek. He kissed her cheek softly and whispered, "I love you, Katie."

Katie stirred, opening her eyes and looked through the dark into his haggard face. She reached up and pressed her hand to his cheek, feeling its rough stubble, and whispered, "Forever."

Andy brushed her cheek with a soft kiss. He changed his clothes, slipped into bed and pulled her close.

With Andy's arm around her, Katie relaxed, and they both fell into a deep sleep.

IT HAD BEEN A full morning, and Andy was glad he'd gone to the RITE2U office early before making his regular deliveries. He had readily agreed when Charlene had asked him to come early to sort some packages that were expected special delivery overnight. Maybe he'd use the extra funds to take Katie to a nice dinner. He needed to do something to make up for being such a jerk.

It was a little after noon when Andy pulled into a space at the RITE2U office. He grabbed an armful of boxes and envelopes and his lunch tote. Inside, Charlene helped him unload.

"Thanks, Charlene," Andy said with a smile, dropping the last box into the bin. Charlene shrugged nonchalantly. Andy shook his head. She was a tough one to figure out. He'd never heard her say much so he figured she treated everyone the same. He'd have to ask around to see if some of the newer guys had figured out what to do to get on her good side. In the two years he'd worked at RITE2U, he sure hadn't, but on her good side was where you wanted to be.

Andy walked to the break-room at the back of the building where a couple of the staff were already eating lunch. Grabbing his lunch after a quick warm up in the microwave, Andy pulled out an empty chair at the table and popped open his soda. He was only half listening to the sports banter as he dished up his first bite. With the fork almost to his mouth, the smell of the hot food reached Andy's nose and his stomach turned a somersault, immediately followed by a severe jolt of pain. His fork clattered when he dropped it to grab the edge of the table. The room was suddenly-spinning.

Conversation stopped abruptly as the other two watched, unsure of what to do. Andy gulped desperately for air as his stomach continued to twist in pain. He could feel cold sweat trickling down the back of his neck and down his forehead. He heard a chair screech and quick footsteps across the linoleum as one of the guys rushed out. The other moved closer and put a hand on Andy's shoulder. A few seconds later, Charlene came running into the room, her round face flushed and her cheeks bright pink from exertion and anxiety.

Andy swallowed a welcome rush of air as the pain subsided as quickly as it had come. Slowly releasing his grip on the table, he attempted to straighten. His hands trembled as he wiped sweat from his forehead. Charlene grabbed some paper towels from the nearby counter and gave them to Andy.

Andy looked sheepishly at their anxious faces. "What?" he tried to quip, taking the paper towels and wiping his face. "Haven't you ever seen a man turn his nose up at leftovers?"

Three pair of eyes continued to stare, wide with concern.

"I'm fine. I'm fine," he tried to assure them. "I must be coming down with something. That's all."

The skeptical looks on their faces told him no one believed that.

Andy put the lid back on the container and the container back in his tote. He stood, placing a hand on the table to steady himself. Charlene and the others watched, unsure of what to do.

"I'll take a quick power nap in my truck," Andy said as he picked up his things. "I'll be right as rain. Just need a few minutes."

"Son, take the rest of the day," Charlene said, watching him with uncharacteristic concern.

Andy looked at her and winced slightly, holding an arm across his abdomen as it continued to spasm lightly.

"I'm fine. I just need a few minutes."

"No. You're done for the day," Charlene said flatly. "I'll clock you out. You okay to drive or do you need one of us to drop you off at home?"

"Thank you, but home is not far. I can make it."

"Alright then," Charlene said. "Go."

Andy glanced back and saw them still watching as he wove his way to the front of the office. Their concern touched him, and he gave them a slight smile as he walked out the door. He made it to his truck and braced his hands against the side. He leaned over, trying to steady his breathing and slow his racing heart. After several minutes, he felt better. He sank weakly into the driver's seat. His stomach ached from the cramping pains but at least the trembling in his hands had slowed. He hated to take time off. This income was important to them. But rather than going home, he decided to schedule an appointment with their family doctor. He hated to give into it, but this had gone far enough. He needed some answers.

KATIE SAT AT HER desk that afternoon, chin resting in the palm of her hand, staring mindlessly at the papers in front of her. She knew she should get them graded and head home.

Home, Andy. Her thoughts went back to last night and then to this morning. Andy had wakened her at 6:30, already dressed and about to leave. "What time is it?" she'd asked, confused.

"It's 6:30. You looked so peaceful, I hated to wake you," Andy said as he sat on the edge of the bed and brushed hair away from her face.

Katie sat up, and he pulled her close before standing to leave. "I've got to run. I'll see you this evening."

"But, Andy, wait. Where are you going so early? You don't have to be at work for another hour at least."

Andy gave her hair a playful yank and then gave her a quick kiss. "I told Charlene I'd come in a little early to help with a special delivery. I'll call you later. Love you."

SCHOOL ENDED AN HOUR ago, and he hadn't called at the usual time. She picked up her phone and dialed his number. It rang only once before she heard his cheerful, "Andy Garrett here. You know what to do." She hung up and laid the phone back on her desk.

"My, my, my. Such a long face. Andy not call in the last fifteen minutes?" Sally asked as she strolled through the room to stand in front of Katie's desk.

Katie sighed with frustration. It had been a long day. She didn't know if it had just been her mood but even her best students had misbehaved today, including Lucas. She hadn't gotten much teaching done, but she'd already resolved to make tomorrow a better day. She stood and started to gather her things.

"Something you need?"

Sally saw the tired circles under Katie's eyes and noted her distracted actions. Sally's eyes gleamed — something was amiss. "I just thought we might discuss next week's computer lab schedule but since you're in such a rush — you probably want to get home to Andy."

Katie stopped, infuriated. Sally had to bring Andy into every conversation. Today was not the day to address that but, she had been pushing Sally to get the lab schedule done and now, of all times, she had it ready. Katie set her things back on the desk, took a deep breath and said, "No rush. Let's get this done."

Sally handed the schedule to Katie and waited while Katie read through it and marked a few changes. "It looks great. I appreciate the times you gave my class. Those will work well," Katie said with a forced smile. She handed it back to Sally and once again picked up her things to leave, but Sally hadn't moved.

"So, who was the blonde?" Sally asked smoothly as Katie stepped around her desk.

"What?" Katie asked, confused.

"You know, the blonde with Andy the other day."

Katie turned and started walking toward the door, her quick steps out-pacing Sally's leisurely stride. She was forced to wait for Sally before closing the door to her room.

"Don't know, hmmmm?" Sally said with a slight sneer.

"Whether you believe it or not, Andy and I have much more important things to talk about than someone at work," Katie said with a pointed look at Sally.

Sally felt the sting of that barb but couldn't let Katie have the last word. "I was just curious, but if my husband was having as good a time with an attractive woman as yours was, I think I'd be asking. Have a nice evening."

Sally turned and sauntered across the hall to her room.

Katie let out an angry huff before hurrying down the hall and as far away from Sally as she could possibly get.

ABERNATHY FIRE CHIEF JERRY Hamilton sat at his kitchen table. In spite of the early hour, coffee was in one hand and phone in the other. Getting the workday underway, he read e-mails, checked personnel and equipment status, and reviewed his calendar. His bright white officer's shirt and black uniform pants were starched and pressed. Natalie, his wife, always made sure his uniform was in perfect order. The gold brass of his officer's bugles and his chief's badge gleamed in the light. He took another sip of coffee and scrolled to an e-mail forwarded by the battalion chief of C shift, Curtis Rogers. The subject line caught his attention: "A. Garrett — Complaint."

Chief Hamilton sighed and set his cup on the table. He tapped the e-mail open.

"Chief, thought you should see this. Thorough report from Bentley. I have made note and responded.

Forwarding for your information. Curtis."

Jerry grinned wryly; "thorough report" was code for long and tedious.

Placing Andy Garrett at Station Two and under the command of Lt. Mike Bentley had been a topic of great discussion among the chief officers. All were keenly aware of the friction between the two. It was also commonly known the animosity came from Bentley, but it was just as well known that Andy often baited Bentley openly. The final decision to place Andy at Two had been his, and his decision was based on a gut feeling that it would prove good for both Andy and Bentley. He pinched the bridge of his nose and shook his head. Only time would tell.

"Something wrong?" Natalie asked as she came into the kitchen.

Taking a last sip of coffee, he walked over and placed the empty cup in the sink before giving Natalie a quick good morning kiss. They had been married for thirty-eight years, and she was more beautiful today than she had ever been.

"No, everything is fine," he replied as he grabbed his command radio and keys. "Bentley is just complaining about Andy again."

Natalie chuckled as she poured steaming coffee into a mug. "That sounds familiar. Do you think they'll ever get along?"

Jerry shook his head and gave a half-hearted laugh. "I'm still hoping, but if they don't get this worked out, my bet would have to be on Andy. That kid has the best instincts of anybody I've seen since Scott —"

Jerry stopped abruptly and Natalie stopped stirring her coffee. Jerry never mentioned his kid brother.

Natalie filled the awkward silence quickly. "Speaking of Andy, I was thinking about giving Katie a call. I haven't talked to her in quite awhile. What would you think about inviting them over to dinner soon so we can all catch up?"

Jerry cleared his throat. "I think that's a great idea. It'd be good to talk to Andy away from work and get his perspective on things at the station. I guarantee you hearing it from him will be much more entertaining than Bentley's long, tiresome emails saying the same thing over and over."

Jerry rolled his eyes dramatically, and Natalie laughed.

"I've gotta run," he said, giving her a quick kiss. "I'll see you this evening. Have a good day, Mrs. Hamilton."

"You too. Be safe, Chief."

Jerry welcomed the morning's freshness as he stepped outside. He thought over the email Curtis Rogers had forwarded as he drove down the quiet neighborhood street. Someone needed to talk to Bentley and Andy, again. Rogers, as C shift's commanding officer, was just the man for the job. Curtis Rogers was his most experienced battalion chief and knew the history between Bentley and Andy. He had talked with them both before, but it seemed like he needed to check in with them again.

BATTALION CHIEF CURTIS ROGERS was studying the staffing roster on the monitor in front of him as he heard Station Four's C shift crew coming in to start their shift. His phone buzzed, and he wasn't surprised to see Chief Hamilton's name on the screen. He'd been anticipating the call since forwarding Bentley's e-mail that morning. Chief Hamilton had told him that putting Garrett at Two would be a challenge given Garrett and Bentley's past, but he was counting on Curtis as the battalion chief to help them work through their differences. It had proved to be a tall order.

Even though Chief Hamilton kept his friendship with Garrett separate from their work relationship, everyone knew what close friends they were. The Chief had befriended Andy while he'd attended the fire academy and some of the old timers said among themselves that the Chief treated Andy as if he was his kid brother. Garrett was a hand full — no question — but he also seemed to know where the line was with the Chief and didn't cross it. Bentley was a trial to them all, but Garrett really knew how to push Bentley's buttons and seemed to take special glee in tormenting him. Maybe Bentley had a point if any of his emails were to be believed, but still, he was the station officer and needed to act like it.

"Good morning, Chief," Rogers said, answering the call.

"Good morning, Curtis. How are things at Four this morning?"

"They're good, sir. Getting the day underway."

"Copy that. And it looks like a nice one, too." Hamilton got straight to business. "I wanted to talk to you about that email from Bentley about Garrett."

"Yes, sir," Rogers acknowledged.

"Why don't you swing by Two today and check things out. Talk to both of them. We've got to get them past this constant bickering. I know Garrett baits Bentley but try to get Bentley to understand he's the officer and should take the lead, no matter his personal feelings. He needs to put the past in the past and move on and Andy . . . well, Andy needs to dial it back a notch. They're both good men *and* good firefighters. Ultimately, I think they'll prove to be a good balance for each other. In the meantime, they've got to stop feuding."

"I agree. I'll go over there this morning. I'll keep you posted."

"Good. Thanks, Curtis," Chief Hamilton said as he ended the call.

Shift was just starting so this would be a good time to catch Bentley and Garrett. After taking a final drink of his coffee, Rogers stood and grabbed the keys off his desk. He walked through the kitchen and said to no one in particular, "Headed to Two for a while. And then I might run to One. I'll be back when I'm back."

ROGERS OPENED THE DOOR to Station Two and walked straight to the coffee pot. He helped himself to a cup and strolled across the empty kitchen to stop just outside the door to the office. Since Station Two was older, the office was small with a worn desk and chairs. The majority of station officers kept necessary binders and notebooks stowed to create needed space. Bentley, however, had already pulled several out and tossed them on the desk where he stood watching the C shift crew at their morning duties.

Leaning against the door frame and quietly sipping his coffee, Rogers scanned the engine bay, but Garrett was nowhere to be seen. Just as Rogers straightened to make himself known to Bentley, Garrett strode nonchalantly across the floor from the back of the bay. His hands were full of plastic packages and supplies for the ambulance. He dropped his load onto the floor of the ambulance. It looked like he and Hedrick were restocking the supplies.

Unaware Rogers was behind him, Bentley flinched when Garrett came into view.

Bentley picked up a folder and then tossed it across the desk, scattering the papers that had been left in neat piles by the A shift commander. Rogers shook his head. Bentley was not known for keeping a tidy desk.

"Good morning, Lieutenant," Chief Rogers said just as Bentley started to sit down.

Surprised, Bentley jumped and stood quickly, shoving the desk chair behind him. "Good morning, Chief," he blurted.

"How are things?" Rogers asked as he motioned with his mug to the bay area and the crew hard at work.

"Fine, sir. We're readying for the day as you can see," Bentley replied.

"Relax, Bentley. Haven't seen you guys in a while so thought I'd swing by. Mind if I sit?" he asked, indicating the lone guest chair.

"Of course. Please." Bentley pulled his own chair back under him.

"I read your e-mail about Garrett this morning," Rogers said, easing himself into the worn chair and eying Bentley's reaction.

He didn't have to wait. Consternation, which quickly turned into annoyance, flew across Bentley's face in quick succession. "Yes, sir. The problems with Garrett continue. I feel it my duty to make command aware of the issues. He is also continually late. That is part of a report I am currently —"

"Mike," Rogers interrupted, holding up an index finger to ward off the barrage of complaints. "Hold on for a second. Take a breath."

Rogers paused and watched Bentley fidgeting impatiently. Several seconds ticked by before Rogers continued. "Mike, you and Garrett are outstanding firefighters. I wish I had an entire station like the two of you, but the bickering and friction between the two of you has got to stop. I know there are reasons for your feelings, but as Lieutenant and C shift's leader at Two, the lion share of the responsibility for making this work falls on your shoulders. You may not like it but it's part of being in command. A good leader learns to lead all of his crew, especially the more problematic ones."

Bentley opened his mouth, but Chief Rogers shook his head. "I will speak to Garrett while I'm here. I know he doesn't make things easy, but he's a good man. This situation will correct itself when you both decide to put the past in the past and work together. Am I making myself clear?"

Bentley nodded grudgingly. "Yes, sir."

"Good. I have every confidence in you." Chief Rogers stood, and Bentley followed him out the office door.

"What's for supper, Hedrick?" the crew asked as they banged the bay door open and filed into the kitchen. Hedrick leaned against the counter while Andy poured cups of coffee for everyone before joining them at the table to wait for Hedrick's response.

"Let me think for a minute," Hedrick stalled, looking around the table. They weren't even an hour into the shift so he hadn't quite decided what the dinner menu would be but these guys would not be put off. They each donated money to the shift food fund and entrusted it to Hedrick. His cooking expertise turned their donations into something hot, filling, and — most importantly — delicious. He loved to cook and becoming a firefighter had successfully brought the two loves of his life together. His specialties included everything firefighters loved from fried and grilled anything to every kind of dessert imaginable. Despite mouthy opinions to the contrary, his meals were heartily consumed and roundly enjoyed.

"I was thinking about grilling some steaks and vegetables," he began, as a menu started to come together in his mind.

"And?"

"And," Hedrick grinned mischievously, "maybe some homemade bread and steak cut fries."

"And dessert?"

"Well, let's see. Oh yeah, how about peach cobbler and ice cream?"

Andy glanced around the table with a grin, then at Hedrick. "Is that all?"

"Is that all?!" Hedrick started, irritation in his voice. "Do you know how long it's gonna to take me to —"

Andy and the others laughed. "Come on, rookie. Just giving you a hard time. It sounds amazing. We're hungry already."

Murmurs of agreement were rippling around the table when Bentley stepped into the kitchen followed by Battalion Chief Rogers. The men stood, chairs scraping against the linoleum.

"Morning, everyone," Rogers said.

"Morning, chief," the group chorused.

Andy stood at the back of the group, looking expectantly at the chief during the small talk that followed. Jernigan shared a joke, and they all laughed, except Bentley, who Andy noticed, looked annoyed. Andy chuckled to himself, guessing what was about to happen.

"Garrett, can I have a word, please," Rogers said.

Garrett nodded with a grin. That was exactly what he'd expected. The room grew silent as the group turned and looked at him.

"Come on, guys," he joked as he shrugged his shoulders. "Chief's probably here to ask my advice on some matter of great importance."

He moved through the quiet group, meeting Bentley's glare, as he followed Rogers down the hall and into Bentley's office. He took a seat as Rogers eased the door closed.

"So, Chief, what's the problem?" Andy asked as he leaned his chair against the wall and crossed his arms.

"What makes you think there's a problem?"

"Why else would you be here so early and asking to see me privately? The LEW-ten-ant been complaining again?"

Chief Rogers sighed. "Yes, Garrett, there is a problem. You know it, and I know it. Bentley is like a dog on a bone, and he's not going to let it go. And, I have a strong feeling you're only giving him more fuel for his fire."

"Chief —" Andy started, but Chief Rogers stopped him.

"Andy, you're a good man, but Bentley's a good man too, and let me emphasize, I believe in you both. I also believe you can complement each other if you work at it, even just a little. I've talked to Bentley and asked him to do the same. Going forward, I expect to hear fewer complaints and see a lot of progress. I'm counting on you to make this work."

Andy stared at Rogers, weighing what he should say, if anything. He wanted to defend himself and felt the need to protect his job. Bentley's treatment was unjustified — mostly — and his constant reports and complaints painted Andy in a bad light. Bentley deserved to be called out. Here was his opportunity to tell his side.

Andy dropped the front of his chair down with a thud and leaned forward, trying to decide. He put his elbows on his knees, his head in his hands. He took a deep breath, sat up and looked directly at Rogers. "Chief, I don't need anyone to fight my battles. I'm not going to run crying to you by filing a report or complaining. I just ask that you remember, there are two sides to every story. You're only getting —"

Andy caught his breath as a quick slice of pain cut through him.

"Garrett?"

Andy pushed the pain down as much as he could and managed to say, "You . . . you only get Bentley's side. You haven't heard mine."

Rogers stood and took a step toward Andy. "You alright, Garrett? You're white as a sheet."

Andy stood. "I'm fine. I just want to make sure —"

Suddenly, the alarm tones came across the speakers and the sound of chairs scraping across the floor came from the kitchen.

"Chief, I..." Andy hesitated and then started to step around Rogers.

"Go," Rogers said, stepping out of the way. "We'll talk more later."

With a nod, Andy opened the office door and joined the others headed to the bay. The tones repeated as Andy and Hedrick loaded into the ambulance, and Bentley and the others piled into the engine. The revolving emergency lights circled the bay and sirens wailed as the ambulance and the engine pulled into an opening in the halted traffic.

Andy glanced up as the ambulance began to roll and saw Chief Rogers watching from the office window. Their eyes met, and Andy saw concern on Chief Rogers' face as he acknowledged Andy with a brief nod.

H EDRICK MANEUVERED THE UNWIELDY ambulance deftly through the
gridlocked traffic and reached the scene of the accident several minutes ahead of the larger engine. He steered the ambulance close to
a concrete mixer, its large, heavy cab wedged tightly into the front of a
passenger car whose collapsed engine hissed puffs of steam. Andy piled
out of the ambulance and hurriedly opened compartment doors, pulling out boxes of medical gear and handing one to Hedrick. They side
stepped puddles of leaking oil and coolant to get to the car as the pun-
gent smell of hot rubber and burnt oil hung in the air and stung their
noses. Traffic noise escalated as more cars were added to the back up.

The angle of the crash allowed Andy to get close to the driver's
door of the car. He maneuvered as close to the vehicles as space allowed
and did a quick assessment, detecting three victims: two females in
the car and one male in the mixer's cab. Worming into the tiny space
beside the driver's door of the car, Andy could see the two women, one
younger and seemingly alert, the second older and semi-conscious. A
light powder hovered in the air from the deployed air bags.

The rumble of the fire engine's diesel motor added to the din of
noise as it pulled in beside the ambulance, its siren ending in an abrupt
squawk. While Andy and Hedrick focused on the victims, the engine

crew swarmed the two wrecked vehicles, flattening inflated tires and placing chocks behind the back wheels of both to make sure they didn't move. The crew checked beneath the wreckage to make sure no sparks or flames were hiding from view and then prepped the jaws of life for action when Andy and Hedrick were ready.

Andy leaned into the car's interior, the younger passenger eying him uncertainly, as he took the driver's wrist to check her pulse. "Hi. My name is Andy," he said, trying to put the younger female at ease. "What's yours?"

The girl in the passenger seat began to cry softly. "My name is Kim," she said.

"Well, Kim," Andy continued in a conversational tone as he worked, "we're going to get you out of here. No worries. Who is this with you?"

"That's my mom. Her name is Sheila."

Hearing her name, Sheila's eyelids fluttered as she tried to focus on Andy, who was still holding her wrist in his gloved hand. Getting a good pulse, he lifted one eyelid and then the other, waving a pin light in front of each of Sheila's eyes. He smiled as he worked and then said, "It's nice to meet you both. Of course, I wish it were under different circumstances, but not to worry. We'll have you out of here in no time."

Andy evaluated the victims with practiced precision as he continued talking in calm, soothing tones, trying to ignore the pulsing pain in his abdomen. When he finished his initial assessment, Andy motioned to Canfield, standing ready to remove the driver's door.

"Ladies, you're doing great," Andy said. "Everything is going to be fine. We will have you out of here in just a few minutes but until then, just relax. You're going to hear a loud motor but don't be afraid. It's a compressor hooked up to the tool that's going to help us move this door out of the way so we can get you out of here."

Sheila started crying and said, "Please don't hurt my car."

Andy gently patted her arm. "If you need me, I'm right here."

Andy stepped out of the way. Canfield took Andy's place and laid a shield across Sheila for protection against loose debris. Clothed in full bunker gear, including his facial mask for protection, Canfield picked up the heavy spreader tool. He gave the cord a firm yank, and it burst into a powerful roar. Canfield's gloved hands held the tool tightly to control the vibration as he stuck the bull nose wedge into the crevice between the door and the frame. He squeezed the handle slightly, and the spreaders started to expand as the metal groaned and started buckling under the pressure.

Andy held his arm firmly against his midsection, hoping to dull the throbbing pain while he anxiously watched Canfield working on the door. He glanced at the women then looked over his shoulder toward the mixer where Hedrick and Hart were working.

Andy turned back when he heard his name in a muffled voice. He saw Canfield pointing at the car door. Stepping close, they lifted the door out of the way together. Andy's breathing was ragged with the exertion and sweat glistened on his forehead. Laying the door aside, Andy now had better access to the car's interior. He removed the protective cover from Sheila and did a quick exam for broken bones and external injuries. He called the information over his shoulder to Hedrick who had come over to help. Andy had been so focused he hadn't heard the additional ambulances and crews arrive on scene and were now assisting the truck driver.

After Andy examined both victims, Hedrick started an IV on each and prepared them for transport. The crew carefully removed the two ladies from the wreckage and placed them onto backboards and into the waiting ambulances. Andy followed the gurney, carrying Sheila into the back of Two's ambulance as Hedrick slipped behind the steering wheel. Taking a seat on the small vinyl bench to the right of the gurney, Andy nodded as the two doors slammed shut, and two bangs on the door signaled Hedrick to pull out.

Andy took a tissue and wiped the sweat from his face and clenched and unclenched his trembling fingers while monitoring Sheila. He checked her vitals and watched her closely as she drifted lightly in and out of consciousness. Inside the insulated sway of the ambulance, Andy heard the siren's muffled wail as they sped through traffic. Minutes later, he felt the ambulance slow and heard the siren end abruptly. He took a quick look outside to see the covered drive of the emergency room at Abernathy's Medical Center.

Mandy Fitzhugh was standing at the nurse's desk when she heard sirens approaching. The first Fire and Rescue ambulance rolled in and cut its siren as it turned into the hospital's emergency entrance. Mandy's heart did a quick flip when she saw Sean Hedrick step out of the ambulance and walk to the back as the two rear doors popped open. She grabbed a pair of gloves and joined the other nurses making their way to the edge of the drive. It was a female victim, semiconscious, with what appeared to be superficial injuries, being wheeled out under Andy Garrett's watchful eye. As they wheeled the victim through the emergency room doors, Hedrick returned to the ambulance and moved it out of the way while sirens from two other ambulances squelched as they pulled in.

Andy relayed the patient's condition as they pushed the gurney through the emergency room and into the first empty examination room. After helping them move the patient to the bed, Andy stepped into the hall to give the nurses room to work. He walked stiffly to the paramedics' computer at the nurses' station to submit the incident report. He held one arm firmly pressed against his side and had just started typing when Hedrick walked up behind him.

"You good?" Hedrick asked.

Andy glanced up at Hedrick and gave a curt nod.

"I'll refill the supplies then," Hedrick said with a questioning glance back at Andy as he headed to the supply room.

Andy, ignoring the activity around him and focusing on his report, didn't hear Mandy walk up. She stood beside him for several minutes before finally clearing her throat.

He looked up and Mandy smiled.

"How's she doing?" Andy asked with a nod in the direction of the exam room.

"She'll be fine. Looks like a light concussion and some serious abrasions but nothing a little time won't heal."

"That's good news," Andy replied.

Mandy nodded in agreement. Stopping Andy before he could return to his report, Mandy took a step closer and in a soft voice asked, "You okay?"

Surprised, Andy turned toward her. "I'm —"

A loud metallic crash shattered the hum of the emergency room's activity. Silence immediately fell as everyone turned toward the source. A red-faced intern stood frozen, a metal hospital tray and its supplies scattered across the floor. After a few seconds of paralyzing embarrassment, several kind-hearted helpers picked up the scattered objects, and the hum of activity resumed.

Mandy turned back to Andy and waited.

Thankful for the timely interruption, Andy said, "Hey, I'm doing great, but thank you for asking. And how are you? You settling in?"

"Settling in?" she repeated with humph. "I've been here six months. I'm pretty sure I'm settled in."

"Ech," Andy said with a laugh. "Hate to tell ya, but at six months, you're still a rookie."

As Andy looked past Mandy, he locked eyes with Hedrick who was coming out of the supply room. Seeing an opportunity Andy grinned impishly. "Speaking of rookies —" He raised his voice. "Hey, Rookie. Over here."

All of the nurses at their stations turned toward Hedrick, who blushed a deep red at the unwanted attention. He reluctantly made his way over to where Andy and Mandy stood. With a knowing grin, Andy hit the submit button on his report and leaned against the counter to watch the interaction between the two.

Mandy watched Hedrick as he walked up, his arms full of supplies.

"Hi, Sean," Mandy said with a warm smile.

Hedrick managed a nervous smile and softly said hello.

Silence hung in the air as Andy grinned wider. The other nurses looked on.

Hedrick shuffled the plastic packages in his arms and blinked, wide-eyed and tongue tied.

"Nice work on the patient you guys just brought in," Mandy offered.

Hedrick's lips parted and nothing but a thank you came out. He turned to Andy but before he could say anything, Mandy went on. "She's going to be fine thanks to you. And Andy, of course."

Andy just grinned, looking between the two.

Hedrick managed a feeble nod and anxious smile before Andy broke in and said, "Well, Rookie, we need to jet."

Smiling expectantly, first at Hedrick and then glancing at Andy, Mandy said, "Well, then. See you next run." She moved toward the nurses' station and the group of nurses pretending not to listen.

Andy slapped Hedrick on the back as they walked toward the doors and slung his arm loosely around Hedrick's neck. Without bothering to lower his voice, Andy said, "So, that was impressive, Romeo." Andy grinned over his shoulder as several of the nurses giggled.

Hedrick turned a deep shade of red and pushed Andy firmly away as he stalked through the automated doors.

"Whoa, whoa, Romeo. What's the rush? It's not busy. No need to hurry back," Andy said as he slowed his steps, still pressing an arm to his side.

Hedrick didn't answer. He walked rigidly to the ambulance and yanked the back door open to stow the supplies. He slammed the door closed, and climbing into the driver's seat, thrust the key into the ignition. He revved the motor unnecessarily while Andy opened his door and slid into the passenger seat. Andy snapped his seat belt in place as he eyed Hedrick warily and reached for the computer to log their status.

"Nice job on the assist," Andy said, trying to break the icy silence as they pulled out.

Hedrick looked out the window silently.

"Looking forward to that fine meal tonight," Andy said, trying again. "I'll fight Jernigan for an extra helping of cobbler and ice cream."

His laugh choked in his throat as Hedrick took a turn too quickly. Andy glanced at Hedrick again. His face was grim and his knuckles were white on the steering wheel. Andy didn't say another word.

Hedrick made the turn in front of the station. Tension hung thick in the air as he backed the ambulance into the bay and turned off the engine. Andy grabbed the box of antiseptic wipes from the console between them and took one before handing the box out to Hedrick. Hedrick took one and started wiping down the steering wheel and dash while Andy stepped out and closed the door behind him.

Andy was still disinfecting surfaces and stowing the additional supplies in the back of the ambulance when he heard the cab door open and slam. He looked out the small window and watched Hedrick as he tossed the used wipes into the sanitary disposal bag at the back of the bay and walk into the living quarters area.

Andy let out a low whistle. He had some serious making up to do.

A<small>T</small> K<small>ATIE'S PERSISTENT URGING</small>, Gloria, Lucas' mom, finally made a reluctant visit one day after school. She confided to Katie that Lucas' dad was not in the picture, and Gloria expected no child support. She was working two jobs to make ends meet and was concerned about Lucas' shyness. She asked Katie if she thought the lack of a good male role model might be the cause. Katie had talked to Andy, and he'd been stopping by the school the past several weeks to spend some time with Lucas. At Katie's suggestion, Gloria had enrolled Lucas in Big Brothers/Big Sisters and with assistance from Jernigan, the fire department's liaison, Lucas had been officially assigned to Andy as his 'Little.' Their visits usually consisted of a quick bite at lunch but mostly, they talked. It always looked like they had a lot to say when Katie observed them together.

L<small>UCAS HAD TOLD HER</small> several times throughout the morning that Mr. Andy was coming to have lunch with him today. Andy hadn't mentioned anything to her about it, but then again, it seemed like he wasn't mentioning a lot to her any more. It was only twenty minutes until lunch, but Katie decided to use those twenty minutes for reading.

"Alright, everyone back to your desk and take out your reading books. We'll take the next twenty minutes to read before lunch." A light tap at the door drew Katie's attention, and her heart skipped a beat as it always did when she saw Andy in uniform. He looked uncomfortable and uncharacteristically nervous as he stepped inside.

"Am I early?" he whispered as Katie met him at the door.

"Just a bit but that's okay."

Andy grinned, looking over Katie's shoulder at Lucas' beaming face. Andy gave a small wave and Lucas waved back, starting to leave his seat.

"Uh uh, mister," Katie said. "There's a few more minutes before lunch."

Lucas eased back into his seat and picked up his book, watching Andy over the top.

Andy grinned at Lucas and looked back to Katie. His face clouded, and she noticed he avoided eye contact as he shuffled his feet nervously.

"I'll just wait in the hall," Andy finally said and stepped outside the door.

Puzzled, Katie followed him. "Andy, you don't have to wait out here," she said, taking his arm to draw him back inside.

Andy gently pulled his arm loose. "I don't want to disturb your class."

Katie dropped her hand and studied him with concern. "Well, okay then. Lucas told me you were coming today, but you hadn't mentioned it so I was hoping he wouldn't be disappointed."

Andy gave a slight frown. "Sorry. I thought I'd told you."

"No, but I know how much he's loved you coming by the past few weeks so I'm just glad you're here. Be warned though, he'll probably talk your ear off."

"Not if I talk his off first," Andy said with a small smile.

"It means a lot to him that you're his Big Brother. I can't tell you how excited he gets when you come by. That little boy needs you in his life," Katie said. "Just like I do."

Katie gave Andy a pointed look as she stepped back into the classroom. He leaned against the wall, jammed his hands in his pockets, and hung his head. It had been a bad morning. He'd upset Hedrick with his teasing, and Bentley had given him a fit, making him clean the bunker gear storage area for the second time in a month. His stomach ached, and he felt lousy. All he wanted to do was lay down and sleep, but this little guy was counting on him, so here he was.

Katie smiled as she watched Lucas keep an eager face trained on the door. He nearly bolted out of his seat when the lunch bell rang, and Andy stepped back inside.

"Whoa there, partner," Andy cautioned as Lucas hurtled up to him. "No need for the rush, my man. We've got time. What's for lunch?"

Lucas ushered him down the hall, followed by the rest of the class. Andy looked back at Katie and gave her a quick grin before he was led away.

Katie frowned as she watched. She could tell Lucas was already talking nonstop. Andy smiled and laughed as he bent over and said something to Lucas. Andy always looked so animated when he was with Lucas. So, why did he seem so bothered when he talked to her? *If* he talked to her, Katie added ruefully.

Sally edged up beside Katie as her class filed past. "Something wrong?" she asked, observing Katie's frown.

"What? Oh no — sorry. Lost in thought," Katie said, covering quickly.

"I'd be lost in thought watching that guy too," Sally said with a snort.

Katie turned on Sally, her patience with Sally's innuendos growing increasingly thin. "That *is* my husband, you know."

"I know. I know," Sally said airily. "But one can certainly still admire right? I am definitely admiring."

Katie whirled and darted into her room, refraining with some difficulty from slamming the door. She fumed as she pulled her lunch from her locker. Yes, Andy was handsome, very handsome. Women noticed him, and some were pretty bold with their admiration. But he was still her husband. The nagging doubt remained in the back of her mind that someday he'd be attracted to one of those women. Andy had always showered her with love so she had never wondered about his feelings for her — until now. Now, something was different. She wasn't sure what it was, but it was coming between them and getting bigger.

Hedrick set the last platter of food on the table as he pulled out a chair and joined the others. Their eyes were wide at the sight of a veritable feast. One platter held a pile of one-inch thick steaks, fresh off the grill, their juices still sizzling and popping. A deep bowl of asparagus, squash, carrots and onions steamed with a tantalizing aroma. Another platter held a heaping mound of steak cut fries, browned and topped with a scattering of sea salt. Another pan held soft mounds of browned homemade rolls just begging for butter.

Canfield reached eagerly for a roll, but Bentley cut him off by clearing his throat loudly.

"Forget something, Canfield?" Bentley asked in a brusque tone as everyone exchanged looks around the table.

Canfield pulled his hand back with a sheepish look.

"Mr. Hart, would you do the honors please?" Bentley asked, turning to Hart on his right.

"Sure, Lieutenant." Hart, along with everyone else, bowed their head as he blessed the food and asked for continued safety and good health for everyone on the crew. Andy couldn't help but cringe at the mention of good health. A hearty amen ended the prayer as forks were raised to spear the steak of choice.

The meal was consumed in silence, except for a 'please pass the potatoes' or 'another roll please' muttered through full mouths. The homemade peach cobbler and ice cream were soon history as well.

Jernigan sighed contentedly and leaned back in his chair as the others pushed their plates back and echoed their contented groans.

"Rookie, you sure outdid yourself tonight," Bentley commented.

Andy kept his head bent over his plate but had taken several sideways glances at Hedrick throughout the meal. Hedrick had avoided him all afternoon. He'd kept his distance even in the tiny kitchen when Andy came in for one thing or another. Andy had made several tries to cajole Hedrick back into good humor but all had failed. When not on the ambulance, Hedrick had sequestered himself in the kitchen creating the meal everyone had just enjoyed. Head down, as the others made their comments, Andy absently pushed his cobbler around in the melting ice cream with the spoon dangling from his fingers.

Hedrick stood and picked up a couple of plates.

"Sit down and take a load off. There's no rush, Rookie," Hart said as Hedrick stacked dishes.

"If it's all the same to you guys, I think I'll go ahead and get the kitchen cleaned up," Hedrick replied in a low voice.

Andy cleared his throat and with a nervous laugh said, "Come on, man. I said I'm sorry." He stood and started gathering plates and bowls.

"Forget about it," Hedrick mumbled as he turned to the sink with a stack of dishes.

"What'd you do this time, Garrett?" Canfield groaned as they all scowled at him.

Balancing the plates, Andy walked to the kitchen counter. "None of your concern, my man," he tossed over his shoulder.

He walked up beside Hedrick who was rinsing dishes and putting them in the dish washer.

Hedrick glared at Andy. "Not another word," he mouthed as he continued to feed the dishes into the washer.

Andy hesitated and then walked back to the table and eased into his chair.

"So, what's the matter with you anyway, Garrett?" Jernigan asked abruptly. He was a keen observer and picked up on the slightest things. His observations were often unnerving.

Everyone looked first at Jernigan and then at Andy.

"What are you talking about?" Andy snapped.

Jernigan shrugged as he ran his fingers over a worn spot on the table. "You didn't eat much. And that was some fine dining."

"Wasn't hungry," Andy retorted and glared around the table to discourage further questions.

"Hedrick, you spent the afternoon in the kitchen. Even though you are a rookie, you shouldn't have to do the dishes too. Let's play to see who has the honor of doing the dishes tonight. I'll pick the game," Andy said, eager to change the subject.

"Why do you get to pick the game?" Canfield groused.

Before Canfield could say anything else, Andy bolted to the TV room and returned seconds later with a rack of pool balls and a stack of miscellaneous items. Dishes forgotten, Hedrick dried his hands and joined everyone in the hallway and began assembling bricks, various pipe lengths, emergency cones, and other objects into an obstacle course.

"Pick your color, my friends," Andy said passing a rack of pool balls among them as they clustered outside Bentley's office. Bentley followed Andy with a fistful of plastic straws for each man to draw.

Canfield glowered when he pulled a runt of a straw. Short straw went first and first was not where you wanted to be. Canfield stepped up to the masking-taped line recently placed on the linoleum as the rest of the crew gathered behind him.

"Come on, show us how it's done," Andy goaded, followed by similar jabs from the others.

Canfield wasn't about to rush his shot, and he wasn't about to lose bragging rights from the last three times he'd won this game. His competitive spirit was in high gear. As he tossed his green-ringed pool ball lightly from hand to hand, he carefully studied the obstacles. He wanted to reach the farthest obstacle without being knocked into the kitchen, or 'the sink,' as it was known for this game. If you were knocked into the sink, the game ended, and you were awarded an automatic round of dish washing.

Crouching low and taking a deep breath, Canfield gave his ball a final toss for good luck, swung his arm back and released the ball gently. It rolled straight and then slowed as it arched slightly, nudging the first two obstacles before finally coming to rest at the midpoint of the last barrier.

The others, crouched in a huddle behind Canfield, straightened as one.

"You have got to be kidding. How is that shot even possible?" Hart asked no one in particular.

A cocky grin spread across Canfield's face as he turned to face his competitors. "Do you just want to call me out now?"

"No way, pard," Hart said, elbowing his way through the huddle. "This is going all the way. Step aside."

Andy stood a few feet away from the group, tossing his pool ball in the air as he watched the game's progress. The ball slipped on one toss and barely catching it, Andy realized his hands were trembling. He glanced around, hoping no one had seen it. But out of the corner of his eye, he saw Jernigan eying him with a keen look.

Andy tried to nonchalantly slip away, but Bentley stopped him in his tracks.

"Garrett, where do you think you're going? This game was your idea. You're not getting out of doing dishes because you don't play. Get over here."

Knowing he couldn't play with his hands trembling, Andy dawdled, trying to come up with a plausible excuse.

"Come on, Lieutenant," Jernigan said suddenly with a sideways look at Andy. "It's not even Garrett's turn. I think it's yours."

All eyes shifted from Jernigan, Bentley, and Andy, as tension started to build. Canfield and Hart moved closer to Jernigan while Jernigan took a couple of more steps toward Bentley.

Bentley glared at each man in turn before taking a deep breath and stepping to the masking taped line.

Jernigan caught Andy's eye and motioned with his head for Andy to step away.

Andy gave a hesitant nod and quickly sidled into the kitchen.

The table, as well as the kitchen counters, were full of dirty dishes, pans and skillets. It looked like every reasonable dish in the cabinet had been pressed into service to cook the meal they'd just enjoyed. Andy glanced over his shoulder as another roar came from the hallway. He looked back to the kitchen as he heard Hedrick let out a whoop. Hedrick had forgotten the kitchen and joined in on the competition. So, his distraction had worked, Andy chuckled to himself.

Andy hadn't realized how much his teasing bothered Hedrick, but Hedrick had been noticeably quiet since the encounter with Mandy that morning. He must really be crazy about her, Andy thought as he started clearing dishes and pushing scattered chairs under the table.

Two hours later, the game broke up with laughter and no clear winner. Walking into the kitchen, they raided the refrigerator for cold drinks, but then Hedrick, followed by the others, stopped and looked around. The kitchen was neat and clean. Hedrick suddenly realized the purpose of Andy's distraction with the game. Every dish was washed, dried and put away, but Andy was nowhere to be seen. Jernigan had made excuses for Garrett during the game, and the rowdiness kept everyone from noticing him in the kitchen working.

Each of them leaned against the counter as they sipped their drinks and exchanged puzzled looks.

"Anyone *seen* Garrett?" Canfield asked.

"Not since the game started," Hart replied.

"He'll be in the bay," someone suggested as the silence quickly gave way to curiosity. They filed out of the kitchen, bent on finding Andy. The search was on.

"He usually checks supplies in the evening when he's on the ambulance," Canfield offered.

"Come on, guys. This is Garrett," Hedrick said. "I bet he's shooting hoops. He can't sit still."

As one, the group moved down the hall to the engine bay. Expecting to hear the station's under-inflated basketball banging against the backboard, they plunged through the door only to be greeted by silence. Giving the empty bay a quick look, their curiosity growing, someone suggested they check the dormitory rooms. There they found success, and Andy, fully dressed, sound asleep on top of his bed.

"Humph," Canfield voiced for the group with a puzzled tone. "Don't know what to make of that."

Huddled around Andy's door, they shook their heads and then moved to the TV room. Each jumped into a recliner before Canfield broke the silence, asking what was on everyone's mind. "What do you think is up with Garrett? He's been acting strange for weeks.

"Anyone notice how much weight he's lost?" Canfield went on. "He hardly touches his food anymore."

A few seconds of silence passed before Hedrick added, "Doesn't work out as often or as long as he used to either. You could almost set your clock by him."

"He's grouchier too," Hart stated flatly.

There were murmurs of agreement.

"But one thing that hasn't changed. He's still late. Every shift," Bentley said.

An unusual silence settled over the room, each rocking in their recliner.

"It sure is quiet," Hedrick ventured after a few minutes, tapping a toe on the linoleum.

"Who'd a thought one guy could make as much noise as Garrett does?" Bentley said with a trace of sarcasm.

Without Andy's banter, the quiet was unusual and uncomfortable. Hart hit the power button on the remote and the TV came to life with the evening news.

Bentley shook his tea glass, loosening the remaining ice cubes at the bottom. Taking a long drink, he set the glass on the table next to his recliner and pushed against the back of the chair, folding his hands behind his head. While the news anchors droned on about the latest happenings, Bentley, along with the others, wondered about the changes in Andy's behavior. It *was* awkwardly quiet without Garrett's constant chatter, and reluctantly, Bentley had to admit, he missed it.

KATIE SAT CROSS-LEGGED ON the sofa that evening as the sun faded into a golden evening fringed with the crisp air of fall. Things were quiet when Andy was on duty, and she always missed him. The screen on her laptop had long since been blank from inactivity. Katie stared out the front window across their lawn, the one big oak tree casting long shadows against the fading green of the grass. She absently sipped a tepid cup of tea. The lesson plans she'd been working on were long forgotten. Her mind was full of Andy. The thoughts she'd tried to put aside during the day, raced back full force tonight. Instead of the thoughts that made her smile, these thoughts were perplexing and troubling. Andy's mood swings were becoming more frequent. She sensed he was hiding something, but she couldn't imagine what might be causing him to act so out of character.

Her phone rang, jolting her from her reverie. It was Natalie Hamilton.

Katie smiled and answered quickly, "Hello, Natalie!"

"Hey, Katie! How you doing?"

"Well, I'm hanging in there. It's great to hear from you."

"Well, it's just been too long since we've visited so thought I'd check in. Jerry said Andy was on duty today so I thought this might be a good time."

Katie sighed with relief. "Natalie, you have no idea how perfect your timing is."

"Oh? What's up?" Natalie asked with concern. She could tell from Katie's voice something was wrong.

"Natalie, I...I don't actually know where to begin," Katie said, suddenly having to hold back tears.

"Katie, dear, just start, and we'll sort it out."

"It's Andy. Something is going on with him, and I just don't know what to do," Katie managed to say before starting to cry in earnest.

When Katie stopped crying, Natalie said, "I'm here. Tell me."

Katie took a deep breath, and everything she'd bottled up inside came pouring out. "He is having mood swings — major mood swings. He's fine one instant and the next he's furious — I mean red in the face angry — and then a little later, he's back to the sweet Andy I know. I'm afraid to say too much not knowing what is going to set him off. He's apologetic afterward and works hard to make it up, but then it happens all over again."

Before Natalie could reply, Katie rushed on. "He used to call — every day after school and the evenings he's on duty — but he hasn't called the past week or so. It seems like he avoids talking to me if he can at all. What is it? Is it me? Am I doing something wrong?"

Surprised at what Katie was telling her, Natalie took several seconds to absorb what Katie had said. Natalie did think this was unusual behavior for Andy. Natalie knew Andy long before he'd met Katie, and she had been just as surprised as everyone else when Andy gave up his bachelorhood to marry Katie. Andy had told her and Jerry a year or two before he'd met Katie that he planned to be a bachelor the rest of his life. He was adamant when he said he'd never be vulnerable or dependent upon another woman the way he had been with his mom.

"I'm controlling my own destiny," Andy had declared. "I'm not tying myself down to anyone. Ever. End of story."

That had changed drastically when he met Katie. She and Jerry observed Andy and Katie while they dated and had even been invited to join them for dinner a time or two. Natalie remembered watching Andy and Katie dance their first dance together as husband wife. She'd never seen two people happier or more in love. She had been, and was still, amazed at the transformation in Andy from a self-centered, rowdy braggadocio to a devoted, loving and thoughtful husband. Something was definitely going on to cause him to act so unlike himself now.

Natalie wanted to help Katie. And she knew Jerry would be in agreement once he heard what Katie had just told her. "Katie, you're right. This doesn't sound like the Andy I know either, and I can't imagine what might be going on. The only thing Jerry ever mentions is the continuing conflict between Andy and Bentley, but that's been going on for years. I'll talk to Jerry and see if he knows anything. In the meantime, why don't you and Andy come for dinner Friday evening? That was another reason I was calling, so it looks like the timing works great. It will give Jerry a chance to talk to Andy outside of work and give us more time to talk, too. What do you say?"

Katie couldn't think of anything she'd like better. "Natalie, that sounds absolutely wonderful, but I'll need to check with Andy. I'm not sure he'll call this evening, but I'll ask him as soon as I can and let you know."

"Sounds great," Natalie said. "I'll look forward to hearing from you. And Katie, please don't worry. We'll figure this out. Jerry has known Andy a long time, and if there's anyone who can get him to open up, it will be Jerry."

"Thank you, Natalie. You have no idea how much this means to me. I was about at my rope's end."

"Well, tie a knot and hang on. We'll look forward to seeing you guys Friday."

After they hung up, Katie was able to finish her lesson plans. She hoped Andy would be agreeable about going to dinner, but she just wasn't sure anymore.

K ATIE FELT GROGGY THE next morning. She wasn't surprised to see the tired eyes or the dark circles beneath those eyes looking back at her from the mirror. She splashed cold water on her face and applied her make-up a little more carefully to camouflage as best she could. She slipped on a pair of pants, a tunic shirt and her favorite pair of flats, thinking of one of her mom's favorite pieces of advice: "always look your best — especially when you don't feel your best."

On the way to school, Katie tried to review the lessons she'd planned for the day but her mind kept wandering back to Andy. He hadn't called last night or this morning. He always used to call in the evenings when he was on duty, but he hadn't the last several shifts. She'd started to call him but then thought better of it. Reaching school, Katie was about to sit at her desk when a soft tap sounded on the door.

"Morning, Sunshine," Sally said sarcastically as she sauntered in.

Katie glanced up. From the look on Sally's face, she knew Sally had noticed how she looked.

"Well, my, my. You certainly look tired this morning. Everything okay?" Sally purred as Katie gathered books to put back on the shelves in the reading corner.

"Of course, I'm fine. What a silly question," Katie said, trying to sound cheerier than she felt.

"Well, you look exhausted," Sally went on, her demeanor sickeningly sweet. "Are you getting enough sleep, dear?"

"What?" Katie snapped back.

Sally threw her hands back, feigning an attack. "Oh my. Looks like there might be trouble in the Garrett paradise," Sally said. "And just a little hint. You might want to pull yourself together before your students arrive. I'd hate for them to be snapped at so cruelly." Sally gave a small sniff of indignation and turned to leave.

"Sorry," Katie said, regretting her tone. "I just have a lot on my mind right now."

Sally humphed as the first bell rang and she left.

Katie sighed with resignation. It was the start of the day, and she already felt tired. As the first students bounced through the door with their bright smiles and chatter, her spirits began to lift. She would make it a good day.

SALLY PULLED HER JACKET close as she stuck her key in the mailbox slot. She'd left school a little late, stopped for groceries and now, it was almost 7:00 p.m. She retrieved her mail and snapped the box shut. As she turned to leave, Sally ran straight into Mandy Fitzhugh, who was looking down as she climbed the two short steps to the mailboxes.

"Mandy!" Sally said, thrilled to have run into her. "How are you?"

Mandy looked up, surprised to hear her name and smiled when she saw Sally.

"Well, hi, Sally! Good to see you. I've been busy, but fine. How about you?" Mandy said over her shoulder as she pulled some mail out of the box.

"I've been good but busy, too. You just getting off work?"

"Yes," Mandy replied. "It's seven to seven shift this week."

"Well, I just picked up some things and was about to fix a bite to eat. Would you want to join me? Nothing fancy, but I promise it will be good."

Mandy paused. "Well, I don't know..."

Sally smiled, but pressed on. "Well, I thought with the fall weather, tomato soup and a hot grilled cheese sandwich sounded good."

Mandy laughed and smiled. "Okay, okay, you sold me. That does sound really good. What's your apartment number again?"

Sally provided the number, and Mandy promised to be over in twenty minutes.

SALLY HAD CHANGED INTO sweats and was heating the soup when Mandy knocked. Sally opened the door and Mandy, along with a gust of cold wind, stumbled in.

"Wow! It's really getting cold out there," Mandy said, pulling off her scarf and gloves.

" 'Tis the season," Sally laughed. "Just throw your stuff over there."

Mandy, dressed in sweats as well, followed Sally into the kitchen. "That smells so much like home," Mandy said as the soup's aroma filled the air. "What can I do to help?"

Sitting across from each other, they chatted comfortably as they ate. Mandy's down-to-earth personality was disarming, and Sally had almost forgotten the primary reason she'd asked her over. "So, what brought you to Abernathy?"

Mandy shrugged, as if there wasn't much to tell. She took a bite of brownie and chewed thoughtfully for a few seconds. "Well, I've been out of nursing school for a few years and worked in a couple of ERs in big city hospitals, but the pace was just too frantic. I still work twelve-hour shifts, but it isn't the lightning speed it is in the big city. You still see illness, injuries and panicked expectant mothers, but it's just a different pace. Abernathy seems to be a great little city too, and the people at the hospital are super nice. I really enjoy the atmosphere."

Sally nodded. "I thought about moving to a bigger city where there's a better chance to meet guys, but Abernathy is home now." She looked down and stirred some crumbs on her plate and sighed wistfully. "Who knows? Maybe there's still a chance I'll meet Mr. Perfect." Catching Mandy's eye, Sally asked pointedly. "So, is there anyone special in your life?"

Mandy looked down and blushed slightly. "No — not really."

"Hmmmm," Sally mused, her eyes gleaming. "Sounds like there might be."

"Well … but no. It will never work out so that's that." Mandy stood and picked up her bowl and plate. "Let's get these dishes done. I'd be willing to bet you've got some papers to grade."

It was Sally's turn to sigh as she followed Mandy into the kitchen. "Yes, papers don't grade themselves. I'm afraid I have quite a few, and I like to take my time. The students worked hard on them so I want to give them my best back."

Sally smiled as she wrapped her scarf around her neck and shrugged her jacket on. "Thanks for supper. We'll have to do it again."

"I'd like that," Sally agreed. She had genuinely enjoyed Mandy's company. After several years in Abernathy, Sally still didn't have many friends and craved the kind of easy-going companionship Mandy offered. "Let's make sure it's sooner than a chance encounter at the mailboxes."

Mandy opened the door and stepped outside, but Sally stopped her. "Mandy, if you're not too attached to your apartment, my neighbors upstairs are moving out in a month or two. It'd be great for you to live closer. Easier commute for meals," she said with a grin.

Mandy stepped back, suddenly looking shaken. "No — thanks. That wouldn't work for me. I only live on the ground level. Thanks again for dinner."

Sally was perplexed at Mandy's reaction. She frowned as she closed the door, and Mandy sped off.

IT WAS FRIDAY NIGHT, and Andy and Katie pulled up in front of Jerry and Natalie Hamilton's house. When Katie asked Andy about the dinner invitation, he had surprised her with enthusiasm. He looked over at her now and smiled. He'd been in a better mood since his last duty shift day before yesterday, and they'd even enjoyed an evening on the couch eating popcorn and watching a movie. She'd reveled in the once familiar — but now unusual — closeness of Andy's arms around her.

Andy took her hand when they got out of the car. They were halfway up the walk when the front door swung open, and Natalie greeted them with a welcoming smile. "Come in! Come in! It's been way too long since I've seen the two of you," she said, hugging Katie first and then Andy. "I'm so glad you guys could come. Andy, Jerry's in the back at the grill. Would you mind seeing what you can do to speed him along?"

Andy gave Katie's hand a squeeze as they exchanged a knowing look. Jerry never needed help at the grill. This was Natalie's way of getting them alone together. Andy obediently made his way through the family room and onto the deck in the back yard where Jerry was at the grill, placing skewers of meat and vegetables on the rack.

When Natalie told Jerry of her conversation with Katie earlier in the week, he was concerned as well. Curtis Rogers had called after talking to Bentley and Garrett, and Jerry could tell Curtis was troubled. Curtis said there was definitely something Andy wasn't saying, but they were interrupted and didn't get to finish their conversation. Jerry was hopeful Andy would open up and talk to him tonight.

Andy stopped a few feet short of the edge of the deck. "So, what's for dinner, Chief?"

Jerry turned and looking Andy up and down said, "Kabobs. Hungry?"

Andy flinched at the Chief's obvious appraisal. Stepping off the deck, he said, "Always, right?" He plopped unceremoniously into the lawn chair Jerry had been using.

Jerry shook his head as he closed the grill lid and reached up to the deck for another chair.

"Why don't you have a seat?" he said with a grin.

"Believe I will, thanks," Andy smirked.

"How are things at the Deuce?" Jerry asked, wiping his hands on a towel.

"Oh, you know, the same ole excitement with the LEW-tenant in charge. We don't dare get anything out of line or else we'll get a fifteen-minute lecture and extra work." Andy launched into an exaggerated tale of a recent infraction of Hedrick's and the extra scrubbing of the ambulance interior and exterior demanded by Bentley. Jerry laughed at Andy's telling of the story. He was glad Andy was taking things in stride, even though Bentley, as usual, was being excessive.

Jerry watched Andy closely while they talked. He didn't see any of the reasons for concern that Curtis Rogers had expressed after his meeting with Andy a few days ago. Andy looked thinner but seemed as relaxed and carefree as usual. But that didn't mean something was going on that wasn't evident.

The shadows in the back yard were lengthening when Jerry stood, chuckling at Andy's most recent comment. He lifted the beef and chicken kabobs from the grill and placed them on the readied platter. Natalie opened the back door. "You guys planning on being out there all night or do we have some kabobs to eat?"

"Coming, dear," Jerry answered. He picked up the platter in one hand and slapped Andy on the back with the other. "Sounds like they're calling us in."

"Indeed it does, Chief. Let's see what the ladies have been up to."

Natalie closed the door, hearing Jerry's answer. "I think they're finally coming. Hope those kabobs aren't burnt to a crisp. Jerry gets distracted when he's grilling, and I know Andy's tales can be quite entertaining."

Katie laughed and nodded. "Don't I know it." She cut up the last strawberry and dropped it into the fruit salad. "How's this?" she asked, holding up the bowl of fresh fruit for Natalie's inspection.

"Perfect," Natalie said, glancing into the bowl as she whisked other dishes to the table.

Natalie appreciated Jerry keeping Andy talking outside for as long as he had. She hoped he'd gotten Andy to talk about whatever might be going on. Natalie and Katie worked side by side, putting finishing touches on the meal and as they worked, Natalie listened attentively while Katie shared more of her worries and concerns about Andy's recent behavior and the distance she felt growing between them. Natalie tried to reconcile the behavior of the Andy Katie was describing with the Andy she'd known for years. This wasn't typical behavior of the man her husband had befriended so wholeheartedly. While Jerry typically didn't grant friendship to rookies at the academy, he'd made an exception in Andy's case. He said he'd seen something special in

Andy that reminded him of Scott, his kid brother, and Natalie knew how important that was.

While Katie placed ice in the glasses for the iced tea, Natalie paused and watched Jerry and Andy walk toward the house. Two handsome men, she thought, but there *was* something different about Andy. She'd noticed it as soon as he and Katie arrived. He looked thinner, yes, but there was something else — something in his eyes she couldn't quite put her finger on. Was it worry or was it fear? She wasn't sure, but there was definitely something.

Jerry opened the door and ushered Andy inside with a wave of the serving tongs and a rush of cool air.

"Where'd you like these, ma'am?" Jerry asked, holding the full platter of kabobs up to Natalie.

"Middle of the table please," she said, smiling.

Andy stepped out of the way as Jerry walked through the kitchen with the platter. "Hey, Chief, is it true you burned a meatloaf so badly when you were a rookie, that it set off smoke alarms at the station?" Andy asked nonchalantly as he popped a grape into his mouth.

Jerry stopped and glared at Andy. "Where are you coming up with such outlandish rumors?"

Andy shrugged. "Oh, you know...a good story never dies." He picked up a couple of the glasses and headed into the dining room.

Jerry followed and set the kabobs in the center of the table. "Well, let me put that rumor to rest right now."

Natalie and Katie, following them into the dining room, exchanged grins as they joined Andy to hear Jerry's answer.

"And ..." Andy prompted with a grin.

"And," Jerry said, "I can neither confirm nor deny such rumors."

Everyone erupted into laughter.

"Oh come on, Chief. You gotta give me something to work with here. That's only gonna stoke the rumor."

"Sorry. That's the best I got," Jerry said, laughing.

"I suggest we eat before it gets cold. Everything in from the kitchen?" Natalie asked as she adjusted the placement of the dishes on the table.

"I sure hope so," Katie said, "I'm not sure we'll even be able to put a dent in this spread."

Jerry pulled out a chair for Natalie while Andy, following Jerry's example, surprised Katie by pulling a chair out for her. He returned her hesitant smile as he pushed her chair in and sat down.

Jerry led grace as everyone held hands, their heads bent over the table. Andy held Katie's hand a few seconds after the prayer ended and then began another tale from the station as the food was passed.

NATALIE HANDED THE LAST plate to Jerry to dry. Andy and Katie had left shortly after dessert and coffee. The dinner had been a success — both the meal and the opportunity to catch up. Andy had been the evening's entertainment regaling them with one story after another about Station Two and Bentley. Natalie had especially enjoyed the story of the call to the historic Piedmont Hotel downtown where the smell of smoke had been reported. Andy's description of the interruption to the wedding reception in the hotel's ballroom brought roars of laughter. Jerry just shook his head and grinned when Andy said he told the bride, "How lucky can you get? You get extra credit in the making memories category. How many brides get to say they had fourteen firefighters show up at their reception?" He had then asked to have his picture taken, in full bunker gear, with the laughing bride and groom. "Now there's a memory," he'd told them as the fire crews exited the building. A small grease fire in the old kitchen had been tapped out, and the wedding reception resumed.

"I don't know what it is, but there's definitely something," Natalie said as she put away dry plates and glasses. "Katie is trying to put on a brave front, but she's scared and really worried."

Jerry leaned against the counter and reached for his cup of coffee. "I tried, but I couldn't get anything out of him. He was all cleverness and smart comments, but he never got serious about anything. And Curtis isn't one to overreact. He wasn't sure what it might be either. I just don't know what to make of it," Jerry said, taking a slow sip of coffee and staring ahead.

"I think there's something seriously troubling Andy," Natalie said. "I have no idea what it is, but it's taking a toll on both of them. Did you notice how thin he's getting and how little he ate? He just moved the food around on his plate, and we both know that's not like Andy."

Jerry nodded. Natalie was right. It was all very unlike Andy.

———

THE DRIVE HOME WAS quiet, the steady rhythm of tires rolling across grooves in the pavement was the only sound. Katie replayed the conversation with Natalie in her mind. It had felt so good to pour her heart out. Katie glanced over at Andy, his strong profile etched in the shadows created by the glow of the dashboard lights. He had been more animated, talkative and funny tonight than he'd been in a long time, but it seemed forced — almost like he was performing a role that was expected of him.

Andy turned and gave Katie a small smile. She returned his smile while hearing Natalie's words in her mind. "Katie," Natalie had said, "I don't know what to think either, but I agree, something isn't quite right. I wish I had some resounding words of advice, but I don't. But I want you to always remember that Jerry and I consider you guys practically family, and we're here for both of you. We'll keep working to figure this out, but we're not going to push or pry. The main thing we want you both to know is how much we love you both."

Katie blinked back tears, remembering the warmth and love in Natalie's eyes. Katie knew Natalie was right. It had taken awhile to put all the random things together, but she finally realized there had been a major shift — not just between her and Andy, but even within Andy himself. His willingness to go this evening had surprised her. He typically didn't want to go out any more; instead he opted to lay on the couch or sit on the patio — doing nothing. Sitting and doing nothing wasn't Andy. She had always marveled at his constant state of motion — at least until the past six weeks or so. And now, his slowing down, his mood swings and bouts of anger were becoming more frequent, and he was more volatile. Katie sighed a heavy sigh as they pulled into the drive.

"You okay?" Andy asked, eying her with concern.

She searched his face for answers but seeing an unusual tiredness etched on his handsome features, she forced a smile. "I'm fine."

ANDY PACED BESIDE THE examination table in the small room. The frigid air was doing nothing to alleviate the chill he felt growing inside. He'd been waiting three weeks for this appointment and had endured tests, pokes, prods, blood draws and what seemed like hundreds of questions from nurses, doctors, and registration desks at three different facilities. The original appointment with Dr Payne, the family doctor, seemed ages ago. It had become just the first step in a series of tests and doctors who had grown increasingly grave as the appointments progressed. He had been told the results were in, a consultation visit was scheduled, and finally, today was the day. He'd had to ask off from RITE2U — again — to Charlene's aggravation but ready approval. He'd told her he had a doctor's appointment and with the incident in the break room still fresh on her mind, she seemed glad to hear he was seeing a doctor.

He had told Katie nothing of the appointments, the tests, or his growing concern. The more the appointments and tests progressed, the more difficult things grew between them, and it was his fault. He was in pain, and he didn't know why. He didn't want Katie to see him struggling, at least not until he knew what he was dealing with. His goal was to spare her, but he was clumsily making things worse. He'd lost count of the number of Katie's calls he'd missed and not returned. He'd either been in the middle of a test or a consultation and couldn't talk at the time, but he never called her back either. He'd even stopped calling her while he was on duty. He just couldn't bear to lie to her any more than he already had. It was easier just to avoid her when he could. It was becoming harder and harder to make normal conversation, but he promised himself that once he got the medicine he needed and started feeling like himself again, he'd make it up to her in a big way. He hung his head as he thought of how things were between them. He might not be feeling well, but she didn't deserve the way he was treating her either.

He paused in his pacing to glance at his watch and then at the closed door. He'd been waiting in this little cube of a room for over thirty minutes and his patience was wearing thin. Where was Dr. Parker? He'd come highly recommended, but Andy had only seen him briefly, once, and then the doctor had sent him off for a barrage of tests. Andy had expected Dr. Parker to have the same warm bedside manner that he himself used at accident scenes, but this doctor was brusque and all business.

He couldn't sit still. He first leaned against the edge of the exam table and then sat in the guest chair across from the doctor's rolling stool, his leg jiggling up and down. He glanced at the magazines in the rack and noticed they were the most current editions. Somehow, that was comforting. If they paid attention to this small detail, surely, they'd be just as meticulous, or even more so, with their patients' care — wouldn't they?

He stood and started to pace again when an abrupt knock at the door startled him. The door popped open and a nurse in navy blue scrubs poked her head in. "Mr. Garrett?" she asked, looking at a chart in her hands.

"That's me," Andy replied with a smile the nurse didn't return.

"There's been a change in plans. Dr. Parker would like to meet with you in his office. If you'll follow me please," she said and walked away.

Andy grabbed his jacket and hurried to catch up to her brisk pace. He followed her down the main hall and deeper into the medical complex. They passed examination rooms on his right and multiple areas that looked like nurse's stations on the left. The stations held a variety of computers and equipment, with nurses scurrying back and forth. Andy followed his guide, side stepping and weaving around nurses, technicians, doctors and lab workers.

After navigating several halls, the nurse opened a glass door that led into yet another hall where the quiet was almost overpowering. The plush, dark green carpet was set off by the deep cream color of the walls which were accented with richly-colored landscape paintings. The doors leading off the hallway were dark mahogany, with doctors' names stenciled in gold lettering.

Andy stopped short when the nurse came to a sudden halt in front of the door stenciled 'Dr. Joseph Parker.' When there was no answer to her brisk knock, the nurse turned the gold doorknob, and the door swung open easily. Unsure, Andy glanced first at the nurse before stepping inside. Almost in his ear the nurse said, "Dr. Parker will be here in a few minutes. Please take a seat and make yourself comfortable."

Andy nodded and turned to thank her, but she had already turned away and was closing the door behind her. Turning back to the office, Andy felt like he'd stepped into another world, world far away from the cold, sterile examination room.

Dr. Parker's office looked like an attorney's office. The large desk commanding the room was solid oak, its honey-tone color a warm contrast to the plush blue carpet. The desk was covered with stacks of files and papers, a tall brass lamp on the front right corner. The desk chair's navy-blue leather matched the two guest chairs of the same material. Bookcases lined the wall behind the guest chairs while the wall behind the desk was covered with certificates, credentials and photographs of Dr. Parker with other distinguished-looking people.

Andy ran his hand along the back of the leather guest chair. This was not what he'd expected. It was intimidating. He felt his already-heightened sense of apprehension escalate even further.

The hall door opened, and Dr. Parker bustled in carrying a stack of folders. He moved behind the desk and pulled out the chair while motioning for Andy to sit in one of the guest chairs. Dr. Parker's crisp white lab coat rustled, and the leather of the chair creaked as he sat.

He laid the folders he'd been carrying to the side and picked up the lone folder laying in front of his chair. Andy noticed the folder was thick as he caught a glimpse of his name on the tab.

"Andrew," Dr. Parker said in greeting.

"You can call me Andy, Doc," Andy replied, his voice a bit hoarse.

Dr. Parker's eyes dropped to the folder and flicked across the pages. He turned one page slowly and then two or three more.

Andy sat silently on the edge of the chair, his hands steepled in front of him. He stared at the edge of the desk, unaware he was holding his breath.

Dr. Parker closed the folder and laid it in front of him. He leaned forward and looked at Andy intently.

Andy looked up and shifted nervously.

"I'm sorry to have kept you waiting," Dr. Parker began. "I wanted to review a few more notes before we talked. In studying your file a bit closer, I see you are married."

Andy nodded, uncertain why that might be of interest. "Yes, sir."

Dr. Parker's eyebrows rose as if were expecting more.

"Her name is Katie," Andy offered.

"I thought she might be with you today to hear your test results," Dr. Parker said, tilting his head in question, waiting for Andy's response.

Andy crossed and uncrossed his legs, rubbing the tops of his thighs with his hands. "Well, sir," he began, "she doesn't exactly know anything about this. I didn't want to worry her, but I'll let her know if there's anything going on. I thought I'd wait to say anything rather than her worry, too."

Hearing himself say it out loud made Andy feel even guiltier about not telling her. He had started to tell Katie, several times, but every time, he just couldn't bring himself to do it. He would have to admit something might actually be wrong and besides, he had a plan. He'd get these tests done, find out what was wrong, get some medicine to correct it, and go on with his life. He met Dr. Parker's eye with an attempt at a confident smile.

Dr. Parker glanced down at the closed file laying in front of him and tapped it once. He came around the desk and sat in the chair next to Andy's. He stared at his hands and rubbed them together, seemingly contemplating what he was about to say. When he finally looked at Andy, the look of concern on his face made Andy cringe inwardly.

Dr. Parker had changed from the abrupt, businesslike doctor Andy had encountered at his initial appointment, to a man leaning toward Andy with friendly kindness. "Andy, I've been in practice for about thirty-five years and have had opportunity to take care of many people — some older, some younger. I've seen things I don't understand and don't pretend I ever will. Some things are just what they are. We have to accept them and know we may never understand the why." He looked at the floor and then back at Andy. "What I have to tell you is not easy to say, and I know it will not be easy for you to hear, but it's best to get it out so we can move forward."

Andy's body tensed while his mind raced.

"You are a fine, young man, but I'm afraid I have some bad news. As you know, we ran a lot of tests to try and figure out what has been causing the pain and discomfort you've been experiencing. The test results are back and all point to the same diagnosis . . . I am so sorry to have to tell you, Andy, but you have cancer — pancreatic cancer to be exact."

Time stopped, and Andy's racing thoughts came to a screeching halt. He struggled to put a coherent thought together but finally managed. "Cancer? I can't have cancer . . ."

"Andy, I'm afraid it's very serious," Dr. Parker continued. "You probably know pancreatic cancer is one of the most serious forms of cancer, but you also need to know that breakthroughs are happening every day, and I intend to do everything in my power to get you through this. There are excellent treatments available, and I'm working up a schedule for you now. Based on the test results, I am recommending chemotherapy and radiation simultaneously. As you've said, and as the test results bear out, this has been going on for awhile, so we need to get you started on these treatments. The sooner the better. The schedule calls for them to start early next week. I want to meet with you and your wife, together, so you'll both know what to expect and how to prepare for what will be happening."

Andy knew Dr. Parker was talking, but his voice sounded far away. Andy could see Katie's smiling face swimming in front of him and feel the crack of the bat as he connected with the ball. He could feel the floor of the fire engine vibrating beneath his boots and see the red emergency lights swirling around the engine cab. He could hear the crackle of flames and hear his raspy breathing through his mask.

He could see the living room at the station with the guys cheering a football game on TV, and he and Jerry visiting over a grill in the back yard. Those things were real. Not this. Not . . . cancer.

Andy leaned forward, put his elbows on his knees and raked his hands through his hair. He'd put his face in his hands when he felt Dr. Parker's hand on his shoulder. "Andy?"

He couldn't think. He couldn't speak. This wasn't happening. He couldn't have cancer.

Dr. Parker gripped Andy's shoulder and said more firmly, "Andy."

Andy shook his head and tried to focus on Dr. Parker, who was eying him with concern.

"Are you sure?" Andy asked, his voice hoarse. "I mean, absolutely sure? There has never been anything in my life to even remotely suggest cancer. I've always been healthy. There's gotta be some mistake — a mix up somewhere down the line." Even as he heard himself trying to rationalize away the reality, he knew in his heart the diagnosis was right. He had cancer.

Dr. Parker shook his head. "Andy, I'm sorry. There is no mistake. That's why there were so many tests. Your symptoms indicated this was what we were dealing with, but I wanted to be absolutely certain before coming to a final conclusion and talking to you." He paused briefly then continued, in a very insistent tone. "Andy, the most important thing to do right now is talk to Katie. Tell her everything. You need her support but most importantly, you need her love. This is going to be hard, very hard, and I don't care how tough you think you are, you can't do this alone."

Andy's phone buzzed. Out of habit, he pulled it from his pocket. It was Katie. He'd sent her two earlier calls to voice mail and did the same with this one before slipping the phone back in his pocket.

"Dr Parker, I don't know what to say to Katie. How am I going to tell her? She knows something is wrong, but I've tried to hide as much as I can."

"Well, Andy," Dr. Parker said, "the answer is simple. Just tell her the truth. Don't hide anything any longer."

Andy nodded absently.

Dr. Parker leaned back in his chair. "Let me ask you this. What if the roles were reversed?"

Andy shifted uncomfortably. "I wouldn't like it. I'd want to know so I could help her." He paused for several seconds. "I'd want her to know that no matter what, I love her and would be there for her."

"I think you just answered your own question. You know exactly what to say. Go home. Tell her. You need her beside you, and it sounds like that's where she's going to want to be."

Dr. Parker hit his palms on his thighs and stood. "Andy, you are a fine, strong young man and all of that plays in your favor. The best thing you can do is be stubborn. I mean make up your mind to really fight. We'll work together on this, and we'll do our absolute best to get it under control. I am sorry to have had to give you this news, but you strike me as a fighter. So, we're going for the win."

He looked closely at Andy who still seemed dazed. "I'm prescribing a pain medication that will give you some relief. We have your pharmacy's number in the paperwork, and the prescription will be there whenever you're ready to pick it up. I know this is new and it's a shock, but do you have any questions I can answer now?"

Andy numbly shook his head. "No, Doc. I just need some time." Andy paused and then asked, "Speaking of time, how much ... will I ..."

Dr. Parker came around the desk and eased back into the blue leather chair beside Andy. "That's not the question right now. The question is, how tough are you and how much are you willing to fight? Those are the questions you need to think about. We're going to give this thing absolutely everything we've got, but you're the one who has to determine how much. I don't go half measures. Do you?"

"No, sir," Andy replied.

"Good. We'll make a good team then. I look forward to meeting Katie. Would you like for me or my nurse to call her so she can pick you up?"

"No … no … thank you. I'm good to get home." Andy tried to sound more confident than he felt.

He couldn't define what he was feeling. Lost? Yes. Afraid? Definitely. He felt like everything he'd ever known had just been pulled from beneath him. No training, no exercises, no practice — nothing could have prepared him for this.

"I've got another appointment," Dr. Parker said. "You have my office to yourself. Take some time. Gather your thoughts."

He trained Andy with an intense look. "Remember what I said. Be positive, but above all, be a fighter. A nurse will be at the end of the hall whenever you're ready for her to guide you out of this maze."

He opened the door and with a quick glance over his shoulder was gone, and the door closed behind him.

Tears came quickly as Andy thought of telling Katie. This would change their lives and interrupt — or possibly even end — their happy life together. He'd heard stories about chemo treatment and about radiation treatment — none good. Stories of pancreatic cancer patients came to mind too — no good news there either. This just couldn't be happening — not now, not him. Stark reality washed over him in an icy wave, and he felt his gut wrench with a different kind of pain. What about being a firefighter? Could he continue to work? How was he going to support them? How was he going to be the husband he'd vowed to be?

He slumped, holding his head in his hands. Even though it wasn't manly, he couldn't stop the tears that came, and he let them fall.

ANDY'S HEADLIGHTS CROSSED THE back of Katie's car as he pulled into the driveway. He turned the engine off. Both the silence and the darkness fell heavily around him. He'd driven for hours after leaving Dr. Parker's office, not knowing or even paying attention to where he was going. Katie had called several times, but each time he sent her call to voice mail. He couldn't bear hearing her voice. Jerry had called too. Andy knew Katie must have called him when he hadn't picked up or let her know where he was. He lowered his head onto the steering wheel, took a deep breath, and exhaled slowly, trying to muster whatever he could from inside to get through seeing Katie. He couldn't give way to emotions he'd been trying so hard to get under control all afternoon. He'd already decided not to tell Katie tonight. There'd be time for that tomorrow — or the next day.

KATIE HEARD ANDY'S TRUCK pull into the driveway and the motor shut off. She looked up expectantly from the book she'd been reading, or actually, the same page she'd been staring at for the past hour.

Katie had been calling Andy after seeing her students off for the day, but when she heard Sally's voice in the hall, she hung up quickly when her call went straight to voice mail. She hadn't heard from Andy all day even though she knew he was working at RITE2U. He usually called or was at least easy to reach but now, nothing seemed easy any longer.

Katie had been preparing to leave when she heard a soft knock and looked up to see Sally striding through the door. She couldn't help but groan to herself. She really didn't want to spar with Sally today.

"Do you have a minute?" Sally asked in a surprisingly kind tone.

Katie looked at Sally quizzically. "Sure," she said hesitantly. "What do you need?"

"Well, it's not exactly what *I* need," Sally said, actually sounding a bit nervous. "It's actually what *you* may need."

Katie frowned and cocked her head. Sally had her attention. "What *I* need?"

"Well, yes. As your team lead, I have noticed that you seem distracted lately. And tired. I was just wondering if there was something I could help with or if you might just need a listening ear."

Katie was stunned. Was Sally actually being nice or just prying for information? "Well, that's very kind of you to offer but I'm fine. Thanks."

Sally was determined to get Katie to open up. "You sure? You haven't looked yourself lately, and I haven't heard you talking to Andy in the afternoon for some time."

At the surprised look on Katie's face, Sally waved her hand nonchalantly. "Don't worry. I'm not eavesdropping. The sound just carries after the kids are gone. I'm just worried about you is all."

Sally waited to see what Katie would say. She didn't have to wait long.

Katie's shoulders slumped as she sat down hard in her chair and putting her face in her hands, started crying.

Katie's strong reaction surprised even Sally, and true alarm started tugging at Sally's conscience.

"What is it, Katie? It will help to talk about it," Sally soothed as she stepped behind Katie and started to pat her back.

"I'm okay," Katie said, looking up and wiping away tears. "Just feeling a bit low right now. Thanks."

"It's Andy," Sally persisted. "I can tell. In the three years we've taught together, I've never seen you like this. And for you to be this upset, it has to be something about Andy."

Katie couldn't stop the tears that fell more freely as Sally put an arm around her shaking shoulders. Sally listened as Katie started talking and continued to talk nonstop for the next half hour. Sally had been prepared to hear about some little something upsetting the Garrett's charmed life, but what Katie was telling her sounded truly sobering. Sally found herself becoming alarmed. This was sounding like Andy might really be seeing someone else, and it was getting serious. Maybe it was even the blonde she'd seen him with and teased Katie mercilessly about.

Well, if Andy was seeing someone else, Katie needed to know, Sally reasoned. Katie needed to prepare herself so she could brace for the worst. The news would, of course, be better coming from a friend and even though she hadn't actually been much of a friend to Katie, Sally thought, she might could be one now.

When Katie finished her tearful account, Sally laid everything out. "I really am sorry, but it's all right there in front of you, kiddo. I hate to break it to you, but everything you've told me points to Andy having someone on the side. All the signs are definitely there. He may just be going back to his old ways with the ladies."

Katie reluctantly had to admit the signs were indeed there. She just couldn't, in her heart, truly believe Andy — her Andy — would break his promises to her and that his professions of love were lies. Logic dictated that it just was something the guy she loved and married would never do. Her hurting heart, though, needed an explanation and reluctantly entertained the possibility. The longer she pondered the possibilities and his unexplained behavior, the more she began to doubt her confidence and belief in him . . . in them.

She'd had hours to turn it over in her mind waiting for Andy. And now he was home. Her mind was still reeling with thoughts she never dreamed of having before her conversation with Sally that afternoon. She closed the book and waited for the truck door to slam, signaling his approach. Several long minutes passed before she finally heard it and then his footsteps came to the door and stopped. She scooted to the edge of her chair and braced herself, ready for a confrontation as the front door opened and Andy stepped inside.

Andy's heart ached seeing his sweet Katie waiting so expectantly. The guilt from ignoring her calls washed over him, but steeling his resolve, he smiled and said, "Hey, beautiful, sorry to be so late."

He tossed his keys on the side table and sauntered to the kitchen. He opened the refrigerator door and waited, unsure of what to say next. He was keenly aware Katie hadn't said a word, and he could feel her watching him.

"So, how was your day?" Andy asked to break the silence and trying to sound casual.

"Fine ... and *yours?*" Katie replied. He didn't miss the pointedness in her question.

Andy closed the refrigerator door and willed himself to look at her. "My day ... well, it was one of *those* kind of days."

He shrugged and plopped into the chair across from Katie, crossing his legs as he put his feet on the ottoman between them. This was the perfect opportunity, and he knew he should tell her and tell her now. She looked so hurt, angry and confused, and he couldn't blame her. He was being terribly unfair. After hesitating, he finally met her look and seeing the hurt and questions in her eyes, he looked away quickly.

"I called RITE2U this afternoon when I couldn't reach you by phone. They said you'd taken the afternoon off."

Andy shifted in the chair. "Yeah — I had some things to do that couldn't wait."

"Really? What kind of things?"

"Oh — just — you know — errands." Andy gave his best effort at another smile and a chuckle that caught in his throat. "No need to bore you. Tell me about your day."

Katie stood. "It's been a stressful day, and I'm tired. I'm going to bed. Good night."

She turned and walked toward the hall.

"Katie," Andy started as he turned in his chair toward her.

Katie stopped, waiting, a hopeful look on her face.

'Tell her' the voice in his head was screaming. 'Tell. Her.'

"Katie…I…" He cleared his throat and opened his mouth to begin again. No — he just couldn't do it. "Sorry — it can wait. Good night."

He saw Katie visibly slump and tears glisten in her eyes before she turned and walked down the hall.

Katie managed to close the door before the tears came. She crawled into bed and curled into a tiny ball. She pulled the sheet over her and cried as the pain washed over her in waves. She was surprised, yes, but hurt and angry too. The special bond she and Andy had shared the past three wonderful years was gone. He had looked her in the eye and lied. Little comfort though it was, she'd also seen guilt cross his face.

What other lies might he be telling her? She replayed the past several weeks in her mind, searching for the clues Sally insisted were there. Katie struggled to put the pieces together where they'd make some kind of sense. She couldn't believe Andy was being unfaithful to her. She had just as many reasons to testify to his faithfulness. She racked her brain for what she'd said or done or could do to fix whatever was wrong but finally fell into a fitful sleep. She woke several times during the night, hoping to find Andy beside her, but he never came.

EXHAUSTED, SHE ROLLED OVER to look at the clock. 6:20 a.m. They both should have been up by now. She had to get to school, and Andy to the station. She sat on the edge of the bed and tried to pull her scattered thoughts together. She glanced at Andy's side of the bed. The sheets and pillowcase were smooth. Not knowing what she would say, she stared at the door several minutes before forcing herself to open it.

She padded down the hall in her bare feet and stepped into the family room, gray with early morning light, her eyes sweeping the empty room. A quick glance told her the kitchen was empty too. She sat down wearily in one of the dining room chairs. She could tell Andy had slept on the couch from the scattered cushions and pillows. She dropped her head into her hands and combed her fingers through her hair.

Everything lately was so unlike him. The nagging voice in her head and the cold dread of fear she wasn't quite ready to acknowledge were beginning to take hold of her every thought.

Suddenly, her head popped up. No, she wasn't giving up without a fight. In a sudden burst of determination, Katie stood and walked to the table. She picked up the phone and dialed Jerry's number. Andy should be at the station today. Jerry would have to get Andy to talk to him.

AFTER KATIE HAD GONE to bed, Andy laid on the couch, staring at the ceiling. He felt guilty for being so deceitful and vague. He knew he would have to tell her — and soon. He heard the bedroom door close but not before he heard a stifled sob. Andy's heart ached. He only wanted to spare her what was coming. He closed his eyes, searching for the right words to say, but they wouldn't come — not tonight. He was too emotionally exhausted, and the constant throb of pain had grown worse.

Wearily, he pushed himself to his feet and picking up his jacket, pulled the bottle of pain killers from the pocket. He'd somehow managed to remember to pick them up at the pharmacy in the haze of the afternoon. He got a glass of water from the kitchen and after swallowing a couple of pills, stumbled back to the couch. He buried his head in the pillows, wrapping his arms around his midsection in a tight grip. It took several minutes but the pain began to ease and mercifully, he slept.

HAMILTON MADE A U-TURN after talking to Katie. He'd stop by Station Two before going to the office. He spotted Andy's truck a few spots over as he parked.

He hesitated when he stepped inside and saw Andy sitting at the kitchen table with the guys from A shift. He glanced at his watch and frowned. It was 6:48 A.M. After Rogers had told him about Bentley's heated reports of Andy being continually late, Andy being at the station early should be a good thing, but Hamilton knew it wasn't.

He walked to the counter and poured himself a cup of coffee. Putting the steaming cup to his mouth, he turned and leaned against the kitchen cabinet. Each man said a friendly hello, and Jerry acknowledged them with a raise of his mug. The low-key early morning talk continued while some read the paper. Andy, Hamilton noticed, was sitting away from the group and was uncharacteristically subdued. He sat at the end of the table, his back to Hamilton, a cup of coffee in front of him, staring blankly into space.

Hamilton casually walked over and claimed the empty chair across from Andy.

Andy blinked and the faraway look in his eyes came to focus on Hamilton. Andy shifted uncomfortably and looked down.

Hamilton took another sip of coffee and silently observed Andy. He looked terrible. His usually tanned face was ashen and there were dark circles under his eyes. His hair was tousled and when Andy finally did look at Hamilton, his eyes were swollen and red, and the usual sparkle wasn't there.

Andy shrugged and smiled wanly.

The talk had slowed, Hamilton noticed. The men at the table were looking between the two of them and waiting expectantly. Andy being at the station early was unusual, but his physical appearance along with the unexpected appearance of the Chief, drew the notice of even the most inattentive.

"Quiet night?" Hamilton half asked, half stated as he turned and looked down the table. He hoped to draw their attention away from Andy. One of the guys commented it had been slow — only a couple of minor medical runs. Others nodded agreement, but conversation still didn't resume.

Andy looked out the window and away from the group.

Someone cleared his throat nervously. It wasn't like firefighters to be at a loss for words. This was getting uncomfortable for everyone so Hamilton tried another tack.

"Thought Everett did a good job quarterbacking the other night."

The tall, balding firefighter at the far end of the table readily agreed. His comment was quickly drowned out with dissents. Hamilton knew the high school starting quarterback controversy would get conversation flowing.

Hamilton stood cautiously so as not to draw the group's attention and catching Andy's eye, motioned with his head for Andy to follow him. They left the A shift guys in heated debate while they walked silently toward the engine bay. Andy walked quietly behind Hamilton, hands stuffed into his pant pockets, head down, his shoulders slumped. Hamilton could tell he would have to start the conversation. He pushed the bay door open and stepped aside as Andy walked to the bunker gear room. Andy picked up his gear and turned to leave but Hamilton blocked his path.

Andy pulled up short and with his eyes suddenly blazing, snapped, "What do you want?"

Taken aback, Hamilton quickly regained control. "What's going on with you? You look awful."

"Nothing's going on. I'm fine … just fine," Andy snarled as he tried to brush past.

Hamilton stood his ground and crossed his arms in front of him.

"Uh-uh. You're not getting out of here until you tell me what's going on. Katie called, and she's really upset. I can't say I blame her, seeing how you're acting."

Andy glared and dropped his gear at Hamilton's feet. He lowered his shoulder and tried to shove his way through.

Hamilton was surprised, but he hooked his arm through Andy's and whirled him around.

"Let go of me," Andy barked, his body rigid with anger. He jerked his arm out of Hamilton's grasp and pushed past him.

"Andy!"

Andy hesitated slightly but continued down the hall. "Leave me alone," he yelled over his shoulder just as the door swung open and the C shift crew entered. Their chatter stopped abruptly when they saw the glare on Andy's face as he angrily shouldered his way through them.

"Garrett!"

They turned as a group when they heard Chief Hamilton, standing with his hands on his hips, controlled frustration radiating from him. He took a deep breath and with a curt nod, brushed his own way past the group.

They trailed behind the Chief to the living area, as he turned and followed Andy to his room. Andy's locker doors stopped banging. They heard the Chief say, "Garrett, take the day. You don't need to be here with the frame of mind you're in." He closed the door behind him as he followed Andy into his room.

Andy whirled on Hamilton, his face distorted with rage. "Why don't you just leave me alone? I don't need you, and I don't need you sticking your nose into my business. If I needed any help, I'd ask for it. Now get out!"

Hamilton listened as Andy continued to yell, slamming gear into his locker.

Hamilton was stunned. He'd never seen Andy so angry or so out of control. Never.

When Andy slowed, Hamilton interrupted and in low, measured tones said, "Garrett, I don't know what is going on with you, but I do know you cannot serve your team or the citizens of Abernathy with the frame of mind you're in. I'm putting you down for a sick day. I want you to leave and when you can come back with the right attitude, come back, but — and I emphasize — *not* before. End of discussion."

Andy, his chest heaving, glared at Hamilton. "I don't need a sick day. I can do my job."

Hamilton stood at his full height, returning Andy's glare. "I said — end of discussion."

Andy hesitated only slightly before throwing his duffel bag over his shoulder, his face a thundercloud about to explode. The door banged loudly against the wall as he threw it open and stormed out. Ignoring the group as he brushed past them, Andy slammed the back door behind him as he left. The silence in the wake of his departure was palpable.

Chief Hamilton stepped into the hall, looking haggard and worried.

The C shift guys were waiting, their eyes wide, staring at him. He took a deep breath and took a step forward, but Bentley, with something akin to glee on his face, strode up to him oblivious to the tension thick in the air. He grinned confidently. "Been telling ya about Garrett, Chief. Now you know what I have to deal with."

Chief Hamilton turned to Bentley. "Bentley, if you're smart, you'll wipe that smile off your face. Now get to work." His eyes flashed as he pinned Bentley with a heated glare before leaving the station through the same door Andy had used.

Meanwhile, the rest of the crew exchanged worried looks. It had been evident for some time things weren't right with Andy. He was a nuisance at times — a big nuisance most of the time — but he was a firefighter and that made him family. It was time to find out what was going on.

HEDRICK BACKED INTO ONE of the reserved spots outside the ER, signaled by the high-pitched beeps of the ambulance's back up warning system. He stowed his gear and crossed the drive to the bustling emergency room. He glanced toward the exam room hall. Hart, who had taken Andy's spot on the ambulance today, was nowhere to be seen. Hedrick glanced toward the nurse's station but didn't see Mandy either. He was disappointed but a bit relieved too.

Before he took his next step, a soft voice behind him said, "Hey there."

He stiffened. Mandy.

"Oh, hi," Hedrick managed as he turned to see her standing a few steps away.

"What's up?" she asked with a mischievous smile.

Hedrick, his heart racing, said, "A...run. We just had a run. Hart's still in with the patient."

"Hart?" Mandy asked with a slight frown, as she thumbed through some file folders on the counter beside her. "Where's Andy? I thought you two rode together."

"Well, we do," Hedrick said, "but the Chief gave Garrett the day off. Garrett was none too happy about it either. I've never seen him so mad."

Mandy's hands stilled as she looked up at Hedrick. "What happened?"

Hedrick stuffed his hands in his pockets and rocked nervously back on his heels a couple of times before answering, "No one knows. Bentley tried to talk to the Chief but was shut down cold. There's an overtime guy riding the engine, and Hart and I are on the ambulance this shift."

"I can't believe I'm saying this, but I actually miss Garrett," Hedrick added with a small smile. "He may be a pain, but I'm worried about him too — we're all worried."

Hedrick stopped as Mandy's eyes shifted from his face to a point behind him. He turned to see Hart approaching.

"Mandy," Hart said as he walked up.

"Hey, Rob. How are you?"

"I'm fine. Thanks," he replied with a stiff nod. He turned to Hedrick. "Ready?"

"Ready if you are," Hedrick replied with an apologetic smile to Mandy. He headed toward the door behind Hart who was already walking out.

Mandy grabbed a notepad and scribbled something down. Tearing the sheet off, she hurried to catch up to them. "Sean," she said softly so as not to attract Hart's attention.

Hedrick slowed and turned. Mandy held the paper out, "Don't forget this," she said, handing it to him. "You'll need it later."

Puzzled, he glanced at the paper and saw a phone number and Mandy's name. He looked at her, unsure. "Call me later," Mandy mouthed so Hart couldn't hear.

Realization dawned, and Hedrick couldn't help the pleased grin that spread across his face. He slipped the paper into his uniform shirt pocket and with a quick wave, followed Hart out the door.

KATIE, SOMEHOW, MADE IT through the school day. Sally checked on her several times and even though Katie called her a mother hen, Sally's concern was soothing to Katie's aching heart. She didn't tell Sally about last night. It was just too painful and would only give Sally more reason to convince Katie of Andy's unfaithfulness. She didn't need that today.

Jerry called around lunchtime. Things had not gone well between him and Andy at the station. She could tell Jerry felt the same frustration she was feeling. Neither of them could figure out how to get Andy to open up. Listless, Katie walked to her car, wondering what kind of day Andy was having at the station. He always seemed better after hanging out with the guys and doing the work he loved so much. Even though she was miserable, she still loved him too much not to want things to be right for him.

She drove the short distance home and slowed when she saw Andy's truck in the drive. Her heart beat faster as she parked behind it. What was he doing home? She exhaled a nervous breath and turned off the engine. She sat quietly, wording a silent prayer before bracing herself for whatever might come as she walked the short distance to the house. She hesitated only slightly before opening the door.

After leaving the station that morning, Andy made the hour's drive to Claremont, where he'd grown up. He parked in front of the little house, a shack really, where he and his mom had lived. His parents divorced when he was just a baby, and they never heard from his dad again.

Andy's mom worked two jobs, sometimes three, if she could get the work and did her best to make ends meet. He tried to help but there was a limit to what a ten-year-old could do. He tried not to eat very much since they couldn't afford a lot of food, and he tried to take care of himself so his mom wouldn't have to worry about him. "You're my sweet angel, Andy," she'd tell him each morning as she hugged him tight before she left for work, and he left for school. Sometimes he wouldn't see her until the next morning, since she went from one job to the next and worked until midnight most nights.

On his tenth birthday, his mom had announced she was taking the whole day off. She'd looked at him with sad eyes. "Andy, you're such a brave young man, and you put up with a lot. I'm so sorry I haven't spent much time with you lately, but we're going to make up for that today. And," she'd said with a flourish, "we're going to start with this." She reached under the table and retrieved a box wrapped in colorful birthday paper.

"For me?!" Andy remembered asking, thrilled, and afraid the box would disappear before he could open it.

"Yes, dear. Just for you. I'm pretty sure you're going to like it."

He eagerly ripped off the paper, his hands trembling with anticipation as he'd lifted the lid. "A new baseball glove!" he'd shouted. Even though it wasn't actually new, it was new to him. The smell of leather tickled his nose as he pulled it on and wiggled his fingers down until they fit snugly into the glove. They'd played catch in the park all afternoon, his mom laughing and pitching the ball back and forth with him.

Andy smiled at the memory. It had been one of the best days he'd ever had until the phone rang that evening. His mom was putting the finishing touches on his favorite dinner, meatloaf and macaroni and cheese, when she'd answered the phone and talked in a low voice. A few minutes later, she sat across the table from him and smiled a fake, glittery smile.

"Darling, I am so sorry," she'd said, "but I have some bad news. I have to go to work. My boss just called and they're short on staff tonight. They're really busy, and he said he'd pay me double time if I would work. At least we got to spend most of the day together. I hope you understand."

Andy tried, but he didn't understand. All he'd wanted was to have the rest of his special day with his mom, like she promised. He did his best to smile, but he hadn't been able to hide the sadness on his face.

His mom hurried off to change clothes and fifteen minutes later rushed back into the kitchen wearing a long coat, even though it was warm outside. She smelled nice and looked really pretty.

"We'll have fun tomorrow, my angel. Now, I've got to run," she said before dashing out the door.

Andy remembered sitting at the table until the front door closed, and then he'd rushed to the front window to watch her leave. She'd stepped onto the drive just as a car pulled in and stopped. She opened the door, and Andy heard her laughing as she spoke to someone inside. When she took off her coat, Andy could tell she wasn't wearing her waitress uniform. She was dressed fancy. She wasn't going to work.

She had lied to him and was going out and the person in the car had probably been the man he'd come to hate in the coming years.

Something changed deep inside him that night. He'd felt abandoned. Andy closed his eyes tight remembering just how alone he'd felt, not just that night, but all the years between then and high school graduation.

"SEE YOU TOMORROW, ANDY," Jill laughed and squeezed Andy's hand before reaching up to give him a peck on the cheek.

Andy smiled and removed his hand from her grasp. "Bye," he said with a wink.

Jill giggled as Andy turned to walk to his car. He heaved a heavy sigh. Only two days until graduation, and he still didn't know what he was going to do. College was certainly out. He had no money. His mother had no way to help him and there certainly wasn't anything to be expected from Donald. He couldn't wait to get away from home. Life had changed drastically after his mother married Donald when Andy was twelve. He seemed to make his mother happy but Andy's feelings of dislike for the man were strongly reciprocated. Donald went out of his way to provoke Andy and when Andy responded, Donald punished him with his mother's full support. Andy tried to spend as much time away from home as possible, but when he was home, he stood up to Donald and defied him at every opportunity, which typically didn't turn out too well for Andy.

In the meantime, he'd turned toward school and learned to look for ways to excel. That turned out to be much easier than he'd thought. Andy was a natural athlete. He enjoyed playing football but his all-time favorite was playing short stop for the high school baseball team. Sports had opened a whole new world of friends — guys and girls. He enjoyed the fun camaraderie with the guys on both the football and baseball teams, but he also enjoyed the 'celebrity' that came with being a high school jock. He never lacked for attention from girls — especially the cheerleaders. He had fun flirting, and it helped bolster his flailing ego.

Jill was the latest cheerleader he'd been dating. That was all coming to an end after graduation, even though she'd been hinting she wanted to continue dating. Andy had already decided with the end of high school, that part of his life was coming to an end too. He was moving on mentally and physically.

"Andy Garrett!"

Andy was just about to unlock his car door but turned to see Barry Giles walking quickly across the parking lot. Barry was the quarterback for the football team, the first baseman for the baseball team, and most importantly, Andy's best friend.

"What's up?" Andy asked as he opened the car door and tossed his graduation gown and cap in the back seat.

"Looking for you."

"Well, you found me. I've got to get home. My mother is fixing a nice 'graduation' meal," Andy said with air quotes and a roll of his eyes. "I'm sure Donald will be there trying to make polite interesting conversation, which we both know isn't possible for him. I can't wait to get out of there."

Barry had been Andy's confidant for quite some time and knew all about his home life.

"That's actually what I've come to talk to you about," Barry said as he leaned against the side of Andy's car.

"About my graduation dinner?" Andy asked with a grin.

"No, goof ball. Thought I'd see if you wanted to move in and crash with me for awhile. Mom and dad are cool with it. I told them we were both getting jobs so we can pay them some room and board. It makes them feel like we're learning how to pay our own way and besides, they both like having you over. And . . . you know my mom's a great cook. What do you say?"

Andy was surprised. This was the first time Barry had mentioned anything. Graduation was just a couple of days away, and all Andy knew he was going to do was find a way to get out of that house.

Andy breathed a sigh of relief. "That sounds great, man. Count me in. Thanks. I'll bring my things over after commencement."

"Awesome. I'll let mom know she'll have another hungry mouth to feed come Saturday. This is going to be great. Let the party continue!"

They shook hands and laughed. Andy was thrilled. It couldn't have worked out better but knowing Barry and his parents, they had probably been planning this for a while. Barry was a great friend and his mom and dad were always so nice. They asked him questions about school and things of interest to him, and not just sports. Andy's mother and Donald, on the other hand, never asked about school and had never come to a single football or baseball game Andy's entire high school career, even after he'd won several awards and the baseball team had made it the quarter finals in state competition this year.

Andy was whistling under his breath, realizing he was happy — at least he was happy until he pulled up in front of his house. Donald was waiting on the front porch with a scowl and stood when Andy pulled into the drive. Andy knew this couldn't be good.

"Where have you been?" Donald snapped, walking toward Andy as he stepped out of his car.

"School. Had to get my graduation stuff," Andy said, reaching in the back seat.

"You were supposed to have been home an hour ago. Your mom has fixed a special dinner for you and this is the kind of disrespect you show her? You're never gonna grow up and be responsible are you, kid?" He kept advancing, but Andy stood his ground.

"She said 6:00. It's only 6:15," Andy said, brushing past him. Andy opened the front door with Donald right on his heels. "There was a line at school. It took longer than I thought."

Andy tossed his cap and gown on the sofa and headed toward the kitchen, but Donald grabbed his arm and whirled him around.

"Don't you turn your back on me and walk away, kid. I've about had it with you and your disrespect."

Andy eyed him. This was the first time in a long time Donald had touched him. Donald knew Andy was stronger and would win any physical confrontation, but Andy didn't want any trouble. He just wanted to get through the next two days, graduate and get out of this house.

"No disrespect intended," Andy said but then added with a smirk, "by the way, my name is Andy — not kid. I thought you might have figured that out after all these years, but guess I was wrong."

Andy turned around to walk to the kitchen.

Furious, Donald yelled, "I said, don't turn your back on me!" He grabbed Andy's arm again but this time, he squared up and landed a solid punch to the side of Andy's face. The pain was sudden but nothing Andy hadn't felt on the football field. He staggered a bit but stood firm.

"Don't touch me again. I'm warning you," Andy said in low even tones. "You'll be sorry."

"Now you're threatening me?!" Donald yelled and suddenly lunged. He caught Andy at his waist and the momentum carried Andy back into the recliner. Andy's mother ran in from the kitchen, screaming at Andy to stop.

Andy shoved Donald off and then punched him in the stomach as hard as he could. Donald went to his knees gasping for air. Andy's mother screamed. She pushed Andy away and knelt beside Donald.

Andy staggered back, breathing heavy, but he felt like he was the one who'd taken the gut punch, as he watched his mother hovering over that awful man. She spoke in soothing tones and helped Donald stand while looking at Andy with accusing eyes.

Andy had reached his breaking point. He went to his room, packed his things, which wasn't a lot, and walked back through the family room where Donald sat on the sofa, still cradling his stomach. Andy walked to his car as his mother followed him out the door.

"Where you do you think you're going?" she asked. She stood on the porch with her arms crossed in front of her. She didn't look worried that Andy was leaving, just angry.

"I'm done here," Andy said as he opened the car door. "You don't care about me. You've made that more than plain. I was just trying to get through the end of school, but I'm done. Hope you're happy. Have a nice life."

Andy got in the car and revved the engine. The tires squealed as he tore down the street.

He showed up on Barry's doorstep after driving around for a couple of hours to cool off. Barry opened the door and his eyes went wide in surprise.

"What happened to you?" he said, eying the dark bruise burgeoning on Andy's jaw.

Andy opened his mouth but nothing came out. He only hung his head.

Barry hesitated only briefly before clapping Andy on the shoulder and pulling him inside.

"Hey, man. No worries. Come in. Let's start the party a couple of days early. Mom, set another plate. Andy's here!"

ANDY STARED AT THE house as the memories flooded his mind. He hadn't noticed the warmth or the brightness of the sun beaming into the truck as the morning slipped away. He sat still, deep in thought.

Barry had been an amazing friend. He was married now and had moved across country with some big fancy job he'd gotten after college.

They kept in touch but not as often as they should. It would be good to talk to Barry. He'd give him a call soon, Andy decided.

He'd lived with Barry and his family for only a couple of months and worked odd jobs until he saw where the Abernathy Fire Department was testing for recruits. It sounded interesting, and he discovered he had the natural disposition for a firefighter. Andy excelled at the academy, making a sworn enemy of Mike Bentley and a true friend in Jerry Hamilton.

He couldn't think about Hamilton right now. Not now, but soon. He took one last look at the house and started his truck. Jerry Hamilton had become more of a father to him than Donald had ever been. A few months after Andy graduated from high school, he heard his mom and Donald had moved somewhere back East. He'd called his mom to tell her about his graduation from the fire academy and his high scores. She'd told him on that call, just once, how proud she was of him. He could still hear the pride in her voice, and he cherished the memory.

After a few letters and a phone call at Christmas, communication with his mom had tapered off. It had been several years since he'd heard from her. He wasn't even sure how to reach her. He had tried to call her when he and Katie were planning their wedding, but the phone number he had for her no longer worked. The wedding invitation was returned as undeliverable.

Andy had been a bit embarrassed to have no family at the wedding, especially after experiencing the closeness of Katie's family, but until today he'd never really missed his mom. But now, he missed her immensely and wished more than anything he could talk to her. When he'd left home that night, he never intended to come back to this house. He wasn't sure what had drawn him here today, but the memories were powerful.

He sighed as he made a U-turn and headed back to Abernathy . . . and Katie. He drove with the radio off and the windows down, taking his time and enjoying the cool air blowing through the cab. His overall mood was better with the help of a steady supply of pain killers. As he drove, he contemplated the best way to approach Katie. He would first apologize for being such a jerk and then break the news to her. But, what could he do to let her know how truly special she was to him? As the miles rolled past, a plan came together in his mind, and he spent the afternoon putting his plan into action.

ANDY SET THE DINNER table with extra care and even lit candles, a firefighter's nemesis. He had gone over the conversation in his mind a thousand times throughout the afternoon. He struggled trying to decide the best way to tell her. He didn't want to tell her, but at least he could try to soften the blow as much as possible. He would do anything to erase the past few weeks and spare her the dismal path ahead.

Andy had just lit the last candle and was shaking the match to douse the flame when he heard Katie's car. He took one more look at the table to make sure everything was just right. Even though this wasn't his area of expertise, he had worked hard to make everything as close to perfect as possible. He used a tablecloth and napkins, both in fall colors, as he'd seen Katie use together, and he set the table with their wedding china. Andy smiled. Katie would definitely be surprised at the china. He hadn't paid attention to china patterns or dishes or towels or anything else when they'd gotten married and picked things out for their new home. He hadn't cared what Katie picked. So long as it made her happy, he was happy. He adjusted the small bouquet of fall flowers he'd gotten as a final touch.

Andy made the drive to Gessupi's late that afternoon and picked up dinner. Mr. Gesuppi winked as he handed Andy the containers with his and Katie's favorites. He took a deep whiff of the aroma coming from the kitchen where their dinners were staying warm in the oven. For the first time in a long time, food actually smelled good.

He heard Katie's footsteps on the porch and with a quick look heavenward, he waited and tapped his fingers nervously on the table. The front door opened, and Katie stepped inside. She closed the door and then turned to see him waiting, the room glowing with candle-light. She took a hesitant step. The candle glow illuminated the surprise on her face as a blush of anxiousness spread across her cheeks.

Andy attempted to smile and in a voice hoarse with emotion said, "Hi."

"Hi," Katie replied hesitantly as she slowly placed her purse on the side table. She glanced around. "You've been busy."

She took a long look at the table and then turned to Andy, look-ing confused. "Is that Gessupi's I smell?"

"It is. Are you hungry?" Andy asked and started toward the kitchen.

"Yes, but hold on a minute. This is lovely," Katie said with a wave of her hand, "but what's it all about? You've been acting like a stranger for weeks and then tonight...tonight there's all of...this. And aren't you supposed to be at the station today?"

Andy opened his mouth to speak but nothing came out.

Before he could begin, Katie rushed on, "Andy, I'm tired, and I'm confused."

Her voice cracked with emotion, and Andy tensed.

"I'm confused about how things have been between us. But mostly," Katie said, with a catch in her voice, "I'm worried about us. You. And me." Her heart thumped painfully as she watched the look of unease on Andy's face melt into confusion.

"What?" he managed. "What do you mean concern about us?" The question hung in the air as Andy frowned in confusion. He was at a loss. This was not even close to how he'd pictured this conversation starting.

"Well," Katie hesitated at first but then said in a rush, "you don't answer my calls or return my messages. You take off work from RITE2U and disappear for the afternoon without telling me where you're going or even that you're taking off. You've been distant both physically and emotionally and ... and ... I'd heard about a pretty blonde you seemed to be having a really good time with at least one time — maybe there were other times too. You haven't been the Andy I know but ..."

Katie paused and folding her arms in front of her, seemed to mentally brace herself. "Andy, I ... well ... I thought you might have lost interest ... in me," she said, ending in a barely audible whisper and light shrug of her shoulders. She glanced at Andy but quickly looked down and trained her eyes on the floor.

Andy took a step back and grasped a chair to steady himself. He knew how hard that must have been for her, how hurt she must be to have said, or even thought, what she did. Caught off guard, he was completely stunned. He felt the weight of the load he'd been carrying the last few weeks crashing in — how badly he'd been feeling, the diagnosis he'd gotten, his altercation with Jerry this morning, and now to this tonight. It hit him like a physical blow, and he moved unsteadily to the sofa and sank beneath the weight of it all. He'd never imagined how his actions could have led Katie to think that he'd ever be able to not love her. "Oh, Katie," he said as he held his head in his hands.

Katie watched Andy sink onto the couch as if weighed down by some unseen force. Her heart raced and sank in the same instant that her breath caught in her throat. Tears pricked her eyes as she waited and watched Andy, his head hanging low, raking his fingers through his hair. "Andy?" she whispered.

His hands stilled at the sound of her voice. He sighed slowly and deeply, his body aching with the effort. Dropping his hands, he looked up at Katie, and she gasped at the sight of the haggard man looking up at her. He patted the cushion beside him and motioned with effort for her to sit. She hesitated briefly, but the look on his face compelled her to move, and she quickly closed the gap between them and sat beside him.

"Katie," Andy said, taking her hands in his, "I am so very sorry. You are right about everything."

He felt her tense, but he held her hands firmly and continued. "You are right about the way I've been acting except, *except*, the reason." He waited a few seconds and then looked her in the eye. "Do you remember the first time we met?"

Katie frowned. "You mean when I threw myself at you, both literally and figuratively?"

Andy gave a small smile. "And I've thanked my lucky stars every day that you did. I've never told you this, but I just played hard to get. I had a playboy image to maintain you know? But in reality, I was a goner the first time I looked into your eyes. All that dating stuff was just a formality. I knew the instant I saw you that you were the one — the only one — for me. I don't know how I knew, but I did, and nothing has changed since or will ever change for me. Never, ever doubt that."

Katie continued to study him silently.

Andy gave a frustrated sighed. "A blonde huh?" he finally said. "I'm guessing that came from Sally."

Katie looked down.

"Katie, that blonde is Lou Franklin. Louisa actually, but she goes by Lou. She doesn't think Louisa sounds tough enough for a police officer. She went through the police academy about the same time I was going through the fire academy. We've been friends for a long time. She was at our wedding. Didn't I introduce you?"

Katie shook her head.

"Well, I must have been distracted by my beautiful bride, but I will introduce you the next opportunity. And for this to have come from Sally, I'd be willing to bet she told you about seeing Lou and I at the grocery store didn't she?"

Katie nodded, her eyes wide.

Andy gave an exasperated sigh. "I ran into Lou at the store. She was getting snacks for she and her partner, and I was getting some things for Hedrick when we ran into each other. I saw Sally before she saw me. It was stupid I know, but I asked Lou to really play things up just for Sally's benefit. She just irritates me so I guess I just saw it as an opportunity to make her look foolish when she started to gossiping and there was nothing real to tell. And that's all there is to it. End of story. Except I forgot to tell you and now, the bad joke is on me. In fact, all of this is totally on me, but please, Sally doesn't need to know what goes on between us, and please don't listen to her gossip. You work with her, but I don't trust her and would rather keep our business between us. Please talk to me if you ever wonder about anything — *not* Sally."

Katie looked down, feeling Andy's gentle reprimand, and nodded agreement.

"As for everything else you mentioned, well, there's a reason for all that too." Andy took a ragged breath. "There is something I need to tell you. I've tried to handle it on my own and hoped it would go away. I didn't want to worry you, but now I see that was a mistake."

Andy looked at Katie, his eyes soft with love. Even tired and worried, she looked beautiful. Her soft auburn hair fell loosely over her shoulders. The one stubborn strand that always fell forward was hanging there now, and he gently tucked it behind her ear. He took hold of her hand again, never taking his eyes from hers.

Katie's eyes were riveted to Andy's. He looked pale and drawn, and his hands were like ice.

Andy took another deep breath and began again. "Katie, I love you. I love you with all my heart, and I'd do anything, and I mean *any*thing for you. You are everything to me."

Andy wasn't usually this vocal about his feelings. A strong sense of foreboding began to creep over Katie.

"The reason for my terrible behavior, the missed phone calls, the messages I didn't return, the afternoons I wasn't at work and gone for the afternoon, I . . . well, I was either at a doctor's office or having tests done that the doctor ordered."

Katie sat up straighter, her heart starting to pound.

"That said," Andy sighed, "I have something very difficult to tell you. It was hard for me to hear, but it is what it is, and I am going to need your help."

"Andy, please. What is it?" Katie said, gripping his hands tightly.

"I haven't been feeling well the past two or three months. At first, I thought it would just go away, but it didn't. I tried to fight my way through it, but it's only gotten worse and now, it's much worse. I finally went to the doctor a few weeks ago . . ." A wave of pain passed over him, and he grimaced.

Katie's lips parted but Andy held up a hand, motioning for her to wait.

He forced himself to go on. "Dr. Payne referred me to a Dr. Parker who put me through a barrage of tests. I had to go through some a second time. I had an appointment yesterday and got the results. That's where I was when you called."

Katie held her breath.

Andy paused, then said, "Katie, I have cancer. Pancreatic cancer. It's serious."

Katie felt her body stiffen as her eyes widened. She took a desperate gulp of air and tried to process what Andy had just said.

A gasp escaped her.

"Cancer?" Her voice was weak and breathy.

Andy nodded solemnly, his eyes focused on hers.

Katie looked away. "You've been going through all of this alone, and I — I've accused you of such horrible things." Her voice broke.

Andy tried to pull her to him, but she resisted.

"Andy, how can you ever forgive me — for my lack of faith in you, in our marriage. I've betrayed your trust at a time you needed me the most. I'm so — so sorry." Katie hung her head and her shoulders slumped.

She ventured a quick glance up at Andy who was watching her, concern on his face.

Everything stopped in that instant.

Katie instinctively reached for Andy and pulled him to her, holding him as tightly as she could.

"Oh, Andy," she breathed, "you should have told me. I love you. I'll always be here for you. She kept repeating words of love until she couldn't go on, her body quivering with involuntary sobs. She gripped Andy even tighter, trying to hold onto him and push this sudden nightmare away.

Andy clung to Katie, needing her, needing her love, needing her strength. He felt her body trembling, and he heard her crying. Guilt threatened to suffocate him as he whispered into hair, "Katie, my sweet Katie. I'm so sorry. I wanted to spare you the worry. I couldn't admit to myself, there really might be something wrong. I thought if I fought hard enough I could get past it. Katie, honey, I'm sorry. I'm so sorry . . . for everything."

Katie leaned back, wiping at tears. "No, Andy. You have nothing to be sorry for. You were looking out for me, and I jumped to some very wrong conclusions. I've thought some horrible things. Things I knew better in my heart, but I was just so afraid . . . I should have had more faith in you . . . more faith in us. I listened to what I was being told rather than listening to my heart. I should be the one apologizing. Not you."

"No . . ." Andy started but Katie put her fingers to his lips when a sudden thought occurred to her.

"What?" Andy asked, seeing that look.

"Andy, are they sure . . . I mean absolutely sure. Do we need to go for a second or third opinion? We need to be sure we've exhausted every possibility and —"

Andy stopped her with a shake of his head and solemn look. "Katie, dear, I asked the exact same question of Dr. Parker. They're sure. Very sure." Andy shrugged his shoulders and looked down.

Katie put her hands on either side of Andy's face and lifting his face to hers, she looked deeply into his eyes. Silently, she put her arms around him and nestled her head against his shoulder. Andy wrapped his arms around her, holding his head against hers. They pulled each other close and sat quietly. The only sound was their soft breathing.

After several minutes, Katie sat back and with determination in her voice said, "Well okay then, we look to the future. I love you, Andy. We're going to fight this, together and with everything we've got. You're a fighter, and I'm placing my bet on you . . . on us."

Andy nodded slowly and smiled. "Dr. Parker said that too. I just needed you both to remind me. I *am* a fighter."

Seeing him brighten and hearing a new resolve in his voice, Katie went on, "Well, alright then. We've got a lot to do. I want you to bring me up to speed on everything — what's happened, tests that were done, doctors you've talked to, and oh, I want to meet them. I need to know what medications you're supposed to take, treatments, options for work. We need to check on insurance, time off...."

As Katie talked on, Andy felt himself relaxing under her love and planning, and he exhaled softly. The pain had been almost unbearable while they'd talked, but he hadn't wanted Katie to know. He watched her. Earnestness and determination were making her face glow and her eyes sparkled with intensity and focus. He basked in her attention and care, and it occurred to him, this was what he'd been needing. His mom hadn't been there for him while he was growing up but when Katie came into his life, everything changed. He wouldn't have to go through this alone. There were rough times ahead, but he knew he could face them ... with Katie.

While they talked and planned and made pages of notes of things to be done, Andy retrieved the food from the kitchen, and they ate. Even though food tasted better tonight than it had in a long time, Andy still ate very little. After washing the dishes, they made their way to their room, mentally exhausted. Tomorrow was Friday, a RITE2U day for Andy and the last day of the school week for Katie but tonight, what they needed more than sleep was each other. Oblivious to everything but their heightened awareness of each other, they spent the night relishing in their rediscovered and intensified connection and loved each other with abandon.

KATIE WATCHED THE GRAY morning light soak through the window blinds as morning dawned. The light found them wrapped in each other's arms, the sheets tangled around them. Katie's eyes, filled with love, roved over Andy's face, studying him as he slept fitfully. Her gaze lingered, seeking to memorize every feature, studying every inch as she fingered his brown scruff more evident in the morning light. He stirred slightly at her touch, and she pulled him closer, draping her free arm over him and burrowing her head into his shoulder. She felt the security of his arm around her, and she willed this moment to last forever.

They lingered as long as possible until they had to part for the day. Andy grabbed Katie's free hand as they walked to their cars. He surprised her by pulling her close and with a grin, gave her a quick kiss on the nose. "See you this evening."

Katie smiled and her green eyes sparkled as she watched him walk to his truck. She fought the urge to run after him, hold him close and never let him out of her sight. Instead, she called, "Hey, handsome." He stopped and turned. "Made you look," she said with a laugh as she got in her car.

Andy flashed a smile and waved as Katie backed out of the drive-way. What a difference a day could make, he thought. It felt like a huge burden had been lifted or at least its weight was shared now. He climbed in his truck and his thoughts sobered as he turned toward RITE2U's office.

Charlene, as usual, was at her desk when he came through the door. "Good morning," he said with a smile as he picked up his delivery box and nodded to the other waiting couriers.

Charlene, focused on her computer monitor, gave Andy a dismissive wave. He shrugged with a grin and joined the others to wait.

She hit the last entry with a flourish and started dropping envelopes and small boxes into each of the courier's trays. Andy waited as the others picked up their boxes and left. Andy reached for his box as Charlene dropped the last envelope in. She placed a hand on his arm, stopping him.

"Well?" she said, eying him closely. Her lipstick today was cherry red and the fingernails on the hand resting on his arm were the same color.

"Well what?" he asked.

"Well, what did the doctor say? You did go, right?"

"Oh, yeah — I went," Andy said uncomfortably. He and Katie agreed to take care of some things before telling anyone . . . *if* they told anyone. They hadn't quite decided who they would tell, but they'd agreed the list would be very short.

"And?" she persisted.

"And, I'm running behind," he said as he managed to grab the box and brush Charlene's hand away.

Charlene plopped into her chair with an irritated harrumph.

Andy started walking quickly to the door. "See you this afternoon."

"We'll talk later," Charlene called after him.

He waved without looking back.

ANDY SCANNED THE LAST envelope and dropped it into the box on the seat beside him. He checked his watch. It was a little after 10:00 a.m. His heart skipped a nervous beat. It was time to face the Chief. He made the short drive to Station One, which also housed Fire Administration, pulling into one of the visitor spots. The Chief's Suburban was in its space, which meant Hamilton was in the office. Andy took a deep breath. He stepped into the reception area as Becky Madrid, the Chief's assistant looked up from her computer.

"Hi, Andy," she said with a smile. "How can I help you?"

"I'd like to see Chief Hamilton if he's available."

"Sure. Just a minute. Let me check."

While he waited, Andy glanced around the lobby and noticed the historic photos on the walls. He stopped in front of the framed pictures of Abernathy firefighters who had died in the line of duty. They were all the typical fire department staff photos, black and white, most from several years in the past, however, a few were more recent. The same pictures hung in the living area at The Deuce, but he had never paid attention to them. Now, though, they seemed to have significance — at least the dying part. Only a couple of minutes passed before the hallway door swung open. Chief Hamilton stepped into the lobby with a look of surprise and concern on his face.

"Chief," Andy said, hesitantly, unsure of his reception.

"Andy," Chief Hamilton said warmly. "Come on back."

Andy followed close behind as Chief Hamilton led the way to his corner office. They stepped inside as the Chief closed the door behind them. Andy had only been in the Chief's office a couple of times, but he was aware, again, how much the office reflected Jerry Hamilton. He was always organized and put together. The top of the desk was nearly empty, there were only three or four sheets of paper, and they were neatly arranged as if he'd been reading them in order. A fire hydrant was in the corner by the floor length windows that overlooked the busy street in front of the station. That fire hydrant was a tradition passed from one chief to another. When a chief retired, a plate was inscribed and placed on the hydrant listing that chief's name and years of service. Andy glanced around at the fire service awards, certificates and mementos on the bookshelves along with fire service and policy manuals. Andy's glance came back around to the Chief, who was watching him and waiting expectantly. He motioned to one of the chairs in front of his desk, and they each took a seat.

Andy cleared his throat nervously. "Sir, I want to apologize for my behavior yesterday." He took a quick glance at Chief Hamilton who sat unreadable, his fingers steepled in front of him. "There is something I would like to talk to you about but not now and not here."

Chief Hamilton sat quietly, but Andy forged on. "Katie and I would appreciate you and Natalie coming over tonight for coffee and dessert. We'd like to talk to you both."

Jerry Hamilton straightened in his chair and studied Andy closely. "Of course, we'll be glad to come. What time?"

After setting the time, Andy stood to leave. "Andy," Chief Hamilton said as he stood, "I'm glad you came by. We look forward to seeing you and Katie tonight."

He put his hand out, and Andy grabbed it and shook it with fervor before opening the door and quickly retracing his steps down the hall.

Chief Hamilton watched Andy leave before moving slowly to sit behind his desk. Instead of going back to work, he stared at the wall across from his desk. The only thing he could see was the look in Andy's eyes. He'd seen that same look once before . . . in someone else's eyes.

KATIE WATCHED AS HER students filed inside after recess. It was a cold but bright and sunny day. She looked up and squinted into the sun's glare. The warmth felt good on her face, but she couldn't help the sigh that escaped her lips. She was tired and worried. She pulled her coat a bit tighter around her as a group of boys from her class rushed past, giggling. When they saw her, they stopped laughing and nervously glanced behind them. Katie's radar went up; something was going on. Miranda, another of her students, skipped into the building and several steps behind her came Lucas.

"Miranda," Katie said, stopping Miranda outside the classroom door. "How was recess?"

Miranda shrugged and giggled. "It was cold, but I bet I was warmer than Lucas."

"And why is that?" Katie asked with concern as she turned to look for Lucas.

"They took his coat away and threw it up in a tree," Miranda said, motioning to the boys ahead of her. "Lucas couldn't reach it, but a gust of wind blew it down."

"I see," Katie said, looking at Lucas as he drew closer. "Thank you, Miranda. You may take your seat."

Lucas shuffled up to the door. His head was down, his hair was tousled from the wind, and his hands were red with the cold. His light jacket hung loosely around his thin frame. "Everything okay?" she asked.

He surprised her with a beaming smile. "Sure, Mrs. Garrett. Everything's fine," he said with a slight shrug.

She smiled back and gave his shoulder a light pat, before he walked to his desk.

The class settled in as Katie walked to the front of the room. This was their normal routine, but today was anything but normal for her. Her thoughts were full of Andy, and she'd been distracted all day. Andy sent a text that Jerry and Natalie had accepted their invitation and were coming over that evening. He didn't say how things had gone that morning, but he had told her of the heated exchange at the station the day before and how much he regretted losing his temper. Katie wasn't worried though. She was confident Jerry would understand and be supportive once he knew the situation. She was glad Andy had such a close friendship with Jerry. Jerry was a friend who would never let you down. Katie looked forward to bringing Jerry and Natalie into their confidence. It would be nice to have strong friends to lean on.

Katie turned to face her students, but she had a sudden inspiration as she looked into their expectant faces. Their eyes followed her as she moved to the bulletin board decorated with a large tree with fall leaves from its empty branches scattered around the base. Curious, the students gathered around her as she removed one of the leaves from the board, a bright red one, and held it out to them in the palm of her hand. "It will be Thanksgiving in just two weeks," she began. "Can anyone remember what happened the very first Thanksgiving?"

Hands shot in the air.

"Cammie, tell us please."

"The pilgrims and the Indians ate together."

"That's right," Katie nodded with a smile. "Why was this so unusual?"

More hands shot into the air. "James," Katie said.

"Because the pilgrims didn't know how to grow food. The Indians showed them how and saved them from going hungry," James said all in one breath.

"That's right! Very good!" Katie said. "Would you say the pilgrims were thankful for the Indians?"

"Yes!" the class chorused.

"Absolutely!" Katie agreed. "So, in the spirit of Thanksgiving and being thankful, let's share some things *we're* grateful for. Everyone is going to get a leaf and then, I want you to think of one or two things you're most grateful for. We'll write them on your leaf and put them back under the tree so when we see our leaves, we'll be reminded of all the things we're thankful for every day. Sound good?"

Heads bobbed excitedly. Katie took the leaves down and handed one to each student, keeping one for herself. Placing a chair near the board and picking up a marker, she asked, "Who'd like to go first?"

Eager, they came one by one, reverently holding their leaf out to Katie and announcing what they were most grateful for. Katie wrote the special item or items on each student's leaf with a black marker and then pinned it back onto the board. Most were what she expected — mom, dad, their dog or cat, possibly a brother or sister, their home, favorite food or a special toy. Some repeated what the person in front of them said and others said silly things which had the desired effect of making everyone giggle.

Lucas, not surprisingly, came last and carefully held his red leaf out to Katie. "And what would you like on your leaf, Lucas?" Katie asked.

Lucas looked at Katie shyly with big, brown eyes and said, "Mr. Andy and fire trucks."

Katie blinked hard several times as tears sprung to her eyes. "That's — very — sweet, Lucas," she managed to say, trying to write on Lucas' leaf as tears blurred the words. She studied Andy's name on the red construction paper. She saw his tender smile and heard him say, "I have cancer." A tear drop fell and smeared the ink on one of the words. She blinked several times, turning away from the children so as not to upset them, or Lucas. The students stilled, sensing something was wrong. Katie cleared her throat and took a couple of quick swipes at her cheeks before pinning Lucas' leaf to the board. She felt his little hand softly pat her shoulder, and it was almost more than she could do to carry on.

She turned to Lucas with a shaky smile and said, "I'm thankful for Mr. Andy too. In fact, I'm going to write his name on *my* leaf."

Lucas smiled as Katie wrote Andy's name on the last leaf and pinned it to the board alongside the others. She stood and with a dramatic gesture toward the board asked, "What do you think?"

The children cheered and clapped their hands.

Katie nodded and smiled at their enthusiasm.

The afternoon passed quickly. Katie had walked her class outside and was almost back to her room when Sally and the first-grade teacher, Sophia Daniels, caught up with her.

"Hey there, stranger," Sally said. "Haven't seen you all day."

Sophia fell into step on the other side of Katie. "Thought we'd see you in the lunchroom but remembered about halfway through that you had recess duty today. A bit cold for that," Sophia said with a dramatic shudder.

Katie laughed. "It wasn't too bad. What are you going to do when it gets really cold?"

"Freeze!" Sophia said emphatically.

They laughed as they reached the first of their rooms.

Sally put an arm out to stop Katie. "Well, how are things?" she asked pointedly. Sophia stopped as well, watching Katie closely.

Katie looked from one to the other. "Is my wellbeing something you two discuss often?"

"Oh no, not often" Sophia said, shuffling her feet and glancing sideways at Sally. "Sally was just worried about you and mentioned some of the trouble you and Andy are having."

"Trouble?" Katie said, anger flaring.

Sally and Sophia looked at each other, not sure whether to respond.

Katie gave them both a cold look. "I want you to know how much I appreciate your concern, your well-intentioned advice and your help getting me through some difficult days. But please let me assure you both, I'm fine. Let me also assure you, I don't appreciate being discussed, however kindly it's meant."

Katie turned to walk away but Sally — too curious to hold back — blurted out, "But how are things with Andy? Are you guys talking?"

Katie stopped and turned slowly. "If you'll excuse me, we have company coming over tonight, and I need to finish getting ready."

"We?" Sally asked in surprise. "We? You go from barely communicating to having guests?"

"See you Monday and have a great weekend," Katie said as she stepped inside her classroom and closed the door. Sally and Sophia were left standing outside, looking at each other with surprise.

Katie waited until she heard them walk away, talking in low voices. She gathered her things and turned her focus toward getting ready for Jerry and Natalie's visit. She paused for a moment and scanned the bright leaves beneath the bulletin board tree. Seeing Lucas' leaf, Katie smiled softly. She was thankful for Mr. Andy too. Very thankful.

KATIE PUT A CHOCOLATE cake, Andy and Jerry's favorite, in the oven as soon as she got home. At five, Andy arrived from RITE2U exhausted, falling into a deep sleep on the sofa.

Working quietly so as not to wake him, Katie washed dishes and straightened the room, and the next time she checked the clock, it was 7:15. The Hamiltons were due around 8:00. She hated to wake Andy, but she shook his shoulder gently. After a few seconds, his face contorted from peaceful sleep to a little boy's pout, and she couldn't help but smile. He really was a little boy at heart. Andy grudgingly sat up, and Katie rubbed his back as he held his face in his hands.

"What time is it?" he asked, still groggy.

"7:15. I thought you might want to take a quick shower before they get here."

Andy nodded and then caught the aroma of chocolate cake and smiled. "Chocolate cake."

"I thought some warm chocolate cake might help smooth the way," Katie said.

Andy placed his hands on hers. "I love you, you know," he said softly.

"I do know," she replied, "but I also know you'd better get busy before our guests arrive."

Wide awake and fresh from his shower, Katie watched as Andy paced back and forth in the living room. "What if he wants me to quit?" he fretted as Katie made coffee.

"He is not going to ask you to quit. You're getting all worked up over something that's not even going to happen. He's coming over as your friend, not as your chief."

"Maybe I shouldn't tell him. I'll make something up," Andy suggested as he watched Katie pull coffee cups and plates from the cabinet. "How can you be so calm?"

"Andy!" Katie said sharply as she turned to face him. "Get a hold of yourself! Jerry is your friend. He is not going to leave you hanging out to dry. Please calm down."

Andy raked his fingers through his hair and then crossed his arms in front of him. "How can you be so sure?"

"How can you be so unsure?" Katie retorted with a slight shake of her head. She picked up a spatula and swirled the last dab of chocolate icing onto the freshly-baked cake. She turned and handed the spatula to Andy.

He took it and twirled it absently, his brows furrowed.

Katie sighed and looked at him with a hint of exasperation. "Now, help me understand —"

The doorbell chimed. They both stopped and looked at each other. Katie placed the plates on the table and walked to Andy's side. "We're in this together, remember? I'm right beside you no matter what. Now, let's greet our guests."

Forgotten spatula still in hand, Andy planted a quick peck on Katie's cheek and opened the front door.

They opened the door to a smiling Jerry and Natalie standing on the porch. Jerry took a look at the spatula in Andy's hand. "You cookin'? We can't stay."

Everyone laughed as Andy gave the spatula a quick lick and waved them inside.

Natalie hugged Andy first and then made her way to Katie and embraced her warmly. Jerry stood just inside the door and turned to Andy with his hand outstretched. Andy shook it and said, "Thanks for coming."

"Our pleasure. Do I smell chocolate cake?"

"Fresh out of the oven. Come on in." Andy took their coats while Katie poured cups of coffee and cut the cake as Natalie passed the pieces. No one was really hungry, or thirsty, but they ate the cake and sipped the coffee, making small talk for the first few moments.

Silence finally fell, and Andy looked at Katie as he took her hand. She squeezed his in return and nodded her encouragement.

Andy cleared his throat. "First of all, Jerry, I want to apologize again for my behavior yesterday. I've been a bit out of control the past few weeks. If it makes you feel better, and I think you already know, but I've been just as bad, or even worse, to Katie."

Katie felt him grip her hand tighter.

"You see, well . . ." Andy faltered as he looked from Katie back to Jerry and Natalie. "You see, I haven't been feeling well. Actually, I've been in quite a bit of pain so I haven't been in the best of moods."

Jerry strained forward, listening closely.

Katie smiled and nodded her reassurance as Andy looked from her back to Jerry.

"Well, it's like this," Andy said, "I . . . I have cancer. Pancreatic cancer. The doctor tells me it's serious."

Shocked silence hung in the air. Natalie put a hand to her mouth. Jerry sat ramrod stiff, unmoving, and staring at Andy.

Katie watched Jerry, his face an emotionless slate, as Andy continued. "I have an appointment Monday to discuss the treatment plan. Katie is coming with me."

Katie nodded as Natalie, her eyes warm with compassion, looked between them.

"The doc says at this stage of the game, I need both chemotherapy and radiation at the same time. Time is critical. It seems I should have gone in sooner, but I thought I could tough it out."

Andy paused as everyone waited for Jerry to say something, but he seemed unable to respond.

Katie felt her face flush as she looked at Andy, tears sparkling on her lashes. She knew that what Andy said had been hard for him, but now, he seemed to relax and talked nonstop for several minutes. He laid everything out, holding nothing back.

"I'm sorry I let this come between us and our friendship. But now, because you are our closest friends, I wanted you to know." Andy faltered, his voice raw with emotion. He cleared his throat, and sat a little straighter. "This isn't easy for me, but I need to ask for your help. Well, not help for me really, but for Katie."

Katie gave a start and turned to look at him, but he avoided eye contact with her.

"We don't know how things are going to go but more than likely, she's going to have a lot to handle taking care of me as things progress. I'd just like to ask that you help her and be there for her." Andy's voice broke, and he ducked his head. "I'm sorry."

Natalie looked at Jerry, who remained stoic and unmoved.

Katie looked at Andy in amazement and scooted closer to him. She had no idea this was on his mind. All of her planning and efforts were going into taking care of him while at the same time, he was thinking of ways to take care of her. Andy might be the fun-loving clown everyone loved, but he was also thoughtful and a deep thinker. Her heart swelled with love for him.

Exhausted, but relieved everyone closest to him had been told, Andy took a deep breath and sat back.

Everyone waited for Jerry to say something, but the silence stretched on. Andy and Katie looked to Natalie, who smiled apologetically but then looked down.

Katie's heart pounded expectantly. They were counting on Jerry. Andy especially needed to hear some type of re-assurance from him about something — his illness, his job, their friendship, his support — What was Jerry waiting for? Why didn't he say something? Katie wanted to shake him.

Jerry looked down at the dessert plate in his hand, a few stray cake crumbs scattered on it. He turned his fork over absentmindedly.

The minutes wore on into an uncomfortable silence, and Andy couldn't wait any longer. He looked at Katie, and the hurt and disappointment on his face broke her heart. He stood rigidly and said in a businesslike tone very unlike him, "Well, I guess that's that. I appreciate you listening. More cake anyone?"

Jerry looked up as if coming out of a daze. He stood and placed his plate on the coffee table. "No, thanks. It's late, so we need to get going."

Katie and Natalie stood in unison, confusion on Katie's face and sadness on Natalie's. Natalie reached for his arm. "Jerry, please . . ."

"Thanks for the cake," Jerry said. "You ready?"

"Jerry . . . I," Natalie faltered, looking between Jerry and then Andy and Katie. Jerry retrieved his coat and walked to the door. He pushed it open and stepped outside. They could hear the car door open and close.

Natalie hugged Katie and then Andy. Cupping Andy's chin in her hand, Natalie looked at him and said softly, "Andy, dear, I'm so sorry, but please don't worry. He'll be in touch. He truly loves you both. He's just having to process things. I'll try to get him to explain but until then never doubt that we're here for you — *whatever* you need."

She reached the front door, and turning back said, "We'll be in touch." With an encouraging smile, she pulled the door closed behind her.

Katie put her arm around Andy as they looked at each other in confusion.

NATALIE STOLE SEVERAL GLANCES at Jerry as they drove home, but his grim look convinced her to keep quiet. She still couldn't believe what Andy told them. It just didn't seem possible that someone as young and energetic as Andy could have something as terrible as cancer. The only thing she'd ever heard about pancreatic cancer was that it was usually terminal, and it didn't sound promising that the doctor told Andy he should have come in sooner. Natalie cringed as she thought of the expectant and disappointed looks on Andy and Katie's faces. She knew Jerry would do anything for the two of them, but they'd needed to hear that from him tonight. Natalie knew how much Andy's friendship meant to Jerry, but she also knew this was something much bigger to Jerry and an internal battle only he could work out. Natalie shook her head sadly as she glanced at her husband again. His knuckles were white on the steering wheel and his jaw clenched.

"Jerry," she started, "do you want to talk about it?"

Silence was the only reply.

"Those kids are hurting, and they're scared. They needed to hear something from you tonight. I know you're thinking about Scott but . . ."

"Good to be home," Jerry said, cutting her off. She looked up not realizing how close they were until Jerry turned into their drive.

Natalie looked back at him, surprised. "Seriously? That's it? That's all you can say?" She had hoped for some type of acknowledgment of what they'd just been told by someone they both cared about.

Jerry killed the engine and opened his door to get out. Natalie grabbed his coat sleeve, trying to prevent his leaving. "Jerry, talk to me please."

Shrugging her off, Jerry stepped out of the car. She slid out and brushed past him into the house but stopped in the middle of the hallway and waited for him to say something. He turned, and Natalie could see the haggard look on his face and the sadness in his eyes. "Jerry, I . . ." but she stopped, not sure what to say.

He gave her a light kiss on the cheek. "You go on to bed. I'll be there in a little while."

She watched him walk to his office, his shoulders sagging under the unseen weight he carried. He closed the office door softly behind him while Natalie stood rooted to the spot for several more minutes. She knew the depth of his feelings, both for those in the past and those in the present. She couldn't help but wonder what was going through his mind. Ultimately, she knew it would be best to let him sort things out on his own.

Jerry eased into his desk chair and closed his eyes, laying his head back. He'd had a feeling since Andy's visit that morning that what Andy wanted to tell him tonight was going to change everything. He wasn't sure what he'd expected, but this was something he'd experienced before and hoped to never experience again. He'd fought hard never to have to live through this nightmare again and this time, it was Andy. He could hear Andy saying, "I have cancer." He could see the uncertainty and fear in both Andy's and Katie's eyes. He could feel their need for some kind of reassurance. Assurance he had failed to provide. There were so many questions he should have asked, so many things he should have said, but instead — he'd sat, wooden and silent. He'd wanted to say something, but the words just wouldn't come.

Jerry shook his head. Andy has cancer. Andy, the life-loving, full steam ahead pain-in-the neck guy who never slowed down. Thinking back over the past few weeks, Jerry realized how hard Andy must have been struggling — his angry outbursts, the occasional pinched look of pain, his short attention span, the weight loss, his moodiness. Unfortunately, all the familiar pieces fit. And tonight, when Andy had carefully chosen him as his confidante, he'd abused that trust with selfishness and cold silence.

Jerry leaned forward and cradled his head in his hands. He frowned as his mind traveled back twenty years to a night that he avoided thinking about. But now, the memories came rushing back as if everything had just happened.

His kid brother, Scott, who had followed him into the fire service, sat across from him with the same uncertain, frightened look Jerry had just seen on Andy's face. Scott had told the family the same thing Andy had just told he and Natalie. Scott had been with the department for three years when he'd gotten the diagnosis of non-Hodgkin's lymphoma. He had lived only fourteen months after his diagnosis.

Jerry didn't want it to be the same with Andy.

Jerry felt an immediate connection to Andy when they'd met. Andy was like having Scott back again, but now, the similarity of their two situations brought back painful memories. Jerry pinched the bridge of his nose, frustrated with himself. He should have pressed Andy for answers when he'd first thought something was wrong. Maybe, if he had, Andy would have gone to the doctor sooner. Just like Andy, Scott had waited to see a doctor, and as Jerry knew, the sooner you are checked out, the better your chances. There were too many similarities: both young and healthy firefighters with no cancer history, receiving a cancer diagnosis.

Jerry suddenly sat up. He grabbed the keyboard to his computer and swished the mouse to turn on the screen. He typed as fast as he could, pausing only to scribble notes on a piece of paper.

SUNDAY DAWNED BRIGHT AND crisp. A brisk wind swirled leaves around their feet as Andy and Katie stood on their front steps. Andy brushed Katie's lips with a kiss and a quick smile before he got in his truck and drove off.

Katie drove the twenty miles to her parents' house to join them for church service. They went to their favorite cafeteria for lunch and over pie and coffee, Katie told them of Andy's diagnosis. Since Katie didn't want Andy to see her upset, she had held back the tears. But in front of her parents, she let herself cry until no more tears came.

"I'm just so scared of losing him," Katie said as her mom held her tight. "I love him so much. He's battling through it, but it hurts me to see him in pain. I'm afraid it's only going to get worse, and I just don't know how I'm going to bear it."

Katie looked imploringly into her mother's worried face. "Why Andy? Why now?" Katie managed before dissolving in tears. She knew there were no answers.

Katie's father, never one for many words, hugged her tightly. "Baby girl, whatever you and Andy need, you've got it. We're here for you."

As they stood in the waning light late that afternoon, Katie said, "I'll call you later this week after we talk to the doctor." She gave them each a kiss, an attempt at a smile and one last hug.

As she turned to get in her car, her dad stepped close. "Katie, you may be a Garrett now, but you are also a Maine, and Maines have always been scrappers. You and Andy are in for a tough fight that's for certain, but you both have to hang in there."

He gave her a firm nod while he looked her in the eye. "We love you and give our love to Andy." He gave her an encouraging smile and pushed the car door closed before stepping back and putting his arm around Katie's mother. They waved as they watched Katie pull out of the drive.

Katie dialed Andy's number on the drive back. She needed to hear his voice. A warmth rushed over her as she heard, "Hey, beautiful," when he answered the phone. She then blushed as a mocking chorus of "Hey, beautiful," echoed behind him.

"Tell them all I said hi back," she laughed.

Andy dutifully repeated her message. She then heard a chair scraping across the floor, and Andy saying, "If you'll excuse me, gentlemen, and you too, LEW-tenant."

It grew quieter, and she could tell he must be walking away from the kitchen.

"Andy, you shouldn't provoke Bentley," she gently scolded. "You're going to need his good will in the coming months."

"I know. You're right. I'll get started on that first thing tomorrow," he said, a trace of sarcasm in his voice. "So, how were your parents?"

"They're fine. They send their love. They said to let you know we can count on them for anything we need. My dad said for us to hang tough."

"Well, there's nobody I'd rather hang tough with." Andy paused. "Katie, I've been thinking, and before we go any further, I just want to tell you now that I am so sorry about all of this."

"Sorry?" Katie asked, confused. "What is there to be sorry for?"

"I'm sorry about this whole thing. This mess — what we've got ahead of us. You deserve better, and I hate putting you through whatever is coming. And well, you know and . . . if . . ."

Katie couldn't talk about this. "Andy, please. Stop. This is something that just happened, and it's no one's fault. Please don't go there."

"I know, I know. But still . . ." he said with a heavy sigh.

"This doesn't sound like you. Has something happened?"

"Nothing I won't have to get used to. You know how a good work out gives me energy, right? I put in a hard one today, and all it did was make me even more tired." She heard him take a deep breath and sigh. "It's just so frustrating."

She tried to remain calm and sound stronger than she felt. "Well, Andy Garrett, I think you'd just better plan on putting your big man pants on because this fight has just begun."

Glad Andy couldn't see the tears in her eyes, she went on, "Don't be wimping out on me. We're just in the first round."

"Whoa, Mrs. Garrett" Andy exclaimed with surprise. "I'm impressed. Where did that come from?"

"Love for my husband. You just have to deal with it."

Andy smiled, hearing the force in her voice. "Well then, yes, ma'am."

"I'm almost home," Katie said with small smile. "I'll see you in the morning."

"Yes, you will," Andy said, his spirits buoyed. "Katie?"

"Yes?" she said, pulling into the drive.

"Remember — I love you, and I will love you forever."

"I love you too. Forever."

HEDRICK, ALONG WITH THE others, watched Andy walk out of the kitchen as he talked on the phone. They looked at each other as Hedrick and Hart started to gather the dishes for washing.

"Great meal, Hedrick," Bentley said as he stood.

"Thanks, Lieutenant," Hedrick answered as Bentley left the unusually-silent group.

"So, what do you think?" Canfield blurted out after Bentley left, looking first at Jernigan, and then to the others.

"About what?" Jernigan countered as he turned his tea glass in circles.

Canfield snorted. "Well, about Garrett of course. There's something going on."

Jernigan looked from one to the other. "Canfield," he finally said, "there probably *is* something going on with Garrett. We've all noticed but ... until it affects his job performance, it's none of our business. I suggest we focus on what is our business instead. Another great meal, Hedrick. Hart, you and Canfield got the dishes?"

They nodded.

"Good. I'm adjourning to the TV room. Great game tonight on Sunday Night Football," he said and sauntered toward the TV room.

Canfield lowered his voice as he stacked dishes. "I don't care what Jernigan says. I'm finding out what's going on."

Deep in thought, Hedrick studied Hart's stocky frame and Canfield's gangly one as they worked together clearing the few remaining dishes from the table to place in the dishwasher. Hedrick pulled the crumpled piece of paper from his pocket and walked down the hall to his bedroom. Tapping the numbers on his phone, he waited until he heard Mandy's voice.

"Hello?"

"Hey, Mandy. This is Sean Hedrick," he said and waited for her reaction. He closed the door to his room but not before four sets of ears heard him say Mandy's name.

"Sean! Hi! How are you?"

He was pleased to hear the warmth in her voice. "I'm fine. Did I catch you at a good time?"

"Absolutely. I'm just driving home from work. Are you working today?"

"Yeah. We just finished dinner, and the guys are doing the dishes."

"I've heard on good authority you're a great cook."

He smiled. "Now, who would be spreading such rumors?"

"Oh, I don't know . . . you know how firemen are . . ."

Sean hurriedly went on. "The guys liked it, but of course, they're not hard to please. So long as it's hot, meaty, and lots of it, they're happy."

Mandy couldn't help but laugh. "I think that's men in general when it comes to food."

"Agreed." After a slight pause, Sean said, "I just wanted to let you know that Garrett — I mean Andy — is back today."

"And?"

"Not sure what happened, but he's more like Garrett today."

"I'm glad to hear it," Mandy said. "I'm sorry I didn't get to see you — I mean you guys — at the hospital today."

Hedrick noted the correction and frowned. "It's been a slow day, but that's good for us and for everyone out there, too."

"Well, yes … yes, it is I suppose," she said as an awkward silence fell. "I'm glad he's better. He's a good guy. Keep me posted. Sorry — got to run."

"Sure, take care," Hedrick said as Mandy hung up. He looked at his phone in confusion. "Well, that didn't go like I'd thought," he said under his breath. He slipped his phone into his uniform shirt pocket and walked to the TV room. The familiar clank of the dishwasher was coming from the kitchen as he joined Andy and the others in the TV room and plopped into one of the recliners.

"Problem, rookie?" Andy asked.

"What?" Hedrick said, unaware he'd hit the recliner hard enough to draw everyone's attention.

"No, fine. Everything's fine," he answered, distracted. Putting his hands behind his head, he leaned back, a slight frown on his face.

Andy and the others exchanged grins. Hedrick was in love, and he didn't even know it yet.

———

MANDY TOSSED HER THINGS on the sofa. Even though she'd look forward to Sean's call, it had been a mistake to give him her number. He was the first firefighter she'd allowed herself to get even this close to, and it terrified her with the memories that still hovered at the edges of her mind. It had been a spur of the minute decision to give him her number and now, she wasn't sure if she regretted it or — if she was honest with herself — she was glad.

Katie's fingers drummed a constant beat on the edge of the chair as her foot pumped up and down. Andy glanced at her from the other chair in front of Dr. Parker's desk.

"Katie," he said, leaning over and placing his hand over her drumming fingers. "Calm down," he whispered. "You're going to make yourself sick. Besides, you're making me tired just watching you."

Katie stilled her foot and clasped Andy's hand.

"Sorry — I'm just anxious to meet this Dr. Parker. You like him, right? You trust and feel confident in him?" Katie asked for the hundredth time. "You're sure?"

Andy patted her hand and patiently answered for the hundredth time, "Yes, Katie, I am, and I do. He came highly recommended by Dr. Payne and has been in practice for over thirty-five years. He knows his medicine."

Katie opened her mouth to reply but just then the door popped open and a tall man in a white lab coat stepped inside. Dr. Parker stopped and looking at the two of them said with a warm smile. "Good morning, Andy. This must be Katie." He reached out and took Katie's hand, as she stood and he shook it with a reassuring clasp.

"Dr. Parker, I'm so glad to meet you." Katie liked him immediately. Dr. Parker exuded confidence and was quite congenial. His prematurely-gray hair was cut short and framed an angular face. His blue eyes were large and round with eyebrows that arched when he smiled. Andy stood when Katie did, and Dr. Parker shook his hand with a firm grasp, a scrutinizing gaze and a quick pat on the shoulder.

Looking back to Katie, Dr. Parker said, "As I am to meet you." He gestured for them both to sit. Stepping behind his desk, he sat down and picked up the folder laying in front of him. He gave them a cursory glance and quick smile before opening the file to skim the information inside.

Andy and Katie exchanged anxious looks as Dr. Parker read the file silently for several minutes. Finally, Dr. Parker took off the spectacles perched at the end of his nose and placed them on top of his head. He looked at Andy first and then turned to Katie with a smile. "Young lady, let me say again how truly glad I am to meet you. When your brave, young husband sat in that same chair a week ago and said he was trying to handle this on his own, I knew he had to be holding something special in reserve. It looks like I was right. Seeing the two of you together, I believe I'm correct in saying that something special is you."

Katie blushed. "Thank you, Dr. Parker. Andy speaks very highly of you." She glanced at Andy and took his hand. "We've talked — a lot — and we're anxious to find out what's next. I understand time is of the essence?"

Dr. Parker leaned back in his chair and pushed his fingers into a steeple. "Yes. Yes, it is," he said thoughtfully. "Pancreatic cancer is difficult to isolate and treat effectively at this stage so we have to go at it with a broader approach. Namely, chemotherapy, and a more localized treatment of radiation."

Dr. Parker looked down at his file as Katie felt Andy stiffen beside her. She tightened her hold on his hand as Dr. Parker pulled a sheet of paper out of the file and handed it to Katie. She glanced at it and saw a time early the next morning noted as Andy's first chemo treatment.

Dr. Parker continued. "I also want to start radiation treatments on the area identified by the tests and scans. This is an intense treatment program to do both chemo and radiation simultaneously, but if we're to have a chance of getting this under control, we need to go at it with everything we possibly can. Are you up for it?" he asked, looking at Andy.

Andy looked to Katie and with her slight nod, looked back to Dr. Parker. "Yes, sir. We're ready."

"Good, good. I thought that'd be your answer." He paused and studied them both. Unsure of his close scrutiny, Katie and Andy glanced at each other. Dr. Parker seemed to come to a decision and taking a deep breath, he moved to sit on the corner of his desk closest to them. "Andy, since you were here last week, and we discussed your diagnosis, I've been doing further research into other treatments, and I've found one that looks promising."

Katie and Andy looked at each other and sat up.

"Now, now, don't get too excited," Dr. Parker cautioned. "This is an experimental drug. It's shown some promise in initial trials but it's far from a cure all. They've been very selective on their test subjects, but I've made some inquiries in case you're interested."

"Absolutely," Andy answered quickly as Katie nodded eagerly.

"I thought so. The good news is I've heard back from them. They're interested in you as a test subject. But first, there are some specific tests they want us to run to determine dosage amount, among other things."

Andy's head was spinning. He'd resigned himself to the chemo and radiation. This was more than he'd hoped possible. "I'm in. When do we start?" he asked, squeezing Katie's hand.

Dr. Parker nodded. "This afternoon. You're set for three additional tests. It will be a couple of days before we hear back from their clinic once the test results are submitted and then a couple more days to receive the drug. Once all of that is done, you'll be ready to start the treatment itself. From what I understand, the medication comes in large capsules, but I don't foresee that being a problem."

Katie and Andy looked at each other, hardly able to contain their excitement.

"In the meantime," Dr. Parker continued, "you will begin the chemo and radiation treatments. This experimental drug is only in addition to these treatments. I want to make sure you understand that."

"Yes, sir," Andy answered, a bit deflated.

"Good," Dr. Parker said. "I'd expect nothing less from one of Abernathy's finest. Everything is set up at the oncology facility for those treatments to start right away. Please read all the information in this folder so you will know what to expect. Andy, chemo affects everyone differently. Don't take as gospel what you read here," he said tapping the folder with his finger. "You may have all of these side effects, and you may have none. We'll hope for the none side of the equation. The important thing is that you don't miss a treatment, and you need to allow yourself plenty of time between each to rest and recuperate. Allowing time to rest is important. We'll start the radiation treatments in about a week to give you a little time to adjust to the chemo. The experimental drug will start soon after. Andy, Katie, doing all three of these treatments at once is going to be tough — I want you both to prepare yourself for that. Andy, you've got to allow your body time to recuperate and rebuild between each. That's critically important."

Dr. Parker saw the worry return to their young, faces. He sighed. "I can tell you're both wound tight. I know you're anxious and that's perfectly natural, but you've got to relax. Go and do something you enjoy doing together. This is a long-haul deal, so you both need to make up your mind to take things as they come. It's natural to imagine the worst but there's no room for that in my treatment regimen.

"So," he said slapping his knees and standing, "off you go until tomorrow. You'll both handle what's ahead much better if you're prepared mentally. Your life could depend on it. Got it?"

Andy and Katie nodded solemnly in unison.

"Good. That's settled. You're worried and hopeful about the experimental treatment — that's natural. You've also got a game plan — a good one — so go. Enjoy each other tonight and try to get this off your mind. Doctor's orders."

He gave them a warm smile as he picked up the phone and dialed for his nurse.

"My nurse will show you out. She'll have a folder for you with additional information about the tests this afternoon, your treatment schedule, medications, frequently asked questions, etc. I could sit here and tell you everything but it seems to stick better if you have the information in hand to read and for future reference. We're here — me, the nurses and staff — at any time when questions or concerns come up. We'll be staying in close touch monitoring what's going on, especially when we start the experimental treatment. We're all on the same team and our one and only goal is to get Andy well."

A soft knock broke the silence, and Dr. Parker's nurse opened the door. Dr. Parker shook Katie's hand first and then Andy's firmly before they followed the nurse out the door.

ANDY AND KATIE SILENTLY followed the nurse to the main hallway. The nurse handed the folder with the information to Katie as they turned to exit. Focused and talking to each other, they didn't notice the young, dark-haired nurse who'd stopped just inside the exit door.

"Andy?" Mandy asked in surprise when they drew close.

Andy and Katie stopped short. "Mandy," Andy managed, surprise then consternation on his face.

"What are you doing here?" Mandy asked, looking first at Andy and then to Katie.

"I . . . We . . ." Andy fumbled.

Katie could tell Andy was irritated so she hurriedly interjected. "Hi, I'm Katie. Andy's wife." She held a hand out to Mandy.

"Katie!" Mandy said, taking her hand. "So good to finally meet you. Andy brags about you all the time. I'm Mandy Fitzhugh — one of the ER nurses. I work with Andy and Sean when they bring patients in."

"Mandy, it's nice to meet you. I've heard about you too," Katie said, smiling. "I hear you tongue tie poor Sean."

Mandy laughed. "Certainly not on purpose. We're getting past that I think. I hope so, anyway."

Katie saw Andy from the corner of her eye, silently looking between the two of them as they talked. He had been afraid this might happen — seeing someone he knew — but she knew he hadn't planned on it being this soon. He'd said repeatedly he didn't want the guys to know — not yet. Now, Mandy would have a pretty good idea something was up.

"We'd better be off," Katie said with a smile and taking Andy's hand, started walking toward the parking lot.

Mandy looked from one to the other but neither offered anything more. She spotted a familiar red folder in Katie's hands, and Mandy's smile wavered, but she turned to Andy. "See you next shift?"

"I'll be there," Andy replied curtly as Katie pulled him toward her.

"Bye," Katie nodded as she kept walking.

"Great, great, great!" Andy fumed as they walked to his truck.

"Andy, don't worry about Mandy," Katie said as they climbed in. "I thought you said Sean couldn't put two words together when he tried to talk to her. Doesn't seem like there'd be much opportunity for anything to be said."

She didn't want Andy to know she was having the same concerns.

"You may be right," Andy conceded. "I know it has to come out eventually, but I'd rather it not be quite yet. I want the guys to know they can count on me."

Katie reached over and took his hand. "They know that, Andy. You being a bit sick isn't going to change their feelings about you. Bentley might even start to like you," she said, a twinkle in her eye.

The corners of his mouth lifted a bit. "Well, let's not get carried away. And what do you think about me qualifying for that experimental drug?" he asked, excitement in his voice. "Sounds like Dr. Parker really went to bat to get me in the program."

"This may be exactly the break we needed, but Andy...I'm worried."

Noting the seriousness in her voice, he asked, "Why? What is it?"

"He said you need to rest between treatments — not continue to work — especially two jobs."

Andy sighed. "Katie, we've talked about this. I am the provider in this family, and I plan to work as long as I'm able. I need you to be on the same page with me on this. Please don't ask me to give up what I love — at least not until I absolutely have to. Okay?"

Katie studied his handsome, intent face. He was stubborn, and she knew she wouldn't be able to change his mind — at least not yet — but she would keep trying.

She smiled reluctantly and said, "Andy, I'm with you on anything and everything. You never need to wonder. I just want what's best for you and what will make it easier and faster for you to get well."

Andy stroked her cheek with his thumb. "Have I ever told you how happy I am being married to you?"

The feel of his thumb on her cheek was intimate and gentle. She closed her eyes, trying to push her fear away. She forced herself to open her eyes and looking at Andy with a teasing smile, said, "Well, I'm sure you have, but I never get tired of hearing it."

"Well, let me just state for the record then that I, Andrew H. Garrett, am the luckiest man in the world because I am married to you," Andy said, and he took Katie's hand and kissed it gently.

"You're crazy, but I love you, Andy Garrett," Katie said with a slight shake of her head.

Andy grinned and looked at his watch. "Mrs. Garrett, I'm sure that poor sub needs a break by now. We'd better get busy. I'll talk to Walt about my schedule and needing to be out again his afternoon." He sighed. "I'm not sure how we're going to make up the money we're losing since I have to cut my hours. Let's hope Walt will just let me cut some hours and not cut me out altogether."

"You worry too much," Katie said, trying to reassure and distract him. She'd worry for both of them. She wanted him focused on getting better. Besides, they were okay for now.

"We'll figure things out as we go," she said, trying to sound more confident than she felt. "This is new territory for both of us, but we'll get there."

MANDY WAVED AS THEY pushed the door open and stepped out of sight. She hesitated slightly before turning and walking down the hall and across a small courtyard to the oncology outpatient clinic where cancer treatments were administered. She wove her way through a maze of cubicles to the front desk where her friend, Deborah, worked as a scheduler.

"Hey, there," Deborah said in surprise. "What are you doing on this side of the world?"

"I was making a delivery for one of the ER docs but got a bit sidetracked." Deborah raised a finger to halt Mandy as she tapped her headpiece and swung to face her monitor.

A few quick keystrokes later, Deborah tapped the headpiece again and turned back to Mandy. "Sorry. It's Monday and busy."

"I need a favor," Mandy hurried on before another call came through. "I need to know if a certain person is on the schedule."

"Well . . ." Deborah hesitated. "I'm not sure that's a good idea. You know how they are about the privacy stuff these days."

"I know, I know," Mandy said. "But I'm afraid a friend may be on the list."

Hearing the urgency in Mandy's voice, Deborah asked in a hushed voice, "What's the name?"

Mandy bent down and said softly in Deborah's ear, "Andy Garrett. Or it might be Andrew."

Deborah's fingers flew over the keys and a second later a calendar popped on the screen. Deborah eyed the configuration and placed a finger on the screen pointing to information below tomorrow's date. There it was: Andy Garrett.

Mandy sighed sadly.

Deborah looked up. "Friend of yours?"

"Yes — of sorts. He's one of the fire department paramedics I work with in the ER."

"I'm so sorry. Looks like tomorrow is his first appointment. And wow," Deborah sat back, surprise on her face.

"What? What is it?" Mandy asked.

"Looks like he's got several appointments scheduled one right after another," she said, her finger tracing down the calendar. "They typically only schedule them like that if it's ..."

She stopped and abruptly closed the calendar. Shaking her head, she said, "Poor guy. It may be a rough go for him."

Seeing the stricken look on Mandy's face, Deborah hurried to add, "But you know it always depends on the patient."

Mandy did know, but it still didn't stop her from being concerned. "Thanks - I appreciate it."

"I'll be sure to take special care of him," Deborah assured Mandy as she started back through the maze of cubicles. Mandy waved and mouthed a thank you before she disappeared.

AFTER HE DROPPED KATIE off, Andy drove straight to RITE2U's office. Without slowing down, he acknowledged Charlene with a wave and walked into Walt's office. As RITE2U's manager, everyone reported to Walt Henderson who was standing behind his desk, studying a schedule in his hands. The half glasses he usually wore on top of his head were currently sitting precariously at the end of his nose. Hearing Andy's approach, Walt looked up and swept the glasses to the top of his head.

"Andy, good morning."

"Morning, Walt. You got a minute?"

Walt grunted assent as he plopped into the chair behind his desk. "What is it? I've got to finish getting the morning calls processed."

Andy sat in the chair across from Walt and cleared his throat. "Walt, I need to cut my hours back..."

"What?! You're already gone one or two days a week to the fire station. I've got regular customers and a full load every day. I can't spare you any more time off." Walt went back to shuffling the papers on his desk, dismissing Andy by ignoring him.

Andy cleared his throat once more. "Walt, I don't want to have to take any more time off, but I really don't have a choice. You see, I..."

Andy stopped abruptly when Walt suddenly stopped shuffling papers. Walt pulled the glasses off the top of his head and tossed them onto a stack of routing slips.

He leaned over his desk and studied Andy. "Does this have something to do with the episode in the break room a few weeks ago?"

Caught off guard, Andy asked, "How do you know about that?"

"Charlene. She may not show it, but she's rather fond of you."

Dubious, Andy said, "I seriously doubt that."

Walt shrugged. "That's Charlene. Back to my question. Is this request related to that incident?"

Andy knew it was only a matter of time before everyone knew, but he wasn't quite ready to become an invalid in everyone's mind just yet. "Yes, it does, Walt. That incident was a bit of a wake-up call, but I can't go into more detail right now. I would really appreciate you cutting my hours by half — just for a while."

Walt stared at the ceiling in thought, absentmindedly rubbing the bald spot on top of his head. After a couple of minutes, he picked up his glasses, perched them back on the tip of his nose and without looking at Andy said, "Sure, kid. Half days on the days you're already scheduled to work. Tell Charlene so she'll know how to draw up the schedules."

The meeting was over. Walt was already re-immersed in his paperwork as Andy stood and headed to the door.

"Thanks, Walt."

Walt glanced up and waved Andy off before going back to the papers strewn across his desk.

That hadn't been too bad, Andy thought. On one hand, it was a relief to have more time to adjust to the treatments but on the other hand, it also meant a lot less money coming in the door.

Andy told Charlene about his reduced hours. The change meant she would have to adjust everyone's schedules. "Sorry for the extra work."

Charlene didn't answer. She nodded to indicate she'd heard but continued to work with her eyes trained on her computer screen. Andy turned and headed to the dispatch area to pick up his morning assignments. He was sure Walt was wrong about Charlene's concern for him. If not for setting the delivery schedules, Charlene probably wouldn't even know his name.

WHILE KATIE POPPED POPCORN that evening, she asked, "How did it go with Walt?"

"Surprisingly well," Andy replied as he put ice in glasses for soft drinks. "He wasn't agreeable at first, but it didn't take much to change his mind."

"Good! I'm glad he didn't make it hard. Do you work at least half of what you were?" Katie asked, trying to sound nonchalant. She wanted Andy to have as much time between treatments as possible, but she also needed to calculate the income they were losing.

"Yeah — it worked out great. Charlene scheduled me with exactly half the hours I was working before." Andy reached over and popped a kernel of popcorn in his mouth. "And, you're not going to believe what else Walt said."

Andy took a handful of popcorn and started tossing one kernel and then another in the air and catching them in his mouth.

Katie laughed and grabbed the bowl from him as he followed her into the living room with their soft drinks. "What amazing thing did Walt tell you," she asked, settling onto the sofa close to Andy.

"He said, 'Charlene is rather fond of you,'" Andy mimicked Walt's voice and then laughed. "I've tried everything I know to get her to like me, but I thought nothing was working. I didn't even think she knew my name except from the work slips." Andy laughed again and put his arm around Katie as she placed the bowl of popcorn between them.

"I think she's a mighty smart lady if she's fond of you," Katie said, reaching up and kissing Andy on the cheek.

"Hey — I've only got room for one special lady in my life," Andy grinned.

"Good answer."

"So, what do you want to watch tonight?" Andy asked, reaching for another hand full of popcorn.

Snuggling closer to him, Katie said, "Well, we're supposed to do something fun, but to tell you the truth, I'm thinking this is pretty fun." She put an arm across Andy, pulling him close.

Andy began to softly stroke her hair.

"Andy?" she asked softly.

"Hmmmm ..."

"Are you scared?"

After a long pause and heavy sigh Andy said, "Katie, with you, I can only be honest, and if you tell anyone I said this, I'll deny it. But, yes — I'm scared."

He stared at the wall and then rubbed his eyes with his free hand. "I'm scared that I'm not going to be able to do the things I've always taken for granted — play baseball, work at the station, peeve Bentley," he said with a low chuckle. "But most importantly, I'm scared I won't be able to be the husband to you I want to be and ... that we won't grow old together. That's what scares me most."

He snatched a kernel of popcorn out of Katie's fingers. "But we're not dwelling on any of that tonight. We've had some great news today. And tonight, we're following the doc's orders and relaxing. I say we draw cards, low man — or woman as the case may be — gets to decide the movie."

"Any movie?" Katie asked, sitting up and looking at him with glee.

"Oh no. No, no, no. We're not watching some sappy romcom. No way," Andy protested with exaggerated horror.

Katie giggled and retrieved a deck of cards.

"Let's just draw and see."

She plopped down on the sofa and fanned the cards. "Okay, big boy, draw your poison."

Andy, drawing the king of hearts, groaned and threw his head back against the sofa cushion.

"Well, well, well, look what we've got here," Katie said, drawing the seven of clubs and waving it in front of Andy's face. "Looks like we're watching a movie of my choice, my friend." She grabbed the remote off the coffee table and drew up their streaming service. She arrowed up and down until she found *Remember the Titans* — one of Andy's favorites. He grinned when it came on and pulled Katie down beside him. He put his arm around her as Katie melted into his side.

In a soft voice she said, "Andy..."

"Hmmm. . ." he replied as the intro played.

"I'm scared too, we're not *ever* giving up. I love you too much..."

Andy brushed Katie's hair with a kiss and whispered, "And I love you too, Katie."

SALLY KNOCKED ON MANDY'S apartment door a second time but still no answer. She checked her watch. She was a couple of minutes late, but not enough that Mandy would have left without her. They'd planned dinner at a popular new bistro known for its single clientele and agreed to meet at Mandy's apartment to go together.

"Sorry I'm late," Mandy said, rushing up the walk. "I got totally side-tracked at work and time was gone before I realized how late it was. So sorry."

Mandy dug in her purse for her keys. "Give me just a minute and then we'll be off."

"Of course," Sally said, surprised by the usually easy-going Mandy appearing ruffled. "You okay?"

"What?" Mandy asked, distracted, as she pushed the key into the lock.

"I said, are you okay?" Sally said, following Mandy inside.

"Oh, I'm fine. I just have some things on my mind." She walked down the hall to her bedroom. "Make yourself at home," she called over her shoulder.

"No rush — we're good on time. Are you hungry?" Sally picked up a magazine off the table and began thumbing through it.

"No — not this very minute," Mandy mumbled as she put on some lip color. "But I probably will be by the time we get there." She fluffed her hair and with one last glance in the mirror, turned and walked down the hall. "Ready," Mandy said, hesitating before grabbing her jacket.

"You don't seem yourself tonight," Sally said. "Are you sure everything is okay?"

Mandy's shoulders sagged as she sat on a bar stool. "I found something out about a friend today that has me worried. I mean, he's not actually a friend. We're more like a work acquaintances, but he's the kind of person you feel like you've known forever."

Sally grinned. "A *he* who's a friend, huh? Is this the special someone you talked about a few weeks ago when you said things would never work out?"

"Hate to disappoint you, but this really is a friend. I met his wife today when they were at the hospital. They're both so nice. It's just so sad ..."

"What's so sad?" Sally asked, concerned at Mandy's evident distress.

Mandy turned to Sally. "From all indications, he has cancer. He hasn't exactly told me himself, but I figured it out. From what I was able to put together, he starts chemo treatments tomorrow, and it looks intense. He's young, a really good-looking guy and a great personality too. He's the total package as they say — even if he is a bit sold on himself," Mandy said with a light chuckle.

"I know someone like that too," Sally nodded. "He's a firefighter. His wife and I teach at the same school. I've hinted to Katie to set me up with one of those good-looking single firemen at the station but so far no luck."

Mandy stood quickly, her eyes round with alarm.

Sally stopped. "Now, you've really got me concerned. What on earth is going on?"

Mandy licked her lips. "You work with Katie Garrett?"

It was Sally's turn to be surprised. "I don't think I've mentioned Katie's last name before."

"No, you haven't. I met her today at the hospital…" Mandy stopped, eying Sally, to see if she would make the connection.

Sally cocked her head and then realization dawned, and she sat down heavily. "Oh no…not Andy. He can't have cancer! Poor Katie, she practically worships him." A few seconds passed and Sally gasped, a horrified expression on her face. "What have I done?"

Mandy looked at her with concern. "What do you mean?"

"I didn't know. I promise I didn't know…" Sally said and started crying, almost hysterical.

Alarmed, Mandy put her arm around Sally. "What is it? What's wrong?"

"I've been so mean to Katie…" Sally took a ragged breath. "I knew something was wrong between them. She has been so distracted and looked so sad and worried these past few weeks. She'd told me how distant Andy had become."

Sally looked sheepish before admitting, "Andy is an incredibly good-looking guy, and I know I'm not the only teacher who enjoys the scenery when he visits the school. I thought I knew what the problem was when Katie told me Andy wasn't answering her calls or returning her messages. There were a couple of afternoons when he didn't go to work, and no one knew where he was. He'd be out of pocket for hours at a time with no explanation. It all just seemed so obvious."

Sally paused and looked tearfully at Mandy. "I told Katie I thought Andy was cheating on her."

Stunned, Mandy stood and took several steps away from Sally. "I'm sorry. You did what?!"

Sally began to cry in earnest and between sobs, repeated what she'd already said.

Mandy paced back and forth before saying indignantly, "Well, Andy may be a flirt and a tease, and he definitely loves being the center of attention, but from everything I know about him, he's not the kind of guy who would cheat on his wife. And, from what I saw today, they're totally devoted to each other."

"That explains why she had a sub this morning," Sally went on as if she hadn't heard Mandy. "She was at the hospital. I have noticed that she's better the last few days — more subdued, but not upset like she had been."

Sally shook her head as if in a daze. "I was so sure I was right."

Trying to control her anger, Mandy said, "So, let me get this straight. To make Katie feel better you ogle her husband when he's around and then tell her he's cheating on her? What kind of friend are you?"

Sally ducked her head and started crying again.

Mandy took a breath and walked over to put a hand on Sally's trembling shoulder. Softly she said, "I'm sorry. Sally, listen. What's done is done. The best thing you and I can do now is support both Andy and Katie."

Unable to look Mandy in the eye, Sally only nodded and dabbed at the tears on her cheeks.

"When I saw them today," Mandy continued, "they gave no indication they wanted to share any information so you cannot, I repeat, you *cannot* let Katie know you know anything. Besides, I could get into big trouble with the privacy laws as they are since I'm an employee of the hospital. I have to have your word that you will say nothing — absolutely nothing — to Katie about this. Can I count on you? I need to know."

Sally looked up at Mandy and nodded, her face glistening with tears. "I promise. I've acted more like a rival to Katie than a friend. I'm ashamed to say I think I was almost hoping Andy was cheating on her."

At Mandy's horrified expression, Sally hurried on to say, "But from this point on, I promise to be a supportive friend. I can't apologize to Katie without explaining how I know what's going on, but I truly am so sorry. Please don't think too badly of me."

Mandy sighed, looking at Sally, and could tell she was sincere. Katie was going to need all the support they could give her. "Sally, your method was harsh, and you were way out of line, but I think you realize that now."

Sally hung her head. "Yes - I do realize that, and I feel terrible. I will do everything I can to make it up to her. I promise to be a much better friend."

"You will have to be, for Katie's sake. The important thing now is to help them both."

"You're right," Sally said and paused.

"I'm not sure I want to ask, but do you have any idea how bad Andy's cancer is?"

"I don't know for sure, but I think it's bad. The treatment is really strong and there's a lot of it. I imagine he's going to have a rough time. Chemo is never easy."

Sally shook her head sadly. "It just doesn't seem possible that someone like Andy can have cancer."

Mandy nodded. "I know. He's total energy, and he sure makes me laugh. I look forward to him and Sean's runs to the ER."

"Sean? Who is Sean?"

"Sean is the rookie at the station. He and Andy are partners on the ambulance."

"Oh, and would Sean happen to be single?"

Mandy blushed. "Yes, Sean is single, quite handsome and from what I hear, an excellent cook too."

"Well, look at you blushing," Sally teased, welcoming the lighter conversation. "Have you guys been out yet?"

The smile on Mandy's face wavered and then disappeared. "No, we haven't gone out, and we won't be going out either." Mandy stood abruptly.

"Whoa there. Looks like you've kinda got a thing for this Sean. Is it mutual?"

"Yes . . . I mean no . . . I mean I don't know. I don't know," Mandy repeated. "What I can tell you, is that it will never work out so I'm not even going there. Hungry?"

Mandy picked up her purse and walked to the door. She stopped, looking down and turned to Sally. "Would you accept a rain check? I'm not really in the mood to go to a singles' hot spot tonight. It still sounds fun but just not tonight."

Sally sighed. "You read my mind. I didn't want to disappoint you but now I don't feel like going out either. Call it a night?"

"Yes — please. Thanks. And Sally, remember, please don't say anything to Katie."

Sally nodded. "I promise. But this is going to be hard. Katie and I interact a lot every day."

"You've *got* to do this," Mandy emphasized. "From what I gathered talking to them today, they aren't wanting to talk about it — with anyone — at least not yet. Until we know differently, we have to do everything we can to honor that. But —," Mandy smiled mischievously.

"That doesn't mean we can't do things to help them without letting on we know about the situation. After all, that's what friends are for, right?"

"Absolutely," Sally quickly agreed.

"So, off with you," Mandy said and waved before she door closed.

Sally smiled in return but grew serious as she turned to walk to her car. She had to do something to make up to Katie, and she had a lot to make up. What could she do and what did Katie need most right now? Sally mulled over several ideas, but then her mind paused, and her lips curved upward in an inspired smile.

Yes, she thought, that will be perfect.

K ATIE WATCHED ANDY CLOSELY the next morning in the hospital. He seemed to be dozing, but she didn't think he was asleep. The treatment room was hushed, the quiet broken only by the soft voices of the nurses, rustles of other patients in their own cubicles and the swish of the automatic door in the lobby. Tubes trailed from Andy's port, inserted for the treatments, ending in a clear bag that hung on a stainless-steel stand. They'd been told the clear concoction in the bag was Andy's special cocktail prepared following Dr. Parker's explicit instructions. Katie reached over and adjusted the heated blanket laying across Andy's legs. Lauren, one of the nurses, had laid it over him when she noticed him shivering. She'd assured them this was a normal reaction to the strong chemicals. Katie looked around at the small cubicle they'd been assigned. The space was small with room for only the blue recliner where Andy sat, a guest chair and a small counter for tools and needed supplies.

As Katie looked at Andy, she wondered how they'd ended up here and why this was happening to them. It didn't seem possible that Andy — the always positive, happy-spirited guy who never wanted to slow down — was now having to make adjustments daily depending on how he felt. Now that she knew what was going on, she could see him fighting the pain and the moodiness and didn't take exception to his angry outbursts or anything out of character he might say. She knew Jerry's failure to offer any words of encouragement or assurance had hurt Andy deeply, but he didn't want to talk about it, and she didn't push him. He knew he had her full support, and she continually offered encouragement. But still, she wished she could do more. She was resolved to protect him from worrying about their finances, but she was also determined to do anything that promised to help him, no matter the cost. Andy still planned to continue working a full schedule, but with the intense treatment plan Dr. Parker had laid out, Katie didn't know how long he'd be able to stand up to it or even if he should try.

Andy stirred slightly. Katie reached over and took his hand. A firm squeeze back confirmed he was awake. After only thirty minutes, they both looked up with surprise when Lauren came over and started unhooking the tubes.

"You're all done for today, Mr. Garrett," she said, smiling as Andy sat up.

"That's it?" Andy asked.

"The first treatment is the shortest. They get a little longer each time as your body builds up a resistance to the drugs," Lauren explained as she continued disconnecting the various tubes and wires.

"Well, that's something to look forward to, isn't it?" Andy replied with a trace of sarcasm.

When everything was unhooked and moved aside, Katie offered her hand to help Andy stand, but he brushed her away. "I'm not an invalid yet," he said with a wry smile.

Katie stepped back, letting Andy push himself up, using the arms of the chair for support. It took him just a second or two but then he straightened and smiled at Katie. He reached for the jacket she held out to him and slipped it on with a slight glower. He took Katie's hand, and they started toward the door.

"Hold on a second, Mr. Garrett," Lauren said as an orderly rolled a wheelchair up beside them. "It's policy after your first treatment that you get a ride to the front door." Lauren smiled matter-of-factly and gestured for Andy to take a seat.

"I'm fine to walk, really," Andy protested, his face starting to flush with irritation.

Katie started to agree with Lauren, but seeing the look on Andy's face, thought better of it.

"Sorry but those are the rules. We've learned that you never know what reaction there might be, whether immediate or a bit delayed. It's better to play it safe."

Andy opened his mouth to object again but the once sweet, now very stern nurse, tilted her head and pierced him with a look that said he would not win this battle. With a sigh of exasperation, he plopped into the chair and waited to be wheeled to the door.

"Thank you, Lauren," Katie said with an apologetic smile.

Lauren, once again kind and sweet, said, "We will see you soon, Mr. Garrett." With a smile and reassuring nod to Katie, Lauren gathered the remaining items from their cubicle and returned to the nurses' station.

As the orderly wheeled Andy to the front door, Katie reached over and took his hand. It felt cold and clammy in her grasp, and she wondered if he was already feeling the effects of the drugs. The information Dr. Parker provided said it took some people days to notice anything, while others could feel effects in a matter of hours. For Andy, it looked like the drugs might be having an even more immediate effect.

Katie retrieved the car and pulled around to where Andy sat in the wheelchair, waiting with the orderly. After Andy climbed into the passenger seat, they looked at each other and breathed a sigh of relief as the orderly closed the door. The first treatment was done.

"Well? How are you feeling?" Katie asked as she turned the heat up when she saw Andy shivering.

"Not bad, actually. Tired, but not too bad."

"Do you feel like going to work?" They had argued this point again just this morning while getting ready. Without knowing what the effects of the first treatment might be, Katie had asked him to stay home and rest, but Andy was determined.

"Right now, all I feel is cold," Andy said and reached over and turned the car heater up a couple more notches. He shifted in his seat to look at her. "Katie, my sweet worry wart. I'll be fine. I'll have a radio with me at all times, and I can call someone if I need to. It's going to be better for me if I keep going. I need to stay busy."

He took a deep breath and waited until he had Katie's full attention. "We talked about this, remember? We're going to need the money."

Katie took his hand and said, "Yes, Andy, I remember, but right now I don't care about the bills or money. All I care about is you and doing whatever it takes to get you well."

Andy patted her hand. "I know, I know. Everything is going to be fine. Just wait and see."

Katie wished she could know that for sure. The best thing she could do for Andy was to be strong, supportive, and positive and that was exactly what she intended to be. She felt Andy's hand tremble as she gripped it in her own. With a quick she nod said, "Well, alright, I'll drop you by the house and then head to school. Who knows what story Sally has dreamed up about me having another sub."

"You need to head that girl off at the pass. She lets her imagination carry her away," Andy said with a sigh as he leaned back against the headrest and closed his eyes.

KATIE HAD ALREADY TALKED to her school principal and explained the need for substitutes the next few months. Betty had been sympathetic and understanding and surprised Katie with a hug at the end of their meeting. Katie wasn't ready to talk to Sally about it yet but their afternoon meeting about the field trip to the fire station would provide Sally with ample opportunity for questions.

Katie's thoughts were interrupted when she neared the door to her classroom and heard pandemonium. Thoughts of the field trip were quickly forgotten when she stepped inside and saw her class in complete chaos. Some of the students were out of their seats and talking, others were drawing on chalkboards while others just ran around the room. The sub didn't look bothered by the chaos, until she saw Katie and the look of fury on her face.

With a firm tone, Kate said, "Class, take your seats ... now. Pull out one sheet of paper and a pencil and wait for instructions. I expect you to wait without talking."

The room fell silent. The only sound was the click of Katie's flats across the floor as she approached the sub.

"Mrs. Garrett ..." the sub stammered.

With a searing look of disapproval, Katie said, "Thank you for your time today. I'll take it from here."

"I —"

"Thank you. Good day," Katie said, cutting her off.

The sub hurried from the room while Katie turned to her class.

Katie was not angry with her class. She was angry with someone who had ignored her lesson plans, mishandled her students and wasted precious teaching time. She took a deep breath and gave the class a short assignment while she gathered her thoughts. She dreaded what this might mean if all the substitutes were like this one.

Lunch came and the afternoon flew by as Katie covered both the morning and afternoon lessons. Class time was intense, but the day ended with smiles and high fives as the students left for the day.

Seeing the students off, Katie sighed a happy sigh of exhilaration and turned back to her room. Surprised, she saw Lucas, waiting patiently by her desk. "Is there something I can do for you, Lucas?"

"No, ma'am. I just wanted to give you this." He reached out and put his little arms around her in a tight hug.

The stress of the day evaporated as Katie patted his shoulder. "Thank you, Lucas," she said softly. "I needed a good hug."

He nodded and turned toward the door.

"Lucas," she called after him. "We're going to the fire station next week. Mr. Andy is looking forward to giving you the grand tour."

A bright smile spread across his face.

"I'll see you tomorrow," Katie said with a wave.

Lucas nodded, still grinning, as he walked out.

KATIE HURRIED OUT OF the bathroom, drying her hair with a towel, the alarm pulsing louder and louder. She tapped the off button and looked at Andy who was laying oblivious, facing away from her. He'd fallen asleep on the couch the evening before when he'd gotten home from work, and they'd gone to bed much earlier than normal. Katie laid extra blankets over him on the couch and throughout the night when he hadn't been able to get warm in bed. By the third blanket, he'd been able to doze off and stayed asleep. He was due at the station at 7:30, but she wasn't sure he'd be able to make it. She glanced at the clock and back at him and whispered, "Andy?"

There was no response. She put one knee on the bed and leaning over, placed her hand on his shoulder and shook him gently. "Andy," she said, her mouth near his ear.

"Hmmm," Andy moaned.

"Andy, it's almost 6:30. Time to get up if you're going to the station." He stirred slightly under the mound of blankets.

"Can you tell how you're feeling?" she asked, rubbing the spot on the blankets where his arm should be.

Muffled by the pillow Andy mumbled, "I hurt all over."

Katie didn't want him to go, but she also knew it would be good for him to be at the station with the guys. "Well, this is one of those big boy pants days," she said, trying to sound strict. "Come on — get up, get your shower and don't be late. You don't want to give Bentley cause to write you up again do you?" She jostled his shoulder gently as he rolled over and eyed her with one eye squinted closed.

He started moving and pushed the blankets aside. "Wow, where did my sympathetic wife go?" he grumbled, pulling first one leg and then the other out from under the layers. He sat on the edge of the bed and raked his fingers through his tousled hair.

In spite of her tough talk, Katie eyed him sympathetically and wondered if he really was up to meeting the physical demands at work so soon after his first round of chemo. She watched him as he came around the bed and stopped where she still knelt. He leaned over and gave her a peck on the cheek and a sleepy attempt at a grin.

A sudden wave of possessiveness washed over Katie, and she struggled not to reach out and pull him close. She wanted to hold him and protect him. With great effort, she pushed those thoughts aside and instead, matched his grin with one of her own. "Shower. Go."

With an amused shake of his head, Andy gave her another quick kiss on the cheek and made his way to the bathroom and a hot shower.

ANDY PULLED INTO A parking spot at the station and looked at his watch. 7:28 a.m. He grinned. Two minutes to spare. Surprised at how well he felt after his shower, he was ready to take the day head on. He opened the back door and stepped into an empty kitchen. Strange, he thought, where is everybody?

He heard papers shuffling from the office. "You're late, Garrett," Bentley groused out his standard greeting.

"Good morning to you, LEW-ten-ant. Check your watch. I'm early," Andy replied. He craned his neck to look down the hall into the bay area in search of the crew. He spotted them in the bay. Ignoring Bentley's muttered comments, he headed down the hall.

Through the bay door window he could see the guys huddled at the back of the engine. Their heads were bent close together, and they appeared to be listening intently to something Hedrick was saying.

Hitting the door with a loud bang, he stepped into the bay and said, "Hey, what's going on here?"

Startled, the four jumped and moved quickly away from each other, looking like they'd been caught doing something wrong.

Several seconds passed with no response. Andy put his hands on his hips and looked from one to the other. He cocked his head to the side and asked, "You guys look guilty as sin. What's up?"

"Nothing," Jernigan said a little too quickly and moved toward the engine's panel of gages to start his morning check. Hedrick mumbled something about a grocery list while Hart and Canfield headed toward the ambulance. Andy remained where he was and watched them suspiciously. Something was definitely up.

Andy shook his head and turned toward the equipment room to get his bunker gear. Jernigan, keeping his eye on the engine's pump panel said, "Gear's already on the truck."

Andy stopped mid track and said, "*My* gear?"

"Yep," Jernigan answered, his back remaining to Andy.

"What happened to each man being responsible for his own gear?" Andy asked of the group in general, irritation creeping into his voice.

"Ehhh," Jernigan shrugged. "It's a one-off. Don't get used to it."

With a humph, Andy headed to the back of the engine to check the hose stacks — one of his routine morning tasks — only to find Hedrick there ahead of him.

"What are you doing?" Andy asked, his frustration mounting. "I thought you were working on a grocery list."

"Yeah, yeah, yeah. I'm gonna work on it as soon as I get done here," Hedrick grunted as he tugged on one of the loads.

"Why don't you work on it now," Andy said, moving in beside Hedrick. "I'll finish this." He stepped up on the bumper and started adjusting the stacks.

Hedrick, hesitated and then shrugged and stepped down. "Suit yourself."

Hedrick headed toward the door to the living area, and catching Jernigan's eye, shrugged and held his hands up in surrender. Jernigan acknowledged him with a brief nod as did Canfield and Hart from where they stood at the back of the ambulance.

HEDRICK BUSIED HIMSELF IN the kitchen, making his grocery list and checking supplies for what they'd need for the day's meals, but his thoughts were on the conversation he'd had with Mandy yesterday. He enjoyed talking to her on the phone which they were now doing often, and they had even been out a couple of times.

They'd met for lunch at a favorite Abernathy hamburger joint on one of Sean's days off a couple of weeks ago. Rock and roll was playing from overhead speakers as they sat across from each other in a booth, eating hamburgers and sharing an order of fries.

Sean smiled at Mandy as he dangled fries in ketchup and took a bite. She was talking about something at the hospital. One of the nurses had gotten a promotion so there was a chance Mandy's schedule might change. Sean enjoyed watching Mandy as she talked, nibbled on her burger, and ate one fry at a time. He rarely saw her out of scrubs but today but she wore a sweatshirt, skinny jeans and slip on tennis shoes. She looked amazing.

"Mandy, you ought to come to the station sometime. You need to meet the rest of the guys," Sean blurted out when Mandy paused. "You've met Garrett but don't judge us all by him." Sean chuckled but stopped short when he realized Mandy was staring at him, her eyes round.

She laid her hamburger on her plate and looked down, smoothing the paper napkin in her lap.

"What's wrong?" Sean asked as Mandy remained quiet, staring at her clasped hands.

"I'm so sorry," Sean rushed on. "I apologize. I interrupted you."

Mandy began to shake her head slowly, still looking down. When she looked up at Sean, tears were glistening on her cheeks.

Stunned, Sean sat back.

"Mandy, I'm so sorry. Whatever I said, I'm so sorry." Sean looked around nervously as if seeking help.

"Sean, please. No. You don't owe me any apologies," Mandy began. "There's just something I need to tell you, and it's very difficult for me."

She took her napkin and wiped her cheeks.

"Besides Andy, you're the first firefighter I've ever talked to and you're definitely the first I've had lunch with." She managed a small smile. "In fact, I've avoided firefighters when at all possible."

Confused, Sean leaned close as she continued, her voice soft.

"When I was six, our house caught fire late one night. I can still hear the wood popping as it burned, the heat from the flames and the dense smoke choking me. The panicked screams of my little brother woke me up as he ran past my door and down the stairs. I heard my parents calling my name as the roar from the fire got louder. And my dad ... my dad."

Mandy stopped and closed her eyes tight.

Sean moved around and sat on the bench seat beside her.

She took a shuddering breath and went on.

"I heard him call my name and then a loud crash followed by hysterical screams from my mother. The next thing I remember was a firefighter carrying me to one of the upstairs windows where he handed me to another firefighter waiting on a ladder. I remember being scared, but I also remember both firefighters being so calm and assuring me over and over that everything was going to be okay."

Mandy looked at Sean, her eyes shining with tears. "Everything had been okay until I saw my dad laying on the ground. He was surrounded by firefighters, and my mom was holding his hand. She was rocking back and forth, crying. I tried to get to them but another firefighter stopped me and moved to where I couldn't see them. I was so confused. I didn't understand what was happening."

Sean looked at her with understanding.

"Go on," he encouraged gently.

"I remember riding in the ambulance to the hospital. My mom was with me. Her face was pale, and streaked with soot and tears. I don't remember anything until later in the hospital room, when I woke up. My mom held my hand tight and told me my dad had gone to be with the angels."

Mandy turned and looked at Sean. "My whole world turned upside down that night. Ever since then I've felt guilty — that it was my fault."

"Your fault?" Sean asked, surprised. "None of that could be your fault, Mandy. It was a terrible, unfortunate accident, but not your fault."

She gave him a watery smile.

"Don't you see? My dad was on the stairs trying to get to me when they collapsed. If I'd run downstairs with my brother, there would have been no reason for my dad to be on the stairs. And if —" Mandy stopped, looking at Sean sadly.

"And if —" Sean prompted.

"If the firefighters had gotten there sooner, they could have saved my dad. They could have helped him first but they were too late —"

Mandy began to cry in earnest and Sean put his arm around her.

Sniffing, she looked up at Sean. "Don't you see? That's why I've tried to push you away. I swore I'd never have anything to do with firefighters and that was easy to do until I started working at the ER. I got to know Andy, and then he introduced me to you and well …"

"As I said," Sean said with a grin, "don't judge us all by Garrett."

Mandy gave a wobbly grin. "Oh, Sean. Andy's a great guy. He always makes me laugh."

"He's a clown alright," Sean countered with a roll of his eyes but then grew somber again. "And now? How do you feel about firefighters?"

"Well, I guess you might say they're growing on me - one in particular."

Mandy smiled sweetly at Sean who blushed red but with a pleased smile.

"One thing you should know though," Mandy said. "Ever since the night of the fire, I've had a fear of being anywhere but on ground level. I only live in first floor apartments, and if I ever absolutely have to ride in an elevator, I'm in a panic until I'm back on the ground."

Sean nodded. "I think that's a normal reaction. You may overcome that fear in time and with the right kind of reassurance, of course."

Sean took Mandy's hand and squeezed it gently. She smiled and squeezed his hand in return.

Since that lunch, they talked often so Sean wasn't surprised when Mandy called yesterday; the surprise was what she told him.

Andy had cancer. It was obvious he didn't want anyone to know, and Hedrick had debated about telling the rest of the crew. After discussing it with Mandy, they'd decided the crew, except for Bentley, should know. They'd agreed telling them would make it possible for everyone to support Andy whether he would actually want or accept the help or not. Hedrick had contacted everyone the night before and requested they arrive early before Andy got to the station. Andy's arrival cut their discussion short, but they'd had enough time to put a rough game plan together. Since they were fairly certain Andy wouldn't want any help, the trick was going to be helping him without him finding out. They knew he wouldn't make it easy, but they were just as determined as he was stubborn.

Booksopen in front of them, Andy, Jernigan, Hart, and Canfield sat around the kitchen table studying the mandatory monthly continuing education chapters. The quiet was broken midmorning when the kitchen door swung open and Chief Hamilton and Battalion Chief Rogers strode in. Andy was just lifting his cup to take a sip of coffee but instead, he took a quick gulp and looked down.

Andy hadn't seen or talked to Chief Hamilton since his and Natalie's abrupt departure Friday. His sudden appearance at Station Two was alarming. Andy fidgeted and kept his head down. Was it possible Hamilton told Rogers about his cancer diagnosis and now they'd come to tell Bentley?

"Gentlemen," Hamilton said to the group.

"Good Morning," Rogers added.

"Chief," the others answered, starting to rise.

"Keep your seats, guys. Where's Bentley?" Hamilton asked as he and Rogers stopped beside the table.

"Lieutenant's in his office," Jernigan answered and after a brief pause added, "doing paperwork."

Bentley's well-known tendency for making a mess of his desk and any kind of paperwork brought a round of grins. Andy grinned too, but he still didn't dare look up.

Chief Hamilton eyed the top of Andy's head but turned to Chief Rogers. "Let's see if Bentley needs any help."

They walked down the short hall to Bentley's office. Andy looked up, watching them with dread. His firefighting days might be coming to an end.

"What do you think all that's about?" Canfield asked, craning his neck trying to see down the hall.

"If it concerns you, I'm sure they'll let you know," Jernigan barked.

Jernigan eyed Andy, whose head hovered just above his book. "You know anything about this unexpected visit, Garrett?"

Andy's head popped up. "What makes you think I know anything about it?" he snapped. He was in no mood for small talk. He was too worried about what might be happening in Bentley's office.

"Seems like you're the reason we get a lot of visits from the chiefs is all," Jernigan went on.

"Can't help it if I'm popular." Andy smirked and looked back down at his book.

"Popular isn't exactly the term I'd use." Canfield chuckled.

Andy pierced him with a glare. "I don't remember asking you," he shot back.

Andy stood and snapped his book closed just about the time the two chiefs came back down the hall. Bentley was hot on their heels, sputtering protests.

Ignoring him, Chief Rogers said, "Jernigan, Garrett, need to borrow you guys for awhile. Grab your jackets and meet us out back."

Jernigan left to get his jacket, but Andy didn't move. He looked with alarm from Bentley to Hamilton to Rogers.

Seeing Andy hesitate, Rogers said, "Garrett, this isn't an option. Get a move on. Now."

While Andy left to get his jacket, Chief Rogers went on. "Lieutenant Bentley, as we explained, we need these guys to evaluate some new equipment before it's put into service. It will take a couple of hours and then they'll be back. In the meantime, there are a couple of guys coming over from Station One so you'll be fully staffed. We all have radios. If a call comes in, and Garrett and Jernigan are needed, we'll get them there. Clear?"

Slipping his jacket on as he came back into the room, Andy, as well as the rest of the crew, sensed this was not going well for Bentley.

Bentley's face was flushed red with anger. "Sir, I believe I'm just as qualified —"

Battalion Chief Rogers cut him off. "Lt. Bentley, I suggest you stop right there. It's decided."

Andy did his best to hide a grin. Bentley, obviously biting back a different retort, said, "Of course, sir."

Hamilton and Rogers stepped aside to allow Jernigan and Andy to walk out ahead of them. The rest of the crew looked at each other in silence as Bentley stomped back to his office.

"You're with me, Garrett," Hamilton said as Rogers motioned for Jernigan to follow him.

Andy walked to the passenger side of the Chief's vehicle but hesitated before opening the door. Wary, he looked at the Chief across the shiny red hood. "So what's going on? Where are we going?"

"Get in," Hamilton said as he got in and started the engine.

Still unsure, Andy hesitated and waited beside the closed door.

Chief Hamilton rolled the passenger window down. "Quit wasting time. Get in."

Andy opened the door and obediently climbed in. He looked at Hamilton with confusion and dread.

"Wipe that look off your face, Andy. You're not going to an execution. Coffee?"

"Coffee? I thought we were going to evaluate equipment?"

"Equipment *is* going to be evaluated. Jernigan is one of our best drivers. I wanted to give him the opportunity to look at the new engine we've bought. It's almost ready to go into service, but I wanted Jernigan's input on some things first. He's been asking to take a look at it, so when I heard Curtis was coming to Two for him, I thought it'd be a good time for you and I to visit as well. So, the question remains, coffee?"

"Sure," Andy said. He braced himself for whatever was about to come.

Hamilton pulled into the neighborhood coffee shop a few blocks from the station and parked. He got out of the car and closed the door, peering through the window and giving Andy an "aren't you coming?" look. He waited at the front of the vehicle as Andy slowly unbuckled his seat belt and followed him inside. After ordering their coffees, they made their way to a table in an out-of-the-way corner. Chief Hamilton settled into a chair as Andy pulled out another and sat down cautiously across from him. Chief Hamilton set a radio on the table between them and finally looked at Andy.

They both leaned back as the waitress set their orders in front of them. They took a sip. Andy kept his fingers wrapped around his cup, enjoying its warmth. He looked up when Hamilton cleared his throat.

"Andy, I want to explain about the other night."

Andy watched his friend's face closely as several emotions played across it in quick succession. Andy couldn't tell if what he was seeing was sadness, anger, regret or something else.

After a long pause, Hamilton continued. "Andy, this isn't easy for me. You brought up a lot of memories the other night I thought I'd buried a long time ago. But the way I treated you was painfully wrong."

Andy leaned forward, confused. His full attention was trained on Hamilton.

"You see," Hamilton said, "twenty years ago, I listened as my kid brother, Scotty, told our family basically the same thing you told Natalie and I Friday night." He took a sip of coffee, eying Andy over the top of his cup. "Scotty joined the fire service three years after I did. He always thought he wanted to do what I did so he applied and was accepted. Like you, he was a natural fit. He was really going places. One year in and he'd already been given a citation for bravery and was studying for the lieutenant's exam. He was popular at the station and a rarity in the fire service, actually in demand as a rookie.

"The sky was the limit...until a fire at a chemical plant on the south side of town. As usual, and again just like you, he was one of the first in and one of the last to leave. Back then, procedures weren't the same as they are now and every man had one set of bunker gear. Gear was cleaned once every six months or once a quarter at best. So, Scotty wore the same bunker gear he wore in that chemical fire for every incident on every shift for at least the next two or three months. He unknowingly continued to breath in PCB's and carcinogens from the chemicals that got on his bunker gear during that chemical plant fire.

"Two years later, he was diagnosed with cancer. It was later determined his cancer was caused by inhaling those lethal chemicals all that time."

Andy's mind was trying to make sense of what the Chief was telling him. He'd never heard the Chief mention a younger brother. And why was he talking about a fire that happened so long ago and one that Scott walked away from? What did any of this have to do with him?

The Chief paused and looked at Andy closely. "I'm sure some of the men have wondered why I've been so insistent about extractors in every station and the mandatory two sets of bunker gear per man. Well, this is why. The studies and information all came too late to save Scott. My biggest goal after becoming Chief was to keep that from happening to anyone else. But ... I failed," he said, his face lined with obvious regret. "I've failed because it's happened to you, and you're someone I've come to think of as another kid brother."

Andy's eyes grew round with surprise, and he swallowed hard, not knowing what to say.

The Chief set his cup down and pulled some papers out of the satchel he'd brought in. Pulling a paper-clipped stack off the top, he laid it in front of Andy. "Do you remember the Warrington warehouse fire several years ago?"

Andy thought for a few minutes. "I think so. It was several alarms; a warehouse close to old downtown?"

"That's the one. If you remember, part of what was stored in that warehouse were old telephone transformers. They were stacked several deep, and the fire originated close to their location."

It was coming back to Andy. He'd only been with the department for a year or so and this had been his first really big fire, and he'd loved every thrilling minute. He had been eager to get inside and had stayed until every spark was out. Andy looked at Chief Hamilton with dawning awareness. "Are you saying ...?"

Chief Hamilton nodded. "I've gone back and analyzed and re-analyzed everything. I've consulted other chiefs across the country with similar incidents and talked to several doctors, including Dr. Parker, who I discovered by accident, is your doctor. All the evidence suggests that the Warrington fire, just like the one Scotty fought, put out a lot of carcinogens — cancer-causing agents. Unfortunately, this particular fire happened before extractors or the extra sets of bunker gear were in place. There were other fires you fought, of course, but that one had the highest intensity level of carcinogens that would have remained on your bunker gear so it is most likely the reason for your cancer."

Chief Hamilton placed the paperwork in front of Andy that detailed the fire along with the reports he'd been gathering. The Chief went on. "Based on Fire Department policy, this means your diagnosis is a result of action in the line of duty, or in other words, a workplace injury. There is a presumptive clause in this state which says that if you're a public safety officer and diagnosed with cancer, it's presumed to have been contracted as a result of your workplace environment."

Confused, Andy asked, "But what does that matter? It is what it is. Where it happened doesn't change the result."

"You're right," Chief said, tapping the sheets of paper in front of Andy. "Except — and this is important — it opens up a whole new world of assistance for you and Katie."

Turning the pages of the report, Andy looked up quickly. "What do you mean? What kind of assistance?"

Chief Hamilton placed the rest of the papers in front of Andy. "Read through this information and then talk to HR again. I've already spoken to the Director so she's aware. She's getting everything ready for you. It doesn't change things, but it will help — at least a little bit."

Chief Hamilton looked at Andy with regret. "Andy, I sincerely apologize for how I walked out on you and Katie Friday night. I felt like I was reliving a nightmare — a nightmare I thought I'd put to rest.

"I meant what I said," he continued. "I think of you as a kid brother. What you shared Friday brought back a lot of painful memories. It made me angry that this was happening at all — but especially to you. I felt — and still feel — guilty as hell that I haven't done enough to protect you and other Abernathy firefighters. You have my promise, though, I will do everything I can to help you going forward. Wait, I'd better rephrase that, *Natalie* and I will do everything we can to help — whatever you and Katie need."

Andy slowly tapped the sides of his cup, processing what Hamilton was saying. "Thank you, Jerry. I appreciate this more than you can know, and I know Katie will too. We will look this over," Andy said and ruffled through the papers. "One thing you haven't told me though . . . what happened to Scott?"

Andy could tell from the stricken look on Jerry's face, it was a question he'd rather not have to answer. He looked down and took a deep breath. Raising his head, he looked Andy in the eye. "Scott died. Fourteen months after the diagnosis."

The words hung in the air between them.

Andy swallowed hard and looked down, staring unseeing at the pages in front of him.

"I thought that would be the answer, but I still had to ask," he said after awhile.

"Andy, listen to me, it doesn't mean that's what's going to happen here. Every case is different, and I've heard on good authority that you're stubborn. They say stubbornness, at least for something like this, is a particularly good thing."

Andy shrugged. "I guess being stubborn might come in handy for more than peeving Bentley after all."

He grimaced as he felt a wave of pain.

Jerry started to laugh but then eyed Andy. "You okay?"

"Just the same old thing," Andy said, breathing easier. "I guess it's time for a pain pill. We've been gone longer than I thought we would be."

Pulling his eyes from Andy's pale face, Jerry looked at his watch. "Whoa, I didn't either. The time got away from us but this was too important to wait. I bet Rogers has dropped Jernigan off by now. Bentley is going to have both our heads." He started to rise.

Andy hesitated, and Jerry sat back down. "Something else?"

"So, you didn't tell Bentley about any of . . . this," Andy said, indicating the papers with a slight wave of his finger.

"Nope. I'm leaving that up to you."

"Me?" Andy asked, surprised.

"If the day and time comes, you'll know, and you'll do the right thing."

"How can you be so sure I'll know?"

"I trust your judgment. You may be a pain in the neck, but you've got great instincts."

Andy stared at the papers in front of him and then looked up at Jerry and nodded. "Well, alright then."

After gathering the papers into a neat stack, they picked up their empty cups and stood to leave. "And one more thing," Jerry said. "Some of the old timers may remember my brother, but let's keep that between us. The younger ones don't need to know any of my back history."

Andy nodded. "Of course, I respect that, but I also think it would be helpful for everyone to know. It might help them understand and appreciate why you're so insistent about the extractors, the bunker gear . . . well, you know. But that's your call. Until you say differently, this stays between us."

CHIEF HAMILTON PULLED INTO the drive at the station, and Andy opened the door. Before getting out, he turned to Chief Hamilton and held up the stack of papers in his hand. "Thank you for this, and thank you for well . . . thank you for everything."

Chief Hamilton studied him for a quick second then said, "Get out of here. Good luck with Bentley."

Andy smiled. "Yeah, I'll probably need it." He watched the Chief drive off. Clutching the papers in one hand, his other arm tight against his side, he headed into the station. He bit his lower lip against the growing pain and tried to look nonchalant as he opened the door and walked inside.

Jernigan was back and everyone was sitting around the kitchen table except for Bentley. Hedrick was at the kitchen counter prepping for dinner. They all turned and looked when he came in. Hedrick stopped working and stepped toward the table, looking at Andy, as he wiped his wet hands on an already-soggy kitchen towel.

"Guys," Andy said, nodding in their general direction as he walked quickly through the kitchen.

"Garrett," they said in unison, eying him and noting the papers he carried.

"You missed lunch," Hedrick called after him.

"Thanks. Not hungry," Andy called back as he dropped the papers on his bed. He yanked his locker door open and pulled out the pain pill bottle from his duffel bag. Gulping one down, he sat on the edge of his bed and cradled his head in his hands, waiting for the pill to take effect.

After Andy's quick appearance and just as quick disappearance, the crew exchanged looks around the table. With a pointed look at the group, Jernigan pushed his chair back and walked to Andy's room. Leaning against the door jam, Jernigan cleared his throat.

Andy looked up. "So how was the new engine?" he managed to ask.

"It's a beauty," Jernigan replied. "You're gonna need an engineering degree to run that panel. You wouldn't believe all the bells and whistles," he said, noting Andy's tightly clenched hands and the beads of perspiration on his forehead. "So, everything okay with you?"

Annoyed, Andy asked, "Why is everyone so interested in my business all of a sudden?"

"I don't really care about your business. I just care if it has anything to do with us," Jernigan replied evenly. "When the Chief comes in and swoops you away for several hours during shift, we figure there might be something that involves us. Just saying." He finished with a small shrug.

"Seems to me a chief swooped you away for a few hours today as well," Andy replied. "Do I need to ask *you* if everything is okay?"

Jernigan shrugged again. "Told you about what I evaluated. How about you? What did Chief Hamilton want you to evaluate?"

"Paperwork," Andy said, motioning to the stack of paper beside him. "He gave me paperwork." The pain pill was beginning to work and feeling better, Andy stood and clapped Jernigan on the shoulder. "Come with me," he said and steered Jernigan back to the kitchen where the others were waiting.

"Guys, it seems like there's a lot of concern pointed my direction, and I appreciate it," Andy began, "but everything's good. Really. If there comes a time I need to tell you more, I will. Come on ... you have my word," he said, seeing their skeptical looks. "For now though, knock it off with all this fretting and speculating. You're driving me crazy! You're like a bunch of old mother hens.

"In fact," Andy said, eying the wet dish towel on the edge of the cabinet, "Let's liven this place up ..."

With a wicked grin, Andy stepped to the cabinet and picking up the soggy towel, threw it at Canfield, hitting him square in the face. Andy laughed and took off running down the hall to the engine bay, throwing taunts and dares over his shoulder. Surprised, Canfield gasped and jerking the soggy towel from his face, took after Garrett in a run.

The others looked at each other and grinned — this was more like the Andy Garrett they knew. They sprinted down the hall and into the engine bay where laughter and wet towels and water flew. The battle raged until Bentley hit the door with a loud bang that echoed around the bay as the metal door hit the wall.

"What the hell is going on in here?" he yelled. The fun and frantic activity came to a sudden halt as all eyes turned to Bentley whose face was contorted with rage.

"Just a little harmless fun, LEW-ten-ant," Andy smirked as he weighed a dripping towel in one hand. "Want to join us?" Andy stepped toward Bentley and raised the towel as if to throw it.

"Garrett, you do that and I guarantee you'll be sorry," Bentley fumed, taking a couple of steps back as Andy advanced.

"Will I be more sorry if I do … or more sorry if I don't?" Andy mused with a smug look, still advancing on the retreating Lieutenant. The others stood frozen in place. They looked anxiously between Andy and Bentley, unsure of what Andy would do.

"Garrett, I'm warning you …" Bentley began again but was interrupted by the tones sounding and the dispatcher's voice announcing a multi-vehicle accident over the intercom. The games and antagonisms were forgotten, at least for the moment.

THE FINAL PLANNING MEETING for the fire station field trip had gone well. Katie's students were so excited about the field trip that they'd asked for a countdown calendar, and Katie had happily obliged. She knew Andy and the C shift crew would make their anticipation well worth the wait.

She had braced herself for the meeting and inquiries from Sally about having another substitute. But the inquires never came. When the meeting concluded, Katie quickly stood to go, anxious to talk to Andy, and was surprised when Sally approached her.

"Do you have a minute?" Sally asked, looking down and nervously rubbing the table between them.

Katie had too much on her mind to deal with Sally's barbs but didn't want to be rude so she sat back down.

Sally cleared her throat. "Well, I owe you an apology." Her eyes darted up quickly to meet Katie's startled look before she looked back down.

"I've said some terrible things to you and been horribly brazen about things I've suggested about Andy. I am truly sorry. I think I was just jealous, and I am horrified at what I've said. Can you please forgive me?"

Katie stared at Sally as the classroom clock clipped the air with loud, crisp strokes.

Sally forged on. "Katie, I would like for us to be friends — true friends — if you're willing. I know that's asking a lot right now, but maybe in time?"

Katie blinked a couple of times. "Well, I..." She stopped and cleared her throat. "Thank you, Sally. I appreciate your apology. You're right. I do have an amazing husband who would never do any of what you suggested." Katie's voice quivered as she stood and quickly gathered her things.

Sally watched Katie, her eyes soft with understanding.

Katie turned and did her best to smile. "And I agree. I would like for us to be friends, too. That would be nice."

Pleased, Sally only had time to nod in agreement before Katie hurried from the room.

KATIE SIGHED AS SHE walked quickly from the school building to her car. Surprised and relieved at Sally's apology and her seeming change of heart, Katie was grateful for one less thing to worry about. She remembered Andy's admonition about Sally and determined to keep her guard up — at least for awhile.

Andy had been on her mind all day but talk about the field trip brought him to mind even more. His treatments were scheduled during school hours, and she never had a second thought about whether to go with him or not. Katie could tell he wanted her with him, even though he'd objected weakly at first about her missing school. She'd made the decision and he'd willingly conceded. She was going.

Unfortunately, being away from her class meant writing lesson plans for a substitute. She cringed thinking about the last substitute and hoped other subs would handle her class better. All she could do would be to prepare and hope for the best.

Finances was the next item on her mental checklist. With Andy working fewer hours at RITE2U, their income was going to be less, which meant expenses would need to be reduced or eliminated. "Where to even start?" Katie mumbled under her breath.

Finally, her mind went to the quiet evening ahead as she turned onto their street. She wished the evening could be with Andy but that wasn't possible with him on duty. She still felt guilty for pushing him to go this morning and hoped she'd done the right thing. She looked at her watch: 4:45 p.m. On a sudden whim, she drove past their house and headed to the station. She'd see how he was doing first-hand.

―――――

ANDY CLUNG TO THE mop handle Bentley had thrust into his hand when they'd returned from the traffic accident. He gripped it to steady himself as Bentley's wrath rolled over him in waves. If he felt better, he'd give Bentley his best smirk, but it wasn't in him — not right now. Bentley had ordered the others out of the bay and had let them, and Andy, know — in no uncertain terms — that the responsibility for the clean-up was Andy's and Andy's alone. No one else could help. Period. Bentley slammed the door behind him as he left, a last punctuation mark to his anger.

Feeling weak, Andy slumped and used the mop handle as a support to ease over and sit on the engine's bumper. A few minutes later, he heard the door from the living quarters quietly open. He stood and started pushing the mop around in half-hearted circles in case Bentley was returning to chew on him some more. Instead of Bentley though, he saw Jernigan's head appear around the corner of the engine, followed by Hedrick's and Hart's.

"Garrett?" Jernigan asked. "You okay?"

"I'm fine. You guys aren't supposed to be in here. I don't want to get you into any more trouble than I already have," Andy said he as pushed the mop shakily around one of the puddles.

"Don't worry — we can take care of ourselves," Hart replied as he handed a mop to Hedrick who nodded and began to mop.

"Well if it's a party, where's Canfield?" Andy asked.

"We're not as dumb as we look," Jernigan said. "We've got a plan. He's keeping Bentley occupied in the TV room while we get this done."

"Guys, really. Please," Andy said, turning to face them. "It was my dumb idea. My responsibility. I've got this. Go on. I'll be there in a minute."

Jernigan stopped in front of Andy as Hedrick and Hart stepped up beside him. Their faces were somber as they studied Andy.

"Garrett, we know there's something going on with you. Whether you want to confide in us now or not, that's your call, but hear what we're saying. It's been discussed, and we're all in agreement. We've got your back. Bentley is in the dark, and it's our plan to keep him that way until you say otherwise. So, in the meantime, give it up. We're taking care of this. Now, you can either stay here and shut up, or you can go inside and risk Bentley's wrath, and ours, if you blow this. Up to you."

Andy bristled with anger. He appreciated their intention, but no one pushed him into a corner and told him what to do. Growing up, his stepfather had made sure no options were available to Andy and since leaving home, Andy had made sure no one limited or took options away from him — ever.

KATIE RANG THE DOORBELL at the guest entrance of the station. Canfield answered and with a broad smile said, "Katie Garrett! Haven't seen you in a while. Come in! Come in!" His smile was extra wide and his voice too sweet, Katie thought, as he opened the door wide.

Unsure what to think of this reception, Katie forced a smile. "Hi, Mark. How are you?

"Well, Katie, I'm doing fine. Just fine," he said as they came even with the TV room from which he deftly steered her away and down the hall.

"Lieutenant and I are in the living room," he was saying, "but I bet you're interested in seeing someone else."

"Yes, please."

"Well, just follow me then."

Katie studied Canfield as she walked behind him to the engine bay. Andy described Mark as a good firefighter but not great. And even though Canfield was a really good paramedic, Rob Hart was still better. Hart had tried to teach Canfield techniques and procedures the 'Abernathy way' when Canfield transferred in, but Mark would have none of it. He was overly confident and obnoxious. Katie remembered the one time Andy confessed being fighting mad at Bentley was when Bentley commented that Canfield was just an older version of Andy. Evidently, Jernigan had been able to keep the conversation from coming to blows when he'd suggested that Canfield *was* irritating and obnoxious, but Andy was irritating and *funny*.

Katie grinned, remembering Andy had been good with that differentiation. She thought they all had Canfield wrong. Her impression of him was a nice guy doing his best to cover up his self-consciousness and insecurity.

While Katie dutifully followed Canfield down the hall, she could see a huddle of men through the small window in the door as she looked over Canfield's shoulder. The group was standing behind the engine. Andy's back was to her, and he was holding what looked like a broom or mop. She could tell he was angry from his rigid stance. The others stood facing him, their faces serious. Jernigan was talking to Andy with an intensity Katie hadn't seen between them before. Hart and Hedrick stood beside Jernigan and seemed to be agreeing with what he was saying to Andy.

Katie barely had time to collect her thoughts before Canfield popped the door open and announced, with a pointed look at the three facing the door. "Garrett, you got a visitor." Turning back to her, Canfield said sweetly, "I have to get back to the Lieutenant. So nice to see you, Katie."

Katie started to smile in response, but her eye caught Andy as he turned around. She gave a small gasp, seeing how different he looked from that morning. His bright blue eyes were dark with dark circles under them. Fatigue seemed to hang on him, and she could see the hand holding the mop was shaking. Jernigan saw it too as he looked past Andy and caught her eye. She forced herself not to rush to Andy's side. He wouldn't want that.

"Katie," Andy said, his rigid stance melting, as he moved toward her with effort. "I wasn't expecting you, but what a great surprise." He took one of her hands and grazed her cheek with a kiss. "The guys and I were just finishing up a little cleaning —"

"Garrett, as we were saying, we've got this. Visit with your wife. Katie," Hart said by way of greeting as he took the mop, none too gently, from Andy's hand.

Katie nodded Hart's direction but couldn't take her eyes off Andy. Hoping to divert the others' attention, she said the first thing that came to mind, "Why are you guys cleaning this late in the day? I thought you'd be eating supper."

A stricken look crossed Hedrick's face as he took a quick glance at his watch and flinched. "Uh oh. My bad, guys — sorry. I didn't realize the time. I'm headed to the kitchen right now." He handed some wet towels to Hart and sprinted to the door. "Good to see you, Katie," he called over his shoulder before the door closed.

Andy smiled at Katie and pulled her toward a couple of lawn chairs that the crew usually set outside when the weather was nice. Jernigan and Hart resumed mopping, giving Andy and Katie plenty of space.

Andy sank heavily into one of the chairs as Katie sat in the one beside him. Leaning toward him, she placed her hand protectively on his arm. "Tough day?"

Andy slumped as his head fell against the back of the chair. "Yeah. It's been tough," he said, closing his eyes. "It's gotten worse through the day, but I'll adjust. Don't worry. It's just the first day after the first treatment."

"I shouldn't have pushed you to come in today," Katie said, shaking her head. "It was too soon."

"No, no - you were right. This is my fault," Andy said as he gestured in the direction of the bay.

"What's your fault?" Katie asked, glancing around the room. Everything looked normal except the few water puddles Jernigan and Hart were mopping up. "I sensed some tension in the room when I came in. Is that what's wrong?"

Andy raised his head, and keeping one eye closed, looked at Katie and said, "Well, I might have threatened Bentley this afternoon. These clowns are taking care of my punishment."

"Threatened? You threatened Bentley?" Katie asked, incredulous, her voice rising. "Andy ..."

Andy held up an index finer, stopping her. "Before you go ballistic, I only threatened him with a wet towel, and ... well, let's just say he didn't take it well. I was ordered to clean up the bay when we got back from the last run. These guys have turned nurse maid and won't let me do anything," Andy said, raising his voice so Jernigan and Hart were sure to hear. They both waved him off. Andy closed his eyes as his head fell back.

"Well, I for one, am grateful to them," Katie said. "There's nothing wrong with accepting a little help now and then is there? Especially now."

Andy rolled his head to the side to look at her and smiled.

"Andy, exactly what is it between you and Bentley? Why does he always seem to have it out for you? It's been like this ever since I've known you, and now," Katie paused as she studied Andy with concern, "now you need his support — or at least his understanding — not additional work or . . . punishment."

"You're beautiful. Did you know that?" Andy said.

Katie frowned. "I'm being serious."

"Well, I'm being serious, too. You *are* beautiful," he said, raising himself with effort. After a long look from Katie, Andy said, "Well, okay. I can't believe I've never told you the story, but now is as good a time as any. And . . . I have to admit, I am really rather famous for it in the ranks."

Katie leaned forward intently. "Well, let's hear it then."

"It happened during the physical agility test the last week of the fire academy. Bentley was acting so confidently, I couldn't help a smirk. Bentley even swaggered a bit, but he had no idea what was about to happen. There were twenty-five of us about to graduate from the fire academy, and the physical agility test was the last test before graduation the next night. I'd drawn an early number and had already gone through the paces. Everyone had practiced daily for this test so it was intense.

"Some of the guys looked my way and grinned when Bentley's turn came up, and the instructor called for a break. My plan was coming together perfectly.

"While some of the other recruits distracted Bentley, me and a few others made our little 'adjustment' to the agility course and quickly resumed our places before Bentley walked to the starting line. The instructors were totally oblivious to what had been planned which made it even easier to catch Bentley by surprise."

Unnoticed by Andy and Katie, Jernigan and Hart had stopped mopping and moved closer. This was a story that never grew old, but to hear Andy himself tell it was a rare treat.

"I knew there would be hell to pay, but it would be so worth it. No one since my stepfather had stayed on my back the way Bentley had since the start of the academy. He singled me out as the guy to beat, and for once in his life, he was actually right. No one was more surprised than I was at how well I was doing, especially since I didn't study — not even a little bit. I was also doing well on the physical tests, which put me at the top of the class ranking. I was the only person higher than Bentley, and he was furious that I was beating him and not studying while he had to scramble for every point. I've never seen anyone want to beat someone more than Bentley wanted to beat me. He wanted top spot in the class, and I did too, but after this little stunt, it wasn't going to happen for me." Andy stopped and seemed lost in thought. "It makes you wonder though, doesn't it?"

"Wonder what?" Katie asked.

"Oh, just wondering if I'd be a lieutenant today instead of him. Looking back now, it just makes me wonder." Suddenly serious, Andy turned to Katie. "I think I'd be a good officer. What do you think?"

Katie smiled at the earnestness in his voice. "I don't have to think — *I know*. You'd be an amazing officer."

Andy's pleased smile was quickly replaced by a wistful look. "I guess it doesn't matter now ..."

Katie started to protest. "Andy —"

He cocked an eyebrow. "Nope — I thought you wanted to hear this."

She looked at him closely then nodded. "Yes, I do."

"Well, all right then," Andy said and sat up in his chair. "From where I leaned against the training tower, I heard the instructor give the signal for Bentley to start. All the guys were cheering, or jeering, as he made his way through each phase. I almost felt sorry for him. He wasn't popular, but it was his own fault," Andy said with a shake of his head and a shrug. "Anyway, he was getting close to the part of the test where you had to drag a dummy."

Jernigan and Hart inched closer, knowing grins on their faces.

"Now we're getting to the good stuff. This is the part of the course where my cohorts and I had worked our magic. I joined the rest of the recruits next to the sideline where Bentley was racing toward the dummy. Now the dummies used in training are like life size rag dolls — only heavy — so they're as much like a real person as possible. Bentley ran to the top of the dummy, which was laying on the ground, and placed his hands under the dummy's arms and lifted. The dummy didn't budge, but Bentley sure did. His momentum carried him backward, and since he'd forgotten to let go of the dummy, it landed on top of him with a thud. You could hear the whoosh of air out of Bentley's lungs as he hit the pavement flat on his back. The dummy landed squarely on top of him. It worked better than I'd thought — it was absolute perfection!" Andy broke into a fit of laughter.

When Andy caught his breath, he went on. "Bentley lay stunned for a few seconds and then started trying to get up, but he couldn't. The weight .... the weight of the dummy held him firmly down," Andy said, starting to laugh again. "No one could help him because we were all doubled over laughing." Andy had to stop talking he was laughing so hard, as were Jernigan and Hart.

Katie laughed with them, almost feeling sorry for Bentley, until Andy added, "But then, his eyes locked onto mine, and the fury I saw on his face caused me to splutter and try to get serious. The instructors finally got control of the situation and lifted the dummy off Bentley. When they examined it, they found the two car batteries we'd stuffed inside to make it a lot heavier than normal. Bentley didn't know who'd planned that little surprise, but even if it hadn't been me, I would still have gotten the blame. I didn't wait for the questions to start though. I went straight to the head instructor and told him the prank had been my idea. I tried to explain it was just a joke and a little payback for the dogging Bentley had given me, but the instructor wasn't amused. The book was thrown at me, and I was lucky to have graduated at all. I didn't even go to the graduation ceremony, another reason for discipline, but at that point, it all just ran together. Bentley got his wish and graduated at the top of the academy class. I'd gained a reprimand in my brand-new personnel file, and I'd also gained Bentley's anger and hatred for the rest of the foreseeable future."

Andy finished with a big sigh and sat back. After a few minutes, he asked, "Well?"

"Well, what?" Katie replied.

"Well, aren't you going to ask me if it was worth it?"

Katie scrunched her face. "Well then, was it?"

Andy cocked his head and shrugged. "I thought it was at the time but then again, here we are today," he said, motioning around the room. "I still get the blame whether deserved or not.

"I have to admit, though," he said, looking between Jernigan and Hart with a mischievous grin, "most of it is warranted. He just begs for it. Anyway, I've got to keep him on his toes. Guys, missed a spot." Andy pointed to a small spot of water near Jernigan's boots. Jernigan jabbed the mop Andy's direction as he and Hart moved away. Andy looked back to Katie and grinned, "Gotta keep *everyone* on their toes." Pushing himself slowly to his feet, he held a hand out to help Katie up.

"Changing the subject," Andy said, "Jerry came by this morning."

Katie looked at him with surprise. "Jerry? Came by here?"

"Yep. There's a lot to tell you, but not here," Andy said, stealing a glance toward Jernigan and Hart. "He gave me a lot of helpful information. I'll tell you everything tomorrow."

Katie was curious and anxious to know what Jerry had said, but for now she just took the hand Andy offered. It was cold and trembling. She looked at him with concern, but he squeezed her hand and held it tightly as they crossed the bay. She waved to Jernigan and Hart as Andy opened the door and with a knowing grin, she waved first to Canfield and then to a scowling Bentley as they passed the living room.

Andy pulled Katie close when they reached her car, clinging to her as she put her arms around him.

"You going to be okay tonight?" she asked, her voice muffled by his shirt. "You look like you've about had it."

"I'll be fine. I'm better — now."

It felt good to be in his arms, but she finally forced herself to pull away. She looked at him with concern but then managed a believable grin. "I love you, Andy Garrett, even though you are a rogue and a scoundrel."

"And I love you for loving this rogue and scoundrel, Katie Garrett," he replied with an impish grin. After a quick kiss, Katie was in the car and waved to Andy as she pulled out of the lot. She watched him in the rear-view mirror as he turned wearily to go inside. She took a deep breath and tried not to cry.

I T WAS GOOD TO be home. Every time he walked through the door, he felt as if the house was welcoming him in a warm embrace. He'd had a place to live growing up, but it wasn't home. Somehow, he'd been lucky to find the home he'd been searching for his entire life, and he'd found it with Katie.

Andy set the file folders on the dining table, stretched, and grabbed a bottle of water from the refrigerator. He unscrewed the cap and took a long, slow drink. It tasted good, unlike everything else he'd tried to eat or drink lately. He'd been told chemo would deaden his taste buds, at least for a while, and that had proved true. He had lost weight, and his clothes hung on him in spite of Katie's best efforts to take them in or have them altered. He knew he should eat something as he perused the open refrigerator, but he saw nothing even remotely tempting. He didn't want to admit it, but high nutrient drinks might be the next thing to keep his strength up. He swirled the water in the plastic bottle; water alone sure wouldn't keep him going. He walked back to the table and pulled the file folders in front of him as he sat down.

Andy sighed. Since he had gotten off duty that morning, he'd had a radiation treatment and then worked the afternoon shift at RITE2U. He was exhausted, but Katie was due home any minute. There was some really good information about available benefits and entitlements in the papers Jerry left with him yesterday. He wanted to go through everything with Katie so they would both understand what it all meant. He flipped the first file folder open and pulled the top sheet out. He had just started scanning the first few paragraphs when a sharp pain suddenly ripped through him, wrenching him double.

He fell to the floor, his chair crashing behind him, as one wave of pain after another racked his body. He gasped for air and clutched his stomach as he inched toward the sofa, trying to reach the duffel bag holding his pain pills. He snared a loop on the bag with a desperate grab and pulled it onto the floor beside him. Between spasms, he found the bottle and with his hands shaking wildly, managed to pop the lid off, causing little white pills to fly in the air around him. After several tries, he finally plucked two off the floor and popped them in his mouth. He couldn't reach the bottle of water still on the table so he worked the pills backward with his tongue until he could swallow them. Their bitter taste was worth the relief Andy

He curled himself into a tiny ball as he laid on the floor. His arms were clutched tightly around his middle, his knuckles white as he fisted his hands in anguish. He gasped between spasms desperately waiting for the pain pills to take effect.

Minutes seemed like hours. His eyes burned, and his midsection was on fire. His breathing was ragged and raspy. He didn't want Katie to see him like this. He braced his shaking hands against the floor and tried to push himself up but collapsed.

From the fog of pain, he heard the clock strike six. Katie would be home from the store any minute. Andy pulled his arms underneath him and after bracing himself one more time, pushed with all the strength he could gather and landed sitting against the sofa, his legs at an awkward angle beneath him. He heard Katie's car door slam shut, and he flinched. Trying one last time to get to his feet, Andy couldn't catch himself before he fell back onto the floor.

Katie opened the door and saw him on the floor. "Andy!" she gasped and dropping her grocery bags, ran to where he lay on the floor writhing in pain. "I'm calling 9-1-1. Hold on," Katie said and started to get up, but Andy grabbed her hand.

"No," he managed to strangle out before another wave of pain gripped him.

"Tell me what to do!" Katie said, desperate. "How can I help?"

Andy gripped Katie's hand tighter. She clinched her teeth and waited. She leaned over him and using her free hand, gently rubbed his back and shoulders until she could feel the tension in his body start to relax.

Andy slowly loosened his grip on Katie's hand and sat up against the sofa cushions, still gasping for air. His breathing slowed as Katie stroked his face and watched him closely.

Andy gradually opened his eyes to see Katie watching him anxiously. "Katie," he managed, "I . . ." as he tried to get up.

Katie gently pushed him back down. "Just stay where you are," she said softly. "I'm here." Andy closed his eyes and rested his head on her shoulder. Glancing up, she now saw the toppled chair, Andy's duffel bag and the tiny white pain pills scattered across the floor. She managed to reach the bottle of water on the table and helped him take a drink. "What happened? Can you tell me?"

Andy, his eyes bleary, took a slow drink of the water and shifted uncomfortably. "It was pain like I've never felt before." He put his head back on Katie's shoulder and shuddered.

"Do I need to call Dr. Parker?" Katie asked.

"No — don't bother him. I think it's passed." With Katie's help, he managed to sit on the edge of the sofa. "That was something else," he said as he exhaled a shaky breath and cradled his head in his hands.

"Why don't you lie down and rest for a while," Katie suggested.

Andy didn't protest. He put his feet up and settled into the soft cushions while Katie placed a throw over him. He was asleep in seconds. Terrified by what had just happened, Katie knelt beside the sofa and watched Andy sleep. She knew he had the heart of a warrior, but it was almost unbearable to see him suffering and in so much pain.

Katie picked up the phone and relayed what had just happened to Dr. Parker's after-hours emergency number. Within minutes, Dr. Parker himself called back, asking for details. She told him everything she'd seen and what Andy had told her. From the numerous questions and pauses while they talked, she could tell Dr. Parker was concerned. He wanted to see Andy the next morning. He had already planned to call them to schedule an appointment since the trial medication had just arrived. Encouraged by this news, Katie brushed her tears away as she hung up the phone. She didn't want Andy to see her cry.

Watching Andy sleep for a while longer, Katie stroked his hair once more and rose. She set the toppled chair upright and noticed the file folders on the table. She looked at the paper on top and, after reading the first several lines, realized this must be the information Jerry brought by the station. She glanced at Andy, still sleeping soundly, and began going through the pages. The papers teemed with valuable information applicable to their exact situation. Katie began highlighting key sections and taking rapid notes.

A couple of hours later, she had finished going through the file and just pulled out their check book, along with the mounting stack of unpaid bills, when Andy moaned and began to stir. When Katie saw him struggling to sit up, she rushed to help him.

"Andy, how are you feeling?" she asked, sitting down beside him.

Andy shook his head and rubbed his eyes. "Better, but not good," he finally managed.

Katie put her arm around him and laid her head on his shoulder. "Andy, I'm so sorry. I wish I could do something to help you," she whispered.

Andy rested his head on hers. "You being close is the best medicine in the world."

Silence passed for several minutes before Katie asked, "Can I get you anything? Are you hungry at all?"

Andy took a deep breath. "Not really, but I know I should eat something. How about some chicken soup but just the juice part — not all the other stuff."

"You mean chicken broth?" Katie asked with a small laugh.

"Is that what you call it?" Andy asked, not sure why Katie was laughing.

"Yes, you silly goose," she teased, trying to lighten the mood. "Broth is the liquid part of the soup."

"Well, then some chicken broth please if you don't mind, chef," Andy said, attempting a smile; a welcome sight to Katie.

She heated some broth and sat next to him while he sipped it tentatively.

"Aren't you going to eat anything?" he asked after several sips.

"Oh, I'm fine. I had a snack while you slept." She watched him take a few more sips. "I called Dr. Parker's office. I thought they should know what happened."

Andy frowned, but before he could say anything Katie continued, "It's a good thing, too, because Dr. Parker wants us to come in the morning. The trial medication has come in."

"Really?" Andy said, instantly alert.

Katie nodded. "Andy, I'm really hoping, this new medication makes a big difference. I don't want you going through again what you did tonight."

"Well, that makes two of us. "I'm counting on that medicine too."

Katie nodded toward the table, "I read the information in the folder. I assume that's what Jerry gave you."

Andy nodded. "Yeah, that's it. I didn't have a lot of time to read it but looks like good stuff."

"Yes — it's really good and all very relevant. I didn't realize cancer was so prevalent in the fire service they had to have special legislation and benefits."

"According to Jerry," Andy said, "the reason it's so prevalent is because today's firefighters are exposed to so many carcinogens. If they're diagnosed with cancer, it's automatically assumed to be work-re-lated." Andy set the bowl on the coffee table and turned to Katie. "You may or may not remember the big Warrington warehouse fire a few years back. That was my first really big fire."

Katie nodded; that was before she knew Andy, but it had been big news. Andy continued, "It was pretty exciting. I was one of the first in and one of the last to leave."

He smiled, remembering. "But, the fire started near a stack of telephone pole transformers. They were really old and filled with PCBs, carcinogens and other lethal chemicals. Once they started burning, all those chemicals were released into the air. Jerry thinks since I was in there for so long, my bunker gear got really contaminated giving me a longer exposure resulting in cancer all these years later. Katie, that's why that paperwork is so important. There's an opportunity to collect benefits we otherwise wouldn't be eligible for and can help with the growing bills I know we have."

Andy noticed a guilty look flicker across Katie's face. "Jerry said he's notified HR about my situation. They're putting together additional information, like phone numbers, to help. We can set up an appointment with the HR Director so she can walk us through everything firsthand. Would you like that?" he asked and reached up to tuck a stray bit of hair behind Katie's ear.

"That would be great," she nodded. "It would definitely help to talk to someone who knows all the ins and outs and how to direct us."

"Good," Andy said as he shifted uncomfortably on the sofa. "I'll call HR and set everything up."

"Andy?" Katie asked.

He tensed, detecting anxiousness in her voice.

"Why did Jerry react the way he did the other night? If he already knew all of this about the cancer, why didn't he explain then? Why did he walk out like that?"

"Katie," Andy began but faltered. He really didn't feel like talking or want to tell her about Jerry's brother. "Can we finish this later? We've got something to look forward to tomorrow, and right now, I need a good night's sleep. Dr. Parker said this pill is big, and I'm anxious to see just how big it really is." He pushed off the throw and stood slowly.

Kate could tell Andy was avoiding her question. She stood and put her arm around his waist to help him down the hall, but he gently took her hand and removed it.

"I may have had a rough time tonight," he said with a weak smile, "but I don't need help walking — at least not yet — but, thank you."

"Okay — but call me if you need me," Katie said as she gave him a quick kiss on the cheek. She stepped back to the table while she kept an eye on him as he eased down the hall. He was keeping something from her, and her intuition told her it wasn't good.

D<small>R. P</small>ARKER WAS SITTING on a short rolling stool when the nurse ushered them into the exam room. He motioned to two empty chairs across from him. On the counter beside him was an official-looking box.

"So, besides yesterday, Andy, how have you been feeling since starting the chemo?" Dr. Parker began as he pulled out a pen to take notes.

Andy glanced at Katie but turned back to Dr. Parker. "The treatment itself goes fine but by the end of the day after, I'm pretty wiped out. Is that normal?"

"Yes. It is. But you're taking the day after each chemo treatment to recoup and rest — right?"

Katie looked at Andy sharply.

Dr. Parker noticed and eyed Andy with a cocked eyebrow. "Well?"

"Well, I rest while I'm at work. There's always some down time at the station, and I mainly just ride around in my truck for my other job."

Dr. Parker sighed. "Andy, your body is going through a lot right now between the cancer, the chemo, the radiation and now, starting this experimental drug. This drug is very potent, and until we know how it's going to affect you, you're going to have to take at least a few days off for us to monitor how your body responds. Is that going to be a problem?"

"No, it's not, Dr. Parker," Katie said before Andy could answer. "He'll rest. I'll make sure."

Andy shifted in his seat. He had no intention of taking off work, but he wasn't going to lose his chance at this experimental drug either. "Looks like I have no choice," he hedged, looking between the two of them. "What kind of monitoring do you have to do?"

Dr. Parker explained the medication was to be taken once a week and then went into detail about the monitoring procedures. While Andy listened, he mentally planned ways around each requirement so he could keep working. RITE2U posed no problem, but the station might prove a bit more challenging. He'd make it work though. The hardest part was going to be Katie, but he had no intention of sitting at home while bills were piling up.

After going through the procedures, Dr. Parker opened the box and pulled out a vial containing a single capsule. It was large but not as large as Andy had feared. Dr. Parker handed it to Andy. "Take this first thing in the morning. My nurse or I will be checking with you throughout the day." He turned to Katie. "We'll need you to stay with him just in case. Nothing challenging has been noted with other trial patients, and I don't expect any problems. But the first day is an important gage."

"Doc, all this precautionary stuff really isn't necessary," Andy hurried to assure Dr. Parker. "I can handle this. I always have a phone nearby."

"I'll be with him," Katie interjected firmly.

Andy sighed. This might prove more difficult than he thought.

Andy took the pill early the next morning and by noon, was flat on his back, unable to raise his head without the room spinning out of control. Katie talked frequently to Dr. Parker or his nurse, relaying what Andy was experiencing. They didn't seem concerned and just urged her to stay close. By late afternoon, the dizziness had passed, but Andy felt like he'd been slammed face first into a wall. He had a monstrous headache and his body throbbed all over. He'd called Charlene that morning to let her know he was taking a sick day. It was the first he'd ever taken at RITE2U, and he could tell it got her attention. "I'll be in day after tomorrow," he assured her. "No worries."

Now, he wasn't so sure, but he also knew he had to focus on feeling good enough to make it to the station in the morning. He couldn't give Bentley any kind of an opening, because Bentley would use anything — even a sick day — to paint him in a bad light.

The next morning, Andy felt better. "I'm feeling fine. Really," he'd promised Katie. "Go on to work. I think the worst is behind me."

Katie looked skeptical but kissed him good-bye and said, "You stay put. Andy. I mean it. I'll call you throughout the day."

Andy smiled reassuringly and stayed in bed until she left. He felt just a little dizzy while he dressed, but it quickly passed. After dreading how he might feel this morning, he actually felt better than he'd expected. His biggest dread now was the storm he'd have to weather when Katie got home that evening and discovered him gone.

He pulled into the station at 7:40 a.m. and frowned. He was ten minutes late. His only hope was that Bentley was in his office and not in the kitchen. When he opened the door and stepped inside, Bentley stood looking right at him, a smug smile spreading across his face.

"Well, let's see," Bentley said gleefully, "according to my watch, you're ten minutes late, Garrett, and that's the second infraction this quarter. One more and you're suspended. That's just one teeny tiny step away from being canned, out the door permanently or to make it simple for you, see ya!"

The rest of the crew eyed Andy with concern. He didn't look right. His face was flushed, and he didn't seem steady on his feet.

"Glad I could make your day, LEW-ten-ant," Andy fired back.

Bentley grinned and with a bounce in his step, headed to his office.

"Garrett, you look like hell. You okay?" Hart asked.

"I'm great. Just great," Andy groused as he made his way through the kitchen to his room and dropped his stuff before rejoining them.

It was a slow day; only a few minor runs, which allowed Andy time to rest. The crew noticed that Katie called several times through-out the day. That was unusual, but they could only imagine what was going on when Katie called late that afternoon. They had never heard Katie yell, but they could hear her yelling on the phone before Andy walked hurriedly to his room and shut the door.

WHEN KATIE PULLED ONTO their street and drew near the house, she hit the brake when she realized Andy's truck was gone. She had talked to him several times during the day, and he had assured her he was taking it easy. Several possibilities flashed through her mind of why his truck wasn't there but none made sense. Why would his truck be gone unless... unless... Her pulse started to race, and she felt a burning anger start to well up inside. She rarely got *really* mad, but if he'd gone to the station, this might be one of those times.

She parked and hurried inside. No Andy. The house was empty, but she found a note on the kitchen counter.

"Dearest, Katie," the note began as Katie's eyes narrowed, "I know you'll be upset, and I am so sorry for that, but I've gone to the station. I'm feeling fine and just couldn't lay around when I needed to be there. I hope you'll not be too mad. Remember how much I love you. I'm just trying to be the best husband I know how to be, which means doing my part to support us. I love you. Forever. Andy."

Katie slowly and carefully laid the note back on the counter. She was absolutely livid. She'd worried all day about leaving him alone and had called him as often as she could. Thinking back on their conversations, he'd never out and out lied, but he sure hadn't been totally truthful either. She stalked back and forth across the living room, trying to get her anger under control, but the more she paced, the angrier she became until it boiled over. She picked up the phone and dialed his number.

"Hey," Andy said timidly when he finally answered after the fourth ring.

"Hey?! . . . Hey?! Is that all you can say to me?! You lied to me, Andy Garrett!" Katie exploded into the phone. "You lied to me! I've been worried sick about you all day; beating myself up for leaving you alone but oh no! You weren't alone were you? When did you go to the station? Had I even pulled out of the drive before you were getting dressed?"

Katie knew she was shouting and knew Andy hadn't said a word since he'd answered the phone, but she couldn't stop. It was as if a dam had burst, and her emotions were spilling over in an uncontrollable torrent. She felt like she was listening to someone else ranting like a lunatic, but when she thought of how Andy was jeopardizing his health and possibly throwing away his chance at continuing the experimental drug, she got even angrier. After taking a quick breath, started again.

"I cannot believe you did this. Not only did you go against doctor's orders, but you had no regard for my concern about you. Don't you care how worried I am about you? Don't you want to get well?"

Finally, after venting her fury, she started crying.

Andy listened on the other end of the phone, feeling like the worst possible human that had ever lived. He felt guilty to have caused

Katie such anxiety and for being the reason she was so angry and out of control, totally opposite the kind, gentle sweetheart he'd married.

When she started to cry, he felt like his heart was being ripped out of his chest. "Katie," he said in an anguished whisper, "Katie, please don't cry. I'm sorry. I'm so sorry, but I'm fine. Really — I'm fine. Katie, honey, please. Everything's okay."

"Okay? Okay?" Katie started again. "You're telling me, Andy Garrett, that everything's okay? The last I heard you have cancer. Has that changed? Has it?"

"No. You know it hasn't," Andy said softly.

"Then how can you tell me everything's okay? It's not okay!" Katie started crying but between sobs she managed, "Don't you understand? The person most precious to me in the whole world has cancer, and he's not taking care of himself. Is it too much to ask for you to take just a little time right now to rest and do what you need to do to help yourself get well? Is that too much to ask? Is it?" She couldn't go on and just sobbed into the phone.

After several long minutes of hearing Katie cry, Andy sighed, a deep, heavy, painful sigh. "Katie, I knew you'd be upset, but I had no idea you would be this upset, and I am truly sorry. I would never, *ever* do anything to cause you so much worry. If I could change things, you have no idea how fast I would, but I can't. As hard as it is for me to even say, I have cancer. But that doesn't mean that I stop living life and doing the things I love. Being at the station and with the guys helps me forget I'm sick. Please try to understand. I've felt fine today — there's been no dizziness at all. I just couldn't lay around the house when I could be here. Please . . . take a second and put yourself in my shoes. I love you, Katie. Please forgive me, but I did what I felt like I needed, and yes — what I wanted to do."

Hearing the anguish in Andy's voice, Katie regretted unleashing her anger at him. Andy was sick — very sick. All she wanted was for him to get well but to do that, he needed to take care of himself and give the treatments a chance to work. She had to acknowledge he was right though. He had a life he wanted to live. She had to give him credit for faithfully going to all the treatments and following the doctor's orders with just this one very big exception.

Andy waited silently, trying to guess what Katie might be thinking as she sniffled on the other end of the line.

"Andy," she finally said, "I hope you have a quiet night. I'll miss you. Be safe and sleep well."

Andy waited, hoping she'd say what he knew would mean she forgave him.

"I love you, Andy. Forever."

He breathed a sigh of relief. "I love you, Katie, more than you'll ever know. Forever."

Katie hung up. She sat alone in their quiet house, her head in her hands. She tried, but she couldn't stop the tears that came again.

When Andy joined them in the TV room over an hour later, he looked totally done in.

"You in trouble?" Jernigan asked with a grin.

"You have no idea," Andy said before sinking wearily into one of the recliners.

KATIE DIDN'T SLEEP WELL. Her outburst the evening before had exhausted her, but she'd also developed a massive headache. She felt guilty for unloading on Andy, but she also felt justified. Maybe he'd give more thought to slowing down and taking time to rest. As she got ready for school, she wondered how Andy had fared during the night. She hoped it had been quiet enough to give him a chance to sleep.

She filled her drink bottle with coffee — she'd need the caffeine today — and gathering her things, walked to her car. When she opened the door, her face melted into a smile. There was a single red rose on the seat and a note. Laying her things aside, she picked up the note. "My dearest, Katie: You have no idea how guilty I've felt for causing you to be so worried and upset. I hope you'll forgive me, and I promise to do better following doctor's orders — at least I'll try. I love you with all my heart. Forever yours, Andy."

Katie smiled even as tears sprung to her eyes. There was no way she could stay mad at him, but ... he was still in at least a little bit of trouble. They could finish talking about it tonight, she thought, as she held the rose to her nose and breathed in its sweet scent. She gently laid it on the seat beside her and started her car. The day ahead suddenly looked really long.

KATIE'S PHONE RANG LATER in the day as Natalie Hamilton's name and number appeared on the screen. Surprised, Katie answered tentatively.

"Katie!" Natalie said when she heard Katie's voice. "How are you, sweet friend?"

"I'm . . . I'm fine," Katie said, surprise evident in her voice.

"Glad to hear it," Natalie responded quickly. "You up for a quick cup of coffee or tea?"

After a brief hesitation, Katie said, "Well, I have a few minutes before I need to get home. Andy was on duty yesterday . . ."

Natalie understood, of course. Katie was anxious to see Andy, but Natalie had been wanting to talk to Katie since last Friday night. She was anxious to explain Jerry's behavior, from a wife's point of view. Jerry told her he'd talked to Andy at the station but encouraged her to wait before contacting Katie to give her a couple of days to absorb everything he'd shared with Andy.

"I understand, and I promise you'll be home long before Andy," Natalie assured her.

Fifteen minutes later, they were at the same coffee shop that Jerry and Andy had visited a few days earlier. After putting creamer in their respective cups of tea, Natalie softly blew on hers before taking a sip and setting the cup back on the table as Katie did the same.

"Jerry tells me he went by the station and talked to Andy a few days ago," Natalie began.

Katie nodded. "He gave Andy a tremendous amount of information, research, phone numbers, contacts. It was amazing and all so helpful. Neither of us knew how prevalent cancer is in the firefighter ranks. This has all been so eye opening. We're certainly learning a whole new side to the fire service; one we didn't know about and still wish we didn't. We really appreciate all the time Jerry took putting that together for us. You guys are great friends." Katie smiled sadly and looked deeply into Natalie's eyes.

"I hope it's easier for you to understand now why Jerry reacted like he did. Andy reminds him so much of Scotty."

Katie cocked her head. "Who is Scotty?"

Natalie looked at Katie with alarm. "Did Andy not tell you about Scott?"

"No...he didn't, but I could tell there was something he wasn't telling me. Who is he?"

Natalie cleared her throat. She and Jerry had both assumed Andy would tell Katie everything and in light of that, Katie would need someone to talk to. But they'd assumed wrong.

Katie sat, studying Natalie, waiting, until Natalie cleared her throat again. "Katie, my dear, I am so sorry. There is something more that Jerry shared with Andy, and we assumed Andy told you but the thing is...well...Scott was Jerry's kid brother. They were three years apart. Scott thought Jerry hung the moon, and he wanted to be just like Jerry. So, when he was old enough, he joined the fire service. A few, short years later, Scott was diagnosed with cancer."

Katie gasped. She'd noted the 'was' and the 'were' Natalie used. The word choice became more ominous when Natalie said the word cancer. "Cancer?" Katie asked weakly.

Natalie nodded. "Yes. Jerry's family was in shock when Scott told them. They'd never had cancer in their family before then or since. I will never forget that night — it was much like last Friday night. And that's why Jerry acted like he did. It brought up a lot of bad —" Natalie stopped quickly, "a lot of upsetting memories. Jerry was up over half the night Friday, went to the office and spent the day there Saturday and Sunday and went in early Monday. I've never seen him so caught up and focused on what he was doing. He knew there had to be a cor-relation of two young firefighters developing cancer with no known history in either family. He contacted other chiefs across the country and turns out, it's a lot more common than we thought ...."

Katie listened intently. Why hadn't they heard about Scott before? "What is that correlation?" Katie asked after Natalie paused.

Understanding dawned on Katie after Natalie told her of Scott's fighting a fire similar to the Warrington fire Andy had described.

"They were both exposed to high levels of cancer-causing chem-icals," Natalie finished. "Jerry's done a lot to advance firefighter pro-tection in Abernathy, but this happening to Andy, brought it all back home. He has been beating himself up with guilt ever since talking with the two of you. He really thinks of Andy as another kid brother."

"Well, that does explain a lot," Katie said with a deep exhale. "But . . .what happened to Scott?"

The stricken look on Natalie's face caused Katie to flinch. "What?" Katie asked, suddenly afraid.

Natalie took Katie's hands and looking her in the eye said, "Katie, Scott died. A little over a year after his diagnosis."

Katie's breath caught, and she jerked her hands away as she leaned back in her chair.

"He died?" Katie felt the ground shift a bit as full realization of hers and Andy's situation struck her. No matter how hard they fought, they were fighting an uphill battle and worse, a battle without much chance of their winning. Andy could only have a few months left, and she'd wasted precious time yelling at him. She'd make it up to him — somehow. She felt a fierce protectiveness of him well up inside, and she resolved, again, to do anything, *anything*, to help him and give him the best possible chance of surviving. Surviving ...

"Katie?" she heard Natalie voice coming from far away. "Katie, dear? Are you okay? I'm so sorry to have to tell you that. We thought Andy told you . . . I am so sorry to add to your distress."

Katie shook her head. "No, but I 'm glad you told me, Natalie. It brings everything into a clearer perspective with what we're fighting. It makes me even more determined to fight harder, and for Andy to be an exception to . . . to . . . He has to be . . ."

Natalie smiled sadly and patted Katie's arm. "Jerry and I intend to fight right beside both of you."

ANDY PARKED HIS TRUCK behind Katie's car, anxious to see Katie, but unsure of the reception he'd receive. He knew he deserved whatever she doled out but still, he was a bit worried. Thankfully, it had been a quiet night at the station and his shift at RITE2U had been an easy one. He'd just taken a pain pill not long ago so he was feeling pretty good and ready, hopefully, for whatever might lay ahead.

He cautiously opened the front door and had barely stepped inside when Katie launched into his arms, almost knocking him over. She threw her arms around his neck and hugged him so tight he couldn't breathe.

"Katie," he gasped. "Katie, honey, I can't breathe."

She loosened her grip ever so slightly and in a quick rush kept repeating, "Andy, I'm so sorry. I'm so sorry about last night. I shouldn't have yelled at you. I'm so sorry."

Andy grinned and was finally able to get a quick word in when Katie stopped for air. "You're forgiven, but I'd gladly be yelled at again if I could get this kind of reception the next day."

They both laughed as Katie tweaked his ear. "But Andy, I really am sorry. It . . . well . . . you scared me. I just want these treatments — whatever it takes — I just want something to work. I don't care what it is — I just want you well. I love you, Andy, so much."

ANDY'S SMILE BECAME A studious appraisal of Katie as she looked up at him so intent, so serious. His beautiful Katie. He could feel the strength of her intensity through her arms and through her body pressed so closely to his. If he could freeze time, this would be the moment, just he and Katie and so completely in love nothing else in the world mattered. Katie was in his arms, showering him with love and saying words more potent than any medicine could ever be. He knew he had to fight to beat the cancer but this woman, this amazing woman and their life together was worth fighting for and to his last breath, that was exactly what he intended to do.

T HE DIZZINESS FROM THE experimental medication had only been temporary, and Andy adjusted to the medication well. The next couple of weeks passed with the regularity of a new routine between the fire station, school, RITE2U, chemo, radiation and taking the trial drug weekly. The trial drug did seem to alleviate some of the stomach spasms and searing pains that had struck him regularly, but the chemo and radiation were taking their toll. Andy's pace had slowed noticeably, but he kept pushing himself to work.

At RITE2U, Andy tried to avoid Charlene as much as possible. He'd caught her watching him a time or two when she thought he wasn't looking. He did his best to smile, but he knew she could tell something was wrong.

Andy felt tired — and weak — but he was determined to make up some of the time he'd missed. He was working fewer and fewer hours, and he'd had to call in sick a couple of more times.

"How are, you feeling, Andy?" Charlene asked one morning when he looked especially pale.

"Doing great!" he quipped a little too cheerfully with an attempt at his best smile.

She acknowledged him with her usual perfunctory nod but made his runs light on purpose.

C shift at Station Two also noticed the changes in Andy but made no comment to Andy or to each other within Andy's hearing. They continued to cover his chores, when possible, but now there was no protest from Andy. His job performance on scene was just as efficient and professional as it had always been and always under Bentley's watchful eye. Andy had dialed his station antics way back and as a result, the atmosphere at the station was subdued — and some even thought — dull.

Bentley, however, was ecstatic. Between Andy being on the brink of suspension and his subdued behavior, Bentley thought he'd finally cowed the mighty Andy Garrett. Bentley rode his own little cloud of self-satisfaction, creating resentfulness from the crew who, as a result, became even more protective of Andy.

Andy knew things were different — he was different. No matter how hard he tried to carry on as before, his body wouldn't cooperate. True to her word, Lauren, the chemo nurse, had increased each chemo treatment until he and Katie were there at least two hours every session. The chemicals were wreaking havoc on his system. but the trial drug was helping with the original pain, at least some of the time. He hoped that the lessening of the pain's intensity meant the drug was shrinking the cancer. He was anxious for the tests scheduled in a few weeks to see if any of the treatments were working.

Dealing with his body slowing down and the anxiousness of wanting to be healthy again, he was also frustrated, and that frustration was beginning to bubble over. He was being short with everyone, including Katie, and he regretted every time he snapped at her.

The times he spent at school with Lucas were the only times he was able to put the discomfort and pain in the back of his mind. Because Lucas was living the same life Andy had growing up, they shared a special bond. Andy remembered when he was younger, wishing for someone he could talk to; someone totally separate from home and away from the verbal abuse he suffered daily. Lucas didn't have a dad so his situation was different, but he still needed someone, a male figure, to relate to and distract him from a lonely home life. Andy was glad he could be that person. The little guy had won Andy's heart with his excitement to know all about being a firefighter and fighting fires. Lucas' questions were endless, but Andy didn't mind. He loved talking to someone about the fire service who was so eager to hear.

And Lucas *was* an attentive listener. With Andy's enthusiasm about the fire service and answering Lucas' questions, their lunch times together flew by. When the field trip to the station was mentioned, Lucas literally bounced from one foot to the other. He reeled off everything to Andy he wanted to see. Andy just smiled and tousled Lucas' long hair. He vowed to make the visit to the station the best experience possible for all of Katie's students, but most especially for Lucas.

IT WAS THE END of the day, and Katie readied her things to leave. Even though Andy had been in a bad temper that morning, she was anxious to see how he had made it through the rest of the day. She could tell the chemo and radiation treatments were getting to him but was thankful the new drug seemed to be helping with some of the pain. It had been a little over two weeks since Andy had started the new drug, and even though it might be wishful thinking, Katie thought she detected some improvement. Andy hadn't mentioned any significant difference, but she was determined to think positively. She had to.

Andy had left his chemo treatment that morning and gone straight to RITE2U. She wasn't sure how much longer he could keep the same pace, but he was determined.

Sally had volunteered to take her class again this morning. In fact, Sally had volunteered to take her class the last several times Katie was out with Andy for his treatments. Somehow, Sally had been managing to ask for Katie's class on the same days as Andy's treatments. Katie wondered how it was happening so often but no matter how, she was just grateful to Sally who was making things so much easier right now.

Afternoon lessons had gone well, and Katie had managed to finish putting the students' individual packets together for them to take home before the Thanksgiving holiday. Each packet included completed tests from the last few weeks, a page of Thanksgiving stickers, some coloring pages, and a list of suggested books to read over the holiday. She had also taken down the bulletin board with the tree and fall leaves with what each student was most thankful for. She had tucked each student's leaf into their project folder for them to take home. She smiled as she tucked Lucas' bright red leaf into his folder with 'Mr. Andy and fire trucks' written on it. She placed the leaf so Lucas would be sure to see it. The underlying excitement about the field trip to the fire station tomorrow afternoon, seemed to make the afternoon longer than usual, but it finally ended. Katie walked her students outside, their excited chatter bubbling up around her. Lucas was so excited about the field trip that Katie wasn't sure he'd be able to sleep that night. He bounced as he walked and turned to give her a bright smile and wave good-bye before he disappeared into the rush of students.

READY TO LEAVE, KATIE was reaching into her purse to pull out her car keys just as Sally stuck her head in the door.

"Leaving?" Sally asked as she came in, her coat already on.

"Yep — headed home. You?"

"Me too. It's been a long day," Sally said, trailing Katie to the door and into the hall. "Tomorrow will be good though. Field trips are always fun — especially to the fire station. Speaking of which, any single, new firemen by chance?"

"You asked that just a month ago," Katie answered with a grin.

"So, I take it that's a no," Sally sighed. "One can always hope."

They walked down the hall for a few more steps before Sally went on. "Too bad Sean Hedrick has a new girlfriend. There's another one off the market I suppose."

"How do you know Sean? And how do you know that he's got a girl-friend?" Katie asked, stopping mid-step and looking at Sally with surprise.

Sally stopped beside Katie. "I must have heard it somewhere. It's not a big deal."

Katie tilted her head and suddenly smiled, catching Sally off guard. "It's Mandy, isn't it?" Katie asked. "Mandy Fitzhugh is Hedrick's new girlfriend, but the question is, how do you know Mandy?"

In the seconds that hung silently between them and the uncom-fortable look on Sally's face, things came together in Katie's mind. Andy had mentioned just last night that Hedrick and Mandy had evi-dently become a couple over the last few weeks. Hedrick was on the phone with Mandy after dinner every shift and had started hanging back at the ER to talk to her when the ambulance had a run. Andy said Hedrick was getting a lot of ribbing from the guys at the station about it and knowing Andy, he was probably dishing out his fair share.

"Well ... I thought I'd mentioned ... that I met Mandy when I moved to my new apartment," Sally said hesitantly. "We live in the same complex and have become — friends."

"And?" Katie said, eying Sally closely.

Sally cleared her throat nervously. "From the first time Mandy and I talked, I sensed she was interested in someone and turns out the guy was Sean Hedrick. She told me later she'd tried to avoid a relation-ship with him because of a bad experience in her past, but evidently Sean is worth getting past it."

Curious, Katie asked, "A bad experience?"

"Well, it seems her dad died in a fire when she was little ..."

"That's terrible. I'm sorry Mandy lost her dad so young," Katie said sympathetically, "but I'm glad she feels differently about firefight-ers now. I think she and Hedrick make a great pair. By the way, I'm just curious. Does she know you and I work together? Since she's talked about Andy, I thought you might have mentioned it."

Sally looked uncomfortable. "I'm pretty sure I told her we teach at the same school."

Katie chuckled, "Is it a problem we teach together?"

"No, silly, of course not," Sally said, opening her car door. Eager to change the subject she said, "See you for the big day tomorrow. I'm looking forward to meeting this Sean character."

"You're gonna like him," Katie said. "He's a great guy, and from what Andy has said, he's also an amazing cook."

Katie got in her car and turned toward home after waving goodbye to Sally. It all made sense now. Mandy was how Sally knew the exact days and times to ask for her class. In spite of their rocky history the years they'd worked together, Sally had become more than just a co-teacher these past several weeks and had been true to her word. She had become a friend.

Pulling in behind Andy's truck, Katie sat deep in thought for several minutes. It was such a relief that Sally knew the situation. Katie had been working so hard to manage everything by herself she never realized what a comfort it would be for someone to know and help. She felt lighter and smiled as she opened her door. She couldn't wait to tell Andy. He still didn't want to tell the guys at the station about his situation or even the people at RITE2U. He was afraid they would think he was weak or couldn't pull his weight. But with the exception of Bentley, Katie knew the others would think just the opposite.

She opened the door and found Andy sitting on the couch with his feet on the coffee table. He smiled brightly as she walked over and sat beside him. Looking into his sparkling blue eyes, she couldn't help but return his smile. She was more deeply in love with this adorable man now than she had been when he'd asked her to marry him. She wasn't sure how she could be; she just knew she was.

Andy put his arm around her. "It's my beautiful wife home from the noble pursuit of teaching children."

Katie smiled, but before she could respond, he pulled her to him and kissed her with a passion she hadn't felt from him in a while. She returned his kiss as he wove his fingers through her hair, pulling her even closer. His nearness, the warmth of his lips on hers, and the urgency with which he kissed her, caused her pulse to race.

"You're feeling better," Katie said breathlessly and smiled before he drew her mouth to his again.

When Andy finally broke the kiss, he placed his forehead against Katie's. "I *am* feeling better," he said with a pleased grin. "I've had no pain today, and Katie . . . I think that trial drug might just be working."

"Oh, Andy, that's wonderful news!"

"I don't want to get ahead of myself, but it's such a relief to feel even a little normal again."

Katie sighed happily as Andy kissed her again and then looking into her eyes, he said solemnly, "But about this morning . . ."

Katie put a finger to his lips and then placed her lips on his in acceptance of his unspoken apology.

ANDY HIT THE STATION'S kitchen door with a bang as he walked in at 7:15 a.m. Jernigan and Hart were already at the table, drinking coffee with another pot brewing. Plastic containers of the cookies Hedrick had baked were spread across one end of the table. Andy plopped boxes of juice drinks down on the other end.

"Well, look who's here early," Bentley spouted as Andy strode in. "What's wrong, Garrett? Clock broken?"

Jernigan and Hart, in turn, scowled at Bentley before turning to Andy. "Anything else need carrying in?"

"There are some plates and a couple of cases of water in the truck if you don't mind."

Andy started to follow Jernigan and Hart out, but before he made it to the door, Bentley said, "Garrett."

Andy turned, eying Bentley.

Bentley sneered, "I know we've gotta give these kids the grand tour, but they'd better not get in the way. Just because your little wife is their teacher, they don't get any special treatment."

Fury welling inside, Andy balled his hands into fists and strode toward Bentley, stopping within inches of his nose. "LEW-ten-ant," he said in terse, low tones, "I don't believe I've asked for any special treatment. You might do well to remember that we are public servants and students are part of the public. You should hang around. Who knows . . . you might even learn something."

"Garrett, I ought to —"

Bentley choked back the rest of his reply when Jernigan and Hart reentered the kitchen carrying the items from Andy's truck.

Both stopped mid-stride.

"Everything okay here?" Jernigan asked, looking between the two, as he set what he was carrying on the table. Hart followed suit, eying the situation and remaining just behind Jernigan.

"Everything is fine, gentlemen," Andy said, still glaring at Bentley. "Just fine. Isn't it, LEW-ten-ant?"

Bentley's jaw muscles jerked. "Yes, it is, and Garrett," he spat out, "you just remember what I said." Bentley quickly sidled down the cabinet and out of Andy's reach before scurrying down the hall.

Andy's taut body relaxed, and he caught himself against the edge of the cabinet where Bentley had just stood.

Jernigan rushed over, but Andy brushed him aside. "Did you guys get everything?" he asked, rubbing his face with one hand as he turned and leaned against the cabinet.

Jernigan and Hart exchanged glances and then looked at Andy with concern.

"Yeah, we got everything," Jernigan said. "What was all that about? We were only gone a few seconds."

Andy moved to the table and dropped into one of the chairs. "Nothing I can't handle." He grimaced with a quick stab of pain and realized he'd left his duffel bag in his truck. "Forgot my bag," he said, standing. "I'll be right back."

Walking in with Hedrick a few minutes later, Andy walked straight to his room and pulled the bottle of pain pills from his bag. He popped one in his mouth and quickly washed it down with some bottled water. He sat on the edge of his bed, waiting for the pill to take effect. A few minutes later, he pushed himself to his feet and opened his locker door to stow his duffel bag, but when he opened the door, a white envelope fell to the floor.

He set the duffel bag inside the locker and looking inside the envelope found $250 cash in tens and twenties. His mouth dropped open. He glanced around and then looked down again at the cash in his hand. The guys . . . it had to have been the guys. Tears started before he quickly blinked them back. How did they know how badly he and Katie needed the money right now? They'd already picked up a lot of his workload and now this? He awkwardly brushed a stray tear away and cleared his throat. He would think of a way to let them know how much this meant to him and Katie. He carefully placed the envelope in his duffel bag, re-zipped the flap and closed his locker door.

KATIE STOOD OUTSIDE THE door of the school bus, clipboard in hand, checking for last minute instructions from the school or the station. The noisy chatter from inside the bus made her smile. There were no absentees today, not surprising for a field trip and especially a field trip to the fire station. Sally stood at the door of the second bus and gave Katie the thumbs up her group was ready to go. Katie returned the thumbs up and nodded to Mr. Kennedy, the driver, as she stepped on board the bus. Katie dropped the clipboard onto the front seat and stepped to the center aisle. She surveyed the bus and in a commanding voice said, "High five!" Sudden quiet replaced the noisy chatter as hands shot in the air, fingers spread wide. She smiled her approval.

They'd been practicing that signal for several weeks preparing for today, and the students had responded right on cue.

"Thank you, everyone! That was excellent! Is everybody ready?" Katie asked as heads bobbed eagerly. "We're about to pull out. Remember that while the bus is in motion, you're not. You're sitting in your seat, hands to yourself. Right?" she nodded, looking into each face.

His eyes trained on Katie, Lucas sat by himself at the front of the bus. In spite of the cold, he wore tennis shoes, no socks and a light jacket, too small for him, but evidently the only jacket he owned. Katie had made sure Lucas always had school supplies and money for lunch, but even with hers and Andy's current money concerns, she made mental note to pick some things up for him. Katie smiled at Lucas who sat perched on the edge of his seat, his face glowing with excitement. "We're ready to roll, Mr. Kennedy," Katie said as she sat down.

"We'll be there soon," she said over her shoulder as the bus jerked into motion.

***

HEDRICK HAD SPENT THE last shift baking cookies, sealed them in plastic containers to keep them fresh and put them in the freezer of C shift's refrigerator. He recounted the containers. Two were missing. Those A and B shift guys . . . he grumbled.

Everyone, minus Bentley, was putting cookies on platters or arranging the plates, bottles of water and boxes of juice drinks on the kitchen counter and table.

"Fire truck napkins? Seriously?" Canfield asked, holding one up by the corner for everyone to see. "Who brought these?"

Hedrick's face went red as he snapped the napkin out of Canfield's hand. "I brought them if you don't mind," Hedrick huffed, placing it with the other napkins beside an overflowing platter of cookies.

Winking at the group, Canfield said, "So, let me get this straight, Hedrick. You went to the store looking for fire truck napkins, and when you actually found them, you put them in your little buggy and bought them just for today? Is that how it all happened?"

Hedrick, looked at the four sets of teasing eyes trained on him and finally said, "Well, not exactly..."

"Oh? So just exactly how *did* it go then?" Canfield said, seizing the opening as he leaned back and crossed his arms in front of him.

"Is it really that big a deal?" Hedrick snapped. "I thought we wanted to make today special for the kids. Right?"

"Well, sure, Rookie," Andy said with a grin. "We just wanted to know what kind of pansy firefighter would buy fire truck napkins."

Hedrick gritted his teeth. "Well..."

They all leaned in closer, waiting for his answer.

Hedrick looked at each of them in turn, shook his head and said in a rush, "If you must know, Mandy bought them for me to bring."

A chorus of oh-ho's and smirks followed, causing Hedrick's already-blushing face to turn deep crimson.

"We knew there had to be more to the story, Rookie," Andy chuckled. "Just took a little digging to get the full scoop."

Hedrick acknowledged the jibes with a slight smile. "I should have known," he muttered.

Andy's phone buzzed. Katie. "Hey there, beautiful," he said, followed at once by the chorus of "Hey, beautiful," from the guys.

Katie laughed. "We're just around the corner."

"Pull around to the back. We'll be waiting for you there."

"Show time, guys. They're around the corner." Everyone, but Bentley, filed into the bay. Jernigan hit the button to raise the back door as the firefighters lined up just inside.

Andy spotted Katie immediately as the first bus pulled in. She was standing and facing the students, who were busy looking out the window and obviously not listening to her. She said something, and all of the students, except Lucas, turned and faced her as their hands shot in the air. Lucas' nose was pressed to the bus window, his mouth rounded into a little "o."

Andy smiled and moved to the door of the bus as it opened. "Hey," he said with a wide smile as he took Katie's hand and helped her down the steps.

In spite of herself, Katie blushed, and her heart fluttered. Andy looked amazingly handsome in his uniform, even after losing so much weight. She returned his smile. It was good to see him feeling so well. "Hey, yourself," she responded, giving his hand a squeeze as she stepped aside to let the children pass. "Gotta go. I need to run some interference." She smiled over her shoulder as she motioned a couple of students back toward the group.

Edging his way through the other students, Lucas stepped in front of Andy and stuck his hand out. Andy smiled and shook Lucas' hand. "Welcome to Station Two, Lucas."

"Thank you, Mr. Andy," Lucas responded in a serious tone. Andy tousled Lucas' hair and grinned as they walked toward Katie. Katie smiled, seeing them approach, as she maneuvered her class against the wall to make way for Sally's class.

Once Katie's and Sally's classes were assembled inside, Jernigan tapped the button to close the door and Andy stepped in front of the group. He waited patiently, with a smile, until he had their full attention.

He caught Katie's eye and with a wink began. "Welcome to Station Two. My name is Andy Garrett. I am a firefighter and a paramedic for the City of Abernathy. The guys behind me are firefighters and paramedics, too." Andy waved them all forward, and each one introduced themselves with Hedrick, being the rookie, going last.

Stepping back in front of the group, Andy asked, "How many of you have been to a fire station before?"

He looked for raised hands and raised one of his own as an example. No hands went up. "What?!" Andy exclaimed, staggering back as if shocked.

The children all laughed, and Katie smiled at his theatrics. He loved this stuff.

"No one?! Oh my! Guys, we've got our work cut out for us," Andy said, feigning seriousness as he looked over at the crew. "We'd better get started."

The students were split into groups with a firefighter assigned to each group. After seeing all the tools and equipment on the engine, each student sat in the driver's seat for a couple of minutes and smiled for photos with his or her firefighter guide. They each examined the ambulance and walked around inside the "box" before sitting behind the steering wheel. After peeking in at Bentley, who was busily acting like he was working, the group took a look at the TV room and took turns sitting in one of the recliners before seeing the workout room, the bedrooms and finally the kitchen where the children eagerly descended on the refreshments.

Andy and Katie, along with Sally and the C shift crew, stood to the side watching the cookies, juice and water rapidly disappear.

Sally edged her way over to Andy and Katie, who were standing together, watching and smiling.

Andy eyed Sally warily as she approached and stopped next to him.

"Hey, Andy," she said shyly.

Andy looked at Katie, who smiled before turning back to watch the children.

"Sally," Andy said with a dismissive nod.

"How are you?"

Andy looked at Sally, confused. He usually had to fend off her advances, even with Katie around, but today, Sally was actually being...nice. "Well, I'm fine and you?"

"I'm doing good," she said and looked at him sadly.

Andy frowned but before anything more could be said, Hedrick walked up.

"Rookie, I think your cookies are a hit," Andy said with a grin.

Hedrick nodded and looked toward Sally, who smiled.

"Hi, I'm Sean Hedrick," he said, extending his hand.

"Sally Morton. Katie and I teach together," Sally offered, shaking his proffered hand.

Hedrick nodded in recognition. "You live in the same apartment complex as Mandy Fitzhugh, right?"

Andy looked between Hedrick and Sally, surprised.

"That's right," Sally answered nervously. "We really appreciate everything you guys have done. This has been great, but we'd probably better get everyone back to school."

"Whoa, not yet," Andy said. "We've got a grand finale. Give us just a couple of minutes."

A few minutes later, Andy steered the group back to the bay area where Hedrick, now fully dressed in bunker gear and air tank waited, holding his mask and helmet. "Anybody recognize this guy?" Andy asked, pointing to Hedrick who waved with a silly grin. The children laughed and nodded. "Well, Hedrick is going to put on the rest of the equipment we wear when we're fighting a fire," Andy said with a nod at Hedrick.

"First, he's going to put on his hood. This protects the back of our necks and ears." Hedrick pulled the hood up over his head and made sure it was securely in place before slipping on his mask. "The mask helps protect our faces and our eyes from smoke and ashes. When the tank is connected to the mask through this place here," Andy continued, pointing to the regulator, "we can breathe fresh air from the air tank on our back."

Hedrick fastened the hose and clicked the breathing regulator onto its place on the front of the mask. Immediately, the sound of his raspy breathing could be heard. "Finally," Andy said, "his helmet goes on, and he buckles the strap under his chin. The helmet protects our head from anything heavy that might be falling," Andy finished as Hedrick pulled on his gloves. As Hedrick stood in front of the group, his breathing loud and scratchy through the regulator, the children's eyes went wide with wonder, or possibly fear.

Andy clapped Hedrick on the shoulder. "Remember the goofy-looking guy with an even goofier smile we saw just a few minutes ago? Let's think a minute..."

Andy looked at the unsure looks on their faces. "Do you remember that guy who put on all this equipment to protect himself when he's fighting a fire?" A few heads nodded tentatively. "Well, that's the same goofy guy on the inside of all this gear," Andy said, resting his arm on Hedrick's shoulder. Hedrick reached over and playfully thumped Andy on the arm, and the children laughed.

Andy smiled. "Show them what we're talking about, Hedrick." Hedrick removed his helmet and then unhooked the hose from the mask to the air tank and finally, pulled the mask and hood off, which lifted his hair into spikes all over his head. Hedrick smiled his goofiest smile and waved. The children broke into cheers and applause as Hedrick bowed with a flourish.

Getting their attention, Andy continued in a serious tone. "So, if you see someone dressed like this, don't be afraid. He's a good guy. Go to him, and he will make you safe. Okay?" Heads nodded solemnly. Lucas stared, mesmerized, his mouth open. He had been less than two feet from Andy's side all afternoon and now sat spellbound at Andy's feet.

"You guys have been great," Andy continued. "It has been C shift's pleasure to have you at Station Two. If it's okay with your teachers, there's plenty more cookies in the kitchen. We'll answer any questions, and as a surprise, there's a bag of goodies for each of you on the bus when you leave." Each firefighter stepped forward and gave a big wave and bow as the children clapped and cheered.

Katie had watched Andy throughout the afternoon, trailed by Lucas, his little shadow. She smiled as Andy laughed and talked with the children, pointing out different things and answering the same questions a dozen times. One time, he'd caught her watching him, and she saw a shadow cross his face, but it was quickly replaced with a wink and the dazzling smile only Andy could give. She smiled back, elated he was acting more like himself. The children, especially Lucas, hung on his every word, and Andy, as always, thrived on being the center of attention.

Her reverie and the children's noisy chatter were suddenly interrupted when tones sounded over the intercom and each of the firefighters froze. "Truck One, Engine Two, Ambulance Two multi-vehicle accident with injuries, Scarber and Warren. Time out 14:09."

Quickly turning serious, the firefighters strode purposefully to the engine and ambulance. Andy gave Katie a quick look and then nodded toward the children as the door to the living area burst open, and Bentley ran across the bay. Eyes wide, the children stood transfixed until Katie called their practiced, "High Five" across the din. Sally called "Class! Class!" Katie's class moved to the side of the bay as Sally's group gathered nearby. They counted their students to make sure all were present before turning to watch what was happening.

From where they stood, they had a clear view of the engine as each firefighter stepped into their waiting bunker pants and pulled the suspenders over their shoulders in one quick movement. Each quickly threw on his bunker coat and jumped into the cab. The bay doors across the front of the station were rolling up as Jernigan cranked the engine. Its roar was soon joined by the motor of the ambulance where Hart and Canfield were clicking their seat belts into place.

Katie watched Andy as he slipped his headset on and adjusted the earpieces before reaching down to click his seat belt. Jernigan flipped the switch, throwing red circles of the emergency lights around the bay. The wail of the sirens began as the ambulance pulled out, followed quickly by the engine. Andy waved to Katie and then to Lucas before they rounded the corner and were quickly out of sight. Katie's heart was racing. No wonder Andy loved it so.

The front bay doors were coming down as the group turned to leave. It was past their scheduled time to depart so Katie and Sally shepherded their classes to the waiting buses. The students bounded onboard and descended on the bags of goodies left in their seats. They held up pencils with "Practice Your Escape Plan" on them, erasers shaped like fire engines or fire hydrants, coloring pages with a safety scene, a miniature firefighter badge and a cardboard fire engine to be punched and folded into a 3-D shape. There was also a plastic drinking cup with the Abernathy Fire Department logo. Each discovery was met with thrilled oohs and aaahs. The guys had certainly gone all out, Katie thought. What a wonderful afternoon they'd provided for the children. Katie glanced at Lucas, who sat transfixed in his seat.

"Lucas, what did you think?" Katie asked, smiling.

With a look of total joy, Lucas said, "That was amazing!" He turned and stared straight ahead, his eyes alight with a sense of wonder.

IT REALLY WAS TOO late to call, but he needed to hear Katie's voice. "Hey," Andy said softly when Katie answered.

"Hey," Katie mumbled, looking at the clock. Andy never called this late. She jolted awake. "Everything okay?"

"Everything's fine," Andy said. "I just wanted to hear your voice."

"Are you sure you're okay? You don't sound like yourself."

There was a long pause before Andy answered. "No, really I'm fine. It's just..."

"Just what?" Katie sat upright on the edge of the bed, the hairs on the back of her neck prickling. Something wasn't right.

"Don't mind me. Sorry I woke you up. Go back to sleep. I'll see you tomorrow."

Katie chewed her bottom lip. Something was bothering Andy.

"Katie? You there?"

"Yes — I'm here ... You sure you're okay?" she asked again, trying to hear what he wasn't saying.

Andy took a deep breath and exhaled slowly. The pain had started weakly that afternoon and grown in strength through the evening. Now his midsection was on fire. The pain pill he'd taken earlier had helped dull the physical discomfort, but it couldn't touch the raw disappointment he felt knowing the reprieve and the hope that he'd allowed himself to enjoy the last few days was coming to an end. The trial drug had helped, but now it seemed that relief had only been temporary. He stifled a groan as he rolled over cradling his abdomen.

"Andy?"

"Really — I'm fine," he managed. "No worries — go back to sleep. Just one more day until Thanksgiving break, and then we've got a whole week together."

"I am so ready," Katie said with a sigh. "And by the way, you guys were awesome today. The kids were thrilled beyond words. I wasn't sure I'd be able to peel them off the ceiling when we got back to the school. You all did a great job of making it fun and educational. Thanks for making it so memorable for the kids."

"I made it memorable for me too," Andy said under his breath but then realized he'd spoken out loud.

Katie gasped. "What?"

"Time to go to bed. Love you, Katie Garrett, and remember, I'll love you forever," Andy managed, trying his best to sound normal.

Katie wanted to ask again what was going on but decided it would be better to wait until they were together. "Sleep well, Andy. I love you. Forever."

ANDY CURLED UP TIGHTLY, clinching his sweat-soaked shirt with both fists as he fought to contain the pain. He moaned softly. How was he going to tell Katie? He — no — *they* — had begun to hope and to think about the future again but now — the pain was back and with a vengeance.

IT WAS EARLY. THE sun's rays were just beginning to slant in the bedroom windows as Andy leaned against the bathroom door, arms crossed in front of him. He watched Katie put on a last touch of make-up. "As I said, you don't need to do this. I've got it."

Katie did a final survey in the mirror and walked over, stopping in front of Andy. She stood on her toes and gave him a quick peck on the cheek and a mischievous grin before continuing into the bedroom. "I'm sorry, did you say something?"

Andy rolled his eyes and turned to see her slipping on a jacket before pulling her hair out from under the collar. "I said," he started again, only to have Katie walk out of the room. She could be so stubborn, he fumed, as he followed her down the hall.

"You'd better get a move on," Katie said, tossing his RITE2U jacket to him. "We're going to be late for work."

"Katie, come on. You're on break this week. You don't need to do my job for me."

"So, explain to me, mister," Katie countered, facing him with her hands on her hips. "How is it that you scheduled yourself to work three days at RITE2U this week? You're taking vacation days from the station if I remember correctly and then signed up for extra work at RITE2U.

That was very nice of you, too, I might add, since so many others wanted time off for the holiday."

Katie eyed Andy. "But don't think I don't know what you're doing. You're trying to pick up some extra time, which means extra pay."

Katie had made her point, and he could tell she knew it. He frowned.

Katie smiled brightly. "Besides, I'd rather spend the day with you than be home by myself."

"What about all that stuff you're supposed to make to take to your parents' for Thanksgiving? When are you going to do that?"

Katie huffed. "We're doing this. You coming with me?" She picked up her purse and walked to the door.

Andy sighed with resignation and pulled on his jacket. Yes, he had married a very stubborn woman. Sometimes it was a great thing, and other times like today, it was really quite annoying.

———

ANDY HAD HAD A rough weekend. He'd tried, but he hadn't been able to hide how bad the pain was. He'd been up most of the past two nights, and Katie had been up with him, rubbing his back, getting an extra blanket, a glass of water — whatever he needed. The trial drug had done wonders, and they both had felt such hope but now, that hope was dimming. Andy was tired and discouraged and couldn't help believe Katie was feeling the same. He could tell she was putting on a brave front for him, just as he was trying to do for her.

They called Dr. Parker, and he had asked Andy some very specific questions and scheduled tests a few weeks sooner than originally planned. He hadn't seemed overly concerned and encouraged them to be patient. He assured them the treatment regimen would mean ebbs and flows in how Andy felt, but it was the combination of all the treatments that would produce the right results. He pulled some strings and rescheduled the tests for the week after Thanksgiving. They were anxious for the tests to be done and just as anxious to get the results.

Katie wasn't giving up, no matter what. She climbed into the truck and settled into her seat. Today, she would be Andy's legs, running in and out picking up packages while he drove and logged the items on the computer.

Andy opened his door and slid in, glancing at her with a half-hearted glare. "Okay. Okay. You win, Mrs. Garrett. But just this time," he said as he turned the key.

Katie smiled convincingly in return. "It'll be fun."

Andy rolled his eyes as he backed out of the driveway. Tons of fun, he thought.

———

ANDY PARKED IN HIS normal spot in front of RITE2U's office and opened his door. Katie started to get out, but Andy held up a gloved hand. "Wait here. I don't want to get Charlene riled up. I haven't been here in a couple of weeks so I don't know how she'll be. Just. Wait. Right. Here," he said pointedly.

Katie lifted her hand off the handle and sat back. "Fine then. I'll wait."

Andy gave her one more warning look before closing his door. She watched him walk toward the building and saw him turn and grin as he opened the office door and disappeared inside.

Charlene looked up at the jingle of the bell. When she saw Andy, her greeting caught in her throat. He was much thinner, his face drawn and gray, and dark circles were under his eyes.

Andy took a deep breath and smiled as he approached her desk.

"Good morning, Charlene. I'm here and ready to go."

Charlene eyed him up and down as she started gathering envelopes and packets into a bin. "So I see. We've missed you."

Andy flinched. He hated letting them down after Walt reducing his schedule. "Yes, well, I'm really sorry, but I hope to make it up to everyone this week."

Charlene plopped the bin onto the counter with a thump. "Son, we're just glad to see you back," she said and turned her usually pursed lips into a smile.

Surprised, Andy smiled in return and reached for the bin. "But," Charlene said, putting a chubby hand out, "take it easy. It's a slow day, so no need to rush. This is the morning run. I'll have a few more things this afternoon. Now, off with you." She waved him away and sat down at her desk. Her hot pink-tipped fingers started clacking on the keyboard.

Andy acknowledged Charlene's instructions with a nod, even though she already seemed engrossed in her computer screen. He picked up the bin and headed toward the door but without Charlene noticing, he took a quick detour to the break room to grab some coffee.

While waiting for a new pot to brew, Andy drummed his fingers on the countertop and couldn't help but hear Walt and Charlene talking.

"He looks awful," he heard Walt state flatly.

Andy peered around the corner to see Charlene nodding silently and looking toward the front door.

Walt shook his head and walked back to his office

Taken aback, Andy stood motionless for a few seconds before stepping over to the mirror someone had left hanging in the corner.

Studying his reflection, Andy had to agree with them. He did look bad — really bad. He shook his head and turned away.

He poured cups of coffee for himself and Katie, snapping the lids on tightly, before grabbing his bin and walking toward the front door. Startled, Charlene jumped when she saw him and then a sheepish look crossed her face. He gave her a quick wave and smile before opening the door and stepping outside.

ANDY HAD TO ADMIT it, this was working really well. He'd scan in the envelope or packet, hand it to Katie who'd take it into each business, get the required signatures and bring the signed pad back for him to finalize the entry. He'd log the information, and then drive to the next address. He glanced over at Katie. Her cheeks were rosy from the cold, and she rubbed her gloved hands together for some warmth. He reached over and turned the heater up. "Cold?"

"Just a little bit but not bad," Katie replied, watching him. "How many more this morning?"

Andy counted. "Just three —" This *was* working really well, and it was great having Katie with him.

DURING THE EVENINGS, KATIE baked pies and sugar cookies — Andy's favorite — while he slept curled up on the sofa. Before they knew it, it was Wednesday.

Andy walked into the RITE2U office a little after noon, having made his last delivery. A lot of businesses had closed early for the long holiday weekend.

"That's it," Andy said, placing the bin on the counter. As he waited, he noticed Walt's office was dark. It had never been just him and Charlene before. She had stopped typing and was studying him.

"So, you going to tell me what's going on?" she asked.

Surprised, Andy hesitated. "I . . . I'm not sure what you mean."

Charlene stood and walked over to him. The top of her head came to just below his nose, but she was still intimidating. "I asked, what's going on."

Andy opened his mouth, but she held her hand up to stop him and shook her head.

"Sorry — I know I'm being pushy and sticking my nose where it doesn't belong, but I just want you to know that the people in this office, and that includes me," she said pointing to herself, "care about you. I'm not getting mushy or emotional . . . just letting you know."

Andy's eyes widened, and he blinked in surprise.

Before he could respond, Charlene retrieved an envelope off her desk and handed it to Andy.

"Walt asked me to give this to you. He said to be sure it made it into your hands today. So, that's done. See you next week?"

Still surprised at Charlene's touching words, Andy began, "Charlene . . . I don't know what to say . . . Thank you. I appreciate it — and yes . . . yes, I'll be here next week."

Charlene suddenly reached out and pulled Andy into a tight hug. He reacted automatically by hugging her back, his arms circling her shoulders. She held him tight for a few seconds before releasing him just as suddenly. "Now, get out of here. I need to wrap things up so I can get home for the holiday too." She sat down facing her computer.

Andy hesitated. "Thanks, Charlene. Happy Thanksgiving."

Charlene nodded once and then started typing.

Andy walked to the door, glancing back a couple of times. He waved before opening the door and leaving.

"What is it?!" Katie asked when he got in the truck. "You look like you've seen a ghost."

"Charlene hugged me!" He sat back, his hands limp in his lap. "But, that was after she told me everyone at RITE2U cares about me." He looked at Katie and shook his head. "That was quite a surprise." Remembering the envelope, he handed it to Katie. He put the truck in reverse and was backing out as Katie ripped it open.

"Andy, wait," Katie said. Andy hit the brake.

The seriousness in her voice alarmed him. "What is it?"

"Look at this," she said, holding the contents of the envelope out to him.

There were two checks. One for a full week's worth of work when he'd only worked three days, and the second check was for an even $1,500. He looked at Katie, confused. "What's going on here?" He pulled back into the parking place to look at the checks more closely. The paycheck was a standard issue paycheck; just made out for more hours than he'd worked. The bottom line of the second check read:

"We care about you!"

Tears were brimming in Katie's eyes when Andy looked up in amazement. He took her hand and squeezed it tightly. She squeezed his in return as an overwhelming sense of relief engulfed her. She could pay bills for two months with this money, maybe more — bills that before now, she hadn't been sure how she was going to pay. She'd been managing on the salaries they were both still drawing but this help was desperately needed and greatly appreciated.

WHAT A TESTAMENT TO Andy, she thought, as she looked at him with pride. His easygoing charisma and fun personality drew people to him, and he seemed totally oblivious. She wished, not for the first time, that she had just a tiny bit of his spark, but he had enough spark for both of them. She sighed happily. It had been fun working with Andy this week and in spite of his resistance the first day, she could tell it had helped him plus he seemed to enjoy having her along. She reached over and stroked his cheek as he drove. He grabbed her hand and with a teasing smile, grazed her fingers with a quick kiss. She smiled back. She was one very lucky lady.

ANDY PULLED UP IN front of the Maine's family home, a stately house nestled on a rolling hill with tall trees in bright and earthy fall tones framing its two-story edifice. A circular brick drive gracefully arched from the asphalt county road to the large front porch. Wicker chairs gently rocked in the cold breeze, dotting the space which overlooked the drive and down a slight hill toward the nearest neighbor's place across the road. Colorful flower beds, rich with autumn colors, stretched to either side of the broad brick walk from the drive which led to the porch steps. Smoke curled lazily from the chimney, and Katie knew a fire was blazing in the family room fireplace and the traditional Thanksgiving Cowboys game was on the TV.

Katie turned to Andy and smiled as they unloaded the food. The woodsy scent of the fireplace smoke drifted on the cold breeze as it brushed past them. Katie's mom threw the door open wide as they stepped onto the porch. The delicious smells of Thanksgiving rushed to greet them as she ushered them in. "Get in here, you two!" She hugged first Katie and then Andy before bustling around, gathering their coats and taking pies and containers of cookies from their hands.

Katie's dad met them in the hallway, hugging Katie and shaking Andy's hand. "Welcome home, kids," he said, looking between them.

"I hope you're hungry. Your mom has been cooking for days." They walked through the entry into the family room where the football game was on the TV, and the fire was popping and crackling in the hearth. "Trenton and his crew will be here after a while. Thought we might enjoy some peace and quiet before chaos descends," Katie's dad said with a rueful smile.

Katie laughed. "Very thoughtful of you, Dad. It will be good to see them. I'll leave you two to visit while I see if Mom needs any help."

Andy and Katie's dad settled into the overstuffed leather chairs in front of the fireplace.

"How are you, son?" he asked with concern as he leaned forward, eying Andy.

"I'm holding my own, sir."

Her dad nodded and sat back. "It's bad, isn't it?"

Andy shifted in the chair. "Yes, sir. I wish I could say differently. We had high hopes for the trial drug, but now, it doesn't seem to be making a difference. Tests are scheduled this next week, but I . . ."

"Is there anything we can do?" Mr. Maine asked.

Andy thought a long time before voicing the concern that had been weighing on his mind. "Mr. Maine, I vowed to take care of Katie forever, and I meant it with my whole heart but now . . . well, hopefully it won't come to it, but if it does, my deepest concern is for Katie. Please take care of her for me, sir." He looked away, unable to go further.

THANKSGIVING DAY WAS A blur once Trenton, Stephanie and their two boys arrived. Katie's older brother, Trenton, was a financial adviser and doing quite well. He was a likable guy, tall and with a commanding presence. While Trenton was fair with light brown hair, Stephanie, his wife, had long dark hair and striking eyes that seemed to change color with what she wore. She was beautiful, and Andy thought she could have been a model. Both Trenton and Stephanie seemed to be oblivious of the striking couple they made. Chaos was a mild term for the mayhem their energetic sons brought with them. Anthony and Drexel were six and eight and went nonstop.

A favorite with the boys, they immediately sought Andy out after careening through the front door. Anthony jumped into Andy's lap, while Drexel pulled a stool close to Andy's chair. Both began talking at the same time, excitedly telling Andy about school, pee wee football, the latest card in their baseball card collection, how long until Christmas, what they were asking Santa for Christmas . . . the topics were endless.

Trenton and Katie's dad watched the game and glanced over, bemused, as Andy carried on an animated conversation with the boys. Katie stepped into the room to let the men know the meal was ready and smiled as Andy lifted Anthony from his lap and stood. Each boy immediately latched onto one of Andy's hands to lead him into the dining room. Andy gave a good-natured shrug and winked at Katie as she fell in step behind them.

Andy tried, but had been unable to eat much of the lavish Thanksgiving dinner Katie's mother had prepared. He felt horrible. The pain pills weren't dulling the pain, but he didn't want to ruin the family dinner. Katie watched him with worry, and he noticed the others stealing looks of concern his way when they thought he wouldn't see.

Following dinner, everyone retired to the back patio where a fire blazed in the outdoor pit.

"Come on, Uncle Andy. Just one game of football," Anthony begged, standing directly in front of Andy, tossing the football in the air. "We'll beat you and Dad again, just like last time."

Drexel, standing beside Anthony, grinned and nodded eager agreement.

"Thanks, guys, but I think I'll sit this one out," Andy said as he tousled first Anthony's hair and then Drexel's. "You guys get out there and show us how it's done."

"Oh, come on, Uncle Andy," Drexel wheedled, taking Andy's hand trying to pull him from his chair. "It's not as much fun without you."

"Guys," Andy began as each boy took a hand and tried to pull him to his feet.

"Anthony and Drexel Maine," Trenton's voice rang out firmly. "I believe Andy has told you he's not playing ball with you right now so you two go ahead. We'll watch from here."

The boys hung their heads and shuffled off dejectedly.

Andy smiled weakly at Trenton. "Thanks. I hate letting them down."

"Does it sound like you've let them down?" Everyone smiled as laughs and whoops resounded from the yard below.

Andy nodded with a small smile and glanced at Katie as she took his hand and squeezed it.

THE DAY HAD BEEN fun, but by early evening, Andy was exhausted and ready to go home. Gathering his and Katie's coats from the front bedroom, he turned to leave but was met at the door by Trenton.

"Can we have a word?" Trenton asked, steering Andy back into the bedroom.

"Sure," Andy replied, surprised.

Stopping midway into the room, Trenton shifted his weight uncomfortably before turning to Andy. "I don't mean to be getting into yours and Katie's business, but Stephanie and I know about your situation and . . ." Trenton paused for several seconds. "Well, we just want you to know we're here — whatever you guys need. Katie's still my little sis, so if there's anything Stephanie or I can do, all you have to do is name it."

Andy blinked a couple of times before looking down and shuffling his feet. "Trenton, I appreciate that, I really do. As a matter of fact, I will probably be calling you in the next few weeks to set some things up for us. There are some funds from work that may be coming our way due to my diagnosis, and I'd appreciate your help making sure those are obtained and invested wisely. It's government stuff so it may not be easy and will take time, but I know you'll make sure it's handled right."

"Of course, I'll make sure of it."

"I just want to make sure we've planned for every eventuality, you know — just in case," Andy said as Trenton eyed him. "But, please, don't say anything to Katie just yet. She has enough to deal with right now."

"Sure, man. No problem. You have my number. Call whenever you're ready and until then, don't worry. This is between you and me," Trenton assured Andy, clapping him on the back. "Stephanie and I want you to know you're in our prayers."

The fervency in Trenton's voice and the look in his eyes gave Andy a jolt. His own voice wavered unexpectedly. "Thank you, Trenton. I truly appreciate that." He took a deep breath, his voice breaking as he spoke. "The hardest part about all of this is Katie."

For a big guy, Trenton was surprisingly gentle. He pulled Andy down into one of the side chairs in the room and took the other. In a low voice Trenton said, "Andy, this kind of stuff isn't easy for us guys is it? We're supposed to be tough, no nonsense men. But no matter what the future might hold, these are hard times for you and Katie. The uncertainty of the future, the hardship on you physically and on both of you emotionally, these are things that no one but the two of you can fully understand. I believe though, these kinds of times make us stronger and can ultimately help us in ways we won't always understand. Know that you both have the love and support of our entire family. Neither of you are alone. It's important you remember that."

Andy nodded. "Thank you, Trenton. That means a lot. We're doing okay, and we talk about things, but she doesn't want to worry me, and I don't want to worry her, so we avoid what's possible to avoid. I don't know what's going to happen. I'm hoping for the best of course, but I just want to make sure she's alright."

"Take that worry off your plate. We'll all work to make sure both you *and* Katie are alright. Deal?" he asked, standing and holding out his hand.

Andy stood and took the proffered hand, giving it a firm shake. "Deal," he said as Trenton clapped him into a loose hug.

"What's going on in here?" Katie's voice came from the doorway. "Everything okay?"

"Of course, everything is okay," Trenton said. "Can't the two most handsome men in your life have a little private conversation?"

"You'd better not let Dad hear you say there are only two handsome men in my life. He might not take that too well."

"Indeed. You are right, little sister. Make that three handsome men in your life," Trenton laughed, giving Andy a perfunctory nod and making his way out the door.

"What was all that about?" Katie asked as Andy helped her on with her coat.

"Guy talk."

"Guy talk, huh," she said, narrowing her eyes as she eyed him closely. "You are not a good liar."

"That's a good thing, right?" he asked and walked to the door.

A ndy dropped his duffel bag on the chair at his desk. After being gone a week, it felt strange to be back at the station. It felt even stranger knowing this would be his last shift for a while. He looked around his room. All was the same. He'd hoped it would feel different, that he might feel a disconnect that would make leaving a bit simpler, but no such luck. This was not going to be easy.

Working up the nerve to tell the guys about his cancer, Andy had decided today was the day, even though they had already, apparently, known something for awhile. He planned to tell them first; he owed them that much, after all the help they'd given him the past several months. But then, he'd have to tell Bentley. That was a meeting Andy wasn't looking forward to, but he had no choice.

Bentley had been on his back constantly that being late one more time would put him on suspension and reminded him at every possible opportunity. Andy knew, if Bentley had his way, he'd be out the door completely. He didn't doubt Bentley would make good on his intentions, but Andy also knew he couldn't and wouldn't let that happen. Without this job, he had no insurance and that was absolutely critical right now. He and Katie had discussed his needing to step away several times, and he was almost relieved this would be his last shift for a while. Andy could feel himself getting weaker and realized that Chief Hamilton had been right when he said he would know the right time to tell everyone. It was hard to admit, but it was time to step aside for his sake as well as for the safety of the other guys.

Andy pulled the fresh sheets out Katie had laundered and began to make his bed one last time. He lifted the mattress to tuck the fitted sheet in when he felt something stiff at the edge where the mattress fit into the bed frame. He pulled out a manila envelope with his name in handwriting he didn't recognize. He flipped the envelope over and pulled out a rubber banded bundle. His eyes widened and his mouth dropped open at the large amount of cash he held in his hand. There were all denominations — from $5s to $100s, and everything in between. He had no idea how much was there. The corner of a piece of paper was sticking out of the envelope; on it was written, "From Your Brothers." Overcome, Andy sank onto the edge of the unmade bed, holding the bundle in his hands.

KATIE SETTLED HER STUDENTS in after Thanksgiving break by asking what fun things they'd done or different foods they'd tried over the holiday. She smiled at their exuberance but kept glancing at Lucas' empty desk. He had never missed class before. While her students ate lunch, Katie checked her mail in the school office and found an envelope containing official notice that her student, Lucas Matthews, had been withdrawn from school. There was no forwarding address, nothing in way of additional explanation or where he'd gone. She slumped against the counter and was reading the notice for the fourth time when Principal Glendon came through the door.

Katie looked up. "Do you know anything about this?" she asked, showing the notice to Ms. Glendon.

Ms. Glendon eyed the paper. "Oh, yes. His mother withdrew him early this morning. She said something about a new job and moving."

Katie's shoulders sagged. She, and Andy, especially Andy, were going to miss Lucas. She didn't know how she was going to break the news to him. Lucas was a bright spot for Andy and now Lucas was gone, and they didn't even get to tell each other good-bye.

Hart was putting the last of the lunch dishes away while Andy and the others sat around the kitchen table. Jernigan was watching a video of his daughter's ballet recital, while Hedrick thumbed through a recipe book. Canfield twirled a pencil, frowning in concentration over a crossword puzzle. Andy fingered his tea glass and looked around the circle as Hart joined them. Bentley had retreated to his office, as he typically did, after every meal. This was it — the perfect time to tell them what he'd been dreading to say.

Looking at each familiar face, he thought about the manila envelope in his locker and how much the fire service brotherhood and these guys in particular meant to him. He knew this was going to be hard, but now, when the time had come, it was even harder than he'd imagined it would be. He'd come to realize that actually telling them wasn't what bothered him — it was having to tell them anything at all. Stepping away from the fire service was something he just didn't want to do, period. He wanted to be a firefighter and be here, working with and beside these guys but . . .

Andy took a deep breath. "Guys, there's something I've been needing to tell you."

They all turned and looked at him expectantly. He looked at each one in turn. "I want you to know I appreciate everything you've been doing for me the last few months. Don't think I haven't noticed all the work you've been picking up for me."

Concerned, they exchanged glances. Garrett sounded unusually serious.

"You see, I haven't been feeling well and —"

Before Andy could continue, tones sounded over the intercom: "Engine One, Truck One, Engine Two, Engine Three, Ladder Three, Battalion 1, structure fire, 1811 Briarcrest. Time out 14:42."

At the naming of Engine Two, they looked at each other and pushed their chairs back in unison. Reaching the bay, the doors were already rolling up when they stepped into their bunker pants and quickly snapped the suspender straps over their shoulders. Andy took his seat behind Jernigan, making sure his headset was securely in place. As the engine pulled out of the station, its red lights turning and siren wailing, Andy pulled on his hood and set his helmet in his lap.

The Briarcrest address was on the historic side of town. These were some of the nicest houses in Abernathy, built during the 1940s. Most had been refurbished and renovated and most had also been enlarged during the process. Each house was exceptional in size for a residential structure. The size alone could prove to be a challenge but the age of the house and number of renovations over the years, could make things demanding on many levels. Andy shifted anxiously in his seat. Seconds later, he could see black smoke ahead and with that much smoke and the equipment dispatched, this might really be a worker.

Jernigan left space for the truck pulling in behind them as Engine Two rolled just past the burning house. Andy could see Battalion Chief Rogers on the radio already directing teams and the multiple pieces of responding equipment from the front seat of the command vehicle parked a short distance away, with an optimum view of the fire ground.

Jernigan deployed the engine where he was directed, and the ambulance pulled up a few feet further out.

Andy heard Rogers on the radio. "Engine Two, you are Attack, Engine One, you are RIT, Truck One, you are Ventilation, Alpha to Charlie."

Andy and Hedrick stepped off Engine Two with full bunker gear on, slipping on their air tanks as they moved to the back to pull the cross lay hose. While pulling hose, Andy made mental note of Chief Rogers' assignments. Engine One was Rapid Intervention, and they were busy pulling equipment and tools off their truck should they be needed for assistance. Truck One had been assigned Ventilation from Alpha to Charlie so Andy knew they would be providing ventilation with either fans or making holes in the house from the front of the house to the back. First lines had been laid and Jernigan was busy adjusting pressure as firefighters deployed around the front of the structure.

When a line and a back-up line were pulled, Andy adjusted the air tank on his back and cinched the straps tight in front. Assigned as the Attack Team, Bentley, Andy and Hedrick picked up a charged hose and made their way to the front of the house. As he stepped onto the front porch, Andy paused to slip his air mask on and made sure it fit tightly to his face. He then pulled his hood up from around his neck and attached the regulator from the air tank to his mask. Putting his helmet back on, he managed to click the chin strap snugly in place in spite of his trembling hands.

Waiting until Bentley and Hedrick completed the same steps, Andy took the lead and stepped forward, carrying the nozzle. His heart was racing, and his body was taut with anticipation. Close behind him, Bentley and Hedrick held the hose, the full weight of the charged line pulsing and heavy in their hands. Gripping the nozzle tightly, Andy took one step at a time, feeling Bentley's gloved hand on his back to make sure they didn't get separated.

Once inside, Andy couldn't help but look around in amazement. The interior was palatial with high ceilings and large rooms on either side of the grand entryway. There was no sign of fire yet, only small puffs of black smoke high overhead, hovering against the ceiling. Directly ahead was a large central staircase leading upward to a wide hallway. Andy pointed upward, and Bentley and Hedrick both nodded their understanding. Pulling the hose behind them, Andy led the way, placing his boot on the first step. His boot sank deeply into the thick plushness of the carpet. The depth of the carpet and the heavy rubber of his boots made each step difficult, forcing him to work hard to lift his legs. Andy grew weaker with each step, but Bentley pushed him impatiently from behind. Finally reaching the landing, Andy had to pause to catch his breath before continuing down the hallway.

Andy could feel the increasing intensity of the heat and smoke was filling the hallway, causing it to grow dark and visibility shrink. As they reached the end of the hall, a sudden loud boom, followed quickly by a wave of pressure, propelled all three firefighters off their feet as a wall of flames shot up on their left. All Andy could see through his mask from where he'd been thrown was a wall of orange.

Immediately, Chief Rogers was on the radio, "Defensive. We are going Defensive. Attack, exit immediately."

"Attack. Copy that," Bentley replied quickly.

Through the muffled closeness of his hood, Andy could hear three yelps from a siren followed by three blasts from an air horn which kept repeating, signaling the change to a defensive fire. He tried to follow Bentley and Hedrick, but he felt weak, his legs were shaky, and he wasn't sure of their strength.

After crawling several feet, Bentley and Hedrick were able to stand and started back down the hallway. Staying as low as possible, they tried to stay below the banking smoke and avoid the extreme heat until they reached the staircase. A slight break in the smoke allowed them to stand and make their way quickly down the stairs, pulling the hose with them.

Finally reaching the landing, Andy saw Bentley and Hedrick make it to the foot of the stairs and run for the door, but he didn't have the strength to follow them. After the difficult climb, his legs were just too weak. As he attempted to stand, he heard a sudden loud boom. The resulting wave of pressure knocked him off his feet and propelled him forward and down the stairs. He felt himself falling, a sudden wrenching pain in one ankle, and then he felt his helmet get knocked off, as he rolled several times. Landing at the foot of the stairs with a jolting thud, he felt something bang into his head and everything went dark.

CHIEF HAMILTON PACED IN front of the command vehicle, watching the crews work. This was one of the oldest, largest, and most historic houses in Abernathy. It had been a small offensive fire at first but with the explosion at the back of the house, it had just turned defensive. Three engines and a ladder truck were pouring water at the fire from every direction, but the flames didn't seem ready to give up. The size of the house made the battle a difficult one trying to deploy equipment and crews the most effectively.

Chief Hamilton watched the calm demeanor of Battalion Chief Rogers directing the crews. After the first explosion, Rogers came across the radio ordering Engine Two to exit the building and declared the fire defensive. Watching for crews to exit, Rogers simultaneously made the adjustment to teams and equipment for a defensive fire. Chief Hamilton knew Andy was with Engine Two. He waited for him and the others to exit. He was confident Battalion Chief Rogers had things in hand, but still, something was nagging at him. He felt anxious.

He heard a second loud explosion and looked toward the front door of the house when he saw Rogers sit up, looking that direction. Two firefighters, carrying a hose, stumbled out followed by a large billow of black smoke. Two men. There should have been three.

Without hesitating Rogers radioed in. "Attack, give me a PAR. I see two of you. Shouldn't there be three?"

Chief Hamilton's anxiousness jumped a notch.

There was no reply.

Rogers radioed again. "Repeat. Attack, Engine Two, give me a PAR."

Chief Hamilton watched the two firefighters who'd exited turn and look around. He could tell from their gestures and their heads craning, they were unsure of where their third person was.

In those long, silent seconds, the air hung static with anticipation.

Finally, Bentley's voice came over the radio. "Attack. PAR times two. Should be three. We have a man inside."

Bentley was out. Who was the second firefighter with him and who was still inside? Chief Hamilton's anxiety was building. This fire was growing even with the large amounts of water being poured onto it, and now, they had a man inside.

Rogers and Hamilton watched as first Bentley, then the second firefighter pulled off their helmet, mask and hood. When the second firefighter turned toward Bentley, they could see it was the rookie, Hedrick. Andy was the firefighter still inside.

Before Chief Rogers could initiate the Rapid Intervention Team, a high-pitched chirp went off. Everyone froze. A firefighter's personal alert safety system device only went off if the firefighter was down and incapacitated for over thirty seconds.

Andy must be down.

Hamilton rubbed the back of his neck and began to pace.

Chief Rogers was on the radio. "Mayday. Mayday. RIT, you are now Rescue. We have a firefighter down inside the structure."

With a "Copy that," Engine One's Rapid Intervention Team made their way quickly to the front of the house from their staging area. They tied off a lifeline to one of the large columns on the porch and moved through the front door and into the thick smoke. Once inside, they bent low and using small flashlights, they rotated a thermal imager back and forth, trying to spot the downed firefighter in the total darkness.

Moving through the main hallway, they caught a glow off what looked like reflective tape among the black smoke. They inched their way forward until the thermal imager picked up Andy's sprawled body, face down on the floor. They came up beside him and with a quick assessment, they knew he was unconscious, but breathing. They tied the other end of the lifeline to one of Andy's arms before gently rolling him over. His mask had been knocked aside, and the alarm on his air tank signaled he was critically close to being out of air. They placed Andy's mask back over his face and unhooking the regulator from his mask, replaced it with the one from the buddy bottle they'd carried in with them and restarted the flow of breathable air. They then gathered Andy, his helmet which had landed near him and the empty air bottle and moved out.

The first floor was coming alive with flames as they carried Andy through the front door, bringing with them another large cloud of black smoke as they stepped outside. Hart and Canfield were waiting at the ambulance and with a sober nod of thanks to the RIT team, they went to work as the rescuers gently laid Andy down.

Hart removed Andy's hood and mask, making sure his airway was clear and then applied a non-breather oxygen mask over his nose. While monitoring Andy's vitals, Hart made sure Andy was breathing as normally as possible in spite of some slight wheezing probably caused by smoke inhalation. He removed Andy's bunker pants and coat, looking for any signs of bleeding or trauma. Canfield cut Andy's pant leg away when he saw one of Andy's ankles swollen with and dark purple and red splotches. Canfield stabilized the ankle with a splint and placed a C collar around Andy's neck, before examining the large knot on the side of his head. Finished with the initial exam, Hart began an IV.

After doing what they could, they lifted Andy onto a gurney and into the ambulance. Canfield ran to the driver's side and Hart stepped inside the box, taking the seat next to the gurney. Hart's focus was on the monitors he was hooking up to Andy as Jernigan solemnly shut the door and gave two sharp bangs to signal Canfield to pull out.

Chief Hamilton watched everything from where he stood a few feet beyond where the doors on the ambulance had just closed. He continued to watch the ambulance as it drove off, and the siren started wailing. As the ambulance rolled away, Bentley came into view, standing next to the engine, a look of uncertainty on his face. Chief Hamilton was confident Bentley, as an officer, was fully aware that his men and their safety were his responsibility. Leaving a man inside a burning house was unacceptable. The Chief didn't want to think this had anything to do with Bentley's ongoing feud with Andy, but he would definitely get to the bottom of it.

He walked toward Bentley and stopping within a few feet, looked him in the eye. "Bentley, I want to see you and Chief Rogers in my office, 8:00 in the morning." Without giving Bentley a chance to respond, Chief Hamilton turned and strode quickly to his suburban and took off in a rush.

Bentley turned and saw a growing group of firefighters watching him, derision on their faces. They turned and walked away, leaving him very much alone.

Katie and her students were focused on the screen in front of them when the back door opened. Betty Glendon stepped inside, motioning for Katie to join her in the hall. When Katie stepped outside, Sally was standing with Betty, concern and worry on both their faces.

"What is it?" Katie asked, sudden fear edging her voice.

Principal Glendon took Katie's hands and speaking slowly said, "Chief Hamilton just called. He's on his way to get you. Sally will take your class for the rest of the afternoon."

Katie's knees went weak, and she fell against the wall. "What's happened? Do you know?" she asked frantically, looking between them.

Sally put an arm around Katie as Ms. Glendon continued, "Katie, we don't know what's happened. Chief Hamilton didn't say much when he called, just something about a fire and . . ."

Katie saw movement at the end of the hall. A white shirt. It was Jerry.

Sally followed Katie's eyes and saw Chief Hamilton striding down the hallway. Turning back to Katie, Sally said, "Katie, get your things. I've got your class. Go."

The firmness in Sally's voice spurred Katie to action. She hurried back into her classroom and gathered her things. "Class, I'm sorry I have to go. You're going to be with Ms. Morton for the rest of today."

Katie's students watched, wide-eyed, as she hurried out the door.

She ran into the hall just as Jerry walked up. With a curt nod to Ms. Glendon and Sally, Jerry took Katie by the elbow and steered her down the hall and out the door.

ANDY FELT LIKE HE was floating in a thick fog. He thought he heard a siren, but it sounded muted and far away. He tried to move, but he couldn't and groaned with the effort.

Hearing Andy's groan, Hart looked down and observed him closely. With a quick glance at the monitors, Hart patted Andy on the shoulder and said in reassuring tones, "You're doing great, Andy. Hang in there. We're almost there . . . just a few more minutes."

Andy thought he heard a voice, but it was garbled and floated away into the fog. He tried to listen, but it was . . . it was just too hard . . . and he drifted off.

———

MANDY HEARD THE AMBULANCE siren long before it squelched right outside. Through the ER doors, she saw Canfield from Station Two jump from the driver's seat and run to the back of the ambulance, throwing the doors open. Mandy pulled on a pair of gloves as she walked quickly outside, arriving at the back of the ambulance as Hart jumped down. She gasped when she saw Andy lying unconscious on the gurney. His face was chalk white with dark soot smudges streaked across one cheek.

A C collar around his neck kept his head from moving, but she could still see an ugly red lump on the right side of his head. She also noticed his splinted left ankle protruding from his pant leg.

"What happened?" she breathed as they hurriedly pushed the gurney toward the automated doors.

Hart, all seriousness, brushed the question aside while hurrying beside them. Canfield managed to say, "We had a structure fire. Andy got trapped inside."

The haggard looks on their faces begged more questions, but Mandy knew better than to ask as she hurried alongside the gurney. She was gathering Andy's vitals from Hart when she noticed activity in the ER had come to a stop. The other nurses, seeing Andy, gathered close in a worried huddle and watched as the procession rushed by.

"Exam one," Mandy said. Steering the gurney into the room, they stopped and gently pulled Andy onto the bed. The ER doctor pushed the door open. He gave them a cursory glance and began examining Andy, asking curt, detailed questions. Hart glanced at Mandy with a questioning look, but she nodded her assurance to continue. After relaying everything they knew, Hart and Canfield lingered momentarily, but with nothing left for them to do, they had no choice but to leave.

Canfield opened the door and followed Hart out. Stepping across the hallway, they leaned against the wall, putting their hands on their knees. After several seconds, Hart shook his head, straightened, took a deep breath and started toward the computer to submit the standard report.

Following close on Hart's heels, Canfield huffed. "I know a report is mandatory, but can't you at least wait a few minutes? That's Andy in there. At least wait until —"

"Wait until what?" Hart broke in sharply as he whirled on Canfield. "Until we know he's going to be okay? You and I both know he's battling a lot more than a bump on the head and a twisted ankle. Who knows what this will do to his chances of —"

Hart paused and looked pointedly at Canfield. "You did notice, Bentley made it out..." The statement hung in the air.

Canfield took a step back, his eyes wide. "You're not saying what I think you're saying — That's a strong accusation."

"I didn't say anything," Hart said and stepped back in front of the computer. "It would just be pretty convenient for Bentley."

Canfield studied Hart closely. "The lieutenant is a jerk to Andy, but surely he wouldn't —"

Before he could finish, the ER doors opened, and Chief Hamilton and Katie rushed in. Chief Hamilton glanced their way but steered Katie to the desk at the nurse's station. "We'd like to inquire about Andy Garrett, the firefighter that was just brought in. This is his wife, Katie."

With a sympathetic look, the nurse pointed to the small waiting room. "If you'll wait over there, dear, I'll find out what's going on and bring you word. He just came in, so not sure there's anything to know just yet, but I'll check."

Chief Hamilton guided Katie to a chair in the waiting room. He made sure she was comfortable before walking over to Hart and Canfield.

"How is he?" the Chief asked softly.

Hart hesitated but then said, "He took a knock on the head and looks like a sprained or twisted ankle. Normally, neither would be a big deal, but in Andy's case, well..." He didn't finish as he looked away from the Chief and glanced at Katie, who was watching them apprehensively.

Chief Hamilton nodded solemnly. He walked back to the waiting room and took a seat by Katie. He put an arm around her and gave her a reassuring hug. "The guys said from what they could tell, he has a bump on the head and a twisted ankle. But try not to worry. I have it on good authority Andy's got a really hard head, so he'll be fine." Jerry's tease succeeded in bringing a small smile to Katie's face. He patted her shoulder and said again, as much to Katie as himself, "He'll be fine. They'll take good care of him."

Canfield and Hart finished their reports and joined Jerry and Katie in the waiting room. The nurse let them know Andy was being evaluated and promised she'd bring word as soon as she knew. The time stretched into an hour and then another. They were still waiting, when the ER doors slid open and the rest of Engine Two's crew walked quickly in.

"How is he?" Hedrick asked.

"We don't know yet," Hart replied. "They've been evaluating and working on him for a couple of hours."

Hart's glance came to rest on Bentley, standing behind the others. "What's he doing here?" Hart growled as he started toward Bentley, his face red with anger, Canfield close on his heels.

Before they could get to Bentley, Jernigan stepped between them and put his hands out to stop them. "Not here, guys. Not here. I gave him no choice," Jernigan said, pushing Hart and Canfield back. Hart flinched angrily, but Jernigan held his ground. "He's the station officer so he's here whether any of us like it or not."

Hart jerked free of Jernigan's outstretched arm, still glowering at Bentley. Chief Hamilton stood and walked to the group.

"Gentlemen, we will discuss this later," he said in low tones. "I suggest we all take a seat."

They walked slowly to the waiting area where Katie sat, her eyes wide, as she looked from man to man, confused at the sudden tension in the room.

Chief Hamilton ignored Bentley as he sat down, placing himself between Bentley and Katie. No one spoke and no one met her eye when Katie looked at each of them. Her concern for Andy was all consuming. She turned to stare at the floor with nothing to do but wait.

The minutes stretched into hours. The frantic rush of the ER gradually subsided. Only an occasional person came through the sliding doors. Their swish and the quiet padding of nurses' rubber shoes on the linoleum, were the only sounds to break the hush. The evening was unusually quiet for an ER. After hearing about the incident, one station crew after another came to check on Andy. Paramedics stopped by the waiting room after dropping off the occasional patient. The ER became so crowded with firefighters that Chief Hamilton sent them back to their stations with the promise to keep them informed.

After the others left, the Station Two crew grew even more restless, occasionally talking in hushed whispers, and somberly staring at Bentley. He squirmed under their glares, turning to avoid them by looking out the window or studying his feet. Jernigan bought coffee for everyone, except Bentley, out of a nearby vending machine. Katie held the cup in her hands, feeling its heat but unable to drink it. As the evening wore on, some of the crew made a quick trip to the cafeteria, offering to bring something back for Katie and the Chief, but both declined.

As the crew milled nervously about or shifted from one vinyl waiting room seat to another, Bentley sat in the corner, alone and apart, until finally, he stood and walked quietly outside. The tension in the room dissipated immediately.

Andy could see a light. It was hazy and far away, but he felt himself drawn to it until it hovered directly in front of him. It was accompanied by a steady beeping noise that continued until it penetrated his foggy mind. He forced one eye open and then the other, peering through slits. He blinked slowly several times until things gradually came into focus.

He could tell he was lying in a hospital bed, but when he lifted his head to see more, a searing jolt of pain made him drop his head back onto the pillow with a strangled moan. He tried to move, but everything seemed to hurt. He glanced down and realized an IV, attached to the back of one hand, led to the beeping monitor. It was joined by a clear tube of oxygen ending in the small tubes he could feel in his nose.

He felt something weighing on his other arm. Rolling his head carefully to the side so as to avoid another stab of pain, he saw the weight was a head of auburn hair. Katie. She was asleep and holding his hand, her head resting on his arm. He smiled weakly. He tried to remember what had happened, but the only thing he could only remember was a burning house and falling. How long had he been here, he wondered? He lifted his free hand and stroked Katie's hair.

"Katie," he tried, his voice raspy and his throat parched dry. She didn't move. "Katie," he tried a little louder and patted her hair softly. Katie's head moved slightly and then jerked up, her eyes wide.

"Andy?! You're awake!" She stood quickly and leaning over, kissed him on the cheek. "You've been out for hours. I've been so worried! How are you feeling?" she said in a rush, studying him closely.

"Katie," he rasped, "My — head — hurts ... and ..." He groaned as he tried to move.

Katie dropped his hand and ran from the room, returning a few short minutes later with a doctor Andy didn't recognize. The doctor was closely followed by Mandy Fitzhugh.

"I'm Dr. Chilcott," the doctor said gruffly, striding into the room, his white physician's coat billowing around him. Dr. Chilcott was a thin, athletic man with a short ponytail tied loosely at the base of his neck with a thick string. His face was angular, and his eyes were hard. He had a no-nonsense attitude that wasn't very appealing, Andy decided.

"I was the on-call ER doctor today when you came in, but I am now your attending physician since you'll be moving out of the ER. But enough of that, how are you feeling?" Dr. Chilcott asked brusquely as he studied Andy.

"My head hurts," Andy repeated with a croak. "And I'm ... I'm thirsty."

Mandy hurried to the other side of the bed and lifted a plastic cup of ice chips and water to Andy's dry lips, maneuvering the straw so he could drink. He lifted his head slightly and took a couple of small sips before the pain in his head became too powerful to allow for more. He dropped his head back onto the pillow with a wince.

"A headache is totally understandable with the blow you took," Dr. Chilcott said, watching Andy. "You'll probably have that headache for several days, but it will wear off eventually. You'll probably feel dizziness for a while, too. Head trauma is always tricky, but you're awake and coherent so that's good. You may have blocks of memory loss for anything that happened from this morning until now but don't worry, it typically comes back; until then, don't force it."

"I understand you're also a patient of Dr. Parker's," he said, consulting his pad. "He's been notified and will probably be in to see you later this evening or tomorrow, but right now, we're going to get you into a regular room. You'll be spending a couple of days with us."

"A couple of days?" Andy tried to sit up, but wincing with pain, he collapsed against the pillow. "I can't..."

Dr. Chilcott, scowled and stepped close to Andy's side. "Mr. Garrett," he began in low, stern tones, "you were lucky today, but you were also injured. You have a concussion and a severely sprained ankle, not to mention some smoke inhalation. You, from what I've read in your file, are also currently undergoing chemotherapy and radiation treatment for pancreatic cancer. Does any of this sound familiar to you?"

Andy looked at Dr. Chilcott, then to Katie, and back to Dr. Chilcott. He nodded almost imperceptibly.

"Well then, there should be no questions. You're staying with us. The injuries you suffered today are serious, but ones you can recover from with time *but* — and I emphasize *but* — combined with everything else your body is dealing with, it needs time to rest and heal. I'd like for Dr. Parker to see you and then we'll determine where to go from there. I'll see about getting you into a room, and Ms. Fitzhugh can get you something to eat if you're hungry."

"I'm just thirsty," Andy said in a coarse whisper. He felt like he hadn't had water for days.

"Of course. Ms. Fitzhugh will take care of what you need. Your throat is probably feeling pretty raw right now — that's the smoke inhalation. It will feel that way for a few days, but we'll give you some breathing treatments which will help." Dr. Chilcott noted something on Andy's chart and then headed to the door, but he stopped and turned around. "Mr. Garrett, your overall condition is serious. I encourage you to acknowledge that and work with me to help you."

Dr. Chilcott's flint-like eyes studied Andy, and suddenly Andy realized how exhausted he truly felt, both mentally and physically. The pain he'd been enduring for months was now joined by a splitting headache, a throbbing pain in his ankle and a burning throat. He had been fighting hard, but it was getting harder every day. Andy exhaled slowly and nodded in resignation. He didn't want to admit it, but the struggle was becoming more than he could manage.

He looked at Katie and saw the worry on her face. He squeezed her hand and did his best to smile.

Dr. Chilcott nodded. "Very good. And now, I believe there's someone else here who'd like to see you. You attracted quite the crowd earlier. They've cleared out, but he's been waiting."

Andy looked at Katie, puzzled, until Dr. Chilcott stepped out, and Jerry Hamilton stepped into the room.

"Let me know if you need anything," Mandy said as she handed the cup of ice chips and water to Katie. "I'll let you know as soon as a room is ready." She closed the door behind her as she followed Dr. Chilcott.

Andy tried to smile. "Chief," he said hoarsely.

"Garrett, we just can't seem to keep you out of trouble can we?" Chief Hamilton asked with a tired grin, his drawn expression betraying his worry.

"Sir, I ..."

Chief Hamilton motioned for him to stop.

"We'll talk about what happened later. Just glad you're doing better."

"Sorry — you waited . . . so long," Andy struggled to say.

"No worries. I was busy keeping everybody updated about you. I'm amazed. You actually have friends," he said with a wry grin.

Andy tried to smile but winced.

"The crowd got too big for the waiting room, so I sent everybody either back to work or home with the promise to keep them informed. It's kept me busy, but it's all been worth it getting to end the evening on a positive note. I assume you're staying here tonight?" he said, turning to Katie.

"Yes, there's no way I'd leave," she said as Andy started to protest.

"That's what I thought," Jerry said. "Natalie pulled a few things together for you," and handed Katie a small bag.

"How thoughtful of her," Katie said gratefully. "Please thank her for me. I can't tell you how much I appreciate everything you've both done today."

"Natalie and I are here — whatever you guys need, any time, day or night. Got it?" Jerry said as he looked from Andy's drawn face to Katie's tired, anxious one. They both nodded. "I'll be back tomorrow." Jerry hesitated briefly but then forced a smile before he turned and left.

Two days later, Katie sat by Andy's hospital bed, trying to read. He'd had a flurry of visitors that morning, including Katie's mom and dad. Trenton, Stephanie and the boys had also stopped by. The boys were fascinated that Uncle Andy had been trapped inside a burning house and wanted to hear every detail. Andy's memory was returning as Dr. Chilcott had promised, and he'd been able to tell the eager boys most of what happened. They'd hung on his every word, while the rest of Katie's family looked between Katie and Andy with worry.

The visitors wore him out, and Andy had been asleep since they'd brought him back from the tests Dr. Parker had ordered. Katie rubbed her forehead with the tips of her fingers as she set the book aside and pulled her phone out to check her messages.

"Hey, beautiful," Andy said sleepily when he roused a bit and saw her.

"Hey, yourself," Katie answered, putting her phone away and taking his hand. "You've been asleep a long time."

"I just feel so tired," Andy murmured.

"That's why you need to rest," Katie said as she ran her fingers through his hair.

"So tired . . ." Andy mumbled before drifting off to sleep again.

Katie watched him sleep for a while and then picked up the book she'd been trying to read. Several minutes later, she was finally turning the first page when there was a light tap on the door. The door opened and a short lady with a plump, round face took a hesitant step into the room. Katie noticed the bright pink lipstick first and then the matching bright pink nail polish on the hand holding a beautiful potted ivy plant. A large mylar balloon attached to the pot said, "*Get Well Soon.*"

Katie stood and said softly so as not to waken Andy, "You must be Charlene. I'm Katie, Andy's wife."

Charlene smiled shyly and nodded. "Yes, I'm Charlene. It's nice to meet you, Katie. This is from all of us at RITE2U," she said and offered the plant with its balloon to Katie.

"Thank you, Charlene. This is beautiful. Andy will enjoy it and especially appreciate your thoughtfulness. I'll put it right here so he can be sure to see it," Katie said, placing it on a nearby table.

Charlene stole a glance at Andy sleeping. "How's he doing?"

"He's hanging in there."

"We heard about the fire on the news and were so worried when we heard Andy was the firefighter trapped inside, — especially since —"

"Since —?" Katie asked.

"Since we know something else is wrong, seeing how he's been feeling lately and all," Charlene said, with sincere concern.

"Well . . . yes. He is struggling with some other issues right now," Katie said, hoping she didn't sound too evasive.

"I really don't mean to pry," Charlene said, "but, well, he's just the bright spot in my day." Charlene looked at Katie with a bit of embarrassment tinging her cheeks pink.

Katie smiled with understanding. Andy was the bright spot in her day, too, but she was surprised when Charlene went on.

"Sure, the other guys are nice, but they only talk to me when they want something — their schedule redone, time off or to give an excuse why they're late — but not Andy," Charlene said with a fond glance at his sleeping form. "When he's working, he comes in and first thing every morning, he gives me a big smile and speaks *to me,* and I know he means it. He's not trying to get something from me and, well, that means a lot."

Katie studied Charlene's face, streaked with concern. Her husband's kind heart and the unassuming way he touched people never ceased to amaze her. "Charlene, that is so kind of you to say, but I know Andy thinks pretty highly of you, too."

The look of pleased surprise on Charlene's face was cut short when they both turned, hearing Andy's voice. "Hi, Charlene," he said, thickly as he tried to sit up in the bed but not succeeding.

Katie stepped to his side. "Sorry. Did we wake you?"

"No — I'm fine. I wouldn't want to miss seeing Charlene. It's nice of you to come by. Missing me?" Andy managed weakly with a tired grin.

Charlene had been standing uncertainly at the foot of the bed. But at Andy's question, raised her head and answered in her clipped business tone. "Well, of course, we're missing you. Everyone is having to share your load."

"Oh," Andy said, taken aback.

"But then again," Charlene hurried to assure them as she broke into a mischievous smile, "they don't mind. They have been emphasizing to customers that you're the one they're subbing for since you were all over the news the other night. It's their ten minutes of fame so they're more than happy to do it."

Andy breathed a short sigh of relief. "Thanks, Charlene. I'm not sure it's a good thing to be in the news but tell everyone thanks for taking care of things. Hopefully, I'll be back soon."

Charlene stole a quick look at Katie's downcast face and knew that probably wouldn't be the case, but smiled at them both. "We'll be looking forward to that."

Pointing to the ivy plant and balloon, Katie said brightly, "See what Charlene brought by?"

Andy smiled. "Why, thank you, Charlene and thank Walt for me too. That's really nice. But speaking of Walt, how is RITE2U functioning without you?"

Charlene gave a start and a quick glance at her watch. "Now that you mention it, I do need to get back. Better run but, Andy," she paused and then said, "get well. We really do miss you." With a curt nod, she turned and gave a small smile before the door closed behind her.

"Wow," Andy said. "And to think, I wasn't even sure she knew my name."

"Oh, Andy," Katie said, shaking her head amused as she resumed her seat by his bed. "Charlene just told me you're the bright spot in her day. I don't think you have any idea how you effect people. You've got a way about you that people respond to. It's just the way you are."

"I'm a bright spot in Charlene's day — really?" Andy chuckled. "You sure could have fooled me."

Andy was thoughtful for a few minutes, then said with a frown, "I don't have that same effect on Bentley though do I?"

"Bentley?" Katie asked, surprised. "What made you think of him?"

Andy shook his head slightly. "While I'm laying here ... and not sleeping," he added with a grin, "I've been thinking, and in spite of, or maybe it's because of what happened at the fire, I'm going to do my best to end the feud with Bentley. It's made things hard on the guys and ultimately it's hard on Bentley and me too."

Katie smiled. "I'm glad to hear you say that. I think Bentley will be glad too."

"Well, that remains to be seen. Bentley always finds a way to complicate things, but at least I'm going to try."

"And that's all you can do. Bentley has to do his part. You surprise and amaze me, Andy. This would be the last thing most people would think of doing if someone had left them inside a burning building."

Andy just shrugged and looked down. A few minutes passed in silence before Katie cleared her throat. She'd been dreading telling him about Lucas, but he should know. "Andy, I haven't told you something you need to know, and you're not going to like it."

Concerned at her somber tone, Andy pushed himself up with effort, and Katie took the hand he offered her.

"What is it?" he asked, looking at her intently. "Are you okay?"

"Oh, no — I'm fine. It's Lucas."

"Lucas? What's going on with him? Is he alright?" Andy asked with alarm.

"I hope so," Katie said, stroking the back of Andy's hand with her thumb. "His mother withdrew him from school Monday with no forwarding address or way to reach them. Principal Glendon said his mom mentioned something about moving for a job opportunity."

Andy's eyes dropped, and he stared at their clasped hands for a long time.

"Andy? What are you thinking?"

"Oh, nothing," he answered vaguely, "I just really liked that little guy. We had a lot in common — how I grew up, how he's growing up. We had a real connection, you know? When we talked about the fire service, I was trying to give him something to hold onto; something to look forward to, something beyond the here and now." Andy paused and sighed heavily. He looked at Katie, his eyes filled with sadness. "I saw a lot of myself in him. I hope some of what I told him sticks."

Katie reached out and stroked Andy's cheek. "Andy Garrett, I can't begin to tell you how much I love you."

Andy gave Katie a long, sad look and pulled his hand from hers. He cupped her cheek with his hand while he looked into her eyes.

"Andy, what is it?" Katie asked, sensing he wasn't telling her something.

"It's nothing . . . I'm just tired."

Katie placed her hand over his and gripped it tightly.

"Please, Andy. I can tell something is bothering you."

Andy sighed and squeezed her hand.

"I feel like the things I've wanted my entire life are slipping away and there's nothing I can do about it."

"Andy . . ."

"No, Katie — you and I both know things aren't looking good. And with this set back, they're looking even worse. I guess I felt like Lucas was my last chance to make the miserable life I'd grown up with count for something. I wanted to make a difference in Lucas' life and now he's gone to who knows where."

Andy sighed and dropped his hand from Katie's cheek.

"I hope he finds someone else to talk to. Someone to confide in." Andy turned away and laid quietly for several minutes. "I hope he'll be okay. I sure am going to miss that little guy."

Katie's heart ached at the sadness in Andy's voice. She patted his shoulder gently, but he didn't respond.

L T. MIKE BENTLEY FIDGETED as he sat in the lobby of the fire administration building. His appointment with Chief Hamilton was supposed to have started twenty minutes ago and in fact, he'd been waiting for three days. The Chief, via his secretary, had canceled the initial meeting and then sent word to be here at 8:00 a.m., three days later.

Bentley told his wife, Amy, what happened at the Briarcrest fire and about the impending meeting. They had discussed, at length, what might happen today.

Knowing this meeting could determine her husband's future with the Abernathy Department, Amy Bentley took time that morning to go over everything with him, again. They'd discussed what would be best to say and what should be left unsaid. She'd encouraged him to keep his temper in check, which always seemed to flare out of control with anything related to Andy Garrett.

Bentley confided his frustrations to Amy and even though he knew he had her support, she didn't always agree with him.

Bentley leaned forward and put his elbows on his knees. His actions and anger were justified toward Garrett. But Amy made him wonder . . . was he sure he was right? *Really* sure?

Bentley stood abruptly and began to pace the floor. What was taking so long?

The rest of shift after the big fire had been miserable. The guys were sullen and ignored him as much as possible. They'd never treat Garrett the way they were treating him, he thought.

Amy's words from this morning ran through his mind again. *"I know what an outstanding and conscientious officer you are. Let them see it, too."*

Why don't the guys see it? Why don't they think I'm a good officer? Bentley pondered as he continued to pace. Why does Garrett get more respect around the station than I do? What does he have that I don't?

Reluctantly, Bentley started listing things, one after another, and the list was long. He stopped pacing abruptly. Could it be that he was *jealous* of Andy Garrett? Had that been the problem since the academy?

The more Bentley thought, the more it bored into the very depths of his being, and he realized he had finally reached the root cause of his animosity. Why hadn't he seen it before? Garrett, with his nonchalant, devil-may-care attitude, assumed things would always go his way, and everyone would like him; which, of course, they always did. Garrett had breezed through everything at the academy and made high scores without even pretending to study. He was popular with the other academy cadets and with the fire department instructors. Bentley had even overheard the instructors talking about their reluctance to punish Garrett for the stunt he'd played. The guys on the C shift crew liked him and always took his side. Garrett was even a favorite of Chief Hamilton's, and they were close friends outside the department.

Bentley's shoulders sagged. Reality hit hard. Garrett was everything he'd always wanted to be. He had what Bentley craved and fought for at the station — respect and admiration of the crew.

Bentley knew, in his heart that, he was a capable officer, and the job was something he wanted to do. He would make the Chief see his abilities and work to gain the respect of his men. He wouldn't let this incident define him forever. He would not be known as the one who'd left a brother behind.

While they waited to get word about Andy until late the night of the fire, he'd sequestered himself in his office while the guys waited together in the TV room. He hadn't been able to even think about what might happen if... Immense relief was shared by everyone when the Chief finally sent a text late that night with word Andy was awake and responsive. Bentley's whole body had gone weak when he read the text. Even that good news hadn't tempered the suffocating weight he still felt knowing he'd failed a fellow firefighter and failed as an officer.

Things had to change. *He* had to change. He wasn't sure how or exactly what to do, but he resolved to figure it out. He would offer an apology and hope Andy wouldn't hold him out for ridicule to the others. Bentley frowned. Things had only gotten worse between him and the crew since the fire. If Andy did embarrass him, and if they couldn't work things out when Andy came back to work, life at the station would be intolerable. And, Bentley knew, depending on how this meeting went today, his days as an officer might even be numbered.

He stood and started to pace again. He knew his crew and their safety were his responsibility. He had no excuse for leaving Garrett inside at the Briarcrest fire. He should have made sure everyone who went in came out. He didn't exactly remember what had happened when Chief Rogers changed the fire to defensive, he just knew he ran and didn't account for his men. That was unacceptable in anyone's book. He had to admit the responsibility...

"Lieutenant?" Becky Madrid, the Chief's secretary was standing in the doorway. How long she'd been standing there Bentley wasn't sure, but she held the door open, waiting for him. "They're ready for you."

Bentley followed Becky to the conference room where he was surprised to see not just Chief Hamilton and Battalion Chief Rogers, but
also both deputy chiefs sitting at the far end of the conference table.
No greetings were exchanged as Bentley walked in, and Becky closed
the door.

"Lieutenant, take a seat please," Chief Hamilton said motioning
to a chair at the opposite end of the conference table.

Bentley sat, looking from one solemn face to the next. The conference room wasn't large, but the space between him and those at the
other end of the table seemed to stretch for miles.

The Chief had an open file on the table in front of him. Bentley
glanced at it, but was quickly distracted as Hamilton began to speak.
"Lieutenant, we are here today to discuss what took place four days ago
at the fire at 1811 Briarcrest. I have talked to Battalion Chief Rogers
and Firefighter Garrett and gotten their statements regarding events
that resulted in a firefighter being left in a burning building with no
support. We are here to get your perspective. Please proceed at your
own pace. This meeting is being recorded for inclusion in the incident
files as well as appropriate personnel files. The floor is yours."

Bentley felt every eye boring into him.

He had no idea what Garrett or Rogers had said in their statements, but remembering Amy's admonition, he was determined not to
let this incident define him as an officer or a firefighter. He cleared his
throat, shifted to where his back was straight, his shoulders square and
with a confident voice began, "I appreciate the opportunity to share my
perspective ..."

And from there, he related with clear and accurate precision, every
detail leading up to the point where the defensive fire alarm sounded.
At that point, Bentley stopped abruptly and looked down, studying

his hands in his lap. The minutes stretched on in silence as the chiefs waited for him to continue at this critical juncture.

Finally, Chief Hamilton glanced at the other chiefs and then at Bentley. "Lieutenant? Are you finished?"

Bentley, knowing he might be jeopardizing advancement or even his career, took a deep breath and chose to do the right thing. He looked up and said, "At the point of the defensive fire alarm sounding, I panicked and exited the building. I have no recollection of what happened from the time the defensive alarm sounded until I heard Chief Rogers asking for a PAR from Engine Two as Attack." Bentley's heart was hammering.

"No recollection?" Chief Hamilton asked.

Bentley shifted in his chair. "No, sir. No recollection."

Battalion Chief Rogers and the other chiefs exchanged pointed looks. Turning to Bentley, Chief Rogers said, "Lieutenant, are you aware some feel that your leaving Firefighter Garrett inside the fully involved structure on Briarcrest was a conscious decision? Before you answer, be aware that your answer is being recorded and can and will be used for legal purposes if necessary."

Chief Rogers' question washed over Bentley in a numbing rush. He must not have heard correctly. Surely, no one would seriously think he would intentionally harm Andy. He looked at the somber faces at the far end of the table, each of them appraising him with narrowed eyes. His heart started pounding while his face flushed red.

"I beg your pardon?" Bentley finally managed, "I don't believe I heard the question correctly. Are you asking if I left Garrett behind *on purpose?*"

"That's exactly what we're asking, Lieutenant," Chief Hamilton responded evenly.

Bentley felt like he was going to explode. He wanted to get up and pace the floor, but instead, he gripped the arms of the chair until his knuckles were white. His men thought he'd left Andy on purpose? Had things really gotten that bad between them? It was in that moment the realization hit. It had gotten that bad. He had failed them as an officer, and as a leader, but more importantly as a fire service brother. He took a deep breath and shook his head, trying to collect his stampeding thoughts.

"Lieutenant?" Battalion Chief Rogers asked. "Please respond to the question."

Lt. Bentley took a deep breath and after looking each chief in the eye, said firmly, "I swear by everything I hold dear that the thought of leaving Andy Garrett, or anyone, *ever*, in a burning building has never even entered my head. My problem with Garrett is ... personal, but under no circumstances would I *ever* consider doing harm to anyone. I am a firefighter and a paramedic, and I took an oath to help and serve others, not do harm. You have my solemn word."

The chiefs exchanged glances and the tension in the room seemed to lessen a small degree.

"Thank you, Lieutenant. We are glad to hear that, but the question had to be asked. Is there anything else you'd like to add?"

"No, sir," Bentley said, still reeling.

"Very well, we have some other questions for you then," Chief Hamilton said. Over the next hour and a half, each of the chiefs took turns questioning Bentley. Some questions were related to procedure and some, Bentley thought, probed his mental wellbeing. He did his best to answer and he felt he'd done well, but he was still shaken and just wasn't sure.

"Any other questions for Lt. Bentley?" Chief Hamilton finally asked. Each chief confirmed their questions were complete before Chief

Hamilton concluded, "Lieutenant, thank you for your time. We will inform everyone involved if any further actions are required regarding this incident. In the meantime, you are to continue at Station Two. You may go."

The chiefs turned and began talking with each other in low voices.

Bentley stood and placed his hand on the doorknob. Before he realized what he was doing, he turned around. "I panicked - okay? I panicked." The chiefs turned, their eyes riveted on him as he continued. "Nothing like that has ever happened to me before, and I swear, I never meant to leave Garrett in there. He and I have had our issues, no question, but I would never *ever* knowingly leave a man behind — Garrett or anyone else."

Bentley looked each chief in the eye and then opened the door and walked out. Closing the door behind him, he exhaled a shaky breath. His career might have just ended.

K ATIE WAS DESPERATE TO stop him.

"I'm just saying — this is a bad idea. You're not ready to go anywhere. You just got home from the hospital yesterday, and you still get dizzy when you stand," Katie pleaded. She was running out of things to say to dissuade him. He could be stubborn — very stubborn — and today, he was holding nothing back. She couldn't remember the last time she'd seen him so single-mindedly focused on anything.

Andy pulled on a shirt and buttoned it before easing on a pair of pants over his swollen ankle. He reached for his crutches as he stood. Gripping the crutches' handles with both hands, he wavered slightly, waiting for the dizzy spell to pass.

Katie could tell he was feeling unsteady and afraid he might fall, she rushed over and put an arm around his waist to steady him.

Silent and uncharacteristically somber, Andy grimaced with each step as Katie helped him down the hall. Finally reaching the dining table, Andy collapsed into one of the chairs. He was exhausted after that brief exertion, and his face was white with pain. Katie was worried, and frightened, at his insistence on going to the station today.

"Would you mind getting my coat?" Andy asked, leaning one elbow on the table, his face drawn.

She had to try one more time. "Andy, please wait — just a few days — at least until you're feeling stronger and more of the dizziness has passed. Please."

Andy looked at her, unfamiliar anger on his face, and in harsh, biting tones said, "I'm going. Either you take me, or I'll find someone else, but I'm going. This is something I have to do myself, and it can't wait ... Nothing can wait any more."

Surprised at Andy's tone but recognizing the determination on his face, Katie began, "Andy, I ..." but stopped as she watched him struggling to stand.

He started toward the front door, one painfully slow step at a time. "Fine," he gritted out between clenched teeth. "I'll figure out a way to get there."

Knowing this could be a mistake, Katie walked past him and pulled both of their coats from the closet. "Here," she said and held his coat out for him to put on. "At least there will be paramedics there if you collapse."

"Thanks for the vote of confidence."

"No problem," Katie replied before picking up her purse and turning toward the door.

Andy reached out and taking Katie's arm, turned her around.

"Katie, honey, I'm sorry," Andy pleaded with an undercurrent of urgency. "Please understand how important this is to me. After you, the fire service is what I love most and today ... well, today I'm having to walk away from it and probably saying good-bye. I need to talk to the guys in person — I need to look them in the eye when I do this. And Bentley ... well, we'll see how that goes, but I need to talk to him face to face too. Please understand."

Katie did understand. She knew how important this was to him and how hard it was going to be, but she still worried he wasn't up to it physically. Hurting for him, knowing what he was struggling to say, Katie took his hand and squeezed it. "It's okay. I do understand. I'll drop you off and won't come back until I hear from you so take the time you need. Just know I'll be anxious to get you home."

"Thank you, my love," Andy said and kissed Katie on the forehead.

———

ANDY TOOK A DEEP breath before opening the back door to the station and hobbling inside. The crew — his crew — were at the dining table and looked up as he came inside.

It was early afternoon. Jernigan, Hart, Canfield, Hedrick and Worth — the guy assigned to Two in Andy's absence — stood as one when the door opened, and Andy entered.

"Garrett, what on earth are you doing here, man? When did you get out of the hospital?" Jernigan said.

Andy took several slow steps toward them. "Mind if I join you?" He sank into an open chair, winded and pale.

They looked at each other and then back at Andy. They resumed their seats as Andy laid his crutches on the floor.

"Yesterday . . . I got out of the hospital yesterday. There were tests and blah, blah, blah. You know the drill," he said as they nodded.

"Can we get you anything?" Hedrick asked. "Coffee? Water? Soda?"

"A bottle of water would be great," Andy said.

Hedrick jumped up and ran to C's refrigerator, returning a few seconds later with a cold bottle of water he set in front of Andy.

"How are you doing?" Hart asked, studying Andy as he opened the bottle and took a sip.

"Well, that's what I came to talk to you guys about actually," Andy said, eying Worth with a pointed look.

Worth took the hint. "You know what? There are some things I need to check in the bay. I think I'll take care of them right now. Great to see you up and around, Garrett. Hang in there, man." Worth walked down the hall and was gone.

The others turned to Andy, waiting. "First of all," he said, looking at each of them, "thank you. Thank you for taking such good care of me when I was hurt. Being on this side makes me understand why so many former victims come by to say thank you. It's hard to put the feeling into words but bottom line, you guys do great work, and I got to benefit from that so . . . thank you."

They all shifted uncomfortably at his praise, high praise from one of the Abernathy Department's best paramedics.

"Come on, Garrett, don't be so melodramatic," Jernigan finally said to lighten the moment. "It was a little slow that day."

They all chuckled and a comfortable silence fell around the table.

Andy looked at each of them and cleared his throat. "There's something else I've been wanting to tell you guys. Ironically, I was about to tell you when we got the call that caused all of . . . this," he said and pointed in the direction of his ankle.

He paused and with great effort forced himself to continue. "What I've been needing to tell you is that . . . well, you see . . . well . . . it turns out I've got cancer — pancreatic cancer to be exact. And it's serious." He looked for some type of response but their faces remained unreadable so he went on.

"As you guys probably already know, from a source who shall remain unnamed," he looked pointedly at Hedrick whose face turned red, "I've been doing chemotherapy and radiation treatments since early fall. I was also chosen to take a new trial drug that's supposed to be the latest, greatest thing. I'm not sure if any of it or all of it is doing any good.

There are good days and there are bad days, as you may have noticed, but the doctors ran some tests while I was in the hospital, so we'll know something soon. I was going to tell you the day of that fire but ...."

Andy paused for several difficult seconds, fighting to hide the sadness about to overwhelm him. Finally, he cleared his throat and said what had to be said. "It's time for me to step away from active duty and go on disability leave. I can't handle the physical demands any more, and I'd just be putting you guys and myself at risk. I'd hoped to work some restricted duty but this," he pointed in the direction of his ankle again, "but this changed those plans."

"Actually," Andy paused and swallowed several times before saying, "I'm not sure I'd be coming back anyway."

Each shifted in his chair, not knowing what to say. They'd discussed Garrett being out because of the cancer treatments and now his injuries, but it had never occurred to them he wouldn't be coming back at all. It had been generally assumed he'd get his treatments, be out for a while and then be back, the same old Andy, and things go on like before. They knew his cancer was serious - just not this serious. They couldn't imagine the station without Garrett, and even harder to think he might not be coming back.

"And guys," Andy continued as they sat deep in thought, "do me a favor ... please."

They all nodded, eagerly. "Name it," Jernigan said.

"I want each of you to promise that if you feel different, see something different, anything different about how you're acting or feeling, please go to the doctor and have it checked out. During all of this I've come to find out, firefighters are especially susceptible to cancer these days because of what we breathe when we're in a fire either while it's burning or after. Chief Hamilton has shown me all kinds of studies, and they're sobering. That's why he's so high on those extractor machines for our gear because our gear absorbs cancer-causing carcinogens. I don't mean to preach," Andy said earnestly, "but this is important. Actually, it's a matter of life and death. I want you guys to be smarter about it than I was. I tried to tough it out, but I waited too long. If I'd seen a doctor earlier, I would have a better chance but now...well, now, I just don't know and the odds aren't in my favor, so..."

Hart stood up. "Garrett, you don't —"

Andy held his hand up to stop him. "I appreciate it — really — but I'd rather not talk about it anymore. I just wanted to be up front and tell you guys myself what's been going on and thank you for all the help you've given me over the past several months. Don't think I haven't noticed everything you've done, because I have. It's been an honor serving with you. I may drop in from time to time, as circumstances allow, you know, to check up on things. Gotta make sure you guys are doing everything right. We all know that without me here, this place is going to hell in a hand basket. Am I right?" he asked, holding his arms wide and grinning.

"Get over yourself, Garrett," Canfield said as they all laughed to break the gravity of the moment.

Andy laughed with them but then grew serious. "Now, for the fun part. I get to tell Bentley. He in his office?"

They all looked at him in disbelief.

"Don't to talk to him! Send an e-mail or we'll deliver a letter from you, but after what he did, how can you even think about talking to him?" Hedrick blurted out.

The others nodded firmly, murmuring their agreement.

"We even heard a rumor you put a good word in for Bentley with the Chief. We know that can't be true. If it is, then that concussion of yours is more serious than we thought," Hart said with a low laugh.

"Guys, guys," Andy said. "You gotta give Bentley another chance. Please. I think he feels really bad about what happened, and it could have happened to anybody so —"

"You have got to be kidding me, Garrett! Jernigan shouted. "After all the times he's tried to sabotage you and your career?! Have you forgotten all the extra work he laid on you for no reason? Or how about him penning the clean up on you after the water fight when you could hardly move? How about him threatening you with suspension and your job over being late a few times? Did the thought ever cross your mind your being left in that house wasn't an accident? Did that concussion knock all that out of your thick head?"

"No — I remember," Andy said. "And he wouldn't, but —"

"What about all the complaints he filed with Rogers that were unfounded? He has waged his own smear campaign against you and tried to get you fired time and time again. And now you're ready to just forget all that and be friends? Sorry — I just can't buy it," Jernigan said.

Silence fell heavy as Andy looked around the circle of faces staring at him in disbelief. Andy was beginning to wonder what he'd been thinking himself.

Bentley suddenly walked in, with his head down, coffee mug in hand. Everyone turned. Bentley nodded to the group but froze mid-step when he saw Andy.

"Garrett, what . . . what are you doing here?" he stammered.

"Actually," Andy said, standing shakily, "I've come to see you."

The shock on Bentley's face was almost worth risking a smile but no one dared.

"Okay, well . . . Okay, good then. We can talk in my office."

Andy hobbled down the hall after Bentley and didn't look back. The group looked from one to the other and shook their heads in frustration, knowing there was nothing they could do.

Andy followed Bentley into his office and gently shut the door. The cramped room was stuffy. It smelled musty and like old coffee. The schedule for the upcoming month was on the computer screen while papers and file folders were scattered across the desk. A stack of books and notebooks were piled in the lone guest chair.

"Do you mind?" Andy asked, motioning to the guest chair. "It's a little hard to stand."

"Oh, no — sorry." Bentley rushed over and cleared the books and notebooks out of the way, maneuvering the chair where it would be easier for Andy to sit.

Andy dropped into the chair, sweat glistening on his forehead. He laid his crutches down and adjusted his ankle, trying to find a comfortable position.

"Garrett, I wanted —"

"Mike, before you say anything, let me say that I hold no grudge about what happened. It was just one of those things that could happen to any one of us. Unfortunately for me, it happened to you when we were in the middle of a raging inferno."

Bentley hesitated, not sure what to say.

"This doesn't come easy for me, but I had a lot of time to think while I was laying in that hospital bed," Andy said, taking a deep breath. "We've been at each other since the academy. What was meant as a joke got out of hand, and I hate to admit it, but I've enjoyed goading you over the years."

"I had a choice to make after that fire. I could believe you left me in that burning house on purpose," he raised his hand before Bentley could say anything, "or, I could believe you were human and something else happened. I chose to believe you were human and knew the same thing could have happened to me."

Andy leaned back and took a deep breath. "I've decided to let it go. In fact, I've decided to let all this animosity between us go. I hope you'll do the same. Mike, I'm not in competition with you. I never meant to be. I don't care about being an officer. I just wanted to be a firefighter — plain and simple."

Andy stopped and watched Bentley's face turn from embarrassment to confusion and finally, relief.

"You know," Bentley said after several minutes, "I didn't believe it when Chief Hamilton said you spoke up for me during the investigation. You probably saved my career, and I sincerely thank you for that."

He hesitated, looking at Andy intently. "There's been a rumor that I left you in that house on purpose. Andy, I swear, the thought never crossed my mind. We've had our differences but I would never—"

Andy held up a hand. "Mike, stop right there. I know . . . I know."

Bentley looked at Andy and slumped with relief. "I'm so glad." He seemed to blink back tears. "I appreciate everything you've just said, and I agree. And if we're being honest here —"

Bentley paused, and Andy tilted his head with a look as if there was any doubt, before Bentley continued.

"I know I get up tight. I'm a perfectionist. And believe it or not, I'm harder on myself than I am on anyone else. If there is someone or something that gets in the way of me obtaining my goal, I hold that someone — or something — in contempt. I thought what happened at the academy had blocked my career goals with the fire department. And from my perspective, you were the reason. You have continually caused trouble for me over the years."

Bentley suddenly stopped and studied Andy for several seconds before his shoulders sagged. "Garrett, what I've come to realize, ultimately, is all this time I've been jealous of you."

Surprised, Andy's face reddened, and he opened his mouth to protest, but Bentley held a hand up, stopping him. "Everything comes easy to you," Bentley continued, glancing down and then back to Andy. "Whether it's scores at the academy or relationships. I've worked hard trying to earn the respect and trust of the guys here as well as the respect of the Chief, but after trying hard, I still don't have what you have with all of them. Everything works for you, and you don't even try. You have no idea how frustrating it has been to work long and hard to have what you just waltz in and have easily without even batting an eye."

Andy sat back, caught off guard by Bentley's candor. "Yeah, well, I think actually, I *do* have a general idea of how frustrated you've been," Andy said. "But let's put all that in the past, and leave it there. We're each who we are, Mike. From my perspective, you're a fine officer," Andy said, shifting to a grin. "And as far as putting a word in for you, don't let that get around. I have a reputation to maintain you know."

Scrutinizing Bentley, Andy continued, "As far as being jealous, don't be. There is something else I need to tell you ..." Andy then relayed the same information he had just told the crew about his cancer diagnosis to Bentley. He could tell he'd caught Bentley totally by surprise.

"If you're doing chemo, why haven't you lost your hair?" Bentley blurted out. "I thought everyone doing chemo, lost their hair."

Andy shrugged. "Can't answer that one. Doc just said some people experience certain side effects and not others. So, I guess that was one I didn't get to experience. Not to worry, there were plenty of others though," Andy said, as he grimaced, shifting in his chair.

Bentley tried to process what Andy had just shared. "So, you're telling me, you've been doing chemo treatments for the past several months and still came to work?"

"Yeah ... and radiation and taking an experimental drug," Andy said with a slight smile. "I've been busy."

"How did I not know?" Bentley asked, incredulous.

"The guys all knew. There was a nurse at the hospital, friend of Hedrick's, who shared the information with them."

Bentley sat back, shaking his head.

"I was going to tell you the day the big fire broke out. I'd hoped to do some restrictive duty but, well, now I'll be going on disability leave. And the rest, as they say, is history. I can't handle the physical demands anymore and for the sake of everyone's safety, this is the only option. I've met with HR. They're taking care of all the paperwork and setting everything up. This is what's best for me and ultimately for you guys too."

Bentley was stunned. "Andy, I . . . I don't know what to say," he managed.

Andy shrugged. "There's not really anything to say. It just is what it is."

Bentley shook his head. "No. I do know what to say."

Andy looked up, surprised at Bentley's tone.

"Even after everything that's gone on between us, I can't imagine being in the fire service without you. From the academy until now, we've served together. You've been a royal pain in my side — whether intentional or not — but you are an outstanding firefighter and para-medic and the leader I've always wanted to be. I thought I had all the answers, but you've shown me time and time again that I don't. Whether I liked the lessons at the time or not, I've learned from you. I hope you'll come by the station when you can. I'm going to think posi-tive and that you'll be back to being a pain in the neck soon. Things just won't be the same around here without your juvenile antics."

Andy studied Bentley thoughtfully and nodded slowly. "Juvenile, huh?"

They both laughed and sat silent for a few minutes before Andy asked, "Mike, can I give you a word of advice?"

Bentley looked up, surprised. "Well, sure ..."

Andy leaned forward to emphasize his point. "Get out there and be with the guys. Don't stay holed up in here," he said and gestured around the cramped space. "You can be a better officer if you spend time with your crew. I know you've got a lot of ground to gain back and even some new ground to break, especially after the last shift or two, but for your sake, and theirs too, you've got to try. They're pretty riled up right now, but they'll come around when they see you're trying."

Andy shrugged. "You have all the makings of a great officer, but you've got to get your men behind you." Andy paused while Bentley sat deep in thought.

"So with that ..." Andy picked up his crutches and struggled to his feet.

"I'll clean out my gear over the next couple of days. Right now, I'd better text Katie to come get me or I'm going to be in even bigger trouble than I already am. It's been an honor, Mike."

Andy stuck out his hand. Bentley looked at Andy with newfound appreciation and shook his hand firmly. "The honor has been mine, Andy."

Andy opened the door and made his way slowly and painfully back down the hall, followed by Bentley. The guys, rejoined now by Worth, waited expectantly around the table, looking from Andy to Bentley and back to Andy again as they re-entered the room.

"Texting Katie," Andy said as he pulled out his phone. "Expect tire squeals any second."

They all tried to smile as Andy looked at the group. His heart sped up. The time had come.

"Well, I guess this is it," Andy said quietly. "I'll see you guys around, but in the meantime, well…it's been an honor and a real pleasure."

They all stood as Andy looked each in the eye and shook each of their hands firmly.

"And remember," Andy said, with a nod Bentley's direction, "everyone deserves a second chance. Even screwball lieutenants." They all looked at red-faced Bentley and then back at Andy in amazement.

Hesitating, but with a firm, final nod to the group, Andy made his way to the back door. Each painful step carried him away from the career he loved. The guys behind him couldn't see the battle raging inside. He fought the urge to look back, just one more time, not only at his compatriots, and friends, but the brothers he'd served with. He wanted one last glimpse *as* a firefighter, and an insider of the brotherhood and the firefighter's life he loved, but it would be too hard. Instead, he stiffened his back, opened the door, and hobbled out.

Before the door closed, Andy heard Bentley say, "Mind if I join you?" There was silence and then the sound of chairs scraping across the floor.

Andy smiled weakly as he slumped against the door when it closed behind him. He leaned his head back with a heavy sigh and looked up, trying his best to blink back the tears.

"ANDY GARRETT, WHAT ARE you doing?!" Katie scolded, her heart pounding as she saw him lean unsteadily against the wall as he tried to walk from the bedroom to the living room. She rushed over and put an arm around him and felt him lean heavily against her. "Just because you made that little trip to the station the other day, doesn't mean you should be up and around. You can't risk a fall with that concussion. Where is it you think you needed to go?"

The little jaunt to the station had almost been his undoing. Andy was completely exhausted afterward and weaker than she'd ever seen him. When they'd gotten home, Katie hadn't been sure she could get him from the car to the house. It had taken every ounce of her energy as he half-leaned, upon her, Katie carrying him as they struggled up the walk and inside the house. They'd managed to get to the sofa before he crumpled. He'd had to sleep there that night as neither one of them had the strength to get him the short distance to the bedroom.

Now, two days later, Katie frowned at his stubbornness.

"Well, not sure there's anywhere I *had* to go, but maybe I just get tired of sitting or lying down. Ever think about that, Nurse Ratchet?" Andy said, trying to smile but feeling lightheaded.

"Maybe I had better sit down though," he said and reached for the arm of the sofa as Katie helped ease him down into its cushions.

The dizzy spells were growing less frequent, but he never knew when they'd strike.

Katie studied him, worried. "Better?"

"Yes — thank you — much better," Andy said and laid his head back. "Katie, honey, I'm sorry to be so much trouble. You should be out Christmas shopping or having lunch with your teacher friends . . . something besides being my nurse maid." Andy tapped the floor with one of his crutches in frustration.

Katie sat down beside him. "I'm exactly where I want to be. With you."

Andy closed his eyes and groaned. "I don't deserve you. I just don't."

"Well, you *are* right," Katie said and gave him a playful punch in the arm. "But you're stuck with me."

Andy opened his mouth to give his own smart reply, when they suddenly heard car doors banging outside and several voices talking at once. Exchanging a perplexed look, Katie left Andy on the sofa and headed for the front window to look outside. She stopped when the doorbell rang. Increasingly puzzled, Andy turned on the sofa to watch as Katie answered the door. When she opened it, the doorway was filled with a huge spruce Christmas tree.

Katie stepped back, surprised. The tree suddenly leaned to one side to reveal Jernigan's and Hedrick's grinning faces. Their heads were topped with bright red Santa hats.

When Andy saw them, he struggled to stand. Katie rushed back to help him as they carried the tree into the room. "What is this?" Andy asked, leaning on his crutches and Katie for support. "What's going on?"

"Well, we've been getting complaints from residents in this neighborhood," Jernigan said. "They're saying this particular house is seriously lacking in Christmas spirit so we're here to remedy the situation.

Now, where do you want this bad boy?" he said, eyeing the tree up and down.

Andy and Katie looked at each other, huge grins spreading across their faces.

"This is so awesome!" Katie almost squealed. "Let's put it over here."

While furniture was re-arranged, another familiar face appeared at the doorway. "Sally!" Katie exclaimed. She ran to her friend and threw her arms around Sally's neck, squeezing her into a tight hug. "What are you doing here?!"

"Well, I have a friend who has a friend," Sally said as Mandy Fitzhugh appeared behind her and pointed a gloved finger at Hedrick, who was helping Jernigan secure the tree in its stand. "Heard there was going to be a party so . . . " Sally grinned. "Besides, I've missed you with you away on leave."

"You got ornaments?" Hedrick interrupted, checking the placement of the tree to make sure it was straight.

"Sure," Katie said before being distracted by more voices outside and a scraping sound against the eaves of the house. Katie went to the window and laughed. "Andy, you've got to see this."

Before Katie could reach Andy, Jernigan stepped in and put Andy's arm around his shoulders. He helped Andy hobble to the front window where they could see the activity on the front lawn. Hart, wearing his own version of a Santa hat, was positioning a ladder on the front of the house. When he saw their faces in the window, he broke into a rare grin. He waved and held up one end of a strand of Christmas lights while to his side stood Canfield, Santa hat on his head and the rest of the string of lights around his neck, ready to unspool them as Hart nailed them into place. Hart caught Andy's eye and looking over his shoulder, jerked his head in the direction of the tree in their front yard.

Andy could see a couple of guys, also sporting Santa hats, putting lights around the trunk. Andy could tell one of the guys was Worth, but when the second person made his way around the trunk and faced the house, Andy's mouth dropped open in surprise — Bentley. Bentley waved with a smile, and Andy waved back.

Andy looked at Jernigan, a bemused look on his face.

"Shut up, Garrett. You know I hate it when you're right," Jernigan groused with a grin, helping Andy back to the sofa. "Don't know what you said to him, but he's coming around. He has a way to go, but he's definitely improving."

Andy smiled, really smiled, for the first time in days. "This is so awesome. Everything — just everything — including those goofy Santa hats," he said, rolling his eyes. "It's wonderful, thank you."

Jernigan took a step back and, with the hint of a smirk, pulled an envelope from inside his jacket. "You shouldn't leave your stuff laying around, Garrett. I believe this is yours." He held the manila envelope out that Andy had found under his mattress.

Andy still had some memory loss from the day of the fire, but he did remember finding the envelope under his bed at the station. He took the proffered envelope from Jernigan.

"I think you'll find a little more in there this time," Jernigan said. "Seems like I'm having money slipped into my hands all the time these days with either a 'this is for Garrett,' or 'get this to Garrett.' We've had a lot of visitors come by the station the past couple of weeks with drop offs," Jernigan said with a grin and walked back over to help Hedrick with the tree.

The lump inside felt significantly larger. Andy was amazed — no, he was humbled. He put the envelope against the cushion behind him as Katie burst back into the room.

"This is so awesome!" she exclaimed, her eyes alight, and her arms loaded with boxes of ornaments. "Let's get this tree decorated!"

"Let's do it!" Sally said. "But wait just a minute...hold that thought. We'll be back in just a second." Sally and Mandy shared a conspiratorial grin and dashed out the front door.

Katie began pulling ornaments from boxes while Jernigan and Hedrick pulled strings of lights from other boxes and handed them to Andy to untangle. In a rush of cold air, Sally and Mandy came sweeping back into the room carrying baskets and covered dishes. The house quickly filled with the delicious smell of hot food. Mandy, wearing her own Santa hat, followed Sally into the kitchen.

"What's all that?" Katie asked, stopping to observe the two working in the kitchen.

Lifting hot pans from the padded baskets, Sally said, "Well, you can't expect all these Christmas elves to go hungry, now can you? How does fire house chili and homemade bread sound on this cold day? Oh, and we've got hot chocolate and homemade Christmas sugar cookies too — all courtesy of one Chef Sean Hendrick. So, I say we've got a party!" Sally exclaimed as she and Mandy laughed.

"Watch who you're calling elves," Jernigan said with a grin.

Amidst all the uproar and activity, Andy watched Katie. She was glowing with excitement and happiness, chatting with Jernigan and attempting to talk to Hedrick when he wasn't busy watching Mandy. Andy smiled.

Katie caught him watching her and reached down and gave him a happy kiss on the cheek and took his hand. "Isn't this something?!" she exclaimed, motioning at the hub bub of activity. "They brought us Christmas!"

"Yes, they did indeed," Andy said, feeling the bulge of the envelope behind him, as Katie hurried off to hang more ornaments. Yes, indeed, he thought. They brought Christmas in a lot more ways than one.

THE HOUSE WAS QUIET after the frenzied afternoon of activity. Katie sat on the sofa curled up next to Andy, his arm around her, as they admired the lights on their Christmas tree. The band of elves had planned well and their house glowed with Christmas spirit. From the Christmas tree to what seemed like a million Christmas lights decking their front yard, their house had never been so dressed up for Christmas. The delicious meal Hedrick had prepared topped the afternoon off perfectly. The group had even attempted a few Christmas carols, but the effort was suspended amid too much laughter and pending recruitment of better voices. Andy wished Bentley had opted to stay, but at least he'd taken part in the afternoon.

He pulled Katie closer as she said, "I'll never forget this afternoon. What a great group of friends. It was all so fun."

Andy was quiet for a long time, gently rubbing his fingers up and down Katie's arm. Finally, with a wistful sigh he said, "It was fun wasn't it? We really are lucky, you know?"

"Lucky?" Katie asked and raised her eyes to him.

"Yeah, lucky. We've got great friends who went to a lot of trouble for us. Oh, and I forgot to tell you about this," he said with a grin as he pulled out the manila envelope and handed it to Katie.

Sitting up, Katie took the envelope, puzzled.

"Open it," Andy said, watching her.

Katie turned the envelope over and reached inside. His grin grew wider as Katie's eyes rounded in amazement. Her mouth dropped open as she pulled the bundle out.

Katie pulled out a huge stack of bills of all denominations. She couldn't even guess at how much she held in her hands. She was already calculating how many past due bills she could pay - bills she was deeply worried about.

She was incredulous. "Andy! Where did this come from?" She turned the bundle over and around looking for some indication.

"There's a note inside," he prompted.

She reached inside and pulled a note out that read: *From Your Brothers.*

She looked at Andy, who was still grinning, just as he'd grinned all afternoon, poking jibes at the guys, watching the chaos and participating as much as he could. The words he'd used to describe the fire service came back to her. *It's a brotherhood. And there's nothing else like it.*

He was so right. She shook her head slowly, awed at the depth of care these firefighters had, not just for the public they serve so well, but also for the care they show their fire service brothers. "It's a brotherhood," she said softly.

Andy pulled Katie closer, her head resting against his shoulder. "Yes, it is, Katie. I'm so glad you see it. It's something that almost defies description — you have to see it and feel it to understand how real it is."

He felt her head nod. When she lifted her face, tears glistened on her cheeks. Words would have spoiled the moment, so he simply put both arms around her as she nestled into his embrace. Cancer had certainly clouded his future, but he had a lot to be thankful for. He had an amazing wife he adored and who adored him; he had the crew and his friends, who always went above and beyond; and Katie's friends, who came through for her when they were needed most. Yes, he thought, as he held Katie close in the sparkle of the Christmas tree lights, he was very lucky indeed.

"**A**RE YOU SURE?" KATIE fretted as she came into the living room, putting first one earring on and then the other. "I can always cancel. I know they'd understand." Katie walked to the kitchen, tugging at the Christmas sweater she'd just put on.

"As I've said for the one-thousand five-hundred and fifty-seventh time, I will be just fine," Andy grumbled. "Jerry is on his way over. We're going to watch the game. He's bringing food so we will both be well-fed and entertained. So go. *Please* go."

He saw the worry on Katie's face. "I mean it. Have fun and don't worry!"

"But, are you ..." Katie started again.

Andy frowned. "I'm not having this conversation again. Good-bye. Have fun," he said as a car horn honked from the driveway. "There's Sally, so off you go," he said, shooing her with his hand.

Katie retrieved her coat and turned back again. Andy cocked one eye-brow, daring her to say anything.

"I love you, Andy Garrett," she said with a half-hearted smirk.

"And I love you, Katie Garrett, but for now - go!"

Katie smiled in spite of his grumpiness and her worry. She opened the door just as Jerry Hamilton was raising a hand to knock.

"Hi, Jerry," Katie said as she slipped past. "Sally's waiting — gotta run." Katie looked over her shoulder one more time and waved to Andy before closing the door.

"Come in, Chief, and make yourself at home," Andy said, shifting on the sofa to ease the pain he'd been trying to hide from Katie.

"Where's Katie off to?" Jerry asked as he carried a couple of bags through to the kitchen and started unloading them.

"Teachers at her school are having a luncheon and a gift exchange. She didn't want to go. She's afraid to leave me alone. Your call about the game was perfect timing. She had no excuse after that. Besides, she needs to get out and not stay stuck at home with me all the time."

Jerry handed Andy a plate heaping with fries, wings and mac and cheese. In his other hand was Andy's favorite soft drink. "This be enough?" Jerry asked as he sat down with his own heaping plate and drink.

Andy laughed and shook his head as he took a couple of bites. "This is enough for two or three games."

"Why does she think she needs to stay with you?" Jerry asked, taking a bite out of a wing.

Andy stopped mid-bite and looked at Jerry. "I'm getting weaker. She's afraid I'm going to fall or pass out, and . . . well, actually she's right," Andy said, setting his plate aside.

Jerry looked at him with concern and set his own plate down. "Tell me," Jerry said flatly.

Still hurting, Andy shifted again. "I have trouble getting around. I feel weak and lightheaded, even after the dizziness from the concussion should have worn off. The pain was better for a while, but it's getting bad again."

Jerry studied him for several long seconds. "Have you seen the doctor since your stay in the hospital?"

"No. I saw Dr. Parker while I was in the hospital, and he ran some tests, but we haven't gotten the results. They called yesterday and rescheduled my appointment from next week until after the holidays. The nurse also said my chemo treatments have been reduced to two before the appointment and no radiation until after the new year. I'd been having two a week of each. They keep telling me all indications are that the experimental drug is having some effect, but I can tell my body is failing. I'm no doctor, but I think it's pretty plain they wouldn't reduce the chemo and radiation and put them off if they thought they were working. Wouldn't they want to keep going at the same rate — holidays or not?"

Jerry leaned forward, elbows on his knees and studied Andy. "Have you told Katie what you're thinking?"

"Nah," Andy shook his head. "She worries enough for both of us as it is. I'm not going to add to it if I can help it. At least for awhile."

"You did the right thing sending her off today," Jerry said. "She needs a break. I'll check in more often and keep a closer eye on things."

Jerry picked his plate up, but he didn't feel hungry anymore. Looking at Andy was like seeing Scotty all over again. It was just as painful watching Andy suffer as it had been to watch Scott's slow deterioration right in front of his eyes. The worst part now, as it had been with Scott, was not being able to stop or even help ease the pain. Jerry could still see the pain on Scott's face and hear the anguish in his voice.

"One more thing, Chief," Andy said hesitantly.

Jerry turned in his chair at Andy's change in tone. "Yes?"

"I'd like your help in making final . . . final arrangements, if you know what I mean," Andy said, uncomfortably. "I don't want Katie to have to worry with anything if . . . well, you know, if it comes to that. I hope I'm just being overly cautious, but you know . . . just in case."

"Andy, it would be my honor. If that time comes, I promise to take care of everything as if you were my own son. I don't want you to worry about anything." Jerry studied Andy for several seconds before shrugging. "But I bet you're right. You're just being overly cautious. Which is great, of course, but it just means I'll have to figure out how to handle you being a pain in the neck for a long time to come."

Andy grinned, visibly relieved. "Thanks, Chief. I knew I could count on you."

Jerry nodded and studied Andy for another moment, and with a forced smile turned in his chair. "Anything else I can get for you before the game starts?" He punched the channel number into the remote.

"Well, no," Andy laughed as Jerry settled back comfortably into his chair. "Wouldn't want you to have to get up or anything."

"Sorry, what?" Jerry said, feigning inattention. "Game's starting."

"Nothing, Chief. Nothing," Andy chuckled.

"Now aren't you glad you came?" Sally asked as they drove back a couple of hours later.

Katie smiled and nodded. It had been a wonderful time and so fun to see all of her teacher friends. "I'm glad I came. It was great seeing everybody. They were all so generous. Andy and I appreciate this so much," Katie said, holding up a gift card to the local grocery store, a gift from the group. "I would ask how they knew what we needed, but then I *do* know."

"Aw, come on. You know how teachers love gossip. Just had to throw a few tempting morsels out there, and besides, how many teachers have their husbands on the news as a local hero?" Sally asked. She put her hand behind her ear. "Huh? How many did you say?"

"Andy wouldn't say he's a hero," Katie hurried to assure Sally. "He'd say the heroes were the guys on the RIT team who got him out."

"You say to-MAY-toe. We say to-MAH-toe. They're all in the same group to me," Sally said, making a circle in the air with her finger.

"You're too funny. We have definitely got to find you a firefighter to marry," Katie laughed.

"I'm totally fine with that."

"Sally, I appreciate you picking me up. And — thanks for encouraging me to go."

"My pleasure, kiddo. Rather selfish of me, actually. I got to spend some extra time with you."

Katie smiled, but then her face grew somber as she turned to look out the window. She needed to talk to someone, but she didn't want to say out loud what she was thinking, what she knew. Katie sighed heavily and her shoulders sagged under the weight she was carrying.

Sally glanced at her. "What is it? You look so sad."

"Andy is dying," Katie said, her voice breaking. "That's the first time I've actually said it out loud."

Sally reached over and took Katie's hand. "Don't jump the gun," she cautioned. "He's still doing treatments, and you said that experimental drug seemed to be helping. Besides, Andy's young and strong. They say that counts for a lot in a situation like this."

Katie shook her head sadly. "I want to believe all that, Sally, I really do. But I also see how he struggles just to stand and walk, and it's getting worse. The trial drug did help with the pain for a while; he thinks I don't notice when he grimaces or flinches, but it's getting worse too."

Katie took a shaky breath. "And Dr. Parker's office called this past week and rescheduled his follow up until after the holidays. They've reduced his chemo and radiation treatments, too. Andy tried to blame it on the holidays, but they wouldn't reduce the treatments if test results showed they were working, would they?"

Katie only allowed herself to feel the depth of her anguish in a few, rare moments and even then, it threatened to overwhelm her ability to recover. She felt like she was crumbling inside, one little bit followed by another and then another and another. Her world was Andy and Andy — her friend, her confidant, her cheerleader, her biggest supporter, her husband, and her lover — was dying and there was nothing she could do to save him. To save them.

Sally could see the look of utter desolation and tragedy on Katie's face. There were no words to say. She simply squeezed Katie's hand and held it tightly as they drove on in silence.

ANDY AND KATIE COULDN'T make the drive to Murfreesboro on Christmas Day, so Katie's parents came to them. It was bitter cold with the threat of snow as Katie opened the door to her parents' knock.

"Come in!" Katie said hugging them as they made their way inside. The cozy warmth of the house and the festive scent of the Christmas tree extending a cheery welcome. Their hands and arms were filled with boxes and baskets of food.

Andy sat on the sofa and tried to stand to greet them but Mr. Maine waved him off as they passed through the living room to the kitchen.

While Katie and her mom started preparing the food, Mr. Maine came back into the living room. He took off his coat and gloves and tossed them over the back of the chair before sitting across from Andy.

"That was quite a load," Andy said with a grin.

"We certainly don't go by the mantra of traveling light," Katie's dad said with a good-natured shake of his head.

"We appreciate you guys making the drive down," Andy said as he settled back into the cushions.

"Our pleasure. The drive wasn't bad. The clouds are looking like it might actually snow."

"Now, wouldn't that be something on Christmas Day in Texas?" Andy chuckled.

A short while later, a feast was on the table. Katie had set the table with their china and best linens. A festive centerpiece of Christmas berries and greenery sent by Trenton and Stephanie was flanked by candles, their flames enveloping the table in a soft glow.

As they sat down to eat, each took the hand of the person on either side. Mr. Maine cleared his throat and with a loving wink at his wife said, "The love talked about and felt at Christmas is special, but we're especially blessed because our family shares a wealth of love year-round."

He looked at each face around the table and squeezed his wife's and Katie's hands. His eyes fastened on Andy, Mr. Maine continued. "Kids, we want you both to know how much we love you. We're here, and we're together. We're family. And right now, that's all that matters. Let's ask the blessing."

Sudden tears pooled in Andy's eyes and then in Katie's as she felt his hand grip hers.

After dinner, a few presents were exchanged. "This one is for you and Andy together," Katie's mom said, handing the package to Andy to unwrap. It was a small square box, festively wrapped with a big bow and streamers that almost engulfed the tiny box.

Andy grinned and held the box up and gave it a good shake.

"Come on, Andy! Open it!" Katie said with a laugh.

Slowly, Andy removed the ribbons and bow and then pulled the paper off the box. Removing the lid, his and Katie's heads bent over the box. They looked at each other and smiled. Andy reached inside and pulled out a large snowflake-shaped frame Christmas ornament. In the frame was a picture taken of Andy and Katie in the Maine's backyard at

Thanksgiving. Arms around the other, they were smiling, looking into each other's eyes.

"We heard about this mammoth tree you guys had and thought you might need another ornament." Katie's mom eyed the tree up and down and then looked at them, grinning.

"Your Dad and I thought that picture depicted you two perfectly."

"We love it!" Katie said wiping at a tear with the back of her hand. "It's perfect."

"Would you do the honor of hanging it on our tree please, Mrs. Garrett?" Andy asked, passing the ornament to Katie.

"It will be my pleasure, Mr. Garrett."

Katie hung the ornament front and center and then stepped back to admire it, taking the hand Andy held up to her.

"You're right, my dear," Andy said, looking up at Katie. "It's perfect."

Katie smiled and patted Andy's hand.

The time passed quickly and after a quiet afternoon of visiting, Katie's mom and dad prepared to leave. Mr. Maine helped Andy to his feet at his insistence to see them to the door.

Katie hugged her mom and dad tightly. "Thanks for making the drive down and for the wonderful Christmas dinner. We've enjoyed the day so much." Andy leaned heavily against her, his arm around her shoulders as she struggled to support him.

Andy echoed Katie's sentiments. "Yes, we've enjoyed everything. We appreciate you guys coming down." He shook Mr. Maine's hand and then hugged Mrs. Maine with his free arm.

They opened the door to see large snowflakes just beginning to fall.

"How wonderful!" Katie and her mom exclaimed together with huge smiles.

"Looks like the perfect way to end the day," Mr. Maine said. He clapped Andy lightly on the back. "Take care of my girl."

"You have my solemn word, sir, as always," Andy said and squeezed Katie as he smiled into her upturned face.

IT WAS JANUARY, AND the new school semester was underway. Katie was back in the classroom but it was only because there were bills to pay. Even though she loved and enjoyed her students, her mind and heart were at home with Andy. Her students had her full attention during the day, but then she'd rush home to spend the evening with Andy.

After Katie went back to school, Andy managed a new routine, not feeling well enough to do anything but lay on the couch. He tried to read, but his eyes would grow weak. He slept most of the time.

There were also frequent fire department visitors as well as surprise visits from Walt and Charlene from RITE2. Andy had called his best friend from high school, Barry Giles, before Christmas to let him know what was going on and now, Barry was calling two or three times a week checking in. The highlight of Andy's day, though, was seeing Katie walk through the door each afternoon.

Unknown to Katie, Trenton and Jerry also made regular visits to see Andy while she was at school. Trenton obtained the needed information and forms from the City's HR Department regarding Andy's cancer diagnosis and was busily making the financial arrangements he and Andy discussed. Trenton also began the lengthy and involved application process to receive funds from the federal government. Jerry and the fire department chaplain, Alex MacShane, made regular visits as well, working with Andy on his thoughts and wishes for a funeral service and other final arrangements.

The routine continued to change as Andy grew increasingly weaker. Katie began to call several times a day and started making a quick trip home on her lunch break to see how Andy was doing and if he needed anything.

Two weeks after school started, Andy and Katie met with Dr. Parker to get results of recent tests. They sat across from him, hand in hand, preparing themselves for what they already knew he was going to say, they just hadn't admitted to each other.

Dr. Parker looked solemnly between them. He sat on the corner of the desk near them.

"Andy, you are a very brave and strong young man. I have never seen anyone fight as hard as you have or continued to work as long as you did while undergoing such intense treatments. That kind of fight and determination says a lot about you and your character. It's something I don't see often, and I admire it.

"Katie," Dr. Parker said, turning to her, "I know you love this fine husband of yours. That doesn't take much detective work. Just seeing the two of you together speaks volumes. I know Andy wouldn't have been able to do as well as he has if not for the extraordinary love and support he's gotten from you. It's rare to see this kind of love, devotion, and commitment between two people. But I've seen that between the two of you."

Andy and Katie exchanged nervous smiles. Dr. Parker took a deep breath. "Having said all of that, makes what I have to tell you that much harder." He reached behind him and picked up the folder laying on his desk. "I have looked at the test results and even asked some colleagues to review them and make suggestions. I'm afraid the news isn't very encouraging."

Andy squeezed Katie's hand, as Katie's heart started thumping painfully.

"The experimental drug actually did hold the cancer at bay, at least for a while," Dr. Parker said. "But I'm afraid the last test results show the cancer growing. Andy, I am so sorry but the treatments are ultimately having no effect. There's nothing we can do to stop it."

Katie felt Andy's grip tighten on her hand as she simultaneously felt the air rush from her lungs. She'd known — deep down that — she'd *expected* this to be what Dr. Parker would say but hearing it said out loud was more devastating than she'd imagined. But this couldn't be the end of it. There *had* to be something more. This was Andy . . .

"There's got to be something else, Dr. Parker. There just has to be," Katie said. She could hear the desperation in her own voice. "Andy hasn't suffered and gone through what he has these weeks and months only to be told 'sorry — that's it.'" Before she knew it, she was on her feet, clutching at Dr. Parker's coat sleeve. "Is there another trial medication, a new style of treatment, an organic treatment, — something? We can't stop. Don't you understand? We just can't!"

"Katie," Andy said softly, trying to pull her down beside him.

"There's got to be something you can do. Please, there's got to be something else," Katie said, breaking into tears. "Please, Dr. Parker."

Andy smiled an apologetic smile at Dr. Parker and grasped Katie with a trembling hand and pulled her down beside him.

"Thanks, Doc," Andy said, holding Katie. "I was hoping for something different, but I thought this would be what you'd say. I appreciate everything you've done."

Katie felt Andy struggling to hold her, as she heard his gracious words to Dr. Parker. She had to gain her composure. Dr. Parker *had* done a lot for them and had gone above and beyond in getting the trial medication. She sat up and swiping at her tears, said, "I'm so sorry, Dr. Parker. I know you've done a lot. I'm just not willing to concede defeat quite yet. I love Andy too much."

Dr. Parker reached over and took Katie's hand. "Katie, my dear, no apology is needed. I assure you, if there was anything...*anything* else that could be done, it would be done without a moment's hesitation. I am so very sorry."

THEY DROVE HOME IN total silence. Andy hadn't said a word since saying good-bye to Dr. Parker. He hadn't even thanked the attendant who pushed his wheelchair or helped him into the car. Katie nodded somberly and mouthed a thank you to the young attendant before he turned to leave. Katie glanced at Andy pensively several times as she drove, but he only stared out the window, mute, his face blank. She'd never seen him this closed off before, and it scared her.

She helped him into the house, where they both sank numbly onto the sofa.

After several long minutes, Katie couldn't stand the silence any longer. "I'm finding another doctor and getting a second opinion," she said matter-of-factly.

"No, Katie. You're not."

Andy's harsh tone caused her to jump, and she turned quickly to look at him.

"But Andy —"

"I said no, you're not. And that's the end of it," Andy said, still not looking at her.

"Andy, don't you want to fight this?"

Andy turned quickly to face her. "Katie, look at me," he said and held up his trembling hands. "Look! See how they're shaking? I couldn't even walk into the doctor's office today on my own power — I had to have a wheelchair! I could barely make it into the house without your help. Katie, don't you see?"

"I see the man I love and don't want to lose. Can't *you* see that?!" Katie snapped back, harsher than she'd intended,

Andy looked at her and studied her for several seconds. Her loved her so much. How he hated to be the cause of the anxiety he saw on her beautiful face. He took a deep breath. "Katie, don't you think *I* want to live? Don't you think I want to grow old with you? Don't you think I want us to have lots of children and grandchildren? Don't you think I want to coach my sons in little league? Don't you think I want to walk my daughters down the aisle? Don't you think I want to . . .'"

He stopped and put his face in his hands, his shoulders shaking as he began to sob.

Katie reached out and placed a hand gently on his arm, but he brushed it away.

"Katie, don't . . . please not right now," he said as he caught his breath. "Don't you see? That just makes it harder. I'm not going to be here to take care of you, to know you're safe, to protect you, to be the husband I promised to be. I even ended my firefighting career being carried out of a burning house. Everyone and everything that's most important to me, I'm letting down. I've failed at everything. Don't you see? I've failed!"

Katie sat, stunned, hearing what Andy was gasping out between sobs. She wasn't sure what to do. She had never seen him so distraught. She felt helpless not knowing how to help him and how to comfort him. After minutes of indecisiveness, instinct took over and Katie scooted closer, gently placing an arm across Andy's shoulders and pulling him close. He stiffened and resisted at first, but Katie continued to gently strengthen her pull until he reached out and clung to her with a desperation that Katie could feel shuddering through his body. She softly rubbed his back, fighting her own tears until gradually, his sobs slowed and stopped altogether. He still clung to her and placed his head on her shoulder.

"Katie?" he said at last.

"Yes?" she said, not wanting to break this fragile moment.

"Katie, I am so sorry ... for everything. There is no way to make up to you what you're going through and what's coming but ..."

Andy sat up and wiped his face with the backs of his hands before taking her hands in his.

Katie tensed, afraid of what he was about to say. Somehow, she knew it was going to make things worse.

"Katie," he said again, looking at her with sadness and a bit of reluctance.

She shifted uncomfortably.

"I didn't want to tell you until we knew for certain, but I've been making ... arrangements."

"Arrangements?" Katie said, confused. "What kind of arrangements?"

"My funeral arrangements."

Katie sat back, feeling as if the wind had been knocked from her. "Funeral arrangements?" she finally managed.

Andy nodded solemnly. "Yes, Jerry and Chaplain McShane have been helping me. They told me it will be a line of duty service since I contracted cancer while working, so it's a bit more complicated. I didn't want you to have to worry about anything so, well ... it's all been arranged."

Katie blinked slowly several times trying to grasp the depth of the man sitting in front of her. He was a clown, no question, but he was also a more giving, caring man than anyone could ever imagine — including herself.

"Oh, Andy," she finally choked out, looking at him with a deeper sense of love and loss than she'd ever thought possible. She felt her face crumple, and it was Andy's turn to take her into his arms to comfort her.

Katie clutched his shirt in her fists and let go of all the emotions she'd been struggling to hold onto for months. She cried, as if she could physically feel her heart breaking.

"Andy, oh Andy," she sobbed as she clung to him. "I can't go on without you. You are the best part of me. I count for nothing without you. You haven't failed . . .not at anything . . .ever, don't you see? I've . . . I've never been good enough for anything until you and .. . . and without you . . ."

She felt Andy stiffen. "Katie, I don't want to *ever* hear that said again. Do you understand me? *Ever*. How can you still not understand?" He stood shakily and moved behind one of the chairs and braced himself for support.

"I have *always* been what's not good enough *for you!* Growing up without any love from my mom after she married my stepdad, I swore I'd never get married. I didn't think there was a woman I could trust to love me back if I opened up and loved them. But then, you came along, and you literally changed, not just my life, but my whole way of thinking and feeling about myself. I was a clown trying to cover up the pain, but then I got attention and it just became who I was. When I met you, I could be me — the real me — the me I wanted to be. That's what I'd been craving all my life, not really knowing it, until I met you. You gave that to me, Katie. You have no idea how incredible you are

and that's one of the reasons I love you so much. I've watched you the past few months — how you've managed our finances, trying to shield me from worrying, how you've gone to school day after day to give those kids your very best when you're exhausted. I've watched you talk and tease with the guys at the station. I love you more than words can ever say, Katie, but I also respect and admire you. Don't *ever* say you're not good enough. *Ever.*"

He sat down beside her and took her hands. "I love you, Katie. And just as I knew what Dr. Parker was going to say today, I also know he's right. My body is tired. I'm tired. I've fought long and hard, but I also know my body can't handle anything else. I'll keep fighting until my last breath to be with you as long as I possibly can, but Katie, Dr. Parker is right. There's nothing more that can be done."

Katie shuddered and grasped Andy's trembling hands tightly in her own as she looked deeply into his eyes.

Andy reached up and cupped her cheek gently in his hand, returning the look in equal measure. He stroked her cheek with his thumb, relishing the softness of her skin beneath its touch. He cocked his head to one side and suddenly it came to him, and he knew. He knew, just as he'd known Katie was the girl for him the first time he saw her, and just as he'd known what Dr. Parker said today was right. He knew, somehow, he'd be with Katie always — just as they'd said in their vows — *forever*. He might not be able to feel her cheek beneath his hand as he did now, but somehow ... he'd be near.

Looking into each other's eyes, they leaned forward until their lips touched, hungry for each other but hesitant. Andy kissed Katie's lips softly, then caressed her cheeks tenderly with his lips, tasting the salt of her tears, before taking her face in his hands and pulling her to him tenderly. Katie gave into his caresses, relishing the feel of his gentle touches as she put her arms around him.

"Katie," Andy said softly, "no matter what, I will be with you — forever. I don't know how, I just know there will be a way. Trust that and never doubt it. Our connection is too strong. It's forever."

Katie stilled as he spoke, and in her heart, she knew it was true. Their connection *was* strong, and Andy would find a way.

KATIE WAS DRAINED, PHYSICALLY and emotionally. Since their visit to Dr. Parker's office, she'd watched Andy decline rapidly, and when he couldn't see or hear her, she cried with sobs that wracked her entire body.

Andy struggled to be with her as much as possible, but the last few days, he'd been unable to muster the energy or overcome the pain to get out of bed. Tonight, Katie sat on the edge of their bed as they talked. Andy, curled in a tight ball, lay on his side, hoping for the pain pills to take effect.

Trying to distract him, Katie asked, "So, you were a jock in high school. Which sport did you like playing best — football or baseball?" She gently ran her fingers through his hair.

"Baseball," he mumbled into the pillow through gritted teeth.

Katie flinched, seeing him in so much pain. Doing her best to sound playful, she said, "But baseball doesn't have the pretty cheerleaders that football does. I thought all jocks liked having cheerleaders around."

Andy tried to smile but another wave of pain bent him further double.

Desperate to divert his attention, Katie went on. "So, what did you like best about being a fireman?"

"Leaving on a call. The lights and sirens … the feel of the engine rumbling beneath your feet … but the best part," he gasped out in staggered breaths, "was knowing you were on your way to help someone … someone probably having one of the worst days of their life."

Katie smiled sadly at his answer. So typical of Andy. "It is exciting," she agreed soothingly. "I know it was exciting to see when we were at the station for the field trip. Lucas was spellbound."

Andy frowned, and Katie regretted mentioning Lucas' name as soon as she'd said it. "I still can't believe the trouble you guys went to that day."

"It was fun for us, too," Andy choked out.

Katie leaned close and gripped Andy's shoulder. "Is there anything I can do?"

Andy shook his head against the pillow and reached for her hand.

"Just hold my hand, Katie … please … I need to feel your hand in mine."

Katie fought back tears and held Andy's hand tightly, until the pain pills took effect, and he drifted into a fitful sleep. She rose slowly so as not to wake him and kissed him softly on his cheek. She went to the dining room and forced herself to work on bills she needed to pay. The money from the guys at the department had been a tremendous help and because of it, she'd been able to breathe a little easier the past couple of months.

She really needed to concentrate, but she was too worried and too exhausted. Her eyes grew heavy and her head nodded until she fell asleep, her head resting on the table, one hand on the computer and a pencil in the other.

Suddenly, she jumped. Something had woken her. And then she heard it again. Andy was calling her, but something was wrong. Her heart hammering in her chest, she ran down the hall. As she stepped into their room, she knew she would never forget what she saw. Andy was on the floor, writhing in pain. He had thrown up some blood, and his face was ghostly white. His eyes locked onto hers, and the terror she saw there almost unnerved her.

"Andy!" she gasped. "Oh, my god, Andy!"

She ran to him and with her own breath choking out of her, she dropped to the floor beside him. Andy tried to grasp her hand, his body convulsing. "I can't ... I can't breathe ..."

Katie grabbed her phone from the nightstand and with shaking hands desperately punched 9-1-1.

THE TONES WENT OFF at 2:11 a.m. It was a medical call. Hart and Canfield were on the ambulance this shift. They were already on the move when Jernigan heard dispatch relay the address a second time — 555 Meandering Lane. Garrett's address. Jernigan threw off the covers, calling to Hedrick and Worth as he jumped into his pants and pulled his shirt and jacket on. "Hedrick, tell Bentley. I'm getting the engine started," he said in a rush as he ran toward the bay.

Hedrick, ran down the hall and called out to Bentley. "I thought it was a medical," Bentley said, shaking the sleep from his voice.

"It's Garrett's address," Hedrick replied urgently.

Bentley jumped up and started grabbing for his clothes. "We're all going. Get everybody up," Bentley said, wide awake and hurrying.

"Done. We're about ready to roll. Box is pulling out now," he said as they heard the ambulance siren start.

"Go. Go. Go. I'm right behind you," Bentley said he as he yanked his jacket off the chair and ran after Hedrick. Jernigan already had the engine running and lights switched on. Worth was in the back seat behind the officer's seat and Hedrick piled in the seat where Andy used to sit. Headsets in place and seat belts buckled, Jernigan hit the siren and the engine pulled out just a couple of minutes behind the ambulance.

KATIE UNLOCKED THE FRONT door and ran back to Andy, who was desperately gasping for breath between convulsions. His face was a sheen of perspiration, and he continued to throw up bits of blood that left a light red stain around his lips. "I'm here, Andy. I'm here," Katie tried to sooth as she held his head in her lap and wiped his face with a cloth. She wasn't sure if he could hear her.

It seemed like hours before she heard the siren and then within minutes, she heard them at the front door.

"Katie?" she heard Hart call from the front.

Thank god, she thought.

"Back here," she heard herself, almost screaming.

Hart rushed to the bedroom but stopped abruptly when he saw Andy on the floor writhing in convulsions, Katie cradling his head in her lap. He took a step forward but stopped.

Canfield rushed up and came to an abrupt stop behind Hart, giving him a slight push.

"Get in there, Hart. We've got to help him."

Hart stood immobile then shook his head as if coming out of a trance. "But that's Andy —" Hart turned to Canfield. "I'm a professional and this is my job but this is Andy — my friend, my fire service brother — it's Andy —"

Andy gasped painfully, trying to breath. The force of the sound cut into the heavy air of the room.

Hart turned and looked at Andy. He braced himself, then took a deep breath and stepped into the room.

"Katie," he said soothingly, "I need to check on Andy."

She didn't respond.

"Katie," he said again softly.

Katie saw Hart. She heard him. But she couldn't move, and she didn't want to let go. She looked down. Andy was in the throes of another convulsion, blood trickling from his lips. But still, she couldn't move. She sat motionless, numb.

"Katie, come with me," Canfield said as he moved to Katie's side and gently lifted her up. He put his arm around her and moved her away as Hart knelt beside Andy. Seconds later, Jernigan and Hedrick, followed by Bentley and Worth, appeared in the bedroom doorway. Jernigan stepped inside the room and Canfield placed Katie into his care so he could assist Hart.

Katie looked on as Hart and now Canfield worked with bags of drugs they were putting into the IV they'd inserted in the back of Andy's hand. "Andy . . . Andy . . ." she heard herself repeating, her voice full of agony and desperation.

"We're here, Katie. We're here," Jernigan soothed as he put his arm around her. "Apart from Andy, Hart's the best paramedic in Abernathy. Andy's in good hands."

Katie felt Jernigan's arm securely around her and felt it tighten even more when she began shaking uncontrollably. She tried, but she couldn't stop.

As Jernigan tried to comfort Katie, he looked over his shoulder to see Hedrick and Worth take off down the hall at a run. Hart and Canfield continued working feverishly on Andy, who now lay pale and motionless on the floor. Just a few, short minutes later, the clang of the gurney came down the hall as Hedrick and Worth brought it quickly into the room. Immediately behind the gurney came Jerry Hamilton.

"Chief, what are you doing here?" Jernigan asked in surprise.

"I left word with dispatch if a medical call came in for this address, I was to be notified," he said flatly, peering in the door. They watched as Hart and Canfield carefully loaded the unconscious Andy onto the gurney and placed several blankets over him. They strapped him in tightly and began wheeling the gurney to the ambulance.

Katie was going with Andy. She had to be with him. In a daze, Katie tried to step around Jernigan to follow, but as Jernigan reached for her, Jerry Hamilton stepped in and motioned for Jernigan and the others to go ahead.

"Katie," Jerry said, taking her and turning her toward him, "They need to get Andy to the hospital as quickly as possible. I'll take you. Go ahead and change your clothes. I'll wait for you in the living room."

Katie looked at Jerry, confused. She tried to focus on what he was saying, but then she heard the ambulance siren as it began to drive away. It was carrying Andy.

The fog suddenly cleared. She had been dressed for bed but hadn't noticed. She quickly pulled on a warm-up suit, put her hair into a pony tail and washed her face. She threw open the door and ran down the hall. Jerry was waiting patiently by the front door. She grabbed a coat from the closet as Jerry opened the door, and they stepped into the night.

HART'S FACE WAS GRIM as he stepped out of the room, leaving the ER doctor and nurses working. He had done his best to stabilize Andy and had mostly succeeded, but Andy's vitals were weak. Very weak. Hart knew Andy's body wouldn't be able to hold out much longer. He shook his head sadly. This wasn't supposed to happen to someone like Andy.

The rest of the crew was watching from the waiting room, empty except for their group. Their faces mirrored his own solemness as he updated them. When Chief Hamilton and Katie came through the door, he walked over to them.

"He's stable," he began. "But ..."

"But what?" Katie gasped out.

Hart glanced down and then looked at Katie. "He's in bad shape, Katie. It won't be long."

Katie slumped against Jerry, and he put his arm around her as the rest of the men looked down.

"I want to see him," Katie said, forcing back tears.

"I don't know ..." Hart said and looked at Chief Hamilton. Chief Hamilton motioned toward the desk with his head. Hart walked over and talked to one of the nurses. The nurse disappeared and minutes later, Mandy walked up to Katie and put her arms around her. Katie shuddered, struggling to hold back the tears.

"Katie, I'm so sorry. I'll be right here with you," Mandy said softly. "Come with me."

She took Katie by the hand and guided her to the exam room. Jerry followed close behind, stopping just short of going in, showing Katie he was nearby in case she needed him.

Mandy stepped inside with Katie, her arm still around Katie's shoulder.

A doctor and two nurses were working on Andy who lay motionless. He looked so frail, Katie thought, and so pale. He was either asleep or unconscious. He never stirred as the staff talked softly checking his vitals, taking his temperature and adjusting the lines and tubes connected to various monitors. She could hear the continual rhythm of the heart monitor and saw the blips on the screen.

The doctor stepped away and gave the nurses a few quick instructions. When he turned to leave, he saw Katie and Mandy. Katie recognized Dr. Chilcott by his ponytail. He was the same doctor who had attended Andy after the fire. He smiled glumly and motioned for them to step outside.

Katie took another look at Andy over her shoulder as she stepped out. She stood next to Jerry while Mandy drifted over to stand with Sean who put his arm around her.

Dr. Chilcott began, "I'm so sorry we have to meet again, but..."

"Well, how is he?" Katie asked.

Dr. Chilcott took a deep breath before answering. "Mrs. Garrett, he's in the final stages of the cancer. There's nothing more we can do besides control the pain. We've given him morphine and can increase the dose until..."

Katie shook her head. She didn't need him to finish.

She felt Jerry's hand on her shoulder.

"I would like to see him now and then I want to take him home. I want . . . *he* wants . . . to be home when . . ." She looked away and couldn't go on.

The doctor nodded. "I understand, and we will make that happen. He's very weak, but you should be able to talk to him. I'll get the arrangements started."

"Doc," Jerry broke in, "we can use the Fire Department ambulance outside for transport, if that will be okay."

Dr. Chilcott nodded. "It will be a couple of hours before he will be stable enough to move, but that will be fine." He opened the door and motioned for the nurses to leave and held the door open for Katie.

Katie gave Dr. Chilcott a nod then walked to the bed and took Andy's hand. He stirred but didn't open his eyes. "Andy, I'm here. I'm right here," she said softly, lifting his hand and kissing it gently.

Andy struggled, but managed to open his eyes. "Katie," he said, his voice soft.

Katie leaned in closer. "I love you," he whispered and squeezed her hand weakly.

Word had spread. By the time they were ready to transport Andy home, the hospital drive was lined with fire trucks, fire engines and ambulances. But Katie didn't see them. She walked beside the gurney, eyes riveted on Andy, holding his hand.

They lifted him into the ambulance, and Katie stepped inside, riding home with him for the last time. Hart rode in the back with them and Canfield drove. Sean hugged Mandy and then joined the rest of the C shift crew as they piled into the engine. Crew members belonging to apparatus lining the drive, stood solemnly beside their equipment watching as the ambulance, Engine Two, and the Chief's suburban pulled out.

The beep of the ambulance back-up alarm split the mid-morning quiet of the neighborhood as Canfield backed the ambulance into Andy and Katie's driveway. The back doors opened and Katie stepped out, reaching back to take Andy's hand as they removed the gurney and set it on the driveway. Katie kept hold of his hand until they reached the front door when she reluctantly let it go to retrieve the house key from her purse. Tears pooled in her eyes as she tried to fit the key into the lock, her hands shaking.

Jerry stepped up beside her and gently patting her back, took the key. He unlocked the door and held it open as Katie stepped through with the crew rolling the gurney directly behind. As she walked through the house, thoughts of hers and Andy's life together walked with her. The living room where they'd spent so many happy times, she curled up on the couch beside him, the security of his arm around her. Their wedding pictures and pictures of the two of them taken since they'd started dating scattered across the room. The kitchen and dining table where they'd prepared and shared so many meals, telling the other about the day they'd had, the frustrations, the laughs — a daily routine that would be no more.

The gurney rolled quietly behind her as she led the way down the hall and into their bedroom. She stopped short when she saw the bed, the sheets still crumpled from the night before when Andy had collapsed onto the floor. Their bed. The bed where they'd loved each other so gloriously and so happily. The bed where she'd slept safely in Andy's arms.

Katie wiped the tears that trickled down her face and quickly straightened the sheets. She stepped aside as the gurney rolled in behind her. Hart and Canfield, assisted as best as possible by Jernigan, Hedrick and Bentley, carefully lifted Andy's thin body from the gurney and gently placed it on the bed. Andy's brow furrowed, and he moaned softly at the slight jostling.

They started to leave but turned as one when they heard Andy say weakly, "Guys."

"Garrett," Jernigan said as they all stepped back toward the bed.

"Thanks...thanks for everything," Andy managed, looking at each of them and trying his best to smile.

They exchanged solemn looks before looking down. Hart, usually a man of few words, cleared his throat. "Don't let it go to your head, Garrett, but we think you're worth the trouble."

Andy attempted a grin and then turned his attention to Bentley. He nodded toward the group. "Mike, keep it going."

Bentley looked at the men around him and then back to Andy. "Understood. I will, and Andy, thank you."

Andy gave a small nod and seemed to slip into a light sleep. They waited a few seconds and then stepped outside, where Chief Hamilton waited with Katie.

"Guys . . ."

Jernigan gathered her in an embrace, followed by the others. Bentley came last, hugging her and gently patting her on the back. They walked away as a group, glancing sadly over their shoulders.

"I think he'd like to see you," Katie said, turning to Jerry.

Jerry nodded and followed her inside.

"Andy," Katie said lightly touching his arm, "Jerry is here."

Andy struggled but opened his eyes. "Chief . . ."

"Save your strength, Andy," Jerry's voice caught, but he went on. "I want you to know I love you like a brother, Andy — a fire service brother *and* a kid brother." Jerry's eyes flickered toward Katie. "And you have my word we'll take good care of Katie."

With effort, Andy extended his hand. Jerry took it and placed his hand on top of Andy's, shaking it gently.

"Thank you, Jerry . . . for everything," Andy managed before dropping his hand limply to his side and closing his eyes.

Jerry looked at Katie and shook his head sadly. He took her by the elbow and guided her outside.

"Katie," he said. "I am so very sorry. I wish there were something I could do . . ."

Katie nodded as she looked down and studied a small crack in the sidewalk.

"I'll be glad to stay until the hospice nurse gets here if you'd like. It's up to you."

"Thank you," Katie said, wiping a tear. "But I'd like to be alone with him. It will probably be our last time."

"I understand. We're all just a call away."

Katie nodded and patted Jerry's arm before walking inside.

KATIE HAD NO IDEA how long she sat holding Andy's hand until she woke with a jerk and realized she'd fallen asleep. She opened her eyes and looked down to see Andy studying her thoughtfully.

"You look so tired," he whispered.

"Andy . . ." she said as she leaned close and tried to smile.

"It was a rough night wasn't it? I remember bits and pieces," he said, looking around the room. Katie followed his gaze.

She could tell it was afternoon from the way the light slanted through the windows.

"It's good to be home," Andy said, looking back at her. "Katie . . ."

"Yes, my love?"

Andy reached up and cupped Katie's cheek in his hand and said softly, "I do remember telling you last night that I love you, but I didn't finish. Katie, I love you forever, and I mean it — I *will* love you forever. Please never forget." He paused to take a labored breath. "I wanted to tell you one more time how amazing I think you are and that the time with you has been the best thing in my life."

He stroked her cheek weakly with his thumb, looking her deeply in the eye as he struggled to go on. "Katie, remember all the good times we've shared and remember, I'll always be with you."

He took her hand and kissed her palm gently before placing it against her cheek, holding it there with a trembling hand. "Whenever you think of me, hold your hand to your cheek like this, and you'll know I'm with you. I'm not exactly sure how, but I know that somehow, someway, I'll be there — with you. You have my promise." He looked deeply into her eyes as he stroked her hand gently with his thumb.

Katie's eyes welled with tears. "Andy, I'm so scared. I don't think I can go on without you."

Taking her hand in his, Andy squeezed it weakly and with a tender smile said, "Katie Garrett, we've talked about this. You're my girl, and you're going to do just fine. You're the most incredible person I've ever known, and I am so lucky to be your husband." Taking a difficult breath, Andy whispered, "And, Katie, always, always remember how very much I love you. Our love is forever."

"Forever," Katie whispered in return. She looked deeply into Andy's eyes and watched as the soft smile on his lips slowly faded. She felt his hand go slack in hers and saw his eyes leave her face and drift upward, becoming fixed, unseeing.

Katie gasped. The air pushed from her lungs as if she'd been punched in the stomach. "Andy?" she strangled out. The silence in the room roared in her ears as she felt her entire world shift irreversibly. Still grasping Andy's hand tightly, she sat back, numb, staring at the face dearer to her than anything on earth.

"Andy," she whispered, "please don't leave me. Not yet. I need you . . . I need you, Andy."

Her words were unheard, and her plea brought no response. In that awful moment, Katie felt trapped, trapped in a silent, lonely void. All she could see was a huge, empty chasm opening in front of her; in it there was nothing but silence and emptiness.

Tears came, finally, silently, unheeded; but tears, alone, weren't enough to express the depth of anguish consuming her. Katie began to sob, uncontrollably, deep, gut-wrenching sobs as she rocked back and forth, clutching Andy's hand.

HER WORLD STOPPED WITH Andy's last breath. She didn't know how much time had passed when she felt a hand on her shoulder. She looked up at a woman she didn't know, looking at her with sympathy and compassion.

"Katie, my name is Harriet. I'm the hospice nurse. Why don't you come with me?" Confused, Katie sat with tears continuing to fall, still grasping Andy's hand firmly in her own. The nurse reached down to take Andy's hand from Katie.

Something welled up from inside, and Katie grasped Andy's hand even tighter. "No!" she said vehemently. "No!" She looked to Andy and saw the nurse had closed his eyes. A suffocating realization washed over her. She'd never see Andy's blue eyes sparkle again. She'd never hear his voice, see his impish grin, feel the thrill of his touch or hear him laugh. Andy was gone, and she felt more alone than she'd ever imagined possible. Her sides already ached from crying, but she started crying again, deep with brokenhearted sobs.

Harriet stepped out of the room and retrieving a file, opened it to a list of phone numbers. She pulled out her phone and dialed the number at the top of the list.

Fifteen minutes later, Jerry Hamilton knocked softly on the front door. Harriett answered and let him in. He walked sadly down the hall, dreading what he would encounter. He prayed to know the right things to say and do. He stepped to the bedroom door and saw Katie doubled over, holding Andy's hand and crying. Jerry glanced at Andy's still form and felt his own anguish as tears welled. He would need to process his own grief for Andy later. Right now, Katie needed him.

Jerry knelt beside Katie and touched her shoulder gently. "Katie," he whispered.

She looked up, her face swollen and wet, her eyes red.

"Katie, come with me. Please," he said softly. He reached down and removed Andy's hand from Katie's grasp and placed it gently by Andy's side. Katie collapsed against Jerry as he lifted her to her feet and steered her into the guest bedroom, closing the door softly behind them. They sat on the edge of the bed, Jerry holding Katie as she slumped numbly against him, unable to stop the tears that continued to fall.

A few minutes later, Harriett answered a light knock at the front door. Chaplain Alex MacShane introduced himself, and Harriett took him to Chief Hamilton and Katie.

Harriett made all the necessary phone calls and in no time, the funeral home had come and gone. Katie heard them through the bedroom door as they moved down the hall and back again. She couldn't bring herself to think about what was happening. Instead, she tried to focus on what Jerry and Chaplain MacShane were saying. She was sure they heard the noise in the hall too but they kept talking, doing their best to distract her.

Katie's parents and Trenton arrived and spent several minutes talking with Jerry Chief Hamilton, who in spite of his own heartache, shared calm reassurances and let them know how much Andy meant to him personally. Chaplain MacShane offered expressions of faith and comfort, telling Katie how much he had enjoyed talking to Andy. He had been impressed with Andy's foresight in making his plans, truly demonstrating the love he had for Katie. Hamilton and the chaplain took turns sharing the details of a line of duty service for a firefighter and some of what Katie and her family could expect over the next few days.

Finally, Jerry stood to leave, his arm still protectively around Katie. Chaplain MacShane and the rest of the family stood while the Chaplain led a brief prayer. Jerry hugged Katie before he and Chaplain MacShane, closed the bedroom door, stepping into the family room where the hospice nurse and Natalie, who had arrived a few minutes prior, waited quietly for them.

Natalie, tears on her cheeks, walked quickly to Jerry and put her arms around him. He put his head on her shoulder and allowed himself to give in to her embrace but just for a moment.

"Thank you," Jerry said to Harriett as he straightened and took Natalie's hand tightly in his own. "You've taken care of everything?" He cleared his throat, trying to check his emotions.

"Yes, sir. All has been done according to the plan Mr. Garrett laid out. I am very sorry. He was so young," she said, shaking her head.

"Yes. It is very sad. Thank you for calling us and thank you for being so gentle with Katie. This is going to be hard for her. They loved each other so ..." Jerry's voice caught, and Natalie squeezed his hand. Jerry felt his grief bearing down on him. Andy was a force unto himself, an incalculable loss in so many ways ... so much like Scott.

The melancholy group glanced down the hall to the closed bedroom door and then back to each other. They followed Harriet out, shutting the door behind them.

K ATIE DIDN'T RECOGNIZE HER own reflection. Her face was pale and drawn, her eyes bleary and tired. The simple black dress she was wearing for the evening's visitation was thanks to a quick shopping trip with Sally. It was princess style, with long sleeves, a rounded neck, and a lacy white collar. Katie closed the clasp on the pearl necklace, and slowly put on her pearl earrings, one at a time. She fingered the necklace that gleamed so brightly against the black of her dress. Andy had given her the necklace and earrings as a wedding gift the night before their wedding. She smiled remembering the proud grin on his face as he watched her open the velvet jeweler's box. He had worked double shifts and some extra odd jobs so he could get them for her.

She still couldn't fathom she'd never talk to him again. She kept expecting him to walk through the door. She'd stood in their living room, looking at the sofa where they'd shared so many wonderful times curled up together, watching a movie, talking . . . and now, strangers sat there eating food that other strangers had brought. Her mom, Mandy, Sally, and Natalie were there all day, every day, helping with the people that came to offer their sympathy. There were so many people Katie didn't know, but they all knew Andy.

His truck sat in the driveway. It hadn't been moved since he'd parked it there a couple of months ago. His keys still lay on the table inside the door. She'd gone to their closet several times the past couple of days, not for something to wear but to gather Andy's shirts in her arms, to smell him, to remember how it felt to have his arms around her, to feel his body next to hers, to see the smile he always wore right before he kissed her. Her lips ached for another kiss. The memories were overwhelming. She forced herself to turn away from the mirror.

The black suit for tomorrow's funeral was laid out on the bed. Sally had taken her shopping for clothes the day after . . . Katie couldn't say it even to herself. Sally was a strong shoulder to lean on, and she'd made herself indispensable. In fact, Katie was grateful for everyone's help, allowing her to gather her thoughts.

She sat on the edge of their bed and fingered the hem of her dress. She hadn't been to the funeral home yet to see him. She wanted to go, but she was afraid. She knew when she saw him there, in that place . . .

She jumped at a knock on the door. "Yes?" she answered tentatively.

"Katie, dear," her father stuck his head in the door. "Chief Hamilton and Chaplain MacShane are here to take us to the funeral home. We'll have some time for family before everyone arrives. They thought you might want that."

Chief Hamilton and Chaplain MacShane had been kind and attentive in ways Katie never realized how much she would need. She thought back to the day it happened, when they had been there. In the very wake of Andy's passing, it had been a comfort to hear Jerry talk about how Andy was like his brother. Chaplain MacShane's kind reassurances in low and comforting tones had soothed her heart as much as her broken heart could be comforted.

Katie sighed. Even with their help, getting through the next couple of days seemed daunting. When Andy had told her he'd made his funeral arrangements, she'd been surprised he hadn't told her what he'd been doing. But now, she loved and appreciated him even more for sparing her that burden.

"Katie?" her father asked again.

Katie gave a small nod. "Yes — coming. Tell them both thank you."

Katie stood, smoothed her skirt, and made a quick glance in the mirror. She gently fingered the gleaming pearls once again and followed her dad out the door.

Chief Hamilton and Chaplain MacShane waited solemnly in the living room. They were dressed in what Andy had called a Class A uniform, a long sleeve white uniform shirt and a tie. Their badges had a black strip of fabric across the middle; a shroud for Andy, Katie realized. Chief Hamilton offered Katie his arm and escorted her and her parents to his suburban, while Chaplain MacShane escorted Trenton and his family to a second fire department vehicle.

CHIEF HAMILTON PARKED NEAR the front door of the funeral home and came around to open the door for Katie and her parents as Chaplain MacShane did the same for Trenton and his family. The funeral director was waiting for them, and Chief Hamilton made the introductions. Katie attempted a smile of acknowledgment, but the double doors to her right had captured her attention. The doors' windows were glazed but through them she could see the colors of an American flag. Following her gaze, the funeral director looked to Chief Hamilton, who nodded.

The director turned to Katie and opened the doors. "Mrs. Garrett, this way." The rest of Katie's family stepped back to allow Katie to go in first, alone.

Katie could sense the room was long and stretched to either side, but her focus was on the oak casket in front of her. Its wood was polished to a high shine, and the brass handles gleamed brightly. A fire department honor guard stood post on either side, each holding the symbolic fire ax; an American flag was on the right side and a Texas flag to the left. The top of the casket was open; the closed portion was draped with an American flag with Andy's fire helmet on top. With a nod from Chief Hamilton, the two men of the honor guard filed past Katie and out the doors as Chief Hamilton pulled them closed, leaving Katie alone.

As she walked slowly toward the casket, Andy's profile came into view. She was at his side, looking into the face of the man she loved. Katie looked at Andy for a long time, willing him to open his eyes and say something, anything, so she could hear his voice again. She searched his face and saw that the anguish of pain so evident the past few months, especially the last few weeks, was no longer there. His face was extremely thin, but still so handsome and endearing. He was relaxed and peaceful. She even thought she detected a hint of his roguish smile at the corners of his mouth. He was dressed in his dress blue uniform, the dark blue, crisp gold braid and shiny brass buttons contrasting the cream-colored lining of the casket. His hands rested naturally on his midsection, his left hand over his right. On his left hand, his wedding band sparkled in the light and Katie blinked away sudden tears. After losing so much weight, he'd stopped wearing it several months ago for fear of losing it. But he'd made sure to wear it now, and it was almost more than Katie could bear.

Looking back to his face, Katie said softly, "Andy . . . I miss you." She gathered a shaky breath and continued, "I'm lost without you. Everyone has been so wonderful but I just . . . I just want you back . . ."

As she brushed away the tears that had begun to fall, she felt an unusual warmth on her cheek. She placed her hand there and as it grew, its intensity and warmth radiated through her fingers, and she remembered Andy's promise. He was there, and he was letting her know. She pressed her hand to her cheek as she looked down into his sweet face and smiled. "You promised, didn't you?" She gazed lovingly at him for several long moments and then touched her fingers to her lips and then to his. "I love you, Andy, with all my heart, and I always will. Forever," she whispered. The warmth on her cheek slowly faded. She stepped back, feeling a strength she hadn't felt since that terrible day.

The doors opened behind her, and the honor guard resumed their places as Katie's family joined her. Katie thought she knew Andy and expected quite a few people, but the outpouring was overwhelming.

Among the crowd was Andy's high school friend, Barry, and his wife, Gina. Andy had told Katie how close he and Barry had been in high school. They'd stayed in touch, so she wasn't surprised when Andy told her he'd asked Barry to be a pall bearer. She hadn't seen Barry since he'd been one of Andy's groomsmen. Barry was charming, not surprising being Andy's friend, and his wife was lively and kind. Katie wished the four of them had had a chance to spend time together.

Katie was listening to Barry tell a story about one of Andy's football heroics when Barry's eyes suddenly shifted to a spot behind Katie, and he stiffened. Katie turned to see a woman she didn't recognize standing beside the casket. Katie looked back to Barry with a questioning look.

"What is it?" Katie asked. "Who is that?"

Barry gritted his teeth and nodded tightly in the direction of the woman. "That's her."

Katie looked back at the woman. "Who?"

"Andy's mother."

Katie gasped. A thousand thoughts flew through her mind — some not very kind — toward this woman who was evidently grieving as she looked into the casket.

Katie gently brushed Barry's protests aside, not sure of what she'd say or if she should even acknowledge the woman's presence, but something compelled her to at least introduce herself.

Katie stopped a few steps away, close enough for the woman to see her. For several minutes the woman continued to stare into the casket, seemingly unaware of Katie's presence. Finally, she turned, and even if Barry hadn't already told her this woman was Andy's mother, Katie would have known. Andy looked so much like her. She was very attractive, a middle-aged woman, hair the color of Andy's, and blue eyes — not as blue as Andy's but still a brilliant blue. She was dressed impeccably in an expensive suit.

The woman turned and studied Katie, finally saying, "You're Andy's wife."

"And you're Andy's mother," Katie replied evenly, trying to keep an accusatory tone from creeping into her voice.

"Yes, I'm Morgan Edwards." She extended her hand, but Katie didn't acknowledge it.

"Why are you here?" Katie asked, fighting the anger quickly building inside. This woman, who Andy had needed and believed didn't love him, was here and seeming to grieve for a son she'd emotionally abandoned.

"Well, I'm here for Andy, my angel boy," she replied, looking sadly to the casket.

Katie blanched. "Your angel boy needed you while he was alive," she said softly but pointedly. "Where have you been for the past ten years? He's looked for you. He wanted you at our wedding."

Morgan Edwards gave a start. "He did?"

"Yes — he did. He also told me he went back to the house where he grew up the day he got his diagnosis, wishing he could talk to you."

Fresh tears started down Morgan Edwards' cheeks. "I didn't know . . . and I didn't know he was sick. I only just heard about —"

"And just how did you find out?" Katie broke in.

"Someone I used to work with always let me know if she heard anything about Andy. I heard about the fire where he was injured. Is that what . . . caused?" she asked, gesturing toward the casket.

"No," Katie shook her head. "But it was work related. He inhaled cancer-causing agents at a fire several years ago. They think that's what caused the cancer. He loved being a firefighter, though, and he was really good at it too," Katie said proudly as she looked at Andy.

As Andy's mom continued to look at Andy, Katie's heart suddenly softened toward this woman. Katie thought of the look on Andy's face when their wedding invitation came back undeliverable. She remembered Andy talking about the high school football and baseball games his mom didn't attend and how disappointed he'd been. Today, though, his mom was here and grieving for her son. Katie knew what Andy would want.

She reached out and took Morgan's hand. "I'm glad you're here, and I know Andy would be glad too."

Morgan pulled Katie into a tight embrace. "Even though Andy isn't here for me to ask, please forgive me. He was always such a dear child, and I . . . well, I was a horrible mother. He really was my angel boy." Morgan went on, seemingly unable to stop. "I was scared . . . scared of being alone and scared of the responsibility of trying to support both of us. When Donald came along, he was a lifeline, but I chose badly when I married him. I know the way he treated Andy, and I stood by and did nothing. Andy didn't deserve it — any of it."

Morgan dabbed at her cheeks with a handkerchief. "I didn't even go to any of Andy's games during high school or any of his other school events. Donald wouldn't let me. He ranted that Andy wasted time on sports." Morgan gave a regretful smile. "I heard he was good."

Katie tried to laugh. "Good? He was a lot more than good. He was a star athlete. Andy excelled at everything in spite of...well, in spite of how he grew up."

Morgan looked to Andy's face as fresh tears fell. Katie couldn't help but go on. "Andy excelled at being a firefighter too," she said proudly. "And, he was one of the best paramedics in Abernathy. He was loved and respected by a lot of people, as you can see." She gestured to the large number of people in the room. Katie forced herself to stop, but she wanted this woman to know what an amazing man her son turned out to be in spite of her neglect.

Several minutes passed before Morgan said softly, "Looking back, I can't believe how awful I was to him, how he must have felt and now," she said, looking at Andy. "And now, it's too late to ask his forgiveness."

"It may be too late for you to ask Andy, but you just told me. I think that would make him happy — and he would be happy knowing you're here."

Morgan looked at Katie and smiled through her tears. "I can see he was much wiser than I was in choosing a partner, and he made a very good choice. He was lucky to find you."

Katie smiled and squeezed Morgan's hand. "I was the lucky one. I assure you."

Seeing Katie talking so warmly with Andy's mother, Barry walked over and tentatively extended his hand. She took it and smiled, relief on her face.

Katie smiled looking between them. It had been an emotional day. She knew it was going to be, but it had been much more than she'd expected. She'd never imagined, or even dreamed, it would be the day she'd meet Andy's mother.

People had been coming for the past two hours, and now, as Katie looked around the room, it was still filled with people. She had always known how drawn to Andy people were but now, she was just beginning to realize the true impact of his life and on so many people.

Thirty minutes later, Jerry cleared the room to allow her one final moment alone with Andy. It was quiet as Katie stood, her hands resting on the edge of the casket. She looked at Andy, memorizing everything she could about him, and then she bid him a silent good-bye, all too aware she'd never see his dear face again. One last time she put her fingers to her lips and then to his, drawing a sense of comfort and peace knowing his spirit was with her and would be — forever.

KATIE STOOD IN THE church foyer beside Chief Hamilton the next morning, her right hand in the crook of his arm. The pallbearers Andy had selected stood on either side of Katie and her family, while Andy's closed casket sat at the front of the auditorium in a circle of soft light, surrounded by flowers and plants. The casket was draped with an American flag, and Andy's helmet was centered on top.

She tugged at the jacket of her black suit and trembled at the thought of what she was about to do. Her parents were behind her and Trenton and Stephanie just behind them. Natalie had taken charge of the boys, and they were already sitting on the second pew from the front along with Andy's mom. Katie still couldn't believe Morgan was here, and she almost felt sorry for her. Morgan seemed almost overwhelmed at the outpouring of love being shown for Andy. Katie only wished she had been around to see herself what an exceptional son she had.

Katie took a shaky breath. Jerry looked down and patted her hand. "You doing okay?"

Katie nodded, feeling anything but okay. The auditorium was full to overflowing with firefighters, police officers and civilians. She knew that once she walked through that door, every eye in the room would be on her. She wasn't used to being the center of attention — that had always been Andy's role and he relished it. She had been happy just to be at his side, but now — Andy was gone. She had to face this service, this day and the rest of her life without him. She wasn't sure how she was going to do that. But today, she would celebrate Andy.

Katie's father's strong hand squeezed her shoulder from behind, and Trenton stepped up to give her a reassuring hug and nod. Katie gave them a trembling smile in return before turning back to see Chaplain MacShane step to the podium and motion for the crowd to stand.

Her heart was pounding. She took a deep breath and gripped Jerry's arm tighter. She could hear Andy's voice reassuring her, "You'll do just fine. You're my girl."

Yes. She would do fine. Katie lifted her chin. She would make Andy proud today.

Ahead of her, the pallbearers walked down the aisle in step by twos. Andy had chosen those he was closest to and knew best: Keevin Jernigan, kind-hearted and nurturing; Andy's partner and the station rookie, Sean Hedrick; the self-assured Mark Canfield; the always rock-solid Rob Hart; his best friend in high school, Barry Giles; and new friend, Mike Bentley. They stopped a few steps before they reached the casket. The five firefighters slowly raised and lowered their right hands in silent salute while Barry studied the casket solemnly.

Jerry patted Katie's hand as he began to walk, and Katie fell into step beside him. The pews passed, mostly in a blur, but she was able to pick some faces out. She spotted Dr. Parker with sympathy and sadness on his kind face. Charlene Todd dabbed her eyes with a white handkerchief trimmed in hot pink and who, Katie guessed, must be Walt Henderson standing beside her frowning sadly. Mr. Gesuppi, Giovanni, and what must have been the entire Gessupi's restaurant crew filled a couple of pews. Mr. Gesuppi nodded sadly to Katie when their eyes met. Katie caught Mandy Fitzhugh's eye as Mandy blotted her wet cheeks with a tissue. They were almost to the front when Katie caught sight of Sally and Betty Glendon. On the row beside them were the students from Katie's second grade class, as well as some of their parents. Katie's breath caught. Sally, tears on her cheeks, smiled encouragement, as Betty stood beside her, watching sadly. Katie tried to smile to her students who were watching, their eyes wide.

Reaching the front, Katie could now see the large picture of Andy on an easel to the left of the casket. It was his official fire department photo but wasn't bogged down with formality. Andy exuded charm and charisma as he flashed a brilliant smile from the photo's canvas. His blue eyes were electric with sparkle. Katie gazed into the blue eyes in the picture and smiled wistfully before sitting down beside Jerry.

Chaplain MacShane spoke first, giving the who, what, where and when of Andy's life along with significant highlights of his career with the Abernathy Fire Department. Chaplain MacShane shared several anecdotes of Andy's skill and ability as a firefighter and paramedic, along with several humorous stories. Katie smiled and laughed with everyone, knowing the antics and pranks were typical of Andy and his fun outlook on life. Following a couple of hymns and a prayer, Chief Hamilton patted Katie's hand and walked to the podium.

He looked out over the large audience and took a deep breath. "We are not here today to grieve Andy Garrett's passing, even though his loss saddens all of us. Instead, we are here to celebrate the Andy Garrett who loved life and was determined to live it to its fullest.

"I met Andy when he was in the fire academy, and I knew right away he was a natural. He grasped firefighting concepts easily, and he was an extraordinarily-gifted paramedic both medically and in the way he related to his patients. Andy touched hundreds of lives, saving many.

But his true gift, as seen by this large gathering today, was leaving lives better off than when he found them. While it's true Andy loved the fire service, there was one thing he loved more. He told me himself that what he cherished most in this life was his beautiful wife, Katie."

Jerry smiled at Katie who blushed as tears burned her eyes.

"Andy was taken from this life way too soon," Jerry went on. "He was only twenty-eight when he died from pancreatic cancer, which is a very painful way to have life taken from you. You might be wondering, especially those in the fire service, why a firefighter who died from cancer is being honored today as a death in the line of duty. Andy's cancer is considered a workplace injury as the doctors and experts who studied his case agree the chances are extremely high one particular fire and exposure to its toxic chemicals and carcinogens were what caused Andy's cancer."

Jerry paused to take a deep breath and went on.

"Andy isn't physically with us, but he wrote a letter and asked me to read it today. So, with your permission," Jerry said, taking a pair of reading glasses from his coat pocket and removing a sheet of paper from his notebook. He read:

"Hello All. First of all, I want to say what a fine organization we work for. Without the rock that is this job and the people I serve with, the last several months would have had a good shot at breaking me. The fire service is a family that takes care of its community and takes care of its own. I guess you might say in fire service terms, we are 'fully involved.' When I had to stop working my second job because of my treatment schedule, you gave money to help with bills. I found money in my locker, under the mattress on my bed or slid into my hand as we shook hands. I needed you more than you knew when we sat around and laughed together, and when we accomplished good things in the field. I couldn't have kept going

without specialized firehouse cooking and encouragement to keep working through my ailments. There were some hard days, but I owed it to all of you to keep going. You made this last Christmas one of the best and most special ever for Katie and I. I can never thank you enough for the laughter and joy you brought us. You helped so much, and sometimes anonymously, there would have been no way to thank each of you individually, but I extend my heartfelt thanks to you now. Unfortunately, life is tragic and human beings suffer. It's the stuff we are involved in that is bigger than ourselves and that make it all worthwhile. Stay mindful of your brothers and sisters when they need you most. We do it for the public, and you did it for me. Thank you for everything. Your friend and fire service brother, Andy Garrett."

Jerry placed the letter back in the notebook and returned to his seat. Andy's simple but compelling words invoked powerful emotions. Katie sat motionless, proud tears falling unheeded. Andy had never mentioned that letter but how fitting that out of the depth of his love for the fire service he would write such meaningful words to share on this day.

Chaplain MacShane took several minutes before coming to the podium and after a final song and prayer, asked the audience to stand. After the crowd exited, the pallbearers lined either side of the casket and slowly rolled it up the aisle as Katie, Chief Hamilton, and the family followed. The Honor Guard positioned on either side of the foyer, called "present AHRMS" and saluted as the casket and pall bearers entered and then exited and took position directly behind Engine Two.

Katie walked close behind the casket between two rows of saluting Abernathy firefighters standing shoulder to shoulder and lining the path to the engine. The pipe and drum corps played softly as the pall bearers transferred the casket to the Honor Guard, who lifted it onto the hose bed of Engine Two.

The procession of apparatus and vehicles then moved slowly down the drive and turned onto the street where a police motorcycle officer had stopped traffic. Katie's breath caught as they turned. As far as she could see, fire engines, fire trucks, ambulances, and every type of fire apparatus lined both sides of the street, their emergency lights flashing and their chrome sparkling in the sun as it shone brilliantly out of the crisp February sky. Beside each piece of shiny equipment, firefighters in dress uniform, stood at attention. As the engine, with the casket, rolled past, wave after wave of hands raised in salute and remained at attention until the procession passed.

"This is all so — overwhelming," Katie began. "We ... I had no idea this would be so — much."

Jerry reached over and patted Katie's hands clutched tightly in her lap.

Continuing to pass fire service equipment until they negotiated the tight turn onto the cemetery's drive, they passed through the gate under two crossed ladders extending from the back of fire engines on either side. Like the others, their red lights were flashing and their crews standing at attention.

Driving down two or three of the cemetery's narrow gravel roads, the engine pulled off to the side and stopped. From the suburban, Katie saw a small green tent several feet off the path. Inside were two rows of folding chairs. A few feet in front of the chairs and just outside the edge of the tent's awning, stood a shiny metal caisson surrounded by the flowers brought over from the church. Katie watched as the pallbearers and Honor Guard made their way to the back of the engine and began to remove the casket.

Jerry opened her door, but Katie couldn't move. The strength she'd felt earlier was waning. She knew Andy was gone, but in her heart, she hadn't really fully admitted it. That tent was the end, and if she went to that tent, standing beside the place where Andy would lay in the ground, it would be . . . over. No. She couldn't do this. She just couldn't.

"Katie?" she heard Jerry's voice coming from far away. "Are you okay?"

Katie's parents and Trenton stepped to Jerry's side, the same look of concern on their faces.

Katie looked frantically from one face to the other. "I can't . . . I just can't do this," she sobbed as she slumped and put her face in her hands.

They looked at each other, unsure of what to do.

Trenton took a deep breath and stepped near Katie. "Sis, you know what I'm thinking about today?" Trenton asked with a slight tease in his voice.

Katie looked up, hesitantly, and shook her head.

"I'm thinking about a softball game about four years ago when I watched my little sister cook up a scheme to meet this cocky firefighter on the department's team. Do you remember that?"

Katie looked down and gave a tentative nod.

"I had never seen my little sister do anything like that before, and I was impressed. It was a gutsy move." Trenton took one of Katie's hands. "Turns out, she married that cocky firefighter. He fell for her really hard and you know, for being so cocky, he really was a smart guy."

Katie looked up with a small smile.

"You're stronger than you think, Katie. Andy saw it in you. What do you think he would he say if he were standing here right now?"

Several seconds passed before Katie said softly, "He already told me. He said I'll do fine."

"And he's right. You will. This will probably be the hardest thing you'll ever have to do, but we're all here with you." Trenton extended his hand to Katie who reluctantly took it and stepped out of the suburban. Trenton embraced her and whispered in her ear, "You've got this. Make Andy proud."

Katie looked again at the tent, the metal caisson, the flowers, the crowd waiting and the Honor Guard carrying the casket ahead of them. It was surreal. It was like watching a tragic play unfolding complete with an audience and actors on a stage. The Honor Guard carefully placed the casket on the caisson and took their place standing directly behind it. Chaplain MacShane stood next to the casket while the pallbearers moved to stand directly behind him.

Katie, her family, and Jerry, with Natalie close beside him, followed in the wake of the Honor Guard and pallbearers, the dead winter grass dusty and crunching beneath their feet. Jerry escorted Katie and Natalie to their seats in the front row then took his place beside Chaplain MacShane. Katie hesitantly sat in the metal folding chair, her parents on either side. Trenton, Stephanie and the boys, along with Andy's mom, were on the row behind. The large crowd gathered close, surrounding the tent on three sides.

Katie looked at the casket. Everything from the colors of the flag laying on top to the scent of the flowers around it were strikingly vivid. The brilliant blue of the sky reminded her of Andy's eyes. It was a fitting backdrop for the stark branches of the trees dotting the little cemetery."

Chaplain MacShane moved forward and stood beside a bronze firehouse bell mounted on a stand. "On behalf of Fire Chief Hamilton and the Abernathy Fire Department, we would like to thank you, Katie Garrett, for allowing each of us to participate in honoring our brother, Andy, today.

"The fire service is rich with ceremony, custom, and tradition. The Abernathy Fire Department's custom of rendering final honors is a long-standing fire service tradition. In the past, it was church bells that sounded when there was a fire. As time moved on, the bell signaled the beginning of a firefighter's shift. Throughout the day and night, each alarm was sounded by a bell summoning these brave souls to place their lives in jeopardy for the good of their fellow citizens. When the fire was out, it was the bell that signaled completion of that call. When a firefighter, paying the supreme sacrifice, dies in the line of duty, it's the mournful toll of the bell that solemnly announces that comrade's passing.

"A special signal of five rings, three times each, represents the end of our comrade's duties. With this rendering of final honors, we pay respect to our departed brother, Abernathy Department Firefighter Andrew Garrett. His tasks complete, his duties well done, to our comrade, it is his last alarm. He is going home."

Chaplain MacShane picked up the bell striker and struck the bell five times, paused, then five more times and after a final pause, five more strikes. Each strike of the bell struck Katie's heart, and she shuddered as the final tone hung on the air. "Ask not for whom the bell tolls," the line from the John Dunne poem ran through her mind, "it tolls for thee." The familiar line seemed appropriate as the solemn tones drifted off on the breeze.

"The signal 5-5-5 has been sounded," Chaplain MacShane continued. "It is with deep sincerity that the Abernathy Fire Department honors our brother Andrew Garrett whose tour is completed. He has returned to quarters."

The Honor Guard moved forward and standing at the four corners of the casket, they removed the flag and folded it into a crisp triangle. Chief Hamilton received the flag and then turned and walked to Katie. Kneeling in front of her, he held it out to her. Katie accepted the flag with shaking hands as Jerry whispered in her ear, "We will all miss him very much, but we, as his fellow firefighters, promise you our support. You will always be part of the fire service brotherhood." Jerry looked her in the eye and nodded firmly.

Katie watched the pallbearers pass by the casket, one by one to say their good-byes. Barry Giles came first, his cheeks wet with tears, as he stood solemnly, deep in his own thoughts and memories. Jernigan was next, placing a gloved hand gently on the casket. Hedrick then stepped to the casket and laid his gloved hands on top and mouthed a few silent words before moving on. Canfield stared solemnly at the shiny oak casket and gave a curt nod before walking stiffly away. Hart, stoic as always, stopped and placed both gloved hands firmly on top. He stared at the casket intensely, standing rigidly silent for several seconds, seemingly reluctant to move on. Last, came Bentley. With the history between he and Andy, Katie was curious what Bentley might do. He walked to the front, looking first to Katie, he then turned and faced the casket. Standing rigidly at attention for several seconds, he slowly moved his hand to his temple in solemn salute. That simple gesture of respect conveyed more than anything else ever could, and Katie's eyes filled with tears.

Chief Hamilton looked at her, and she stiffened. The moment had come for her final good-bye. Everyone waited expectantly as Katie, clutching the flag Jerry had given her, slowly stood and walked to the casket. She placed her left hand on the smooth wood, gripping it until her wedding ring dug into her finger. Katie bent near the top of the casket and said softly, "Andy Garrett, I'll love you — forever, and I will never, *ever* forget."

I**T HAD BEEN TWO** months since Andy's death. It hurt to even think those words. Katie knew in her heart it wasn't Andy's fault, but she still couldn't help being angry. He'd left her behind to live without him. She screamed over and over that it wasn't fair as she lay in bed alone each night. This hurt was worse than anything she could have ever imagined. Part of her, the best part — Andy — had been ripped away and the wound left gaping and raw. Suffocating grief surrounded her like a fog that never seemed to lighten.

Andy had made her world bright, colorful, and filled with endless possibilities. Her world without Andy was dull, a somber black and white. Nothing felt worth doing any more. Most of the time she found herself on the sofa where they'd often sat together, Andy's arm around her. Her heart still skipped a beat thinking of how he'd looked at her, how he'd laced his fingers with hers, how perfectly their bodies fit together, how their hearts beat in unison when Andy held her tight. They had been so happy together, but now...

The guys from the station came by regularly to help around the house or just to check on her. She would visit with them briefly but the effort to be social was just too much. In the last few weeks, she had withdrawn from everything and everyone but then, Jerry showed up with an invitation she found she couldn't refuse.

Jerry stood in the doorway when Katie opened the door. "May I come in?"

Katie stepped aside for him to enter.

"How are you doing?" Jerry asked tentatively as they both sat on the sofa.

Katie shrugged her shoulders and looked away as she said softly, "The same."

Jerry took Katie's hands in his. "Katie," he began, but she stood and walked a few steps away.

"Jerry, please don't . . ."

He followed her and handed her an envelope. "Please take a look at this," he said, placing it in her hands.

Katie opened the flap and pulled out an invitation. It was to the grand opening of the new Station Two. Katie remembered how excited Andy had been about the new station. "It's going to have great showers," he'd said with a teasing grin and wiggle of his eyebrows. Katie sighed before taking a closer look. The bold Abernathy Fire Department logo blazed across the top of the cream linen and beneath it read:

"You are cordially invited to the official grand opening of the
Abernathy Fire Department's
Andrew H. Garrett Fire Station Two,
dedicated to the service and memory of
Firefighter Andrew H. Garrett,
Years of Watch 1994 - 2001"

The date of Monday, May 7, 2001, and the time of 10:00 a.m. were below with an RSVP phone number at the bottom.

Katie looked sharply at Jerry. "What is this?"

"It's Bentley's doings," Jerry said, steering Katie back to the sofa. "I've worked for the City a long time and never seen anything like this. Bentley spearheaded an absolutely monumental effort to get this station named for Andy. It's something a city typically will not do, but Bentley took it through the ranks of the department, through the maze of red tape and regulations at City Hall. Late last week word came down that he'd succeeded. I think Andy would be pleased. What do you think?" Jerry asked, anxious to get Katie's reaction.

Katie stared at the invitation, her fingers skimming the words. She looked up at Jerry, tears in her eyes. "He'd absolutely love it. But he'd be the first to acknowledge so many others deserve an honor like this. For this to come at Bentley's initiative, that alone would have meant the world to Andy." Katie couldn't help but return Jerry's smile.

"I thought the same thing," Jerry said. "I'm so glad you feel that way. I've been sent on a special errand from Bentley."

"An errand for Bentley?"

Jerry turned on the sofa and once more took Katie's hands. "Katie, I know what your first reaction is going to be, but please just hear me out."

Jerry looked serious and it took Katie aback. "Well, of course. What is it?"

Jerry looked at her intently then said, "On behalf of the Abernathy Fire Department, we would appreciate your saying a few words about Andy at the dedication service. I and a few others will, of course, speak but nothing would make the dedication of this station more appropriate or more meaningful than hearing from the one person Andy cherished most in this world."

Katie gasped and tried to pull away, but Jerry held her hands firmly.

"Jerry, you don't know what you're asking," she said, her voice thin. "I can't do this. I'm not a public speaker. I can't even have a regular conversation about Andy without breaking down, let alone make a speech. Please don't ask me to do this." Tears began to course down her cheeks as her insides churned with fear but also, she realized, with a twinge of desire — desire to do this for Andy.

As if reading her mind, Jerry said, "I'll let Bentley know you're thinking about it."

Katie opened her mouth to object but closed it again. She *was* terrified, but somehow, she would find a way to do this. For Andy.

That had been four weeks ago and now, the day had come. Katie paced the floor and stopped to glance at the clock. Sally was supposed to pick her up at 9:45 a.m. They were meeting the rest of her family at the station. Katie pulled out the folder with her comments and flipped it open to reread the few words she'd put together. She just hoped she wouldn't break down and cry.

Katie walked to the window just as Sally pulled into the drive. She took a deep breath and started to the door but suddenly stopped. Her hands began to tremble, and she felt a bead of sweat trickle down one temple. What had she been thinking when she'd agreed to this? She wanted to do it — for Andy — but it was a challenge just making it through each day. She laid the folder back down on the table and placed a trembling hand on top before stepping away. No. She couldn't do this. She would offer her apologies to Jerry and Bentley, but she wasn't up to it. Katie took a deep breath and leaving her comments on the table, walked to the car. She tried to give Sally a convincing smile as she slid into the passenger seat.

As Katie buckled her seat belt, she felt Sally's eyes on her in a dis-approving frown.

"What?" Katie asked. "Something wrong?"

Sally frowned deeper. "Not buying it."

"Sorry?" Katie asked.

"I'm not buying the fake smile thing. You can't show up and look like you'd rather be anywhere but there."

"You have no idea what I'm —"

"This station is being dedicated in your husband's honor. Don't you think a little enthusiasm from his wife would be in order?"

Katie's face went white, and her lips pursed angrily into a thin line. Her chest heaving, she blurted out, "You want to know what I think? I think I don't want to go at all today. I'm not a public speaker. I want to do this for Andy, but I'm terrified. I know how much they're all counting on me, and I don't want to let anyone down — especially when it's for Andy. Don't you understand how hard it's going to be seeing all those guys in their uniforms and remember how Andy looked in his? I don't want to hear all the fire station talk about how they serve the public and save lives. Doing all that didn't help Andy, now did it? He died because of what he did to help other people. I don't want to hear all the nice things they'll say, expecting a gracious reply from me. I don't have any gracious replies. I'm sad. I miss my husband. What I want to do is go back inside my house and curl up in a tight little ball. I can't do this — I just can't. Does that answer your question? Are you happy now?" Katie's voice kept rising until she was almost screaming.

Sally watched Katie's pale face, tight with anger, and listened patiently to her tirade. This wasn't Katie talking. It was raw grief. Maybe asking her to do this today *was* too much too soon.

Sally studied Katie, her head now clasped in her hands, her shoulders sagging. Katie looked so frightened, so unsure of herself. Sally didn't know if she was about to do the right thing, but she reached over and pulled one of Katie's hands away from her face and held it tightly in her own. "Katie, please look at me."

Katie ducked her head and looked away, but Sally clasped her hand firmly and patiently waited. Katie eventually turned and looked at Sally with eyes that held such profound sadness, Sally momentarily froze. She took a deep breath and looking Katie in the eye, offered a small, encouraging smile. "Katie Garrett," she began, "Do you know what? I *am* happy. I am happy to be sharing this extraordinary day with the wife of the remarkable young man being honored today. Andy loved his job, he loved the men he served with, he loved serving the public. But most especially, he loved you."

Katie choked back a sob, but Sally continued. "You have shown an almost inhuman strength through the darkest times that you will probably ever experience. You showered Andy with love, attention and support right until the very end. Andy knew, without question, how much you loved him, and you know just as strongly how much he loved you. Put a smile on the face Andy loved so much and go out there and tell the world how proud you are of him. Let them hear from you what a difference Andy made in your life, and I would imagine others will remember what a difference he made in their lives, too. Can you imagine what a powerful effect that will have on you . . . on everyone?" Sally gripped Katie's hands. "You can do this, Katie. Do it for Andy."

Katie stared at Sally, unable to look away. The hum of the car engine was the only sound penetrating her numb mind as Katie searched her heart for the right thing to do. She could hear Andy encouraging her as he did so often, "You're my girl, Katie Garrett. You've got this." Katie could see his sparkling blue eyes smiling and hear him whisper, "And don't ever forget how much I love you — forever — remember."

It was at that moment Katie knew. She *could* do this.

"That's all I'm going to say so now, what do *you* say?" Sally waited and watched the conflicting emotions play across Katie's face.

Katie's lips parted in a timid smile. She pulled her hand gently from Sally's grasp and swatted a stray tear. "I say we'd better get a move on. We don't want to be late."

C SHIFT WAS ON duty so it was Andy's team mates who met Katie at the door of the new Station Two. Sally gave Katie a smile and a gentle push as Jernigan and Hedrick led her away on a personal tour. The new Station Two was huge compared to the old one. Katie admired the spacious kitchen and dining area, she commented on how roomy and comfortable the bedrooms looked. But as the group came to the family room, she stopped abruptly, seeing a large picture of Andy on the wall behind the recliners.

Exchanging a concerned look with Hedrick, Jernigan stepped up beside Katie. "I hope you don't mind. We thought Andy could always be part of things this way." Katie didn't move, so Jernigan continued. "The picture's placement was up for debate, but this spot won out." Jernigan glanced at Hedrick as they waited anxiously for Katie to say something.

Katie surprised them with a slight smile and took a seat in one of the recliners. Not daring to look at either of them quite yet, Katie's toe tapped lightly as she rocked back and forth. A few minutes later, she stood and said, "He'd get a kick out of it. I just wish *he* was here instead, but this means a lot."

"We miss him too, Katie," Jernigan said. "Never doubt that. He was and will continue to be a huge part of C shift, Station Two and the department, and we're so —"

Before Jernigan could finish, Chief Hamilton strode in. "Time to get things rolling. Everyone ready?"

The ceremony was compelling in its sincerity. Rows of Abernathy firefighters and city officials filled the spacious new bay area. Katie sat with her family in chairs close to the front along with Natalie, Sally and Mandy. Chaplain MacShane led a prayer asking for safety and good health for the men and women who would be serving the City of Abernathy out of Station Two. In his prayer, Chaplain MacShane also mentioned Andy and his contributions to the Abernathy Fire Department and asked for blessings on Katie and her family. The city manager said a few words and then Chief Hamilton stepped to the podium.

He cleared his throat, uncharacteristically nervous, and looking around the bay, began. "It is my honor to stand before you today on this occasion to honor Firefighter Andy Garrett. Andy was an exceptional young man. A dedicated firefighter and a caring, insightful paramedic. He is greatly missed. Not long after Andy told me of his cancer diagnosis, I confided something to him which he encouraged me to share. Today seems the most appropriate time and place."

Jerry paused and took a deep breath. A hush descended over the crowd. "Years ago, I had a younger brother, Scott, who followed me into the fire service. Andy reminded me of Scott in so many ways. They were both full of energy, enthusiasm and" — he paused with a slight smile — "they were both willful, more than a little stubborn and loved to have fun. Their excitement while at the station was infectious. They loved everything about firefighting.

"Our family, though, was stunned when just a few years after becoming a firefighter, Scott was diagnosed with cancer. He lost his battle fourteen months later. There was no history of cancer in my family so I wondered — why? Scott was young and strong. It didn't make any sense. I began researching cancer in the firefighting community. What was being discovered, even years ago, shocked me. The dangerous agents firefighters are exposed to every time they get near a fire far exceed even the most lenient of safety boundaries. Firefighters succumb to cancer-related deaths at a 14% higher rate than the general public and certain cancer rates can increase further based on factors such as number of fire runs and the amount of time spent at fires.

"Percentages are increasing rapidly. As research proves — and you know from personal experience — modern homes burn hotter. Not only do materials ignite quickly and more violently, they also leave toxic carcinogenic soot behind that sticks to firefighters' gear which can transfer to the skin when gear is being removed. These non-natural pollutants can also become breathable as smoke and toxic exposure risk becomes far greater.

"Just like every firefighter here, Scott and Andy fought many fires. But in each of their cases, they were involved in a particular fire that exposed them to chemicals extraordinarily high in carcinogens."

Chief Hamilton stopped and looked down for a long time. Finally, he cleared his throat and looked up, tears glistening in his eyes. "Andy knew firsthand how important this information is and asked me to find a way relay it to you for this reason: You are his fire service family, and he doesn't want what happened to him to happen to any of you. Andy doesn't get to continue fighting fire and doing what he loves. Most importantly, he won't get to live the long and happy life he and Katie were planning. But — and this is important — he wants each of you to have that opportunity.

"As Chief of the Abernathy Department, I assure you steps are being actively studied, pursued and implemented to combat these cancer-causing agents. Firefighter safety is of paramount importance. Andy asked me to encourage each of you to take every precaution. If you notice something that doesn't feel or look right, get it checked. Don't wait and try to tough it out. If even one life can be saved by hearing and following Andy's advice, his loss will have served a significant purpose.

"And now, I would like to introduce Andy's wife Katie, the one person who meant more to Andy than anyone else in this world. We are grateful Katie has agreed to say a few words this morning on hers and Andy's behalf."

Katie felt her heart lurch and her breathing quicken. Her knees trembled, but she managed to stand and walk to the podium. She looked out over those gathered. The large bay was full of people, all looking at her and waiting expectantly. She glanced over at Jerry who smiled and nodded encouragement. She saw Lt. Bentley standing proudly beside the C shift crew. She wished Andy stood there with them, handsome in the Abernathy Fire Department uniform he loved so much. She looked down, trying to collect her thoughts and recall some of what she'd written, but then, she decided to simply speak what was on her heart. She quickly blinked tears back before looking up at the crowd and nervously cleared her throat. Her voice was weak but grew stronger with each word.

"I loved Andy Garrett not just because he was an amazing firefighter, and not just because he was an exceptional paramedic. I didn't love Andy because he saved lives or because he took a little boy under his wing and filled him with hope and exciting stories about being a firefighter. I didn't love Andy just because he was fun and loved adventure. I didn't love Andy just because he was thoughtful, sweet, and gentle. I loved Andy because —"

Katie paused and in the hush, she saw Andy, standing with the C shift crew, beaming with pride, as he watched and listened. Katie blinked. The image was gone but she felt him near. "I loved Andy Garrett because he believed in me more than I believed in myself. Yes,

I was the lucky one married to Andy, and he took me along the great adventure of sharing his life, but he brought nothing but good to all those he came in contact with — whether it was a patient, a softball teammate, a member of the C shift crew, a friend or his wife. With the dedication of Station Two in his name, his legacy will continue to provide inspiration, especially to those in the fire service he loved and cared so much about. On behalf of Andy, we thank you for this tremendous honor."

Katie stepped back and the room exploded with applause. Those sitting in the chairs stood as one, applauding. Katie glanced over to Chief Hamilton and Lt. Bentley who were both applauding and smiling broadly as were the rest of the crew. Her lips trembled as she tried to smile at them.

The applause eventually died down and C shift, along with those on Station Two's A and B shifts, came to stand on either side of Katie. A coupled fire hose lay on the cement floor in front of them. Chief Hamilton and Bentley lifted the hose and handed the coupled joint to Katie. In the fire department's version of a ribbon cutting, Katie took the coupling, and with their help, turned the lever and the two hoses came apart. As everyone clapped and cheered, three broad bay doors folded open allowing bright sunlight to spill in. The polished chrome and sparkling red of Engine Two in the middle doorway was dazzling. Katie's breath caught, remembering Andy's smiling face as he waved to she and Lucas at last year's field trip.

Chief Hamilton then led Katie outside where he asked her to remove a velvet covering from the plaque hanging in the alcove of the station's front door. Katie removed the cover and gasped when she saw the beautiful bronze plaque bearing Andy's resemblance, the years of his life and the words of dedication Chief Hamilton had read in his remarks. The artist had captured Andy's personality perfectly and in spite of her sadness, Katie smiled.

"It's perfect," she whispered as she turned to Chief Hamilton and Lt. Bentley standing behind her, hugging first one and then the other. "It's absolutely perfect. Thank you." Battalion Chief Rogers then stepped to the flagpole to oversee the raising of the American flag for the first time on the station's new pole. Katie joined everyone in applauding as the flag unfurled from the firefighters' hands and began waving gently in the breeze.

Chief Hamilton's voice boomed over a megaphone, asking everyone to step away from the engine as an arch of water dowsed the engine for the traditional spray down. Katie knew, after hearing Andy talk about some of the fire service traditions, that the spraying of the water came from past eras when the transfer from an old engine to a new one meant water spilling and then having to be wiped up.

Katie hadn't really been interested at the time but had indulged Andy, listening as he went into detail about the time-honored traditions of the fire service. Now, watching some of those traditions come to life in front of her, she felt stirrings of the same pride Andy must have felt. She glanced over her shoulder at the bronze plaque with Andy's likeness and then back at the firefighters in their dark blue uniforms handing out towels to dry off the engine. Oh, how Andy would have loved this, she thought, remembering how his face had lit up when he talked about the ceremonial "pushing in" of an engine into a new station. It originated, he'd said, during the times of horse drawn equipment when an engine couldn't be backed by horses, so it had to be pushed by hand instead. That ceremony's tradition evolved to include members of the community, symbolizing the station's coming into service for the people.

Katie looked at the bustling scene in front of her, and she suddenly felt compelled to take part in these traditions that had meant so much to Andy. She made her way to the front of the crowd just as Hart passed by with a basket of towels. He gave her a rare grin as Katie reached in and pulled a towel from the basket. She stepped up to the engine, Sally and Mandy beside her with towels of their own, and they joined the others drying off the engine. Jernigan stepped into the cab a few minutes later and cranked the engine. He placed it in reverse, letting it idle as everyone gathered around. With everyone having at least one hand on the engine, it began to slowly back into its new bay.

Katie looked around at the hum of activity and looked fondly at the circle of firefighters who were Andy's friends. She saw Chief Hamilton talking with her family, and Sally and Mandy's smiling faces beside her. Katie looked up into the brilliant blue sky and knew she'd come into her own. Andy had given her that. He had fallen in love with her — just for her. In spite of any disappointments and insecurity she'd experienced before, this amazing, generous, loving man had fallen in love with her. Today, she'd found the confidence he'd left with her. *You're my girl, Katie Garrett. Never forget that."*

And today, she hadn't. Today she had honored him in a special way and with the fire service he loved so much. Katie felt the engine vibrating beneath her hand and then she felt a smile — a real smile — bloom for the first time in a long time. It was a start. Andy would have been pleased.

KATIE LAID THE MAIL and her purse on the small table by the front door. Since she and Sally were both retired, they didn't see each other very often. Getting together for lunch today had been fun but now, she was tired. It was hard to admit, but old age was gaining on her. Katie sat on the sofa and pulled the scrapbook she'd been looking through that morning back onto her lap. It was hard to believe it had been forty years since the grand opening of the Andrew H. Garrett Station Two. But it had, and Bentley was requesting photos of that day to commemorate the re-grand opening after the recent renovations, and she was determined to find them. She smiled as she turned to the pictures from the Christmas before Andy died. What a fun time that had been, in spite of Andy being so sick. He smiled at her from the pictures, but she could see the pain on his face. She shook her head sadly. He had suffered so much more that she realized only later.

Andy had been on her mind more than usual lately, and she wasn't sure why. He was always on her mind but the last few weeks, he seemed especially close. She still missed him terribly. Through the years, she had caught herself still turning to tell him something or reaching for his hand, only to remember he wasn't there. After all this time, she still felt as if he would walk through the door any minute. Well-intentioned others, not understanding her feelings, had tried to set her up on dates.

The other guys were nice, but none were Andy. The special magic she and Andy had shared didn't spark with anyone but him.

She turned a page and smiled as she saw a picture of Sally holding a bowl of chili and wearing a Santa hat and big grin. Sally never married her firefighter, but she did marry a high school football coach. They'd been married almost thirty years now and had two grown sons in college. Sally would always be her best friend. As Katie turned the pages, she saw other pictures from that Christmas — Keevin Jernigan and Sean Hedrick wrestling with the monster Christmas tree, Rob Hart and Mark Canfield dangling from the ladder and the house as they hung the Christmas lights.

In another picture, Bentley grinned at the camera, his arms reaching around the tree in the front yard as he wrapped it with Christmas lights. That picture made Katie smile most of all, thinking what close friends she'd become with Mike and his wife, Amy.

Not long after Station Two's grand opening, Chief Hamilton had approached Katie and asked her to become a spokesperson and advocate for creating awareness of the carcinogenic dangers firefighters face. Chief Hamilton had said as the widow of a fallen firefighter, she would have a strong impact and would increase awareness more effectively than someone without the emotional attachment. Katie wanted to do something to prevent other firefighters from suffering as Andy had and became determined to overcome her fear of public speaking. The more she spoke, the more her confidence grew, and she became in demand as a speaker by fire departments across Texas and neighboring states. She had also become a successful fund raiser for smaller departments and had lent her voice to their efforts to purchase safer equipment and gear.

Bentley, after rising in the ranks of the Abernathy Department, joined her, adding a firefighter's expertise and perspective. Katie and

Bentley often sat on the same dais as speakers, worked together and over the years, became close friends. Bentley was now a depty chief and would retire this year. This re-grand opening was his last large event to coordinate, and he'd told her it was going to be his best ever. He'd had a stellar career and was known among Abernathy firefighters as a firefighter's chief. There was no higher compliment. Bentley had told her many times over the years he owed his career to Andy.

The next few pages of the scrapbook were filled with pictures from Hedrick and Mandy's wedding. What a fun day it had been celebrating with them. They had three boys now, the first one they'd named Andy. Several years after Andy's passing, she'd asked Hedrick what it was he'd said over Andy's casket at the cemetery that day. Sean smiled and said softly, "I thanked him for showing me what true courage and bravery look like. He suffered more than any of us knew, and we'll never know how he kept going. He'll always be one of my heroes." Even though that conversation had been years ago, Katie remembered it like it was yesterday. She was and would always be so proud of Andy.

On the next page there was a picture of Jerry and Natalie in front of their old house. They'd moved to Colorado a few months after Jerry retired. Katie sighed. She missed them. They'd grown even closer after Andy's passing. Katie had spent a lot of time with them and had taken them up on the offer of their guest room many times when she felt especially lonely. They'd asked her to move to Colorado with them, but even though Katie would have loved to be near them, Abernathy was home.

Katie shivered. There was a chill from the fall air, and she pulled a throw around her shoulders before settling back to look at the next pages with pictures of her parents. They were both gone, but Trenton and Stephanie lived nearby. They were grandparents now. Anthony and Drexel were both married and had five children between their two families. Katie enjoyed being a big part of their lives and especially enjoyed spoiling her great nieces and great nephews every chance she got.

Katie stared at a picture of Trenton and Andy taken the Thanksgiving before Andy died. They had been so indifferent to each other when she and Andy married, but had become close the last few weeks of Andy's life. Katie had been surprised the first time she met Trenton leaving their house after he'd been to see Andy. She ran into him a few more times, and Andy had finally explained that Trenton was researching and helping with the federal grants and monies available to firefighters diagnosed with cancer, and Trenton had been successful. He had discovered two large benefits firefighters battling cancer and their families could receive due to presumptive laws in the state. Thanks to Trenton's tenacity, it had taken awhile, but he had been able to successfully acquire those grants for Katie. While working on those grants, Trenton had become familiar with the complicated process and made impressive contacts at the state level along the way. He saw the need to assist the increasing number of firefighters dealing with cancer and adapted his financial expertise to what he'd learned and made it his full time work to help them receive the government funds they had due. Trenton had joined Katie many times when she spoke and had helped numerous firefighters over the years.

As the coziness of the throw relaxed her, Katie soon drifted off to sleep. She felt herself floating until she became aware of a steady warmth enveloping her and growing stronger. She felt herself slowly open her eyes. Several feet in front of her, surrounded by a soft glow, stood Andy, smiling his impish smile, looking so happy and so healthy — just like he had before he'd gotten sick.

"Andy? Andy!" Katie exclaimed excitedly. She felt herself running toward him and as she ran, she felt the years fall away until she was a young woman again. And then, she was in his arms and he swung her around as they laughed together. He set her down in front of him and looking at her, his bright blue eyes sparkling with happiness, he bent his head to kiss her. Her heart was pounding, her lips eagerly waiting to feel his . . .

Something woke her. She waited to see if she'd hear it again, and then the doorbell chimed. She had no idea how long she'd been asleep, but she blinked several times as she pushed off the throw and laid the open scrap book on the coffee table. The dream had been so real, just as it had been when she'd dreamed it many times before. Unfortunately, the aching sense of loss was also just as real and all too familiar.

She stood when the doorbell rang again and took a second or two to steady herself before she made it to the door and opened it to the mid-afternoon sun. A silhouetted figure stood in the brightness, but all she could make out was that the person on her porch was wearing a firefighter's uniform. "Andy?" she said, still a bit groggy.

"Mrs. Garrett?" the figure said and stepped to the side to block the sun. Able to see him better now, Katie studied the man for several long seconds. He looked to be in his late forties or early fifties with blondish brown hair that would be considered long for someone in uniform. He continued to look at her expectantly with large brown eyes that seemed to radiate warmth.

"Do you remember me?" he finally asked as he tilted his head and searched her eyes for a hint of recognition.

Little things about him seemed familiar. The large brown eyes that looked at her with expectation, the kindness she felt from him, the tilt of his head, his shy uncertainty. He was a past student, she was sure of that, and so familiar, but beyond that, she just didn't know.

Sensing her dilemma, he smiled and pulled out his wallet. Opening it, he removed a faded and creased piece of paper. As he unfolded it, Katie gasped.

"Remember this?" he asked and held out a leaf cut from construction paper, now faded to a light red. "Mr. Andy and Fire Trucks" were written on it with a black marker in her handwriting, one of the words was partially smudged. He smiled and handed it to her.

Katie's eyes opened wide as she took the leaf from the gentle man standing in front of her. "Lucas?! Lucas Matthews?!" Katie asked almost breathless.

He relaxed and smiled broader. "Yes, ma'am."

"Lucas! Oh my goodness! Lucas!" she exclaimed and grabbed him into a tight hug. "Lucas! Let me look at you!"

She stepped back, looking at him with astonishment. "It's been forty years at least," she finally said as she tried to process this grown man from the second grader she'd known.

"Actually, it's been forty-one years," he said with a broad smile.

Katie regained some composure. "What am I thinking? Come in, come in!" She stepped back and held the door open wide. Lucas stepped inside and hesitated before Katie motioned for him to take a seat.

"What a wonderful surprise!" Katie exclaimed. Lucas smiled shyly as Katie continued to eye him with wonder. Now, she could see that little boy in the grown man across from her — the eyes, his mannerisms, his shy smile were all there.

"I've thought about you and Mr. Andy so many times over the years," Lucas said as he stopped and chuckled lightly. He looked at Katie and grinned. "All these years later, and I still think of him as Mr. Andy."

"I love it. I think that's incredibly sweet," Katie said, her eyes shining with delight.

"As you can see," Lucas said, motioning with his hands, "I became a firefighter. In fact, I never had a doubt about what I wanted to do and be after that field trip to the fire station in second grade. You have no idea how those few short months in your class and the time I spent with Mr. Andy shaped my life. It has always been my dream and my plan to come back to Abernathy and surprise the two of you." Lucas then smiled that shy smile Katie now recognized. "You see," Lucas went on, "I'm in town today because I had an interview with the Abernathy Department."

He paused and looked at Katie.

Katie furrowed her brows, thinking. "Interview? I'd heard they were interviewing for a new —" She stopped and then beamed at Lucas as realization dawned — "a new chief."

"Yes, ma'am," Lucas said with a proud smile. "I'm happy to say the interview went well, and I will be starting as Abernathy's new fire chief in just a few weeks."

"Oh, Lucas!" Katie said and clasped her hands with pleasure. "What wonderful news!"

Lucas smiled but then grew serious. "It's been my dream ever since I moved away in second grade. Things weren't easy for my mom and I after we moved. In fact, they were much worse than when we lived here. But once we moved, we had no money to come back and then my mom died a couple of years later. I went from one foster home to another. I was lucky enough to eventually end up with a nice family, but I had to pay my own way through school and through the fire academy. It all just took time — too much time I know now. It was my plan to surprise you and Andy when I came to interview but then I saw his picture on the wall at Station One. Until then, I had no idea that..." Lucas paused and looked at Katie who nodded. "That he had died. I know it's been a lot of years, but when I saw his picture and realized it happened only a few months after we moved, I felt the loss like it just happened."

He looked at Katie sadly. "I thought about all the times he had lunch with me, and we talked about the fire service. He always got so excited when he talked about a fire he'd been to or medical call he'd made. He got me excited just listening to him. All these years I've been looking forward to swapping stories with him. And now, to find out he's gone, well, I can't tell you how sad it makes me."

Katie listened and saw the same look on Lucas' face that Andy always had when he talked about the fire service. The light in Lucas' eyes faded when he mentioned Andy's passing, but it returned as he finished and looked at Katie.

"I'm talking too much. I'm just so happy to finally get to see you," he said as the innocent smile of that second grader spread across his face.

Katie reached out and took his hand in hers. "On the contrary," Katie assured him, "I could listen to you talk about Andy all day. The past forty years, for the most part, have been good but they've been a long forty years too. I still miss Andy so much." Her eyes drifted to the open scrapbook on the coffee table, and Andy's smiling face looking up at them. Lucas followed her gaze and waited, but Katie brightened and turned to him with a smile.

"Tell me about your family. Are you married? Do you have children? I've wondered about you so often — where you moved, how you were doing, if you ever got a heavier coat." She stopped and laughed. "Isn't it funny the things you think of?"

Katie fixed coffee, strong like she knew every firefighter liked, and she and Lucas visited nonstop until Lucas reluctantly set his coffee mug on the table and stood. "Mrs. Garrett," he said, "I look forward to seeing you and visiting with you more after Jill and I move to Abernathy. You will be our first dinner guest once we get settled."

"I'm already looking forward to it, and I can't wait to meet Jill," Katie said as she stood. She reached down and picked up the faded red leaf from the coffee table. She looked it and smiled as she handed it to Lucas. "I think you need to keep this, Chief."

Lucas took the little leaf, refolded it carefully and placed it back in his wallet. "Yes, ma'am. I think you're right," he said with a small smile. "And you know, you're the first one to call me Chief. Very fitting I think."

As they walked to the door, Katie said, "I can't begin to tell you how wonderful it is to see you and how glad I am you came by. I wish Andy could see you and know you're a firefighter and about to become Chief! He would have been so incredibly proud." Katie hugged Lucas tightly and said, "I am looking forward to those visits and meeting your wife."

"I look forward to introducing the two of you." Lucas walked down the sidewalk and waved as he got in his truck.

As Katie stood in late afternoon sunshine and watched Lucas drive away, she held her hand to her cheek just as Andy had told her to do when she missed him. Suddenly, a steady warmth began to grow beneath her fingers. Blinking back tears, she looked up into a sunbeam of golden light threading its way to her through the tree's fluttering leaves, and she remembered when she'd felt this same sensation before. Holding her hand securely to her cheek, the heat radiating strongly between her fingers, she whispered, "Andy," and then she smiled. Andy *was* here, with her, but then she knew, he had been all along.

ACKNOWLEGMENTS

THIS BOOK HAS CERTAINLY been a labor of love. Ever since the idea took root, it has truly been an inspiring journey of discovery into the depth of the fire service brotherhood. There are so many to thank who helped make this book possible but the only place to begin is with my brother, Chief Larry Bell. My brother not only told me about Larry Kraus, but over the years he consistently and constantly encouraged me to see this dream through to completion. He answered a myriad of questions, proofed the fire scenes for accuracy, encouraged me to participate in the Plano Citizens Fire Academy to get firsthand experience, was there for moral support, and made interviews with fire service personnel and information readily available. Thank you for your faith and trust in me to bring more awareness to this unseen danger firefighters face and to tell the "behind the station walls" story of these brave but humble public servants.

Along the way, many fire service personnel contributed their expertise, time and insight to ensure the book's accuracy. From the Abilene, Texas Fire Department, I'd like to thank Captain Jeremy Wolfe whose moving email written for the occasion of my brother's retirement was adapted for Andy's letter to his fellow firefighters. Jeremy, you should be a writer! My thanks to Chaplain Chris Hale for the information and verbiage he shared regarding a line of duty service. It was invaluable for the accuracy of the funeral and graveside ceremony and to know you wrote parts of it, made using it even more special. Thank you, Elise Roberts, AFD's Public Information Officer, for securing Larry

Kraus' photo and arranging the cover photo shoot at Station 7. My thanks to Lacy Dickey of Jynnifer Lacy Photography, whose husband, Isaac, is an Abilene firefighter, for the beautiful cover photography. You captured the tenor of the book perfectly! My thanks to Chief Candy Flores, Deputy Chief Michael Burden, and Deputy Chief John Brunett for your time to meet and discuss this book and for permission for the cover photo shoot.

What an incredible experience and learning opportunity it was to participate in Plano Fire Rescue's Citizen's Fire Academy. From Plano Fire Rescue, many, many thanks to Captain Peggy Harrell and Battalion Chief Forest Harrell for making the course so enjoyable, informative and participative. Thanks to all of the fire station personnel who welcomed me into the stations and took me along for the ride on calls to see what they do so capably day in and day out. It was an honor and a privilege. Thank you. (Shout out to Station 5 — Recognize the game played to do the dishes?) My thanks to Lt. John Barrett, Community Outreach and Education Officer, for sharing statistical and research information regarding cancer awareness and its increase within the fire service. You know your stuff — thank you for sharing.

The book wouldn't be what it is without the incredible editing by Sean Linton. Thank you, Sean, for helping take what I'd written to the next level. I owe a HUGE debt of thanks to Dr. Laura Cheshier and Betty Wiesepape for their expertise in proofing, editing, suggestions and valuable insights which greatly improved and fine tuned the manuscript. Thank you, Dr. Jerry Barker, for sharing your medical and oncology expertise about cancer. To Andrew and Kelsey Caprio — you guys are adorable and perfect as models for the cover. Thank you for your enthusiasm for the project and your willingness to participate. And to Dayna Linton — wow — you are an amazing professional.

Thank you for taking such good care of my dream. You are a jewel, and I can't thank you enough.

Please note that anything amiss factually or procedurally in Fully Involved is totally on me as some adaptations were made for the story line.

Cara (Kraus) Pilgrim, it was a pleasure to visit with you and an honor to have you share memories of Larry and his cancer battle. I admire your becoming an oncology nurse to help others suffering from the same disease.

As always, heartfelt thanks to my Mom and Dad for their rock solid support and steady encouragement to see this dream through to completion. To my family and friends, your support and excitement for this book has spurred me on.

We all owe firefighters our gratitude and appreciation. It's not what they do every day, it's what they're willing to do at any given moment that make them so incredibly special. Do something for a firefighter to show your appreciation. Their humble thanks will make you appreciate them all the more.

ABOUT THE AUTHOR

A PROJECT TEN YEARS IN the making, *Fully Involved* is Lindy Bell's debut novel and avidly reflects her admiration and love of the fire service. Thoroughly researched, the quest for accuracy for the book led Lindy to participate in the Plano Citizens Fire Academy, attend classes and accompany firefighters on ride outs. With a retired fire chief and a current paramedic/firefighter in the family, Lindy has witnessed firsthand the dedication and humbleness of first responders which fueled the impetus to convey the importance of the legendary fire service brotherhood and create cancer awareness and its growing effect on the fire service.

Lindy's first book, *Jane Austen Celebrates~Holidays & Occasions Regency Style,* is a showcase Regency Era holidays and their impact on modern holiday celebration traditions. A member of the Jane Austen Society of North America, Lindy has spoken to a variety of groups and taught Continuing and Adult Professional Education courses at Southern Methodist University (SMU).

A graduate of Abilene Christian University, Lindy currently lives in Plano, TX and works from home for a governmental executive recruitment and training firm. As hobbies, Lindy enjoys supporting Plano Fire Rescue by volunteering with the Plano Fire Rescue Association, writing, reading an engaging novel and cross stitching.

Website: lindybellwrites.com   Twitter: @LindyBellWrites

Facebook.com/LindyBellWrites/   Instagram: LindyBellWrites